PENGUIN BO

THE PENGUIN B
MODERN INDIAN SH

Stephen Alter is an American who was born and brought up in India, where his parents worked as missionaries. He completed his education at Wesleyan University, Connecticut. He has published four highly regarded novels, *Neglected Lives*, *Silk and Steel*, *The Godchild* and *Renuka* all of which are set in India. He has also edited *Great Indian Hunting Stories*.
Stephen Alter teaches at present in Cairo, Egypt.

*

Wimal Dissanayake is assistant director of the Institute of Culture and Communication at the East-West Center in Honolulu, Hawaii. He received his doctorate in literature from Cambridge University and has written several books and a large number of scholarly papers on literature, films and communication. He is an award-winning broadcaster and poet and is the editor of the *East-West Film Journal*.

Albuquerque Academy
Library
6400 Wyoming Blvd. N.E.
Albuquerque, N.M. 87109

THE PENGUIN BOOK OF
MODERN INDIAN
SHORT STORIES

Edited by
STEPHEN ALTER and
WIMAL DISSANAYAKE

Albuquerque Academy
Library
6400 Wyoming Blvd. N.E.
Albuquerque, N.M. 87109

PENGUIN BOOKS

Penguin Books (India) Limited, 72-B Himalaya House.
New Delhi-110 001, India
Penguin Books Ltd., Harmondsworth, Middlesex, England
Viking Penguin Inc., 40 West 23rd Street, New York, N.Y. 10010. U.S.A.
Penguin Books Australia Ltd., Ringwood, Victoria, Australia
Penguin Books Canada Ltd., 2801 John Street, Markham, ontario, Canada L3R 1B4
Penguin Books (N.Z.) Ltd, 182-190 Wairau Road, Auckland 10, New Zealand

First published by Penguin Books India 1989

Copyright © Penguin Books (India) Ltd.
All rights reserved

Typeset in Palatino by Macrographics, New Delhi

Made and printed in India by Ananda Offset Private Ltd, Calcutta

This books is sold subject to the condition that it shall not, by way of trade or
otherwise, be lent, resold, hired out, or otherwise circulated without the
publisher's prior written consent in any form of binding or cover other than that
in which it is published and without a similar condition including this condition
being imposed on the subsequent purchaser and without limiting the rights
under copyright reserved above, no part of this publication may be reproduced,
stored in or introduced into a retrieval system, or transmitted in any form or by
any means (electronic, mechanical, photocoping, recording or otherwise),
without the prior written permission of both the copyright owner and the above
mentioned publisher of this book.

891.47
PEN

To Natalie Augden (S.A.)
To Doreen (W.D.)

Contents

Acknowledgements

Every effort has been made to ensure that permissions for all materials included in the book were obtained. In the event of any inadvertent omissions, the publishers should be notified and formal acknowledgements will be included in all future editions of this book. Special thanks and acknowledgements are given to:

Pritish Nandy for *The Discovery of Telenapota* by Premendra Mitra published in 1984 in *The Illustrated Weekly of India*. Translated by Pritish Nandy.

Amrita Pritam for her story *The Weed* published in 1978 in *The Aerial and Other Stories*, United Writers, Calcutta. Translated by Raj Gill.

Penguin Books Canada Ltd for *Nostalgia* by Bharati Mukherjee published in *Darkness*.

Gangadhar Gadgil for his story *The Dog That Ran in Circles* published in 1961 in *Modern Marathi Short Stories*, Kutub Popular, Bombay.

U.R. Anantha Murthy for his story *The Sky and The Cat* published in1980 in *Indian Literature*, Sahitya Akademi, Vol. XXIII No. 3 & 4, New Delhi. Translated by D.A. Shankar.

Gopinath Mohanty for his story *The Somersault* published in 1979 in *The Ant and Other Stories*, United Writers, Calcutta. Translated by Sitakant Mahapatra.

Oxford University Press for *Companions* by Raja Rao published in 1978 in *The Policeman and The Rose*, Oxford University Press, New Delhi.

Jhayu Mani for *A Loss of Identity* by S. Mani 'Mowni' published in 1978 in *Tamil Short Stories*, Authors Guild of India, New Delhi. Translated by Albert Franklin.

William Heinemann Publishers for *A Devoted Son* by Anita Desai published in 1978 in *Games At Twilight*, 1985.

Jaico Publishing House for *The Snake Charmer* by Chunilal Madia published in 1982 in *Selected Stories From Gujarat*. Translated by Sarla Jag Mohan.

Manoj P. Rege for *Savitri* by P.S. Rege published in 1968 in *Indian Literature*, Sahitya Akademi, New Delhi. Translated by Kumud Mehta.

T.S. Pillai for his story *A Blind Man's Contentment* published in 1976 in *Malayalam Short Stories*, Kerala Sahitya Akademi, Trichur. Translated by V. Abdulla.

Sahitya Sahkar Trust for *Ghisa* by Mahadevi Verma published in *Mahfil, The Journal of South Asian Literature*, Vol. XX No 1, Chicago. Translated by Sudha Chandola and Susan Tripp.

O.V. Vijayan for his story *The Wart*.

Bhisham Sahni for his story *We have Arrived in Amritsar*.

Sunil Gangopadhyay for his story *Shah Jahan and His Private Army* published in 1986 in *Mahfil, The Journal of South Asian Literature*, Vol. XXI No. 1, Chicago. Translated by Phyllis Granoff.

Nirmal Verma for his story *Deliverance*. Translated by Kuldip Singh.

Devanuru Mahadeva for his story *Amasa*. Translated by A.K. Ramanujan and Manu Shetty.

Introduction

Of any literary form, the short story is perhaps the most accessible. Unlike a novel, it can be read at one sitting and at the same time it does not offer the density of images that might make a poem difficult to understand. A short story usually deals with only a handful of characters and gives us no more than a brief glimpse of the setting. This is not to say that it is a simplistic form; some short stories can be as complex in design as a full length play or novel. Many are as intricately drawn as a Moghul miniature. The brevity of the form often allows the writer to experiment with style and theme in a way that would be unthinkable in a longer work.

It is possible to trace the origins of the short story in Indian literature back to the earliest writings from the subcontinent. The *Mahabharata* and *Ramayana* can be read as story cycles in which each episode is a self-contained narrative. The *Jataka* tales and the *Panchatantra* also offer some of the earliest examples of short stories. But the modern Indian short story probably owes more to oral traditions and folk-tales than it does to the ancient texts. Many of the selections in this anthology employ narrative techniques and images which can only have come from a folk tradition. This is probably true in many other countries as well, for the short story shares much in common with oral narratives, not just in length but also in its capacity to express a universal experience through very specific characters and events.

Many of India's short story writers have also been influenced by European and American literature. While an earlier generation of writers probably admired the works of Maupassant, Chekov, Tolstoy and many others, the writers of the fifties and sixties were certainly influenced by Kafka, Camus, and Hemingway, it is likely that the youngest generation of writers in India are looking beyond Europe and America to stories from as far away as Japan, Brazil, or Nigeria. More important than this, Indian writers are looking at themselves. Through more and more translations and through the interpretive medium of cinema, Bengali writers are now being exposed to Malayalam writers and so on and so forth. There is an enormous amount of translation yet to be done, not only from regional languages into English and Hindi, but also from one regional language to another.

Literature has always been recognized as an important vehicle for inter-cultural understanding. As many fine translations have shown, the barriers of language are not as formidable as they might seem. A reader can explore the jungles of South America through the works of Gabriel Garcia Marquez almost as easily as entering the streets of Dublin through the pages of James Joyce's novels and stories. It should be noted that most of the works which are considered 'classics' in British and American universities are translations themselves from Greek and Latin. It is true that sometimes the nuances of a language can be lost but there is no reason why an English translation from Hindi, Kannada, Urdu or Malayalam cannot be as immediate or evocative as a translation from any other language.

This collection hopes to offer some of the best examples of Indian short stories written in the last fifty years. It should be admitted that not all of these stories are the most contemporary examples of Indian fiction. Some were written several decades ago and one or two are now considered 'classics'. Younger writers certainly need to be translated and collected but the purpose of this anthology is to present a general selection of writers, old and new. To anyone who is familiar with Indian literature, the three most glaring omissions would be Rabindranath Tagore, Prem Chand and Saadat Hasan Manto. We have chosen not to include their works because they have been widely published and would seem to represent a distinctly separate generation from the authors in this collection. These eighteen writers were all born within this century and the bulk of their writing comes from the period following independence. Though several of these stories have been anthologized before, to the best of our knowledge, none have shared the covers of the same book.

The table of contents in an anthology ultimately reflects an editor's personal preferences. To some the stories selected may seem arbitrary or unjustified but there is probably no collection in the world which would satisfy every reader. In order to avoid some of the pitfalls of earlier anthologies, we have not used linguistic or regional guidelines to make our selection. We chose these stories on their literary merits alone and were gratified to find that the final list of authors reflects a diversity of languages and regions. Several well-known authors have not been included. This is not because we judge their work inferior but because their strengths may lie in other genres such as the novel or because the existing translations of the work were unsatisfactory.

January, 1990   *S.A,W.D.*

Premendra Mitra

The Discovery of Telenapota

When Saturn and Mars come together, you may also discover Telenapota.

On a leisurely day, after hours of angling without a catch, when someone comes and tempts you, saying that somewhere there is a magic pool filled with the most incredible fish anxiously waiting to swallow any bait, you are already on your way to Telenapota.

But finding Telenapota is not all that easy. You catch a bus late in the afternoon. It is packed with countless people and by the time you get off, you are drenched in sweat and dust-smeared. Actually you are even unprepared for the stop when it comes.

Before you even know where you are, the bus disappears in the distance, over a bridge across the low swampland. The forest is dense and dark, and night has arrived even before the sun has set. There is a strange wind that blows, an eerie quiet. You will see no one anywhere. Even the birds have flown away, as if in fright. There is an uncanny feeling, a strange dread slowly rearing its head out of the lonely marshland.

You leave the main road and take the narrow muddy track that winds into the forest. After a while, the track gets lost in thick groves of bamboo.

To find Telenapota you need a couple of friends with you. You will be going there to angle. What their interests are you have no clue.

Your first problem will be mosquitoes. They will arrive in hordes and you will try to scare them away. Failing, all three of you will stand and look at each other, wondering what to do. And slowly it will grow quite dark. The mosquitoes will become more insistent and you will wonder if it would not have been better to get back onto the main road and catch the return bus.

Just then a strange noise will startle you. A noise from that point where the mud track loses itself in the forest. Your nerves being on edge, you will imagine this phantom scream coming from the dumb forest and you will immediately become tense and perhaps a little scared as well. And then, you will see in the dark a faint lamp gently swaying. Slowly a bullock cart will amble out of the dark forest.

It is a small cart. The bullocks are also very small. They will all seem dwarf-like, and yet the three of you will climb onto the cart and huddle together in the dark interior where there is only room for one.

The cart will return the way it came. The dark, impenetrable forest will yield a narrow tunnel as the cart slowly enters. The bullocks will move forward, unhurried, as if creating with each step the path they slowly tread.

For sometime you will feel terribly cramped in the dark. But slowly you will drown in the depths of the blackness around you. From your familiar world you will enter another. An unknown mist-clad universe, bereft of all feeling. Time will stop dead in its tracks.

And then, suddenly, a howl of drums will wake you. You will look around you and find the driver of the cart furiously beating an empty drum. The skies will be full of countless stars.

You will ask what the matter is. And the driver will casually tell you that this din is to drive the tigers away. When you wonder how one can scare away tigers by just raising a racket, he will reassure you that these are not real tigers. They are panthers; and a stick and a drum are enough to keep them at bay.

Tigers! Within thirty miles of the metropolis! Before you can raise your eyebrows, the cart will have crossed a wide moor lit by a late moon. Ruins of deserted palaces will gleam in the phantom moonlight. Lone colonnades, broken arches, the debris of courtyard walls. A ruined temple somewhere further down. They will stand like litigants, waiting in futile hope, for the recording of some evidence in the court of time.

You will try to sit up. A strange sensation will once again make you feel as if you have left behind the world of the living and entered a phantom universe peopled only by memories.

. The night will be far gone. It will seem an endless dark in which everything lies stilled, without genesis or end. Like extinct animals preserved in museums for all time.

After a few more turns the cart will stop. You will collect your tired limbs and climb down, one by one, like wooden dolls.

14

There will be a strong smell in the air: the stench of leaves rotting in the pool just in front of you. Beside the pool will stand the feeble remains of a large mansion, its roof caved in, walls falling apart, and windows broken—like the battlements of a fort, guarding against the phantom moonlight.

This is where you will spend the night.

First, you will find yourself a room, somewhat habitable. The cart-driver will fetch you from somewhere a broken lantern and a jug of water. It will seem to you ages since someone had walked into that room. Some futile efforts have been made to clean it up and the musty odour will reveal that this was a long time back. With the slightest movement, plaster will peel off and bits of rubble will fall on you from the roof and the walls, like angry oaths from a resident spirit. Bats and flying foxes will shrilly question your right to stay there for the night.

Of your friends, one is a sod and the other would have snored through a holocaust. Your bed will be hardly ready before one of them hits the sack and the other the bottle.

The night will wear on. The lantern glass will gather soot and the light will softly dim. The assault of mosquitoes will become unbearable. This is the blue blooded anopheles, the aristocrat who carries malaria in his bite. But, by this time, both your companions will be in worlds of their own, far removed from yours.

It will be hot and oppressive. You will take a torch and try to escape to the terrace, to beat the heat. The danger of the staircase giving way will scare you at every step. But something will draw you on, irresistibly. You will keep on climbing till you arrive.

On reaching, you will find the terrace in ruins. Trees have taken firm root in every crevice, every nook. As if they were fifth columnists, making way for the inexorable advance of the forest.

And yet, in the wan moonlight, everything will look beautiful. It will seem that if you searched long enough, you would find that inner sanctum of this sleep-drenched palace where the captive princess has been asleep through countless centuries.

And even as you dream of such a princess, you will notice a faint light in one of the windows of the tumbledown house across the street. And, then, you will see a mysterious shadow walk up to the window. Whose silhouette is it? Why is she awake when everyone sleeps? It will baffle you: and even as you wonder about it, the light will slowly go out. Was it real? Or did you see a dream? From the abysmal dark of this world of sleep, a dream bubble surfaced for a while, floated silently in the world of the living, and then suddenly melted away.

You will walk down the staircase carefully and fall asleep beside your friends.

When you wake up some hours later, you will find morning already there, with the delightful chatter of birds.

You will remember what you had come here for. And very soon you will find yourself sitting on a broken, moss-covered step beside the pool. You will cast your line into the green waters and wait patiently.

The day will wear on. A kingfisher perched on the branch of a tree beside the pool will occasionally swoop down, in a flash of colour. A snake will emerge from some crack in the steps and slither slowly into the water. Two grasshoppers, their transparent wings fluttering in the sunlight, will keep trying to land on the float of your line. A dove will call out from the distance. Its lazy notes will bring on a strange ennui, as your mind will wander far and wide.

The reverie will break with the sudden ripples on the water. Your float will gently rock. You will look up to find her pushing away the floating weeds and filling up a shining brass pitcher. Her eyes are curious; her movements unabashed and free. She will look straight at you and at your line. Then, she will pick up her pitcher and turn away.

You will not be able to guess her age. Calm and sorrowful, her face will tell you that she has already walked the pitiless road of life. But if you look at the thin, emaciated lines of her body, you will think that she had never grown out of her adolescence.

Even as she turns to go away, she will suddenly pause and ask you what you are waiting for. Pull hard, she will say. Her voice is so mellow and tender that it will not surprise you that she should have spoken to you, a complete stranger, with such familiarity. Only the suddenness of it will startle you and, by the time you pull the line, the bait would have gone.

You will look at her somewhat abashed. And she will then turn and go away with slow, unhurried steps. As she walks away, you will wonder if you saw the hint of a smile breaking through her sad, peaceful eyes.

Nothing will again disturb the loneliness of the afternoon. The kingfisher will fly away. The fish will ignore you. Only a strange feeling of unreality will remain. How could she have come to this strange land of sleep?

And then, after a long while, you will pack up—a little disappointed with yourself. When you return, you will find that the news of your fishing skills has preceded you. You will ignore the wisecracks of your friends and ask them how they knew you had fared so poorly.

Why, Jamini told us, the tippler will reply. She saw you there. Curious, you will ask him who Jamini is. You will learn that she is the same person you saw beside the pool, a distant relation of your friend. You will also learn that you are going over to her place for lunch.

You look at the ruins across the street—where you had watched last night's silhouette framed by the broken window in the wan moonlight—and you are surprised by its wretched condition. You had not imagined that the veil of night, now stripped rudely by the harsh daylight, could have hidden such an ugly nakedness. You are even more surprised to know that Jamini lives there.

It is a simple meal. Jamini serves it herself. Looking at her now, closely, you are struck by the tired sorrow writ on her face. It seems as if the mute agony of this forgotten and lonely place has cast its dark shadow across her visage. A sea of infinite tiredness swirls in her eyes. You know she will crumble slowly, very slowly with the ruins around her.

You will notice there is something on her mind. You may even hear a faint voice calling from a room upstairs. And every now and then you will notice Jamini leaving the room. Each time she comes back, the shadows lengthen on her face and her eyes betray a strange anxiety.

After the meal is over, you will sit for a while. Jamini will first hesitate, and then call out in despair from the other side of the door: Manida, can you please come here once? Mani is your friend, the tippler. He will go to the door and you will hear his conversation with Jamini quite clearly, even though you have no intention to eavesdrop.

Mother is being difficult again, Jamini would say, in a troubled voice. Ever since she heard you were coming with your friends, she has become quite impossible to handle.

Mani would mutter irritably: I suppose it is because she imagines Niranjan is here.

Yes. She keeps saying, I know he is here. He hasn't come up to see me only because he is embarrassed. Go, fetch him. Manida, I don't know what to say. Ever since she went blind, she has become rather difficult. She won't listen to anyone. She is always angry. I am sometimes scared she will collapse and die during one of her fits.

If only she had eyes, I could have proved to her that Niranjan is nowhere around: Mani would reply, somewhat annoyed.

A shrill, angry scream will come from upstairs, this time more clearly audible. Jamini will beseech him: Please come with me once, Manida. See if you can make her understand. All right, Mani will reply a bit roughly. You carry on; I'll come.

Mani will mutter to himself: Why, for heaven's sake, does this mad woman refuse to die? She can't see; she can hardly use her limbs; and yet she is determined not to die.

You will ask him what the matter is. Mani will reply, annoyed: Matter? Nothing very much. Years ago, she had fixed Jamini's marriage with Niranjan, a distant nephew of hers. The last time he was here was about four years ago. He told her then he would marry Jamini as soon as he returned from abroad. Ever since then, she has been waiting.

But hasn't Niranjan returned? You will ask.

Of course not! How can he return when he never went at all? He was lying; otherwise, the old hag wouldn't let him go. Why should he marry this rag-picker's daughter? Yes, he is married all right and rearing a family. But who is to tell her all this? She won't believe you; and if she did, she would die of shock immediately thereafter. Who's going to take the risk?

Does Jamini know about Niranjan? You will ask.

Oh yes. But she can't speak about it to her. Well, let me go and get it over. Mani will turn to go.

Almost unaware of it yourself, you will also get up then and say: Just a moment. I will come with you.

You? With me? Mani will be very surprised.

Yes. Do you mind?

No, of course not, Mani will reply, a trifle taken aback. And, then, he will lead the way.

After you have climbed the dark, crumbling staircase, you

will enter a room that looks like an underground vault. There is only one window, tightly shut. At first, everything will look indistinct. And then, as your eyes get used to the dark, you will see a large, decrepit wooden cot. On it you will notice a shrivelled up woman, wrapped in torn rags, lying still. Jamini stands beside her, like a statue.

At the sound of your footsteps, the bag of bones will slowly move. Niranjan? My child! You are back at last! You have come back to your poor wreck of an aunt! You know, I have been waiting, keeping death at bay, knowing that you will be here someday. You won't slip away again like last time?

Mani will be about to say something but you will interrupt him by blurting out: No, I promise you I won't.

You will not look up but you will feel the stunned silence in the room. You could not have looked up even if you wanted to, for your eyes are rivetted to the sockets of her old, unseeing eyes. Two tongues of dark will emerge from the empty sockets and lick every inch of your body. To feel, to know. You will feel those moments falling like dew into the vast seas of time.

You will hear the old woman saying. My son, I knew you would come. That is why I am still in this house of the dead, counting the days. The sheer effort to speak will leave her panting. You will look up at Jamini. You will feel that somewhere, behind the mask of her face, something was slowly melting away, and it will not be long before the foundation of a vow—a vow made up of endless despair, a vow taken against life and fate—will slowly give way.

She will speak again: I am sure Jamini will make you happy, my son. There is none like her, even though I, her mother, should say so. I am old and broken down, and often out of my senses. I try her beyond endurance. But does she ever protest? Not once. This graveyard of a place, where you will not find a man even if you search ten houses, is like me, more dead than alive. And yet, Jamini survives, and manages everything.

Even though you may want to, you will dare not lift your eyes should someone discover the tears that have welled there. The old woman will whisper: Promise me you will marry Jamini. If I do not have your promise, I will know no peace even in death.

Your voice will be heavy. You will softly mumble: I will not fail you. I promise.

Albuquerque Academy
Library
6400 Wyoming Blvd. N.E.

And soon it will be late afternoon. The bullock cart will appear once again to take you back. One by one, the three of you will get inside. As it is about to leave, Jamini will look at you with those sorrowful eyes of hers and softly remark: You are forgetting your tackle.

You will smile and reply: Let it be. I missed the fish this time—but they won't escape next time.

Jamini will not turn her eyes away. Her tired face will softly light up with a smile, tender and grateful. Like the white clouds of autumn, it will drift across your heart and fill you with a strange and beautiful warmth, an unexplained happiness.

The cart will amble on its way. You will not feel cramped this time; nor will the monotonous creak of the wheels bother you. Your friends will discuss how a hundred years ago, the scourge of malaria, like a relentless flood, carried off Telenapota and left it here, in this forgotton no-man's land, just beside the frontier of the world of the living. You will not be listening; your mind will be drifting elsewhere. You will only listen to your own heartbeats echoing the words: I will come back, I will come back.

Even after you get back home to the city, with its hectic pace and harsh lights, the memory of Telenapota will shine bright in your mind like a star that is distant and yet very close. A few days will pass with petty problems, the usual traumas of the commonplace. And even if a slight mist begins to form in your mind, you will not be aware of it. Then, just as you have crossed the fences, prepared to go back to Telenapota, you will suddenly feel the shivering touch of the oncoming fever.

Soon the terrible headache and the temperature will be on you and you will lie down under a lot of blankets, trying unsuccessfully to ward off the fever or at least come to terms with it. The thermometer will register 105 degrees Fahrenheit and the last thing you hear before passing out will be the doctor's verdict. Malaria.

It will be many days before you are able to walk out of the house and bask in the sun, weak and exhausted by the long fever. Meanwhile, unknown to yourself, your mind will have undergone many changes, the inevitable transformations. Telenapota will become a vague, indistinct dream, like the memory of a star that has fallen. Was there ever such a place? You will not be sure. The face that was tired and serene. The eyes that were lost and lonely, hiding an unknown sorrow. Were they real? Or were they, like the shadows of Telenapota's ruins, just another part of a phantom dream?

Telenapota, discovered for one brief moment, will be lost again in the timeless dark of night.

Translated from Bengali by Pritish Nandy

Amrita Pritam

The Weed

Angoori was the new bride of the old servant of my neighbour's neighbour's neighbour. Every bride is new, for that matter; but she was new in a different way: the second wife of her husband who could not be called new because he had already drunk once at the conjugal well. As such, the prerogatives of being new went to Angoori only. This realization was further accentuated when one considered the five years that passed before they could consummate their union.

About six years ago Prabhati had gone home to cremate his first wife. When this was done, Angoori's father approached him and took his wet towel, wringing it dry, a symbolic gesture of wiping away the tears of grief that had wet the towel. There never was a man, though, who cried enough to wet a yard-and-a-half of calico. It had got wet only after Prabhati's bath. The simple act of drying the tear-stained towel on the part of a person with a nubile daughter was as much as to say, 'I give you my daughter to take the place of the one who died. Don't cry anymore. I've even dried your wet towel.'

This is how Angoori married Prabhati. However, their union was postponed for five years, for two reasons: her tender age, and her mother's paralytic attack. When, at last, Prabhati was invited to take his bride away, it seemed he would not be able to, for his employer was reluctant to feed another mouth from his kitchen. But when Prabhati told him that his new wife could keep her own house, the employer agreed.

At first, Angoori kept *purdah* from both men and women. But the veil soon started to shrink until it covered only her hair, as was becoming to an orthodox Hindu woman. She was a delight to both ear and eye. A laughter in the tinkling of her hundred ankle-bells, and a thousand bells in her laughter.

'What are you wearing Angoori?'
'An anklet. Isn't it pretty?'
'And what's on your toe?'
'A ring.'

'And on your arm?'

'A bracelet.'

'What do they call what's on your forehead?'

'They call it *aliband*.'

'Nothing on your waist today, Angoori?'

'It's too heavy. Tomorrow I'll wear it. Today, no necklace either. See! The clasp is broken. Tomorrow I'll go to the city to get a new clasp...and buy a nose-pin. I had a big nose-ring. But my mother-in-law kept it.'

Angoori was very proud of her silver jewellery, elated by the mere touch of her trinkets. Everything she did seemed to set them off to maximum effect.

The weather became hot with the turn of the season. Angoori too must have felt it in her hut where she passed a good part of the day, for now she stayed out more. There were a few huge *neem* trees in front of my house; underneath them an old well that nobody used except an occasional construction worker. The spilt water made several puddles, keeping the atmosphere around the well cool. She often sat near the well to relax.

'What are you reading, *bibi*?' Angoori asked me one day when I sat under a *neem* tree reading.

'Want to read it?'

'I don't know reading.'

'Want to learn?'

'Oh, no!'

'Why not? What's wrong with it?'

'It's a sin for women to read!'

'And what about men?'

'For them, it's not a sin.'

'Who told you this nonsense?'

'I just know it.'

'I read. I must be sinning.'

'For city women, it's no sin. It is for village women.'

We both laughed at this remark. She had not learned to question all that she was told to believe. I thought that if she found peace in her convictions , who was I to question them?

Her body redeemed her dark complexion, an intense sense of ecstasy always radiating from it, a resilient sweetness. They say a woman's body is like a lump of dough, some women have the looseness of underkneaded dough while others have the clinging

23

plasticity of leavened dough. Rarely does a woman have a body that can be equated to rightly kneaded dough, a baker's pride. Angoori's body belonged to this category, her rippling muscles impregnated with the metallic resilience of a coiled spring. I felt her face, arms, breasts, legs with my eyes and experienced a profound langour. I thought of Prabhati: old, short, loose-jawed, a man whose stature and angularity would be the death of Euclid. Suddenly a funny idea struck me: Angoori was the dough covered by Prabhati. He was her napkin, not her taster. I felt a laugh welling up inside me, but I checked it for fear that Angoori would sense what I was laughing about. I asked her how marriages are arranged where she came from.

'A girl, when she's five or six, adores someone's feet. He is the husband.'

'How does she know it?'

'Her father takes money and flowers and puts them at his feet.'

'That's the father adoring, not the girl.'

'He does it for the girl. So it's the girl herself.'

'But the girl has never seen him before!'

'Yes, girls don't see.'

'Not a single girl ever sees her future husband!'

'No....,' she hesitated. After a long, pensive pause, she added, 'Those in love...they see them.'

'Do girls in your village have love-affairs?'

'A few.'

'Those in love, they don't sin?' I remembered her observation regarding education for women.

'They don't. See, what happens is that a man makes the girl eat the weed and then she starts loving him.'

'Which weed?'

'The wild one.'

'Doesn't the girl know that she has been given the weed?'

'No, he gives it to her in a *paan*. After that, nothing satisfies her but to be with him, her man. I know. I've seen it with my own eyes.'

'Whom did you see?'

'A friend; she was older than me.'

'And what happened?'

'She went crazy. Ran away with him to the city.'

'How do you know it was because of the weed?'

'What else could it be? Why would she leave her parents. He brought her many things from the city : clothes, trinkets, sweets.'

'Where does this weed come in?'

'In the sweets : otherwise how could she love him?'

'Love can come in other ways. No other way here?'

'No other way. What her parents hated was that she was that way.'

'Have you seen the weed?'

'No, they bring it from a far country. My mother warned me not to take *paan* or sweets from anyone. Men put the weed in them.'

'You were very wise. How come your friend ate it?'

'To make herself suffer,' she said sternly. The next moment her face clouded, perhaps in remembering her friend. 'Crazy. She went crazy, the poor thing,' she said sadly. 'Never combed her hair, singing all night....'

'What did she sing?'

'I don't know. They all sing when they eat the weed. Cry too.'

The conversation was becoming a little too much to take, so I retired.

I found her sitting under the *neem* tree one day in a profoundly abstracted mood. Usually one could hear Angoori coming to the well; her ankle-bells would announce her approach. They were silent that day.

'What's the matter, Angoori?'

She gave me a blank look and then, recovering a little, said, 'Teach me reading, *bibi*.'

'What has happened?'

'Teach me to write my name.'

'Why do you want to write ? To write letters? To whom?'

She did not answer, but was once again lost in her thoughts.

'Won't you be sinning?' I asked, trying to draw her out of her mood. She would not respond. I went in for an afternoon nap. When I came out again in the evening, she was still there singing sadly to herself. When she heard me approaching, she turned around and stopped abruptly. She sat with hunched shoulders because of the chill in the evening breeze.

'You sing well, Angoori.' I watched her great effort to turn back the tears and spread a pale smile across her lips.

'I don't know singing.'

'But you do, Angoori!'

'This was the....'

'The song your friend used to sing.' I completed the sentence for her.

'I heard it from her.'

'Sing it for me.'

She started to recite the words. 'Oh, it's just about the time of year for change. Four months winter, four months summer, four months rain! ...'

'Not like that. Sing it for me,' I asked. She wouldn't, but continued with the words:

> Four months of winter reign in my heart;
> My heart shivers, O my love.
> Four months of summer, wind shimmers in the sun.
> Four months come the rains; clouds tremble in the sky.

'Angoori!' I said loudly. She looked as if in a trance, as if she had eaten the weed. I felt like shaking her by the shoulders. Instead, I took her by the shoulders and asked if she had been eating regularly. She had not; she cooked for herself only, since Prabhati ate at his master's. 'Did you cook today?' I asked.

'Not yet.'

'Did you have tea in the morning?'

'Tea? No milk today.'

'Why no milk today?'

'I didn't get any. Ram Tara....'

'Fetches the milk for you?' I added. She nodded.

Ram Tara was the night-watchman. Before Angoori married Prabhati, Ram Tara used to get a cup of tea at our place at the end of his watch before retiring on his cot near the well. After Angoori's arrival, he made his tea at Prabhati's. He, Angoori and Prabhati would all have tea together sitting around the fire. Three days ago Ram Tara went to his village for a visit.

'You haven't had tea for three days?' I asked. She nodded again. 'And you haven't eaten, I suppose?' She did not speak. Apparently, if she had been eating, it was as good as not eating at all.

I remembered Ram Tara: good-looking, quick-limbed, full of

jokes. He had a way of talking with smiles trembling faintly at the corner of his lips.

'Angoori?'

'Yes, *bibi*.'

'Could it be the weed?'

Tears flowed down her face in two rivulets, gathering into two tiny puddles at the corners of her mouth.

'Curse on me!' she started in a voice trembling with tears, 'I never took sweets from him...not a betel even...but tea....' She could not finish. Her words were drowned in a fast stream of tears.

Translated from Punjabi by Raj Gill

Bharati Mukherjee

Nostalgia

On a cold, snowless evening in December, Dr Manny Patel, a psychiatric resident at a state hospital in Queens, New York, looked through the storefront window of the 'New Taj Mahal' and for the first time in thirteen years felt the papercut-sharp pain of desire. The woman behind the counter was about twenty, twenty-one, with the buttery-gold skin and the round voluptuous bosom of a Bombay film star.

Dr Patel had driven into Manhattan on an impulse. He had put in one of those afternoons at the hospital that made him realize it was only the mysteries of metabolism that kept him from unprofessional outbursts. Mr Horowitz, a three-hundred-and-nineteen-pound readmitted schizophrenic, had convinced himself that he was Noel Coward and demanded respect from the staff. In less than half-an-hour, Mr Horowitz had sung twenty songs, battered a therapy aide's head against a wall, unbuttoned another patient's blouse in order to bite off her nipples, struck a Jamaican nurse across the face and lunged at Dr Patel, calling him in exquisite English, 'Paki scum.' The nurse asked that Mr Horowitz be placed in the seclusion room, and Dr Patel had agreed. The seclusion order had to be reviewed by a doctor every two hours, and Mr Horowitz's order was renewed by Dr Chuong who had come in two hours late for work.

Dr Patel did not like to lock grown men and women in a seven-by-nine room, especially one without padding on its walls. Mr Horowitz had screamed and sung for almost six hours. Dr Patel had increased his dosage of Haldol. Mr Horowitz was at war with himself and there was no truce except through psychopharmacology and Dr Patel was suspicious of the side effects of such cures. The Haldol had calmed the prisoner. Perhaps it was unrealistic to want more.

He was grateful that there were so many helpless, mentally disabled people (crazies, his wife called them) in New York state, and that they afforded him and Dr Chuong and even the Jamaican nurse a nice living. But he resented being called a 'Paki scum.' Not even a sick man like Mr Horowitz had the right to do that.

He had chosen to settle in the US. He was not one for nostalgia; he was not an expatriate but a patriot. His wife, Camille, who had grown up in Camden, New Jersey, did not share his enthusiasm for America, and had made fun of him when he voted for President Reagan. Camille was not a hypocrite; she was a predictable paradox. She could cut him down for wanting to move to a three-hundred-thousand-dollar house with an atrium in the dining hall, and for blowing sixty-two thousand on a red Porsche, while she boycotted South African wines and non-union lettuce. She spent guiltless money at Balducci's and on fitness equipment. So he enjoyed his house, his car, so what? He wanted things. He wanted things for Camille and for their son. He loved his family, and his acquisitiveness was entwined with love.

His son was at Andover, costing nearly twelve thousand dollars a year. When Manny converted the twelve thousand from dollars to rupees, which he often did as he sat in his small, dreary office listening for screams in the hall, the staggering rupee figure reassured him that he had done well in the New World. His son had recently taken to wearing a safety pin through his left earlobe, but nothing the boy could do would diminish his father's love.

He had come to America because of the boy. Well, not exactly *come*, but stayed when his student visa expired. He had met Camille, a nurse, at a teaching hospital and the boy had come along, all eight pounds and ten ounces of him, one balmy summer midnight. He could always go back to Delhi if he wanted to. He had made enough money to retire to India (the conversion into rupees had made him a millionaire several times over). He had bought a condominium in one of the better development 'colonies' of New Delhi, just in case.

America had been very good to him, no question; but there were things that he had given up. There were some boyhood emotions, for instance, that he could no longer retrieve. He lived with the fear that his father would die before he could free himself from the crazies of New York and go home. He missed his parents, especially his father, but he couldn't explain this loss to Camille. She hated her mother who had worked long hours at

29

Korvette's and brought her up alone. Camille's mother now worked at a K-Mart, even though she didn't need the money desperately. Camille's mother was an obsessive-compulsive but that was no reason to hate her. In fact, Manny got along with her very well and often had to carry notes between her and her daughter.

His father was now in his seventies, a loud, brash man with blackened teeth. He still operated the moviehouse he owned. The old man didn't trust the manager he kept on the payroll. He didn't trust anyone except his blood relatives. All the ushers in the moviehouse were poor cousins. Manny was an only child. His mother had been deemed barren, but at age forty-three, goddess Parvati had worked a miracle and Manny had been born. He should go back to India. He should look after his parents. Out of a sense of duty to the goddess, if not out of love for his father. Money, luxuries: he could have both in India, too. When he had wanted to go to Johns Hopkins for medical training, his parents had loved him enough to let him go. They loved him the same intense, unexamined way he loved his own boy. He had let them down. Perhaps he hadn't really let them down in that he had done well at medical school, and had a job in the State set-up in Queens, and played the money market aggressively with a bit of inside information from Suresh Khanna who had been a year ahead of him in Delhi's Modern School and was now with Merrill-Lynch, but he hadn't reciprocated their devotion.

It was in this mood of regret filtered through longing that Manny had driven in Manhattan and parked his Porsche on a side-street outside the Sari Palace which was a block up from the New Taj Mahal, where behind the counter he had spied the girl of his dreams.

The girl—the woman, Manny corrected himself instantly, for Camille didn't tolerate what she called 'masculists'—moved out from behind the counter to show a customer where in the crowded store the ten-pound bags of Basmati rice were stacked. She wore a 'Police' T-shirt and navy cords. The cords voluted up her small, rounded thighs and creased around her crotch in a delicate burst, like a Japanese fan. He would have dressed her in a silk sari of peacock blue. He wanted to wrap her narrow wrists in bracelets of 24-carat gold. He wanted to decorate her bosom and throat with necklaces of pearls, rubies, emeralds. She was as lovely and as removed from him as a goddess. He breathed warm, worshipful stains on the dingy store window.

She stooped to pick up a sack of rice by its rough jute handles while the customer flitted across the floor to a bin of eggplants. He discerned a touch of indolence in the way she paused before slipping her snake-slim fingers through the sack's hemp loops. She paused again. She tested the strength of the loops. She bent her knees, ready to heave the brutish sack of rice. He found himself running into the store. He couldn't let her do it. He couldn't let a goddess do menial chores, then ride home on a subway with a backache.

'Oh, thank you,' she said. She flashed him an indolent glance from under heavily shadowed eyelids, without seeming to turn away from the customer who had expected her to lift the ten-pound sack.

'Where are the fresh eggplants? These are all dried out.'

Manny Patel watched the customer flick the pleats of her Japanese georgette sari irritably over the sturdy tops of her winter boots.

'These things look as if they've been here all week!' the woman continued to complain.

Manny couldn't bear her beauty. Perfect crimson nails raked the top layer of eggplants. 'They came in just two days ago.'

If there had been room for a third pair of hands, he would have come up with plump, seedless, perfect eggplants.

'Ring up the rice, *dal* and spices,' the customer instructed. 'I'll get my vegetables next door.'

'I'll take four eggplants,' Manny Patel said defiantly. 'And two pounds of *bhindi*.' He sorted through wilted piles of okra which Camille wouldn't know how to cook.

'I'll be with you in a minute, sir,' the goddess answered.

When she looked up again, he asked her out for dinner. She only said, 'You really don't have to buy anything, you know.'

She suggested they meet outside the Sari Palace at six thirty. Her readiness overwhelmed him. Dr Patel had been out of the business of dating for almost thirteen years. At conferences, on trips and on the occasional night in the city when an older self possessed him, he would hire women for the evening, much as he had done in India. They were never precisely the answer, not even to his desire.

31

Camille had taken charge as soon as she had spotted him in the hospital cafeteria; she had done the pursuing. While he did occasionally flirt with a Filipino nutritionist at the hospital where he now worked, he assumed he did not possess the dexterity to perform the two-step dance of assertiveness and humility required of serious adultery. He left the store flattered but wary. A goddess had found him attractive, but he didn't know her name. He didn't know what kind of family fury she might unleash on him. Still, for the first time in years he felt a kind of agitated discovery, as though if he let up for a minute, his reconstituted, instant American life would not let him back.

His other self, the sober, greedy, scholarly Dr Patel, knew that life didn't change that easily. He had seen enough Horowitzes to know that no matter how astute his own methods might be and no matter how miraculous the discoveries of psychopharmacologists, fate could not be derailed. How did it come about that Mr Horowitz, the son of a successful slacks manufacturer, a good student at the Bronx High School of Science, had ended up obese, disturbed and assaultive, while he, the son of a Gujarati farmer turned entrepreneur, an indifferent student at Modern School and then at St. Stephen's in Delhi, was ambitious and acquisitive? All his learning and experience could not answer the simplest questions. He had about an hour and twenty minutes to kill before perfection was to revisit him, this time (he guessed) in full glory.

Dr Patel wandered through 'Little India'—the busy, colourful blocks of Indian shops and restaurants off Lexington in the upper twenties. Men lugged heavy crates out of doubleparked pickup trucks, swearing in Punjabi and Hindi. Women with tired, frightened eyes stepped into restaurants, careful not to drop their shopping-sacks from Bloomingdale's and Macy's. The Manhattan air here was fragrant with spices. He followed an attractive mother with two preschoolers into Chandni Chowk, a tea and snacks-stall, to call Camille about the emergency that had come up. Thank god for Mr Horowitz's recidivism. Camille was familiar with the more outrageous doings of Mr Horowitz.

'Why does that man always act up when I have plans?' Camille demanded. '*Amarcord* is at the rep tonight only.'

But Camille seemed in as agreeable a mood as his goddess. She thought she might ask Susan Kwan, the wife of an orthodontist who lived four houses up the block and who had a son by a former marriage also at Andover. Her credulousness depressed Manny. A woman who had lived with a man for almost thirteen years should be able to catch his little lies.

'Mr Horowitz is a dangerous person,' he continued. He could have hung up, but he didn't. He didn't want permission; he wanted sympathy. 'He rushed into my office. He tried to kill me.'

'Maybe psychiatrists at state institutions ought to carry firearms. Have you thought of that, Manny?' she laughed.

Manny Patel flushed. Camille didn't understand how the job was draining him. Mr Horowitz had, for a fact, flopped like a walrus on Dr Patel's desk, demanding a press conference so that the world would know that his civil liberties were being infringed. The moneyless schizos of New York state, Mr Horowitz had screamed, were being held hostage by a bunch of foreign doctors who couldn't speak English. If it hadn't been for the two six-foot orderlies (Dr Patel felt an awakening of respect for big blacks), Mr Horowitz would probably have grabbed him by the throat.

'I could have died today,' he repeated. The realization dazed him. 'The man tried to strangle me.'

He hung up and ordered a cup of *masala* tea. The sweet, sticky brew calmed him, and the perfumed steam cleared his sinuses. Another man in his position would probably have ordered a double Scotch. In crises, he seemed to regress, to reach automatically for the miracle cures of his Delhi youth, though normally he had no patience with nostalgia. When he had married, he burned his India Society membership card. He was professionally cordial, nothing more, with Indian doctors at the hospital. But he knew he would forever shuttle between the old world and the new. He couldn't pretend he had been reborn when he became an American citizen in a Manhattan courthouse. Rebirth was the privilege of the dead, and of gods and goddesses, and they could leap into your life in myriad, mysterious ways, as a shopgirl, for instance, or as a withered eggplant, just to test you.

At three minutes after six, Dr Patel positioned himself inside his Porsche and watched the front doors of the Sari Palace for his date's arrival. He didn't want to give the appearance of having waited nervously. There was a slight tremor in both his hands.

He was suffering a small attack of anxiety. At thirty-three minutes after six, she appeared in the doorway of the sari-store. She came out of the Sari Palace, not up the street from the New Taj Mahal as he had expected. He slammed shut and locked his car door. Did it mean that she too had come to the rendezvous too early and had spied on him, crouched, anxious, strapped in the bucket seat of his Porsche? When he caught up with her by the store window, she was the most beautiful woman he had ever talked to.

Her name was Padma. She told him that as he fought for a cab to take them uptown. He didn't ask for, and she didn't reveal, her last name. Both were aware of the illicit nature of their meeting. An Indian man his age had to be married, though he wore no wedding ring. An immigrant girl from a decent Hindu family—it didn't matter how long she had lived in America and what rock groups she was crazy about—would not have said yes to dinner with a man she didn't know. It was this inarticulate unsanctionedness of the dinner date that made him feel reckless, a hedonist, a man who might trample tired ladies carrying shopping-bags in order to steal a taxi crawling uptown. He wanted to take Padma to an Indian restaurant so that he would feel he knew what he was ordering and could bully the *maitre d'* a bit, but not to an Indian restaurant in her neighbourhood. He wanted a nice Indian restaurant, an upscale one, with table-cloths, *sitar* music and air ducts sprayed with the essence of rose-petals. He chose a new one, Shajahan, on Park Avenue.

'It's nice. I was going to recommend it,' she said.

Padma. Lotus. The goddess had come to him as a flower. He wanted to lunge for her hands as soon as they had been seated at a corner booth, but he knew better than to frighten her off. He was mortal, he was humble.

The *maitre d'* himself took Dr Patel's order. And with the *hors d' oeuvres* of *samosas* and *poppadoms* he sent a bottle of Entre Deux Mers on the house. Dr Patel had dined at the Shajahan four or five times already, and each time had brought in a group of six or eight. He had been a little afraid that the *maitre d'* might disapprove of his bringing a youngish woman, an Indian and quite obviously not his wife, but the bottle of wine reassured him that the management was not judgemental.

He broke off a sliver of *poppadom* and held it to her lips. She snatched it with an exaggerated flurry of lips and teeth: 'Feeding the performing seal, are you?' She was coy. And amused.

'I didn't mean it that way,' he murmured. Her lips, he noticed, had left a glistening crescent of lipstick on a fingertip. He wiped the finger with his napkin surreptitiously under the table.

She didn't help herself to the *samosas*, and he didn't dare lift a forkful to her mouth. Perhaps she didn't care for *samosas*. Perhaps she wasn't much of an eater. He himself was timid and clumsy, half afraid that if he tried anything playful he might drip mint chutney on her tiger-print chiffon sari.

'Do you mind if I smoke?'

He busied himself with food while she took out a packet of Sobrani and a book of matches. Camille had given up smoking four years before, and now handwritten instructions THANK YOU FOR NOT SMOKING IN THIS HOUSE decorated bureautops and coffee tables. He had never got started because of an allergy.

'Well?' she said. It wasn't quite a question, and it wasn't quite a demand. 'Aren't you going to light it?' And she offered Manny Patel an exquisite profile, cheeks sucked tight and lips squeezed around the filter tip.

The most banal gesture of a goddess can destroy a decent-living mortal. He lit her cigarette, then blew the match out with a gust of unreasonable hope.

The *maitre d'* hung around Manny's table almost to the point of neglecting other early diners. He had sad eyes and a bushy moustache. He wore a dark suit, a silvery wide tie kept in place with an elephant-headed god stick-pin, and on his feet which were remarkably large for a short, slight man, scuffed and pointed black shoes.

'I wouldn't recommend the pork vindaloo tonight.' The man's voice was confidential, low. 'We have a substitute cook. But the fish Bengal curry is very good. The lady, I think, is Bengali, no?'

She did not seem surprised. 'How very observant of you, sir,' she smiled.

It was flattering to have the *maitre d'* linger and advise. Manny Patel ended up ordering one each of the curries listed under beef, lamb and fowl. He was a guiltlessly meat-eating Gujarati, at least in America. He filled in the rest of the order with two vegetable dishes, one spiced lentil and a vegetable *pillau*. The *raita* was free, as were the two small jars of mango and lemon pickle.

When the food started coming, Padma reluctantly stubbed out her Sobrani. The *maitre d'* served them himself, making clucking noises with his tongue against uneven, oversize teeth, and Dr Patel felt obliged to make loud, appreciative moans.

'Is everything fine, doctor sahib? Fish is first class, no? It is not on the regular menu.'

He stayed and made small talk about Americans. He dispatched waiters to other tables, directing them with claps of pinkish palms from the edge of Manny's booth. Padma made an initial show of picking at her vegetable *pillau*. Then she gave up and took out another slim black Sobrani from a tin packet and held her face, uplifted and radiant, close to Manny's so he could light it again for her.

The *maitre d'* said, 'I am having a small problem, doctor sahib. Actually the problem is my wife's. She has been in America three years and she is very lonely still. I'm saying to her, you have nice apartment in Rego Park, you have nice furnitures and fridge and stove, I'm driving you here and there in a blue Buick, you're having home-style Indian food, what then is wrong? But I am knowing and you are knowing, doctor sahib, that no Indian lady is happy without having children to bring up. That is why, in my desperation, I brought over my sister's child last June. We want to adopt him, he is very bright and talented and already he is loving this country. But the US government is telling me no. The boy came on a visitor's visa, and now the government is giving me big trouble. They are calling me bad names. Jealous peoples are telling them bad stories. They are saying I'm in the business of moving illegal aliens, can you believe? In the meantime, my wife is crying all day and pulling out her hair. Doctor sahib, you can write that she needs to have the boy here for her peace of mind and mental stability, no? On official stationery of your hospital, doctor sahib?'

'My hands are tied,' Manny Patel said. 'The US government wouldn't listen to me.'

Padma said nothing. Manny ignored the *maitre d'*. A reality was dawning on Manny Patel. It was too beautiful, too exciting to contemplate. He didn't want this night to fall under the pressure of other immigrants' woes.

'But you will write a letter about my wife's mental problems, doctor sahib?' The *maitre d'* had summoned up tears. A man in a dark suit weeping in an upscale ethnic restaurant. Manny felt slightly disgraced, he wished the man would go away. 'Official stationery is very necessary to impress the immigration people.'

'Please leave us alone,' snapped Manny Patel. 'If you persist I will never come back.'

The old assurance, the authority of a millionaire in his native culture, was returning. He was sure of himself.

'What do you want to do after dinner?' Padma asked when the *maitre d'* scurried away from their booth. Manny could sense him, wounded and scowling, from behind the kitchen door.

'What would you like to do?' He thought of his wife and Mrs Kwan at the Fellini movie. They would probably have a drink at a bar before coming home. Susan Kwan had delightful legs. He had trouble understanding her husband, but Manny Patel had spent enjoyable hours at the Kwans', watching Mrs Kwan's legs. Padma's legs remained a mystery; he had seen her only in pants or a sari.

'If you are thinking of fucking me,' she said very suddenly, 'I should warn you that I never have an orgasm. You won't have to worry about pleasing me.'

Yes, he thought, it *is* so, just as he had suspected. It was a night in which he could do no wrong. He waved his visa card at the surly *maitre d'* and paid the bill. After that Padma let him take her elbow and guide her to the expensive hotel above the restaurant.

An oriental man at the desk asked him, 'Cash or credit card, sir?' He paid for a double occupancy room with cash and signed himself in as Dr Mohan Vakil & wife, 18 Ridgewood Drive, Columbus, Ohio.

He had laid claim to America.

In a dark seventh-floor room off a back corridor, the goddess bared her flesh to a dazed, daunted mortal. She was small. She was perfect. She had saucy breasts, fluted thighs and tiny, taut big toes.

'Hey, you can suck but don't bite, okay?' Padma may have been slow to come, but he was not. He fell on her with a devotee's frenzy.

'Does it bother you?' she asked later, smoking the second Sobrani. She was on her side. Her tummy had a hint of convex opulence. 'About my not getting off?'

He couldn't answer. It was a small price to pay, and anyway he wasn't paying it. Nothing could diminish the thrill he felt in taking a chance. It wasn't the hotel and this bed; it was having stepped inside the New Taj Mahal and asking her out.

He should probably call home, in case Camille hadn't stopped off for a drink. He should probably get dressed, offer her something generous—as discreetly as possible, for this one had class, real class—then drive himself home. The Indian food, an Indian woman in bed, made him nostalgic. He wished he were in his kitchen, and that his parents were visiting him and that his mother was making him a mug of hot Horlick's and that his son was not so far removed from him in a boarding school.

He wished he had married an Indian woman. One that his father had selected. He wished he had any life but the one he had chosen.

As Dr Patel sat on the edge of the double bed and slid his feet through the legs of his trousers, someone rapped softly on the hotel door, then without waiting for an answer unlocked it with a passkey.

Padma pulled the sheet up to her chin, but did not seem to have been startled.

'She's underage, of course,' the *maitre d'* said. 'She is my sister's youngest daughter. I accuse you of rape, doctor sahib. You are of course ruined in this country. You have everything and think you must have more. You are highly immoral.'

He sat on the one chair that wasn't littered with urgently cast-off clothes, and lit a cigarette. It was rapidly becoming stuffy in the room, and Manny's eyes were running. The man's eyes were malevolent, but the rest of his face remained practised and relaxed. An uncle should have been angrier, Dr Patel thought automatically. He himself should have seen it coming. He had mistaken her independence as a bold sign of honest assimilation. But it was his son who was the traveller over shifting sands, not her.

There was no point in hurrying. Meticulously he put on his trousers, double-checked the zipper, buttoned his shirt, knotted his tie and slipped on his Gucci shoes. *The lady is Bengali, no?* Yes, they knew one another, perhaps even as uncle and niece. Or pimp and hooker. The air here was polluted with criminality. He wondered if his slacks had been made by immigrant women in Mr Horowitz's father's sweat-shop.

'She's got to be at least twenty-three, twenty-four,' Dr Patel said. He stared at her, deliberately insolent. Through the sheets he could make out the upward thrust of her taut big toes. He had kissed those toes only half-an-hour before. He must have been mad.

'I'm telling you she is a minor. I'm intending to make a citizen's arrest. I have her passport in my pocket.'

It took an hour of bickering and threats to settle. He made out a check for seven hundred dollars. He would write a letter on hospital stationery. The uncle made assurances that there were no hidden tapes. Padma went into the bathroom to wash up and dress.

'Why?' Manny shouted, but he knew Padma couldn't hear him over the noise of the gushing faucet.

After the team left him, Manny Patel took off his clothes and went into the bathroom so recently used by the best-looking woman he had ever talked to (or slept with, he could now add). Her perfume, he thought of it as essence of lotus, made him choke.

He pulled himself up, using the edge of the bathtub as a step ladder, until his feet were on the wide edges of the old-fashioned sink. Then, squatting like a villager, squatting the way he had done in his father's home, he defecated into the sink, and with handfuls of his own shit—it felt hot, light, porous, an artist's medium—he wrote WHORE on the mirror and floor.

He spent the night in the hotel room. Just before dawn he took a cab to the parking lot of the Sari Palace. Miraculously, no vandals had touched his Porsche. Feeling lucky, spared somehow in spite of his brush with the deities, he drove home.

Camille had left the porch light on and it glowed pale in the brightening light of the morning. In a few hours Mr Horowitz would start to respond to the increased dosage of Haldol and be let out of the seclusion chamber. At the end of the term, Shawn Patel would come home from Andover and spend all day in the house with earphones tuned to a happier world. And in August, he would take his wife on a cruise through the Caribbean and make up for this night with a second honeymoon.

Gangadhar Gadgil

The Dog That Ran in Circles

I was walking lazily towards the bus-stop. I had to go somewhere, oh—anywhere. I was feeling so restless and so depressed,
I knew I had to write a story. So I was walking to enjoy the restful pause at the end of each step. 'I want to write a story...a
story...a s-t-o-r-y....' I was saying to myself mechanically, over
and over again. 'A story...a s-t-o-r-y.'

The word became bloated and shapeless. It stared at me and
drove my consciousness into a stupid daze. Deeper down, in the
half asleep wakefulness something was astir. Meandering circles
were being traced with a weak insistence. They were dully luminous. Caught in the tangled web of the circles would appear a
shape like a mark left by a faded flower in a book. Mute shapes
that paused on the brink of life and meaning! Suddenly they
would acquire bold outlines. But before they could mean anything to me, they would become spreading blots of ink,
shapeless and dead. I stared at them, hoping to see through
them. But they gave away nothing . . . .

I was utterly engrossed in this tantalizing search—lost in a
dark brown cloud of concentration tinged by fleeting moods and
fancies. I wanted to see nothing, hear nothing. I reached the bus-
stop and stood there staring blankly at the street.

I was seeing a shape, although I did not in the least want to
see it. It was out there in the street. A brownish shape—a dog,
faded and limp, lying in the street. I couldn't take my eyes off its
starved and heaving belly. It heaved in quick spasms, as if it
wanted to get the whole thing over and done with. The dog lay
still in the midst of the endless scribble of traffic and movement
on the street. Possibly it had bumped against a passing car and
had fainted.

A crowd had gathered on the sidewalk. It was swelling and
imperceptibly edging forward over the curb into the street.
Vagrant boys, hoodlums gambling at the street corner, old
women stooping and shrivelled, hawkers and labourers! The
white collared gentry stood at the bus-stop, stiff and indifferent,

giving the dog now and then an anaesthetized look. They wouldn't stoop to anything as plebian as a mouthful of pity or a squirt of casual curiosity.

The crowd stood there, hesitant and slightly ashamed of its concern over a street-dog. Yet, they all felt relieved as each car swerved to avoid running over the dog. Unwittingly, they started signalling to the cars that came along.

One of the old women started muttering. She looked around to gauge the attitude of the crowd and then raised her voice.

'You there! You brat! Go and get a pot of water. Pour it on the dog's head, will you?' she said, and shoved a boy in the direction of a restaurant.

'Well auntie! That's a good idea. But why don't you do it yourself?' said a man who stood behind her.

Everybody laughed, and the interest in the dog became more lively. A couple of boys ran forward. A thin straggling line of people followed them hesitantly. Soon the whole crowd was standing on the street around the dog.

I couldn't quite see what was happening. The boy whom the old woman had shoved ran to the restaurant and came back with a pot of water. The whole crowd leaned forward. Those at the back stood on their toes. The people watching through their windows leaned out and craned their necks. 'Hey!' everybody cheered happily. The crowd made way and the dog emerged, still dazed, but now on its feet. It staggered towards the curb. The crowd followed it.

It was a starving, shrivelled dog. It had a pitifully meek expression—the kind of dog that gets in everybody's way and is always kicked. But for its eyes, I wouldn't have looked at it twice.

The eyes were moist in a queer way. It wasn't the kind of moistness that calls forth pity, but different. The eyes asked for nothing. In fact, nothing had any meaning for them any more. They expressed no hunger, no fear. They had nothing to do any longer with the world of dogs. If they expressed anything at all, it was compassion—the kind one sees in the eyes of a saint. But this of course was my crazy fancy.

The queer moist look in the eyes made me uneasy. I had a feeling that apart from the people, the vehicles and the shops with their gaudy makeup, there was something else present there, something more substantial and compelling. It was right there in front of me, and those eyes were seeing it.

Mechanically, the dog sniffed at the ground and at people's feet. It wagged its tail and licked its nose. It settled down near the curb, resting its head on its paws.

The crowd still stood around and looked at it with pity. People walking along the sidewalk stopped and asked eagerly what the matter was? Most of the time they didn't get any reply, and if they got one it said nothing. Many in the crowd had come there too late to know what had happened, and even those who had seen everything had nothing to tell. Nothing really had happened.

But there was one in the crowd who had seen everything and, whenever asked, he would look straight ahead with a very solemn face and narrate everything in tedious detail. His listeners would look puzzled, for what he said didn't lead to anything at all. They would conclude that it was all a silly fuss about nothing. Some of them walked away. But others stood there because of the crowd, and looked at the dog with an affectation of sickening pity.

I was losing interest in the whole affair. It seemed to be one of those incidents that holds a promise and then hangs in the air inconclusively, like the loose end of a thread. I tried to think of the story I wanted to write.

But, by now, everything was tangled and adrift. I had lost track of everything that had so tantalizingly remained beyond my reach. All I could think of was that silly incident. It had left a scratch across my consciousness—a scratch that hurt but didn't bleed.

'I want to write a story...a story...a s-t-o-r-y....' I said to myself, and the words soothingly ran over and around the scratch, like a massaging fingertip. Slowly, I got back into that state of daze. Wandering circles began to be traced again—circles potent with the insubstantial presence of a shape, a form. It was there all the time, not caring to be seen.

Wandering circles—dully luminous!

All of a sudden the dog stood up and started running in circles, tottering and slipping all the time. At first it moved in little circles, in a corner of the street. But, gradually, the circles grew bigger and crazier.

There was a stir in the crowd. Everybody perked up and looked intently at the dog. 'Ch-ch!' 'Sit down in a corner, you crazy dog....!'

The old auntie darted forward and tried to catch hold of the dog. That little push threw the dog off its balance and it yelped.

'There, auntie! Don't you get mixed up with that dog. It seems to be loony. It might bite you.'

'Oh woman! Oh!' cried the auntie, and jumped back to the sidewalk with unsuspected agility. She barely missed having a fall and everybody laughed. The crowd decided to stay away from the dog and shuffled back a couple of steps.

The dog ran in crazy circles seeing nothing with its queer moist eyes. It was now right in the centre of the street. Horns were honking, brakes were screeching and cars were turning and swerving madly to avoid running over the dog.

Sometimes the dog ran in big circles, as wide as the street. Then suddenly, it would trace a ridiculously small circle at the edge of the big one, and achieve a precarious and impossible balance between the two. Sometimes its path had a beautiful oblong shape that contrasted oddly with its ridiculous figure. At times the path wobbled like a reflection in the disturbed water of a pool.

'Stop it! Stop it!' 'Come here you crazy dog. You will get killed.' 'I wish it would get run over so everything was finished.' The people in the crowd gesticulated and talked wildly.

But the dog saw nothing, heard nothing. It wasn't bothered about getting killed. It was possessed, held in thrall and driven by some mysterious impulse that sought this odd fulfilment.

People at the wheels of cars expected the dog to behave normally and get out of the way, when they honked their horns. But the dog wouldn't budge and the cars veered at crazy angles, barely missing the dog. It almost seemed to have a charmed life.

The crowd watched tensely in terror. They knew the dog would be run over sooner or later and, in a way, they were resigned to it. Yet they were signalling wildly to the cars, and bursting into happy hysterical laughter whenever the dog had a particularly narrow escape. They were somehow deeply involved in that absurd drama of the street.

'Hey there! Somebody buy a biscuit and offer it to the dog. Tie him up with a piece of string!' the old auntie cried, unable to stand the tension any more.

'Very well, auntie! Give me a couple of coins. I will buy a biscuit for the dog,' said a man in the crowd, grinning slyly.

Dear old auntie laughed, opening wide her toothless hole of a mouth. It was a cunning laugh, and yet innocent. Everybody laughed. But the strain was getting unbearable. So somebody bought a few biscuits and offered them to the dog. The dog wagged its tail and licked its nose mechanically. But it didn't stop. It was tired and staggering at every step. Yet it went on.

Nothing could be done for that dog. It wanted no kindness and no help. So all we could do was to play the uncomfortable role of spectators. Everybody felt very foolish about it.

'Shoot the bloody dog! Kill it!' screamed a man in English. He had been sucking at his pipe and reading a paper, trying to affect the indifference of an Englishman.

A woman on the upper storey of a house was leaning out of the window and watching. She would press her head in her palms and grimace in pain when the dog seemed to be going under the wheels of a car. When it escaped, she would scream with joy. She was gesticulating wildly and calling everybody in the house to the window to watch the fun. The lipstick on her lips made her look even more queer and frightening.

People in the crowd were all talking at the same time. 'The municipal staff must have poisoned the dog,' they were saying, which of course was not true. But the crowd wanted to get mad at somebody.

The dog was certainly being protected by some invisible deity. It escaped death for more than ten minutes on that busy street. The absurd drama continued in the midst of a high voltage circuit of tension and jitters.

Then came a double-decker bus—a huge, brash, red box on wheels. The driver was perched high, sealed in a glass cabin. He was sitting very erect, as if he had a steel rod for a spine. He was wearing outsized sun-glasses that covered half his face and made it look like a fiendish mask.

The dog staggered on unconcerned and in a moment was right in front of the bus. The crowd screamed. The driver jammed the brakes on with an awkward jerk. But the bus kept rolling on. I saw the dog going under a wheel. I closed my eyes and waited for an infinitesimal fraction of time to hear the final yelp. It was a very weak yelp, conveying no pain and no reluctance to die. It was just a motor response of the body.

The woman at the window crushed her head in her palms and screamed. She then burst into an idiotic laughter. Because of the lipstick, it looked as if her lips were smeared with blood.

There were screams all around. The huge, red bus hesitated for a moment on its ponderous wheels, and then moved on with a jerk that was very much like an indifferent shrug. It moved on inexorably in a straight line, gathering momentum amidst the rising roar of its engine.

The dog lay on its side with all its legs outstretched. Blood was trickling from a corner of its mouth.

A few people gathered around the corpse. But they had already lost interest. The rest of the crowd walked away in a hurry, brushing the whole incident off their minds with little impatient gestures.

'I want to write a story...a story...a s-t-o-r-y . . . .' I said stupidly to myself.

Then a bus came, in all its mechanical dignity. I had been almost praying all this time that it should come and take me away before the dog met its inevitable end. It swallowed up the waiting queue in which I stood, and then moved on.

Translated from Marathi by the author

U.R.Anantha Murthy

The Sky and The Cat

Jayatheertha Acharya listened to Govindan Nair till nine in the night; then he slept; and, at five in the morning, making a sound as if being sawn into two, he died. He was bedridden for hardly twenty days. At the time of his death, all his dear ones were there; his son who had heard of his father's illness and had come from Delhi with his family; Govindan Nair, a Communist from Kerala, a friend of his youthful days who had not seen him these forty years; Acharya's wife; his widowed daughter and her twelve-year-old son; and, more importantly, even Gangubai was present—his mistress these twenty years. She was from Shimoga and she had come without a second thought, when the news of Acharya's illness had reached her. It was rumoured and was sort of known that he had a mistress; but it was only now that she was seen in the flesh. When she came, Acharya did not raise any objection. His wife Rukminiyamma, of course, made a rumpus—talked of decency, of honour, and of fear of pollution, etc., with her daughter. But her husband's state of health and her awareness that one's *karma* had to be lived had kept her in check. Gangubai talked to everyone with a smile on her face and quietly took over the nursing of Acharya. She saw the bed they had put him on was hard and lumpy. She got another, softer one made. She washed the sheets, neatly pressed them with a charcoal-heated iron and daily made the bed. When Acharya began to talk to her about the cows she had left behind, the milk that was to be distributed, and so on, she said she knew how to manage things, that he should not worry, and that she had made the necessary arrangements. To his question, 'How long will you be on leave?' she had laughingly said, 'Till you get well.' Acharya's widowed daughter, Savithri, felt somewhat at ease when she came to know that Gangubai had a teaching job in a primary school. Acharya had never spoken about his mistress to his wife. Now it appeared as if he had accepted her as one of the members of his own family.

Krishna Moorthy wondered whether his father knew that his

end had come. If not, why would he have asked his friend to come, a friend he had not seen these forty years? True, now and then, he had remembered Nair. Whenever reports of Nair's violent political activity appeared in newspapers, Acharya had expressed his disapproval of it to his son. For example, an incident that some five years ago headlined in the national newspapers. It seems Nair had gone to see a minister to discuss the payment of bonus to workers in a coffee plantation. According to the minister's statement, word led to word and Nair took out of his bag an acid bomb and threw it at the minister. According to Nair's statement in the court, his intention, of course, was to kill the minister but he had unfortunately missed his target. He had only succeeded in beating up the minister with his *chappals*. The minister, in his bid to escape, had fallen against a table and had suffered a head injury. Nair was sentenced to five years imprisonment. After his release he had issued a statement saying that his mission henceforth would be to eliminate corrupt men who were enemies of the people. Acharya had, then, immediately thought of writing to Nair, condemning his activities. He, however, had not. Perhaps because he did not know what or how to say anything to a friend of his youth, whose way of life had become so completely different from his own. Or, perhaps that may not have been the only reason. He was so engrossed in settling property disputes of the local rich, in drafting documents and in going up and down the steps of law courts pursuing his other cases, he, perhaps, did not have the patience to understand his old friend who was prepared to sacrifice his life for a cause. After this incident, an article had appeared in a weekly about Nair. Did his father, the son wondered, have the faintest idea that Nair—with whom he had joined the Railways in Delhi—would one day shape like this? They had, apparently, shared a room. Nair had taken Acharya into his confidence, and had told him all his secrets. Since Acharya was a brahmin he would do the cooking. Nair would do the shopping, cut vegetables, etc. When Acharya was busy preparing the dishes, Nair, smoking a *beedi*, would read aloud a story. The stories that were dear to both were ones by Goldsmith and Reynolds. So far as Acharya's memory went, Nair was a man who loved his pleasures. Why did such a man set out to subvert a system which protected those very pleasures?

Acharya lost his job because he was found to be medically unfit; it was malarial fever and the consequent tumour in his tummy that had cost him his job. Later he became an accounts clerk and worked on a part-time basis in several shops. He did this for two years and then got fed up. Added to this, remembrances of his young wife who had not yet come of age, his father, his father's job in the town temple made him leave Delhi.

Nair also lost his job. But that was for participating in a strike. And that was again in post-independent India. Nair went back to Kerala, his home state, began to work with the peasants and became a Communist. To him the Congress party was a party of treacherous men. When his party began to work with the Congress under orders from Russia he resigned his membership and became a loner, but still continued to be a Communist. The weekly had picturesquely presented his life: 'At night, he sleeps on the verandah of someone's house. Wakes up. Washes his clothes in well-water, has a wash himself and then leaves. He collects wrappers of bound notebooks from schoolchildren, makes fans out of these wrappers. He takes the paper-fans to the hospital, enquires about the patients and leaves the fans with them. In the afternoon, he sits in the hotel at the town's centre. He does odd jobs for the workers and peasants and eats whatever they give him. Drinks the tea, smokes his *beedi* and walks the town streets. He visits ration-depots, public-offices, police stations, argues, quarrels with officials on behalf of the poor and the ignorant, gets their job done. Again, in the evening, sits in the hotel, drafts petitions for them, eats whatever they buy him and spends the night on somebody else's verandah. He never keeps a paisa in his pocket for the next morning. And while working for the poor he educates them on Exploitation, Revolution, the New Society, etc. This is his daily routine. This was not the first time that he had beaten people's enemies with his *chappals*. But because the person who got beaten this time was a minister, it had hit the headlines. That was all.

'Dressed in a white *dhoti* and a shirt, and with a pencil stub in his hairy ears and paper-fans in his hands, he walks the town streets and people know him by one name, "Master".'

Acharya read the article, sat with a pinch of snuff between his fingers and thought deeply. Like him, Nair too lived for others; but how differently. He made his son too read the article, began to say something but stopped halfway, abruptly. All this took on a mysterious meaning for Krishna Moorthy after his father's death.

As soon as he fell ill Acharya had written to Nair, the man without a postal address—that was the title of the article in the weekly—and had asked him to come. He had written to Gangubai too, but had not asked her—as he had asked his son and Nair—to come. But since Nair was involved in a plantation workers' strike, he could come only a day previous to Acharya's death.

It was Krishna Moorthy's firm belief that his father's name defied all abbreviations. But he was surprised when Nair walked in, put down the sling-bag which contained everything that could be called his possessions on the floor, sat on the bed, and said with spontaneous affection 'Jaya.' Nair took a look at the medicines Acharya was taking, felt and pressed his swollen feet as if he had left Acharya only the previous day. Was he not from Kerala? Like Acharya, he too was an admirer of Ayurveda. He felt Acharya's pulse, made him open his mouth, looked at his tongue, pulled his eyelids down and peered into the eyes, sighed, took some powder from his bag, mixed it with honey and made him eat it. While attending to the sick man, he spoke rapidly and said how allopathy had destroyed the native medical system, how this was inevitable in the neo-colonial set-up and how, from this point of view alone, Nehru was a traitor. As he was speaking, he took out a pamphlet he had written and published and gave it to Acharya— as if somehow Nehru was the cause of his illness. When he heard that Krishna Moorthy was working at the Delhi School of Economics, he laughed a sad laugh and said, 'You are all slaves either of Russia or of the States; there is not a single patriot left among our educated young men.'

At the beginning, Nair's total absorption in the thing he was doing looked a little ridiculous to Krishna Moorthy; but gradually it began to worry him. Consoling and gently stroking the brow of the sick man whose body was all swollen, Nair looked so feminine and gentle; and at the same time he was shredding to pieces the entire socio-political set-up so savagely. Krishna Moorthy did not know how to understand such a man. Should he not, for the sake of courtesy, ask father what he had been doing these forty years? Father did not say, because he was not well. Anyway he could not make out what father wanted to say or hear from Nair. Then why had he got him here? And, did Nair know that father would not survive and was that why he asked him to eat whatever he liked? Father said he had lost all taste for food. When Nair, recalling the forty-year-old memory of their Delhi days, said 'Well, you were always dying to eat mango chutney,' father had smiled. Krishna Moorthy had rarely seen his father smile like that and he had certainly not seen father smile after he had fallen ill. He would spend much of his time either staring vacantly at the roof-beam or studying the almanac or the *ashtanga hridaya*. To father's question, 'Doesn't mango chutney cause acidity?' Nair said, 'I have an antidote, don't worry.'

Then Nair sat beside father and read the pamphlet he had written. He seemed to read without any expectation of a response. When it was night Gangubai helped Acharya sit up. His daughter brought him rice and mango chutney. He ate a morsel or two, said he had no taste for any dish and then lay down. He turned towards Nair and said 'Now what next?' The way he said it and the way Nair took it, was significant to Krishna Moorthy as the whole thing occurred the night previous to his father's death. Nair struck a match, lighted a *beedi* and spoke in a quiet tone.

'You mean what I intend doing? Well, I am like the seed which hopes for and wishes to fall into fertile soil. Look, what I wrote in my diary just before I came here.' He opened his diary and read. 'The coffee plantation workers were with me. They used to listen to me but now they have become greedy and have deserted me. They were duped by the greatest scoundrel of Kerala politics, M.V. Wariyar. One of these days I want to stop him on the main thoroughfare and put a knife into his heart.' Shutting the diary and putting it back into his bag he said as if they were going to be his last words— 'See I have put it all down here, and I go tomorrow.'

What kind of a person was this who brought in the entire nation in his answer to a personal query? Father didn't say anything. Why? Perhaps he could not grasp. Or, was he too tired? It was hard to guess what transpired in the silence of his mind. Father did not survive to see Nair translating his words into action. He did what he had said he would. In the main thorough-fare, in the presence of a large number of people, he stopped Wariyar, pulled out a knife, and proclaimed his intention loudly and clearly. Anybody could have guessed the outcome. Wariyar fell back and then ran. Nair pursued him. People gave chase, caught hold of Nair and took away his knife; later he was arrested on a charge of attempted murder.

Did Nair who was sixty years old really think that he would succeed in killing Wariyar who was younger by twenty years? How serious was he in his life's mission? Was not the whole thing a bit too melodramatic? Such thoughts often passed through Krishna Moorthy's mind. This was because Nair had, in fact, become a challenge to Krishna Moorthy's way of life.

Nair left the moment father died and said while going, 'Your father lived and died a foolish man. You too seem to be treading his path.' Krishna Moorthy could not speak, but managed to mumble haltingly, 'What about the last rites?' True, the violence in Nair's words was not seen in his eyes and yet the harsh words had shaken Krishna Moorthy. 'Nothing much left now. Bury him, he will make good manure. But you are brahmins. You cremate. Because it was a friend I came, leaving aside all my work. But now I don't have any more time to waste. And you must pay my expenses. A day's food and the bus fare come to twenty-five rupees.' He had felt like giving him a little more than twenty-five but had become afraid. The minute Nair left, Krishna Moorthy's wife, Meera, who had intensely disliked him for his bushy eye-brows, hairy ears, the pencil stub behind them, etc., grumbled loud enough for him to hear, 'What an indecent fellow! Should one sit beside a dying man and make street-corner speeches? And should one, while leaving, speak such words?' Nair's beha-viour had irked Krishna Moorthy also but he snubbed his wife, 'Don't talk of things you don't understand.'

Why did father wish to see a man like Nair after these forty years? Krishna Moorthy often worried himself over the strange friendship between his father and Nair and over the last, puzzling meeting between the two. And more so when he got tired of Delhi, of his wife and of his futile research on 'Five Year Plan and Land Reforms Act.'

Perhaps an incident which took place much before father's death made him feel this way. He had of course been surprised by the fact that father, a much respected man of the town, did not show any sign of embarrassment at Gangubai's presence. What had, however, equally surprised him was the contempt with which father had treated Vishnu Moorthy —the rich landlord who had been father's benefactor. These two incidents, he felt needed to be understood to know his father's mind in its last dying moments.

*

It was Acharya who had practically conducted the cases connected with the adoption of Vishnu Moorthy by Narasimha Bhatta. After the death of Narasimha Bhatta it was his wife who had brought up Vishnu Moorthy. She had a brother who was dear to her. When a son was born to him her affection flowed towards her nephew. Vishnu Moorthy was no longer a minor. And his parents advised him to be careful regarding the family property and the gold kept in an iron safe. Vishnu Moorthy had another lock put on the safe. With it started the legal disputes. Vishnu Moorthy beat up his foster-mother and drove her out. She filed a suit stating that Vishnu Moorthy was not her adopted son, that the records pertaining to the adoption were all fabricated and that she was the legal owner of all the family property. She, with her brother and her relatives, tried to force her way into the house. But in the meanwhile Vishnu Moorthy broke open the lock she had put on the safe, collected all the gold, put it in a trunk and left it in the safe custody of Jayatheertha Acharya. Acharya got him an advocate and advised him at every step. After that Vishnu Moorthy regularly carted rice to the Acharya's household every year.

Everybody knew that Vishnu was a smooth man. Dressed in a silk shirt, a gabardine jacket and white *mull-dhoti*, he always looked elegant. Whenever he visited Acharya's house Rukminiyamma was most deferential. Wasn't he the man who was feeding them all? Of course, Acharya was not unaware of Vishnu Moorthy's selfish and violent nature. He knew how Vishnu Moorthy had driven out his foster-mother. But since Acharya had seen a point of law in favour of Vishnu Moorthy and had also known the foster-mother's deceit it looked legally all right to Acharya. Father used to understand all moral values within the legal framework. But an act of Vishnu Moorthy put him in a painful dilemma. There was, in Vishnu's household, a servant by name Venkappa Naika. He was muscularly built and dark-skinned. Since he was also rather close to Vishnu, there were few family secrets he did not know. It was he who drove the master's covered bullock cart. Vishnu himself was very proud of the pair of bullocks he owned. They were so tall and handsome. Vishnu had left two acres of paddy-field on lease to his trusted servant.

There aren't any survivors left now who can say whether it was Venkappa who took a liking for Vishnu's widowed sister-in-law or whether it was the well-formed girl herself who fell for him. Be that as it may, the young widow became pregnant. Venkappa Naika was murdered. The widow underwent an abortion and kept her mouth shut. This was how he was murdered. There was a cousin of Venkappa Naika who had been his sworn enemy. The cousin murdered him and buried the body in the forest. Someone filed a suit. Vishnu had also become a suspect. He ran to Acharya and fell at his feet. By now, the news had reached Acharya. It certainly caused him much moral anguish; and yet he did not insist he should be told the truth. On the other hand, he came to willingly believe in Vishnu who declared that he did not know anything, that he was innocent, that it was Venkappa Naika who had first assaulted his cousin, that there were marks of injury on his body and that the cousin had killed Venkappa Naika purely in self-defence. Not only did he believe in Vishnu, he had enough evidence manufactured to convince others too that there was bad blood between the cousins from the beginning. He engaged the best criminal lawyer, got Vishnu Moorthy released on bail and ultimately won the case. Vishnu was declared innocent. After all this was over, Acharya told his son in confidence; 'Kittu, if there is what they call hell-fire, this Vishnu will surely roast in it. A beast of a man, that's what he is.'

'But you got him out.'

'No, it was the law. And, the law would rather let go ten guilty men than punish an innocent individual. The police case was rather weak. That's how Vishnu escaped.'

Father's sincerely spoken words and the importance law had gained within his framework of reference had surprised Krishna Moorthy. Was the legal system, to him, a diamond-hard breast-plate invulnerable to all moral questions till the moment of death? Perhaps it was. Nair's words about his work in the Delhi School of Economics were in a similar vein. Krishna Moorthy was quite aware of arguments like 'social science research cannot be free of values, etc.' But they frightened him, especially when he remembered father who died slaving for the rich.

Do we give up such consolations when death suddenly confronts us? Recalling the way father, in his dying moment, had treated Vishnu, Krishna Moorthy began to doubt the strength of beliefs and convictions. The adoption case had not yet been decided; it was still before the High Court. Added to this, there were fresh legal complications because of the new Land Reform Act. Vishnu's uncle had taken on lease a fertile piece of garden land which he was trying in vain to get back from him. The uncle was a much bigger rowdy than Vishnu. And it had also been said that Vishnu had kept gold and jewellery worth over a lakh of rupees with Acharya. As soon as he came to know of Acharya's illness, he must have got worried. Father did not even look at Vishnu who had come dressed in a silk shirt and white *mull-dhoti*. Displaying his gold teeth, he had enquired after Acharya's health. Father in reply had merely said ah, yes, no, yes, etc. Rukminiyamma made coffee specially for him and brought it in a silver tumbler. Vishnu, sipping the hot coffee, had said, 'Acharyare, shall I get you a doctor from Shimoga? If there are any drugs you need, I shall get them. Please, don't stand on any formality with me.' Father perhaps knew that this was only a prologue, a prefatory speech.

'I am tired, I can't talk much. Tell me what you want?' Acharya had said coldly. 'Nothing special Acharyare. I heard you were not well. And then I had some work in the Shimoga Bank. My wife, she has an abcess on the neck. She is to undergo an operation and it means expenses. You know my court cases and how they swallow up all money. So, I thought of pledging a few jewels...' Acharya had called his wife. She had come and stood there playing with her nose-ring. She had looked so enthusiastic. Her eagerness to please the man who supplied them the yearly quota of rice had angered Acharya. Coldly he had said, 'Give him that trunk.' Give him the trunk, which had been locked and kept in a big wooden box! Whenever she saw Vishnu open it, how irresistibly she was drawn to glance lovingly at the gold jewellery! It was a festival to her. She had only a pair of gold bangles and a *tali* on her person. But the fact that she was in charge of the trunk had in itself a matter of pride to her. Vishnu had got up saying, 'No, I shall come. No need to bring it here.' 'See, Vishnu, I have not been well and you can never say. Take the trunk. And, from next year, you don't need to send us any rice. As soon as I get well, we will all be going with our son to Delhi.' Acharya's cutting tone had made Vishnu say, 'No, no, Acharyare, you must not say such things, you are like a father to me.' 'See, Vishnu, when it comes to money there is neither father nor mother nor son. I am tired of my life—a life spent in slaving for the rich.' Acharya had spoken and as if he did not want to hear or say any more had turned on his side and kept his eyes closed. Vishnu had wrapped the trunk in a rug, had it put in the boot of the car and sneaked out like a thief.

*

While the case of attempted murder against Nair was still going on, Krishna Moorthy wrote him a letter in which he described the Vishnu Moorthy incident in detail. 'You cannot, therefore, call my father a fool. He too was disgusted with the rich. Yet he lived a full life and compared to him you look like a simple-minded and self-dramatizing person.'

Nair wrote back in English and the letter began with 'Revolutionary Greetings.' 'I intensely hate the society which is designed by the rich for their own happiness. Awakened by a love-affair, and desiring to escape from what Marx calls 'the idiocracy of rural life', your father left for Delhi forty years ago. What was it that destroyed the bubbling life spirit of the man? Slaving for the rich! That's what killed him. Money, the Moloch-image of the capitalist system, destroys our *dharma*, our culture and our dear relationships and our everything. It's only through the struggle of men like me that man will recover his genuine humanity. This is possible only through the Marxist way. I want my life itself to be an example of such a thought-process. If my actions appear to be that of a self-dramatizing person, suggest a better mode. I will follow that. My intention to kill the fat pigs of the capitalistic system is certainly no play-acting. I only wish that your life won't go to waste as your father's did. And I don't give much importance to awareness that comes at the point of death. What is important to me is the effect each living moment's work has on the community. Victory to Revolution.'

Krishna Moorthy didn't know the love-episode Nair had referred to in his letter. The one who knew of it, the one who was thinking only of it at the time of Acharya's death, was Gangubai.

*

Acharya's body was removed from the bed and placed cross-legged on the floor. Lamps in coconut-shells were lighted and kept; one near the head and the other near the feet. Govindan Nair left as soon as this was done. It must be said that his leaving the place gave some relief to Rukminiyamma. She sat weeping and as a last act of service to the dead applied some oil to the feet and head of her husband.

This death lay heavy on her. She felt as if the sky had fallen on her head. Who knew how much he was in debt to the local shops and the bank? He lived and died a proud and envied life. This son—perhaps he no longer even wore the sacred thread around his neck. What would the *purohit* say? He turned a deaf ear to those who bore him and married a North Indian woman. God knew what language she spoke or to what caste she belonged. He half-killed himself worrying over the son. True, in a passing fit of anger he had told Vishnu that they would all go to Delhi and stay with Kittu. Would that ever be possible? And that too with the widowed daughter and grandson? Through signs and gestures Savithri had to tell this North Indian daughter-in-law the simple done-things and not-done-things in a brahmin family. If Kittu was asked to tell her he got angry. And, to add to it that accursed woman had also come from Shimoga—even those who came to have a last look at the dead man, lingered on and cast inquisitive glances at her.

She felt lightened in spirit when she saw Vishnu get out of his car and come in. He would not desert her on this occasion of heavy expenses even though Acharya had been angry with him. Vishnu stood in a corner with his hands folded. Since not many of his status had come, he said in a weeping tone; 'You know, Kittu, there was none equal to him in the whole of our district. There was not a law or a legal point he did not know. It was because of him that men like me could manage to retain some land in these vicious times and live with some dignity. I could not even dream of such a thing happening when I was here two days ago. Making us all orphans, he left; a great soul.'

His last words aroused a fresh spasm of grief in Rukminiyamma. Her daughter Savithri came and took her in. Vishnu also followed them. People who had come from nearby villages did not know how to console Krishna Moorthy who stood there composed and serious, without any visible sign of grief on his face.

Father looked as if he was sleeping peacefully. And this exhibition of sorrow appeared to Krishna Moorthy an insult to the dead. He had never seen father weep. He had lived and died a self-respecting man. Perhaps Nair too had not wanted to witness such scenes. Perhaps he too knew father's way of showing love and affection. Once when Krishna Moorthy was in Mysore at school, he had suffered from a serious sore throat and almost lost his speech. He was running a high fever too. One morning, all of a sudden father had come. In his black waistcoat-pocket, there was a newly bought thermometer. Saying, 'I somehow felt you were not well. So, straightaway I bought a thermometer and came,' he had stayed for two days and nursed him. Father had lightened the strain of illness by peeling for him sweet lime and by talking of astronomy which was so dear to him.

While discussing astronomy father had also brought in subtle points of law connected with property. The world of law was as wonderful to him as the sky and stars. This had always seemed strange to Krishna Moorthy. Though father had to depend on the mercy of the rich men of the village, he himself had no particular fondness for money. Strangely, again, father had taken upon himself the job of saving those who had some property as if this was a big challenge life had thrown at him. Maybe father was a fool after all, as Nair had said.

His marriage must have been a rude shock to father. He had talked of what one owed to the gods. He who had never spoken of his personal feelings had thundered in his letter; 'You are marrying outside the caste because you don't want to perform my last rites.' Since father would not accept any money from him he had begun to send it to his mother. After the birth of a grandson, he had forgotten it all, accepted son and daughter-in-law and stayed with them as though he had never been away from them.

Again, just before his death he had said he would go and live with him in Delhi; he had come to accept Gangubai also; he had sent for Nair. All these spoke of one thing; father had digested the bitterness of his son marrying outside his caste.

He stood watching the lamps burn and the men busily engaged in making a bier with bamboo sticks. He noticed that Meera was trying to draw his attention. She was engaged in her perpetual and daily warfare with their son, Srinath, who was refusing to sit on the yellow, plastic pot. She needed her husband's help. But if his sister and mother saw him helping, he would look henpecked. The thought embarrassed him. He did not know whether it was proper or not for him to move away. Meera, an alien to whom such niceties did not exist, glared at her husband and forced the boy to use the pot.

Krishna Moorthy, pondering over what Nair had said of father, took up his son and went into the backyard. The bullocks, tied to pegs, were breathing heavily and slowly munching the grass. A dog stretched itself in the sun. There were heaps of cowdung on the floor since the routine cleaning had not been done because of father's death. To the right, at a distance, was the cowshed; beside the shed, as a witness to father's modern thinking, stood the *gobar* gas cylinder.

Today's fire had not been lighted in the kitchen. The cows had not been milked and they were tugging at the ropes. Savithri was now freeing them. Mother had never let the cows out without first milking them. Every day she would milk the cows, give them grass and some cattle feed and then tie round the calves' mouths a thorny basket. Her son would protest against such cruelty. Mother would laugh and say, 'You are a city-fop; how would you know things here? These calves drink up all the milk. And Gowri is so clever. She somehow hoodwinks us and has all the milk herself.' For the calves today it was a festival as nobody had taken care of this job.

Krishna Moorthy kept the plastic pot in a corner of the yard which was fairly clean and tried to make his reluctant son sit upon it. The child had grown up in a world of clean cement floors and found the dirty backyard repulsive. Meera too feared coming to this house. The done-things and the not-done-things of the place and the doorless lavatory curtained off with bamboo sticks were what she most disliked.

Temptation and threats made the boy sit on the pot. Meera seemed to be trying to say something to her husband now that she had chanced to meet him alone. The dog which was asleep in the sun got up. An old cow moved out of the cowshed and came towards the bullocks which were munching dry paddy grass. The bullocks tugged at the ropes, breathed audibly and moved as if about to make a charge. In the courtyard to the right the men continued to piece together bamboo sticks for the bier. The old cow grabbed a mouthful of grass, stood at a distance and ate. His son was using the pot now; the smell made it evident. More evident was the happiness of Meera who had sensed it. Her face, the way she stood with an arm on her waist and even her bobbed hair tied with a ribbon spoke of her inner happiness. When Savithri motioned to him to come, he was struck with a thought; he had never felt that father would die on such a wretchedly ordinary morning. The boy saw a millipede slowly, silently moving towards him, got frightened and jumped off the pot. Meera touched it with her feet and it rolled itself into a circle. Krishna Moorthy picked it up with a stick and threw it away. The boy was happy.

While walking towards the cowshed Krishna Moorthy remembered again how Nair had summed up father's life and said to himself, 'No, he did not die a fool. He had decided to come and stay with me in Delhi and to sever himself from the things he was doing here.' His sister took him to a corner where they could not be seen. He became curious and was struck with another thought. Father had always dreamt of retiring from the service of the rich and staying with his son. He had wanted to live in Delhi and pursue his study of astronomy, his lifelong interest. Or, perhaps father had thought of sending away mother and sister to Delhi, and staying with Gangubai. The day he rushed back from Delhi, father had with difficulty moved his heavy and swollen limbs and sat up against the pillows Gangubai had brought for him. He had said, 'Oh, you have come. You must have come by air. Very expensive it must have been. That's all right. Glad you have come.' He had then added, 'I have also asked Nair to come. I feel much better now.' Then, he had begun to talk about an article he had read with wonder during the week.

It was about the dark holes in the sky. 'Listen, it seems they really are stars. Huge stars. And, they are falling. While falling they develop an enormous gravitational pull and do not allow anything, not even a ray of light, to escape them. These giant stars keep sucking everything into them. Time has no movement there. Isn't it amazing? See, Kittu, that's why they say; if like Shankaracharya one thinks that the world is an illusion, to him there are no wonders, no puzzles. He has them all solved easily. But for our Ananda Thirtha this world is real. It's a real thing. Contradictions too are true. It's therefore possible to look at the world in amazement. And because this world is true there is knowledge in understanding the contradictions. But if you want to speak of the Absolute, then....'

From this topic, father had moved on to a condemnation of the concept of equality, of the importance of property rights, of the legal system, etc. What had it all meant? When Krishna Moorthy was thinking such thoughts, Savithri took something out from a knot in the corner of her *pallu* and said, 'Remove your shirt.' 'Why?' asked Krishna Moorthy. 'To wear this.' She was rolling the sacred thread in her grimy palms—to give it a much worn look on her brother's chest. 'I don't like this play-acting.' 'You might say so. But aren't you a brahmin? Won't you perform the last rites?' 'See Savithri. Father had no faith in those things. That's why he and Gangubai...' 'That's all one's *karma*. Nobody can escape it.' Savithri stood aside. Krishna Moorthy removed his shirt and put on the sacred thread. 'Look, Savithri, father was disgusted with the work he was doing for these rich bastards. That's why he sent for Nair. You know, Nair's aim was to kill all rich landlords. Father too had no faith in brahminic do's and don'ts. If he had any he would not have lived with Gangubai.' Savithri did not like to discuss the topic. 'You mean to say these are in our hands? I say it is all one's *karma*. See, how you were bossing over us all before you were married. But look how you have changed now.' Savithri had not meant to taunt him; the words had simply slipped out, that's all. Krishna Moorthy was to recall this incident on a Sunday at lunch time in his Delhi flat. Though he was happy that his father at the time of his death had thought of staying with him, he came to realize that it would never really have happened. The twenty-five-thousand-rupee-debt father had bequeathed killed all his life's pleasures. He had to keep apart five thousand rupees towards the loan. He had to withdraw his son from a good school and put him into an ordinary one. He had to stop taking his wife and child out to cinemas and hotels. He had also to send at least two hundred rupees to his mother without his wife coming to know of it. 'You know, father spent his life slaving for the rich. But he was a most self-respecting man. He would not accept any money from them. That's why he died in debt. To educate me he sacrificed much. He might have become a renowned astronomer or practised at the bar of the Supreme Court.' He would say this loudly. Meera would listen in stony silence and express her anger and displeasure, which was quite understandable to Krishna Moorthy. Yet he had to fight with the memory of his father for days to come. On one such Sunday, at lunch time, when Meera icily remarked: 'They were wise who said cut your coat according to your length of the cloth,' Krishna Moorthy thought of Nair who was rotting in jail. He argued that Nair was the one who could transcend pettiness, reach out to something big and that's why he was dearest to father. Since he had failed to take her to a picture that afternoon, Meera hissed at him and said, 'Why do you fornicate with words? Go, if you have the courage, with a knife in your hand too.'

Krishna Moorthy had become depressed. He wondered whether Gangubai, friends like Nair and the dark holes in the sky were only means to escape for a while the tiredness that comes in the perpetual pursuit of money. Prior to her marriage, Meera's face was full of beauty and gentleness; and now anger had become the dominant emotion and was carving deep lines on her face. In those lines, he tried to trace the meaningfulness of father's way of life. He remembered Nair who smiled even when speaking most cruelly. But since he also felt that Nair was a somewhat ludicrous looking eccentric, his questions became more and more knotty. Did father's life, in spite of its many possibilities, run to seed? Why? Was he also going the same way? There was no answer here.

*

The impermanent body was to be returned to the five elements it was made of. Krishna Moorthy, dressed in a short *dhoti*, had a dip in the river; on the river bank the body, given its last ritual bath, lay on the bier. He carried water in a pot that had holes in it, went round the body, then threw it backward and it broke. He lit fire to the body, soaked in kerosene and sat watching the leaping, multicoloured flames. The fire spread, spluttered, and the flames, bud-like and flower-like, burnt and enveloped the body. The flames converged with all their fiery strength at the skull. While Krishna Moorthy, with an effort to still his mind, remembered father bringing a thermometer when he was ill, the rest of father's innumerable friends, for their consolation, were talking amongst themselves. Krishna Moorthy was surprised to see how a cremation ceremony turns into a picnic. Somebody was talking loudly and had made the rest into an audience. 'Acharya was a very wise man. He saw much before others could that the Land Reform Act was in the offing. He was a man of this world, very much so. You know the Peasants' Association was formed and Venkappa Naika began to say that the tiller of the land was its owner. Acharya immediately sent for us and told us: "You settle all your property disputes right now. Keep whatever land that justly belongs to you. And sell the rest for whatever price it fetches. If your tenant wishes to buy it, sell it to him. It does not matter even if he pays a little less. After all he has to sweat for you. It does not matter even if he is not grateful. That is another issue altogether. Otherwise, there will be a bloodbath." We who listened to him prospered. Those who did not lost all that they had. His knowledge of the laws has saved many a scoundrel. We by ourselves would never have managed to survive the wretched Peasants' Association.'

Krishna Moorthy, watching father's skull burst, like a coconut shell into colourful flames, felt like shouting, 'No, this is not the whole truth.' He recalled this too in his Delhi flat. He discussed it with his leftist friends, and yet remained unsatisfied.

*

After the body was removed, Gangubai went and sat under the jackfruit tree that was beyond the cowshed. The prospect of the womenfolk thinking of the pleasures her fair and tall body, still without a wrinkle, might have given Acharya, embarrassed her. If she took herself away, the others might weep or praise Acharya uninhibitedly. Let her presence not leave a bad taste in their mouths.

She knew of Acharya's boyhood life. He had told her everything. He had talked to her of the sky, of the legal system, of the son who was dear to him, and of Nair—nothing had been held back from her.

Their twenty-year-friendship had begun when Acharya put up his office on the first floor of the hotel her mother ran in Shimoga. Then its name was 'Landlords' Association'. Acharya was its secretary. Later it had become 'Malnad Cultivators' Organization'. She then had a teaching job in a primary school. She first met him when she had to get papers drafted for pledging the house to someone. She was married too. But her mother did not know that she had given away her daughter to a cruel widower. Gangubai had left her husband to become a teacher. It was Acharya who had advised her on the ways and means of getting a divorce.

Their relationship had started then. The hotel had to be closed after the passing away of her mother. With Acharya's help and with the money that was left, she had bought a few cows and opened a dairy. Acharya had become closer to her than the man she had married. She did not want him to suffer more humiliation than he was already undergoing; and had, therefore, got herself aborted twice. However, at the time of his death he had accepted her and that gave a sense of grateful fulfilment.

*

His was a life of adventure. His father was a priest at Sri Rama temple. The son was taught *mantras* and *tantras* at home. The temple itself was located in a village on the banks of the Tunga. There were some twenty brahmin families in the village. The annual car festival of the temple was a much admired event in the surrounding areas. Acharya's boyhood was spent in performing rites and rituals in brahmin families or in assisting his father. Acharya was from the beginning a discontented man—a man of aspirations. He knew the names of many stars and would often sleep in the courtyard of the temple under the *champak* trees and study the star-studded sky. One day while returning after performing the Sathyanarayana *pooja* at somebody's place, he met a padre who was riding a bicycle and from him caught a desire to learn English. The passion for the sky and the passion for learning English made Acharya dream strange dreams while engaged in making sandalpaste for the Gods. He learned the alphabet from educated, godfearing men who came to the temple to worship. He also learned to read. He got a 'Teach-yourself-English' and learned enough to be able to write English. The desire to go to far-off places grew in him.

Acharya married at the age of sixteen. His wife Rukminiyamma was then eight years old. It seems when Acharya's father went to see the bride, she was sitting on the branch of a mango tree. Acharya's father asked her the way to Gopalacharya's home and she said, while still on the tree and eating a mango, 'See, there,' and pointed the way. Now Rukminiyamma looked a woman to whom such pleasures were never known.

Since she was still a girl, she had remained at her father's place for about five or six years after the marriage. Acharya's income, however, went up as he was now married and could officiate at various ceremonies.

It was at this period that a most significant event took place in Acharya's life. There was in the village a very rich *desashta* brahmin family. The temple honours went first to the master of the household. His wife was blind. He had no son, but only a daughter who was very beautiful. Naturally they did not want to give away the girl to somebody from outside the family and had her married to her maternal uncle.

She stayed with him ten years, got tired and came back to her father's place. The fact that she had remained childless made people wonder whether her husband was impotent. Her father died of worry and sorrow. After his death, in that palatial mansion, there were only two; the blind mother and her daughter. Of course, there were in various parts of the house, widows and destitutes who did the cooking and attended to odd jobs, and innumerable guests who came to worship at the temple. In the main hall of the house were pictures of Gods in silver frames, and swings with silver-rimmed wooden planks. The house had a high roofing and was always cool.

This girl was older to Acharya by about four years or so. Her name was Alaka Devi. After performing the *pooja* at the temple, it was part of Acharya's duty to visit her house and perform the *pooja* there. He was then eighteen or nineteen. Alaka Devi always wore silk saris, parted her hair, as the fashion was in those days, to the left, and wore blouses with puffed sleeves. She too knew a little English. It was her father who had taught her. She would give Acharya books by Scott, Dumas, Goldsmith and others from her father's library. He would read the books, hiding them from his father to whom English meant pollution. He would go with the books to Alaka Devi, begin to explain what he had read hesitantly at first, and then, as she sat on a swing and swung herself to and fro, he would grow bolder. His uninhibited narration of the stories would make Alaka Devi's eyes dilate in wonder. This way, in the forest-surrounded village, under the silent presence of the temple God, Alaka Devi became the queen of his enlarging dream world.

Alaka Devi would behave as if the two of them were characters from those tales of wonder. She thought of Acharya—dressed in priestly clothes and sporting a huge tuft at the back of his head—as a prince incognito or as a soldier. Wasn't the mother of this beautiful lady blind? And who else was there to keep a check on this young woman? She wore a different silk sari every day, sat on the swing, talked to the parrot in the cage and waited for Acharya to bring *thirtha* and *prasada* from the temple. She would receive Acharya, make him sit on the swing beside her and talk of this and that.

Acharya spent the whole day waiting for this moment. Whenever he had to go out of the village to perform a marriage or a ceremony, he would feel bored. Also Alaka Devi would get angry. It appears that she once said she would buy him a horse so that he could come back soon from wherever he had gone.

There were several phases in their growing relationship: of the lady and her trusted servant, of the queen and soldier, of a goddess and devotee, of the heroine and the hero of romances. Acharya would convulse with a strange, ethereal passion when he heard in the evenings cows coming home, their bells tinkling; when, on moonlit nights, he heard the nightingale sing in ecstasy; when the Tunga, full to the brim, softly flowed and murmured in the December cold. And, the reasons for his convulsive hunger were the hunger to know Alaka Devi and the sky.

Acharya, it seems, was afraid that even if his little finger touched her, he would be burnt to ashes. Alaka Devi, in an oblique and suggestive way, had told him everything. She told him that she had remained a virgin as her husband was deficient in manliness. Acharya, it appears, was much worried as to what 'deficiency in manliness' meant.

One afternoon when Acharya made his usual visit, Alaka Devi looked at him with her large eyes and asked, 'Will you do me a favour?' Acharya's face spoke of his willingness. 'If you touch me, will you have to take a bath again?' 'Well, that is no problem.' 'Then, keep the *pooja* plate there and get me some sandalpaste. There is an abcess on my back. Please, apply some paste to it.' Acharya grew red in the face. She looked at him and laughingly said, 'You are a good man, aren't you? Then, close your eyes and apply it, without looking at me.' She turned, let down the *pallu* of her sari and unbuttoned her blouse. On the milk-white skin of her back, in a corner, there was a tiny red boil. While Acharya softly and with trembling finger was applying the paste, she suddenly turned round, took his face in her palms, as if it were the face of a child, and said, 'I am wicked, aren't I?' It seems there was, on her face, a triumphant smile. Acharya felt he was perspiring all over. Before he knew what he was doing, he had pressed her to him. He felt his body slowly dissolving itself against her softly-pressed body; a shiver ran down his spine and his thighs became wet. Hoping to god that Alaka Devi would not notice it, he sank onto the swing, and she sat near his feet.

From that day began his irrepressible desire for her, and with it a fear. The next day when he came from the temple, she stood before him, demure and like a little girl, inspiring love in him. With trembling hands, he gave her the *prasada* and returned without knowing what to say. The desire to have her grew in him the whole day. At night, while lying under the *champak* trees and looking at the moonless but star-brimming sky, the desire made him spring up as one possessed. In the dark of the night, gasping in excitement, he walked to her house. It was past twelve and there wasn't a living soul around. He went and stood before Alaka Devi's house. Knocking on the main door was out of the question. The men who were whitewashing the house the previous day had left their ladder at the back of the house. Acharya went up the ladder, got on to the balcony, and holding his beating heart with his left hand, ascended the staircase and came to Alaka Devi's bedroom.

She was lying on her cot. Beside her the lamp was still burning. On her breast was a book, half-open. The parrot in the cage fluttered and screeched. He thought it was not proper for him to touch and wake her up when she was asleep. For a long time he stood there, gazing at her peaceful face. Softly he whispered her name, once, twice, a hundred times as if he was repeating the name of a goddess. Slowly she opened her eyes and, without getting worried or confused, recognized him. She stretched out her hand and made him sit beside her, as if accepting the worship he offered as rightly due to her. Acharya was not himself, he was like a man possessed. She saw him trembling helplessly in passion, made him lie beside her, and stroking his body said gently, 'I've wed you in my mind; but wed you in body I can't.' The closeness of her body made Acharya pass the extremity of his passion and he could no longer feel any desire for her. The next night, again he went to her, pleaded with her but she gently pushed him away. When, the day after, he saw her, he begged her to accept him. She asked him, 'But what afterwards?' Acharya said, 'Let us get married.' She said, 'That's not possible,' and sighed. And, she had been right, it would not have been possible. Acharya was a priest at the temple and was married. Moreover, Alaka Devi herself was a married woman, and she was older than Acharya. After this incident, Acharya was like a man demented. Whenever he found time he would go and beg her to accept him. She would fondle him, but as soon as Acharya responded and became passionate, she would withdraw. This went on for two months and Acharya's body wasted away. One day, it appears, she said, 'Leave this place. Find a job for yourself. And, then, you can take me there.'

It sounded right to Acharya too. But every time the day neared on which he had decided to leave, she would start nagging. 'You want to go because you want to be away from me. You want to forget me.' When Acharya, in reply, said he wouldn't and that they should now live together, she would taunt him, 'All that you want is my body, isn't it?'

One day, however, Acharya left the village. Alaka Devi had given him enough money to meet his travel expenses and had begged him to take her away. The previous night she had even expressed her willingness to sleep with him. Acharya wanted her to realize how truly he loved her and therefore said 'No.'

After his two years' stay in Delhi and in Nair's company he came back and saw Alaka Devi. She had changed. She had got her thin and emaciated husband back. He wore thick, sodabottle glasses and his head looked like a malformed areca-nut. On the whole, he was a ridiculous-looking man. Acharya's own wife was a woman now. His father was also happy that his son had returned as an educated man. Alaka Devi did not wear silk saris now. Her blind mother had passed away. She now wore plain saris and came to the temple herself. Her husband himself offered worship to the family god—the only manly thing he could do.

Acharya was disappointed. He decided to leave the place. Alaka Devi, to show how devoted a wife she had become, would not even look at Acharya. One day, when he knew she would be alone, he went and told her, 'I am leaving this village.' Acharya now had his hair cut in the English fashion and wore shirts. Alaka Devi did not raise her head. She wept silently. Acharya held her hands, pressed them gently and said, 'What else can I do now?' 'You don't want me now, do you?' said Alaka Devi and withdrew her hands. Her words again made him want her. He embraced her and Alaka Devi kept her face on his bosom and wept.

Acharya became a postmaster in a nearby village. He gradually began to see how clever Alaka Devi was. Saying that her husband had little knowledge of the world of business, she appointed Acharya as a clerk, and requested him to manage her estate for her. She had an office built on a thickly-wooded hillock. Acharya would go there after his office hours. She would also come in the evening. As she was rich, people were afraid to talk. Yet, much of the energy and intelligence of the two got wasted in planning their secret meetings. What had once deeply haunted him as a profound passion had now become a body-and-mind-satisfying necessity. It was while settling the disputes connected with the estate that he became bitten by the law bug.

A discontentment and a sadness began to leave hard lines on the face of his young wife. Acharya felt like running away from the whole thing. The hypocritical play-acting was becoming too much to bear. But Alaka Devi made her body yield new pleasures, and since the pleasures could be had only in secrecy, their sharpness was felt more keenly and her hold on him increased.

Gradually, there began to grow a feeling in him that he was slowly losing his self-respect. Noticing this, Alaka Devi became more and more adept in the art of love-making and made her body yield a new and stronger taste. She gave herself to him every day but it was as if on each day she was a different woman. She taught him how they could come together in an ever fresh and unending mystery of the body, and the wonder bound him fast to her.

Two years passed. Alaka Devi was with child. Her husband held his tongue but walked about proudly as if he had done it all. Acharya found his humility most disgusting. Alaka Devi, however, remained untouched and looked as if she was beyond all morality. With the child in her womb, she shone like a goddess. She again wore her silk saris and sparkling diamond earrings. She was least worried about what others might say and accepted Acharya's love as if he really owed it to her. She gave him money so that he could buy for his wife saris and jewels. As the child in her womb grew, her body, like a bud, hid within itself all its unexhausted mystery. A sigh of relief escaped Acharya and he turned to his study of law and the sky.

Alaka Devi died while giving birth to a still-born baby. Acharya was rudely shaken. He tried to become friendly with his wife, but failed and one day he left the place to settle down here.

It is hard to say whether Acharya became an addict to law and legal disputes because he wanted to forget Alaka Devi or whether the pursuit of law became an inevitable necessity or whether the rich were only a pretext for his addiction. Whatever it is, Gangubai had been to him those twenty years an island of peace. Perhaps it was because of her that he could bear the shock of his dear son's marriage.

*

Gangubai saw men returning after consigning Acharya's mortal remains to the flames. She got up from under the tree and walked into the house. She took five thousand rupees from her trunk and gave it to Rukminiyamma. She was surprised and said

69

'No.' 'I brought it to be of use to him. It belongs to him. Please accept it. Let me be of some help,' she said with tears in her eyes. At home, there was little money. Rukminiyamma did not know if her son had any. She wondered if she could ask Vishnu Moorthy. And, so declining and saying 'No,' she took the money. When Gangubai said, 'I am going to Shimoga now. I shall come for the fourteenth day ceremony,' Rukminiyamma wiped her eyes and said, 'The deeds of our past life have brought us together. Why don't you stay on?' Gangubai said she had little leave left and took the evening bus.

*

Two years later Krishna Moorthy was sitting in an armchair and fanning himself on a summer evening in Delhi. It had been an unbearably warm and sultry day. His wife sat beside him and sewed buttons onto their son's shirts. After a long time Krishna Moorthy had found some peace, the main reason for which was his son's recovery from diptheria. Both husband and wife had kept watch over the boy, sat up together day and night without any thought of food or water. This had brought them closer. Money and other related problems had looked small and inconsequential. And, besides, Krishna Moorthy had worked for three months and written a *Guide for the I.A.S.* under an assumed name. Though he was ashamed of what he had done, it had brought him fifteen thousand rupees in a lump sum and he had cleared much of the debt. The money had solved his hundred and one small problems.

Suddenly it struck Krishna Moorthy: Had father lived and died a foolish man and had awareness come to him only in his dying moments? How to answer it now? The words he had spoken just before he died had not, so far, appeared to him of any particular importance. But now they seemed so. Father had fallen asleep even as he was speaking to Nair. Krishna Moorthy had been half-awake. A cat had given birth to a litter in the lumber room right on top of father's room. Harikumara, his nephew, had gone up to remove them as they were making a lot of noise. The cat had seen the boy come up, had sprung at him, and tried to claw him. Father, half-conscious, had moaned in pain. 'Hari, why do you bother the poor cat? Let it stay there, poor thing.' These were his last words; compassion for the poor cat had brought a lump in his throat and the voice had quivered.

Krishna Moorthy asks himself why, then, does he burn in anguish as if this was not enough.

Translated from Kannada by D.A.Shankar

Gopinath Mohanty

The Somersault

The day Jaga Palei of Sagadiasahi defeated Ramlawan Pande of Darbhanga to enter the finals of the All-India Wrestling Competition—being held in the Barabati Stadium—the sky was rent with the jubilant shouts of thousands of spectators. It was not the victory of Jaga Palei that excited them so much. It was Orissa's victory. Orissa had won. This was the feeling everywhere.

At that moment, Jaga Palei became a symbol, the symbol of the glory and the fulfilment of the hopes and aspirations of the Oriya people. A sea of humanity surged forward to greet him, to meet the heretofore unknown, unheard-of wrestler. The waves broke on each other, there was a stampede. At least twenty-one persons had to be removed to hospital. The situation became so riotous and uncontrollable that the police had to be called out.

The crowd that returned home that evening had among its numbers those who had their shirts torn, watches and fountain pens lost, and their bodies sore. But everybody carried in his heart the Oriya national consciousness. And something else, which may be termed as the intoxication of heroism. As if each one of them was a Jaga Palei! Newspapers flashed photographs of that momentous wrestling match. All the Oriya papers raved in Jaga Palei's praise! 'Jaga Palei—Orissa's glory'; 'Jaga Palei—Orissa's honour'; 'Jaga Palei, the unparalleled Oriya wrestler'. 'Never-heard-of-before wrestling at Cuttack!' 'Jaga Palei, Emperor of athletics'; 'the Newest Success of the Unbeaten Wrestling Artist' and so on.

Excitement spread rapidly to the rural areas as soon as the newspapers published the news. Many cursed their bad luck that they could not be witness to such an epoch-making event.

The week that followed could legitimately be called 'Jaga Palei Week'. In buses and in trains, in hotels and in the village *Bhagabat-tungi*, the talk was only about Jaga Palei's wrestling feat. This news completely over-shadowed all other daily news like the 'Rocket to Mars', 'Man's flight in Space', 'Death of Lumumba' and the subsequent daily events of Congo's politics,

'Success and Failure in *Panchayat Samiti* and *Zilla Parishad* Elections', and many other exciting changes in the country. Since there were no auspicious marriage dates in the coming year, hundreds of marriages were solemnized in the fortnight following this event and in these festivities a frequent subject of discussion was Jaga Palei's wrestling.

'Did you go to see the wrestling?'

'How did you like it?'

Even if one had not gone, one had to answer, 'Oh, yes, of course; it was simply wonderful.' It was almost as if to say otherwise was to do worse than confessing to a hidden guilt.

During that 'Jaga Palei Week', a small five-page booklet could be seen on sale in crowded places. The poet: 'Abid'. The price: Ten paise. Hawkers were seen hawking the songbook with harmonium accompaniment in front of the *cutchery*, railway station, bus-stand and big squares. Glass-framed photographs of the wrestling event went up on the walls of photographers' studios, and also at sweetmeat-and-tea-stalls and *paan*-shops in the town. Alando Mahila Mandali, Olangsha Yubak Mandal, Gababasta Grama Samaj, Bamphisahi Truckers Club, Ganganagar Sanskritika Sangha, Uttarward Kuchinda Minamandali, Ghusuri Abasor Binodan Samaj and many other institutions passed resolutions congratulating Jaga Palei and sent them to the press.

Even though his name had become a by-word everywhere, Jaga Palei of Sagadiasahi still followed his traditional profession of carrying gunny bags in the *malgodown*. He had done this job ever since he was fifteen; from the day his father Uddhab Palei had returned the bullock carts of the money-lender, had come home, slept on the spread-out end of his *dhoti* and had never woken up again. Uddhab Palei had got an attack of pneumonia. The Chhotamian of Mohamaddia Bazaar had come and tried to exorcise the evil spirit. Govinda Ghadei of Janakasahi who kept different tablets in his shop inside the *cutchery* premises for curing different diseases, had administered four different tablets, bitter, *kasa*, *raga* (hot) and saline respectively. For this he had taken one rupee seventy-five paise. Karuna Gosain, the monk of Tinigheria had prescribed that he should feed eighteen bundles of straw to stray cattle on a Wednesday and then lay himself prostrate on the dust of the street. Uddhab had obeyed this prescription as well but nothing had helped. He died without discovering whether mankind had discovered a cure for pneumonia.

It was thus that Jaga Palei was left fatherless in the big city, with no job, no savings, no help and the greedy eyes of the well-to-do on his two-roomed thatched house and three *gunths* of land. Widowed mother, two minor siblings—Khaga and a twelve-year-old sister Sara. The well-wishers arrived and proffered their advice to the family : 'Sell the plot of land, build a small house elsewhere and with the balance start some business.' The argument appeared *prima facie* reasonable. The ancestral plot of land may have been in a congested locality of town but a little way away was the main road where a *gunth* sold at seven hundred rupees. With two rooms on it, it could fetch three thousand rupees. Wouldn't it be so much cheaper to purchase land and build a house in Tulsipur Bidanasi, Uttampur and around the Dairy Farm?

This is what the plot of land looked like: at its back a dirty, dark drain, on the right a tank whose rotten water threw up bubbles constantly; on the left a washerman's house and a *bustee* that extended far; in the front, a lane hardly six to seven cubits wide and the back of the boundary wall of the double-storeyed building belonging to the money-lender Garib Das. Through the chinks in the boundary wall black waters tumbled down and accumulated in the plot, grew, extended, putrefied.

But Uddhab Palei had never sold that small plot of his ancestors, nor did his wife and son sell it. The advice of the well-wishers remained unheeded.

Another bit of advice from the same well-wishers was that the members of the household should take up service as domestic servants. Or else who would maintain them? At fifteen Jaga looked quite a man. Various offers came; an apprenticeship in driving bullock carts, operating machines in a saw-mill, service in shops. A *babu* suggested he do some domestic service with the chance of a peon's post later. Another person came and told him that Jaga was very fortunate as his sahib wanted him to be his personal valet. No work—Jaga only had to accompany him wherever he went, a little bit of miscellaneous work as per his orders and there would be no end to the good food, tips and a salary to cap it all! Jaga was given the dream of flying in cars and planes, sleeping on thick mattresses, wearing costly clothes and eating good food. Many would come seeking little favours through him, flattering him in diverse ways. It would be for him to make or mar them. He would be a strong, stalwart person. The *babu* had done everything for persons who depended on him. After all for him money was just like earth and pebbles!

Jaga Palei listened to everything in silence. Somebody seemed to whisper inside him: 'Do not listen Jaga, close your eyes, say "No". No, you will not take to servanthood. However ferocious a dog with a thick blanket or fur, thick tail, huge body and large teeth—a dog remains a dog at the master's call. It can only lick his boots and lie chained to a post. A dog seen from a master's car staring from behind the glass-panes with big open eyes at the road and licking its tongue may excite the onlooker's admiration. Nobody, however, can ever forget that he remains only a dog.'

To fifteen-year-old Jaga Palei such thoughts came naturally; for in his blood was the tradition of endless ancestors—people who tilled their soil and preserved an unbending tensile dignity which three generations of town life had not corroded.

Jaga turned his back on all the offers and persuasions to choose for himself the life of a daily wage-earner, carrying loads every day. His mother did not object. With the help of her daughter she opened a small snack-shop in the front room of the house. His mother had a knack of preparing good and tasty food. Sales were brisk. Khaga went hawking ground-nut and *bara bhaja*. Thereafter he took a job rolling *beedis* in a factory. Somehow, the family of four members lived on; nobody died, the house was not sold. From the outside everything looked the same. Four persons became of one mind, suffered hardships and privation. Nobody came to know anything of this.

Jaga had one obsession in life. Physical culture. Early inspiration for this came from his father's godfather, the old *khalipha* of Sagadiasahi. Jaga remembered his mango complexion, the body of a young man, the flowing beard, the look of a child in his small blue eyes, and the green turban. Once he had tugged at Jaga's shoulder and asked him why he did not attend his *akhara*. He had asked Uddhab to hand Jaga over to him so that he could make a wrestler out of him. Uddhab had smiled and agreed. That was the beginning.

A couple of small rooms in an old building near a tamarind

tree with a compound wall. That was the *khalipha's* house. No wife, no children; nobody knew if ever there were. Only a single pleasure in life, the *akhara*. Only the *akhara* inside his compound. Early in the morning, before the darkness lifted, Jaga would go to the *akhara* and do various types of gymnastic exercises including practice with the club, the *lathi* and wrestling. Many joined the *akhara*; many also dropped out. But there wasn't a sunrise when Jaga Palei would not come out from the *akhara* after his exercise.

The *khalipha* knew people in the other *akharas* in town. When wrestlers from other towns came he would arrange a competition. Jaga was unbeaten in these competitions. The town people who cared for wrestling soon knew his name. They would praise his iron-like body, the lightning speed of his reflexes and the marvellous tricks he had learnt from the *khalipha*. But rarely were these people from among the higher circles of society.

Mostly they were shopkeepers, tailors, butchers, drivers, carpenters and so on. This lack of fame in all sections of society was in the part due to the *khalipha's* regulations. No showing-off, no publicity. Only during Dussera and Muharram was there a tradition of his team going round demonstrating their skill. Besides this, there would be competitions.

While growing up as a wrestler, Jaga had various other offers of jobs. One was a watchman's job guarding somebody's house with a rifle or a *lathi*. Good pay. The other proposal was still more astonishing. Enough food, monthly salary, special payment for special items of work. And the work would be of the age-old, time-honoured variety: to act as a Kichaka; in modern terminology, goondaism. King Virata had been defended by Kichaka. Now new empires had opened up in business, trade and industry. And empires always needed Kichakas. It was for the master to point a finger at the enemies. Then there would be work of all descriptions: staring hard at somebody, rendering somebody lame, breaking somebody's neck, confining somebody illegally, locking someone up in a house, throwing stones at somebody's house at night, accosting somebody on the way and so on. If dragged to the court the master would defend his Kichaka through lawyers without getting identified.

There was another proposal too. He would be somebody's son-in-law and remain in that household and enjoy the property.

Somebody had perhaps appreciated his health and beauty while looking down through the window of the first floor of a building. This proposal he turned down as well. What remained was the old work—carrying grey bags of cement from one place to another and getting paid per bag.

After the big wrestling match that day he found strangers crowding round him and jostling one another. Lights flooded on him from many directions and snaps were taken. Then came the rain of questions. Questions and more questions even before they could be answered: 'How long have you been in wrestling? Who is your guru? Ah, Omar *khalipha*! Whom did you defeat earlier? Please give a list. What prizes did you win? What is your diet and in what quantities? Are you married? How many children? What do you consider necessary for health and long life?'

Somebody from the crowd shouted, 'Do you agree that vegetable *ghee* is very conducive to good health? Ah, you have never taken that!'

More questions. 'How many cups of tea do you take per day? What tea? You never take tea? Couldn't you please tell us the truth, sir? What *beedi* do you prefer? Which *gurakhu* do you use? Which party do you support? What do you think of the recent changes in the country? Oh, when can you grant an interview? We would like to publish your photograph along with your signature and your views on our commodities: flash it in cinema slides and finalize the dues. Please, your autograph please.' And all the time, more jostling and pushing about. The waves were breaking. And that solved many questions for the questioners could hardly remain in their places. Jaga Palei felt suffocated. He stood in grim silence and folded his hands. That too was photographed. Then he turned and ran through the crowd, still afraid that they might follow him.

First he went to his guru and fell at his feet. The *khalipha* embraced him, his flowing beard touching his chest and back and said: 'That's a good boy; you have preserved my name.' Jaga hardly noticed the praise from other quarters. He knew somebody always wins and somebody always loses. Just as in this contest he had won and the other man was defeated.

From the *khalipha* he went to the temple and listened for a time to peaceful music sung to the accompaniment of the tambourine. On the way back he heard the radios blaring forth news of the wrestling. A little later the newspaper-vendors, carrying bundles of papers, were shouting the same news. His head was reeling. Instead of returning home directly, he went to the Kathjuri embankment. Returning late at night, he found an elaborate meal awaiting him: rice, *dal*, mashed potato, fried brinjals, fish curry. His family members embraced and patted him and praised him in their own way. Excepting a few neighbours, no one else came to look at him. He was relieved.

Before dawn the next morning he was back at his exercise and then the daily carrying of bags. He did not say a word to anybody about his profession and his private life. Newspapers gave out the fact that he was a labourer. He was not aware how news about him had spread; but news of his achievements also circulated in that area of the *malgodown* where he earned his daily wage, and people would stop him on the way to congratulate him and ask about his wrestling. They would tell him about his high place in the world of Indian wrestling and how he had raised the prestige of Orissa. They said he would have a great future if only he won the last round. That would bring him great prestige and status and take him to wrestling matches outside Orissa and even outside India. He would go to Ceylon, Singapore, Mongolia, Peking, Japan, Russia, Germany, America, Africa and so on. Along with prestige he would also earn a lot. For all this, he had only to win the last round of the All India Wrestling Competition.

And there was also a lot of useful advice! He should take greater care of his diet, health and practice; he must take fruits, mutton, milk, vitamins; he ought to be careful. After all he had to hold aloft the prestige of Orissa and later of India.

The flood of advice made him sigh wearily. He only saw mutton when walking down the tired streets. Milk was a dream. And by fruits he understood banana or at the most coconuts. All that he aspired for was a seer of *chura* per day but his domestic budget was tight and rarely permitted more than half a seer.

A few days later a large number of unemployed labourers came to town from down South. They camped in the open under a tree and all that they wanted was to earn some wages and somehow exist. The wage rate went down. To his utter misfortune, his younger brother, Khaga, met with an accident while returning from the *beedi* factory. He had fractures and multiple injuries and was carried to the hospital. This added to the woes of the family and Jaga's daily worries.

A newcomer opened a small hotel at the end of the village street and started selling various types of delicacies and sweets and cakes and tea. Benches and chairs were provided and food was served on sparkling clean plates with a fan overhead and music from the radio. Customers started dwindling at the shop run by Jaga's mother and sister. Wants stared at him from every side.

And yet Jaga Palei persisted with his wrestling. His diet came down from half-a-seer to a quarter seer of *chura* and fried rice worth only four annas a day and one coconut in three days. He would fill his stomach with some rice and whatever green leafy vegetables were available. Hunger would burn fierce in his stomach. When there was no work, Jaga could be seen sitting in grim silence, lost in thought. He would feel how lonely he was, how friendless, forsaken! Everybody had forgotten him a few days after the wrestling match.

Three months passed. Then came the fateful day of the final test: Dilip Singh of Punjab versus Jaga Palei of Orissa. When it was over, the newspapers flashed the report along with an analysis of the match. All were agreed that the wrestling, the artistry and skill which Jaga applied against the heavily-built, massive Dilip Singh were superb but the odds were heavily against him. It appeared that Dilip Singh would fall flat, but ultimately he won.

Dilip Singh's life-sketch appeared in the papers. All the great men in the wrestling world were his patrons. There was also information about the variety and quality of his diet, how his weight was taken every day and many other facts about him. Jaga Palei was again in the wilderness. Fresh discussions started in trains and buses and in crowded corners. Some people even expressed resentment against the man who had soiled Orissa's name; many were unhappy and crestfallen. Even that was quickly forgotten. But the day after the wrestling match, like any other day, Jaga Palei quietly went back to his exercise and the carrying of bags.

Translated from Oriya by Sitakant Mahapatra

Raja Rao

Companions

Alas till now I did not know
My guide and Fate's guide are one.

— Hafiz

It was a serpent such as one sees only at a fair, long and many-coloured and swift in riposte when the juggler stops his music. But it had a secret of its own which none knew except Moti Khan who brought him to the Fatehpur Sunday fair. The secret was: his fangs would lie without venom till the day Moti Khan should see the vision of the large white rupee, with the Kutub Minar on the one side and the face of the Emperor on the other. That day the fang would eat into his flesh and Moti Khan would only be a corpse of a man. Unless he finds God.

For to tell you the truth, Moti Khan had caught him in the strangest of strange circumstances. He was one day going through the *sitaphul* woods of Rampur on a visit to his sister, and the day being hot and the sands all scorching and shiny, he lay down under a wild fig tree, his turban on his face and his legs stretched across a stone. Sleep came like a swift descent of dusk, and after rapid visions of palms and hills and the dizzying sunshine, he saw a curious thing. A serpent came in the form of a man, opened its mouth, and through the most queer twistings of his face, declared he was Pandit Srinath Sastri of Totepur, who, having lived at the foot of the Goddess Lakshamma for a generation or more, one day in the ecstasy of his vision he saw her, the benign Goddess straight and supple, offering him two boons. He thought of his falling house and his mortgaged ancestral lands and said without a thought, 'A bagful of gold and liberation from the cycle of birth and death.' 'And gold you shall have,' said the Goddess, 'but for your greed, you shall be born a serpent in your next life before reaching liberation. For gold and wisdom go in life like soap and oil. Go and be born a juggler's serpent. And when you have made the hearts of many men glad with the ripple and swing of your shining flesh, and you have

80

gone like a bird amidst shrieking children, only to swing round their legs and to swing out to the amusement of them all, when you have climbed old men's shoulders and hung down them chattering like a squirrel, when you have thrust your hood at the virgin and circled round the marrying couples; when you have gone through the dreams of pregnant women and led the seekers to the top of the Mount of Holy Beacon, then your sins will be worn out like the quern with man's grindings and your flesh will catch fire like the will-o-the-wisp and disappear into the world of darkness where men await the birth to come. The juggler will be a basket-maker and Moti Khan is his name. In a former life he sought God but in this he sits on the lap of a concubine. Wending his way to his sister's for the birth of her son, he will sleep in the *sitaphul* woods. Speak to him. And he will be the vehicle of your salvation.' Thus spoke the Goddess.

'Now, what do you say to that, Moti Khan?'

'Yes, I've been a sinner. But never thought I, God and Satan would become one. Who are you?'

'The very same serpent.'

'Your race has caused the fall of Adam.'

'I sat at the feet of Sri Lakshamma and fell into ecstasy. I am a brahmin.'

'You are strange.'

'Take me or I'll haunt you for this life and all lives to come.'

'Go, Satan!' shouted Moti Khan, and rising swift as a sword he started for his sister's house. He said to himself, 'I will think of my sister and child. I will think only of them.' But leaves rustled and serpents came forth from the left and the right, blue ones and white ones and red ones and copper-coloured ones, long ones with short tails and short ones with bent tails, and serpents dropped from tree-tops and rock-edges, serpents hissed on the river sands. Then Moti Khan stood by the Rampur stream and said, 'Wretch! Stop it. Come, I'll take you with me.' Then the serpents disappeared and so did the hissings, and hardly home, he took a basket and put it in a corner, and then he slept; and when he woke, a serpent had curled itself in the basket. Moti Khan had a *pungi* made by the local carpenter, and, putting his mouth to it, he made the serpent dance. All the village gathered round him and all the animals gathered round him, for the music of Moti Khan was blue, and the serpent danced on its tail.

When he said good-bye to his sister, he did not take the road to his concubine but went straight northwards, for Allah called him there. And at every village men came to offer food to Moti Khan and women came to offer milk to the serpent, for it swung round children's legs and swung out, and cured them of all scars and poxes and fevers. Old men slept better after its touch and women conceived on the very night they offered milk to it. Plague went and plenty came, but Moti Khan would not smell silver. That would be death.

Now sometimes, at night in caravanserais, they had wrangles.

Moti Khan used to say: 'You are not even a woman to put under oneself.'

'But so many women come to see you and so many men come to honour you, and only a king could have had such a reception though you're only a basket-maker.'

'Only a basket-maker! But I had a queen of a woman, and when she sang her voice was all flesh, and her flesh was all song. And she chewed betel-leaves and her lips were red, and even kings....'

'Stop that. Between this and the vision of the rupee....'

Moti Khan pulled at his beard and, fire in his eyes, he broke his knuckles against the earth.

'If only I could see a woman!'

'If you want God forget women, Moti Khan.'

'But I never asked for God. It is you who always bore me with God. I said I loved a woman. You are only a fanged beast. And here I am in the prime of life with a reptile to live with.'

But suddenly temple bells rang, and the muezzin was heard to cry *Allah-o-Akbar*. No doubt it was all the serpent's work. Trembling, Moti Khan fell on his knees and bent himself in prayer.

From that day on the serpent had one eye turned to the right and one to the left when it danced. Once it looked at the men and once at the women, and suddenly it used to hiss up and slap Moti Khan's cheeks with the back of its head, for his music had fallen false and he was eyeing women. Round were their hips, he would think, and the eyelashes are black and blue, and the breasts are pointed like young mangoes, and their limbs so tremble and flow that he could sweetly melt into them.

One day, however, there was at the market a dark blue

woman, with red lips, young and sprightly; and she was a butter woman. She came and stood by Moti Khan as he made the serpent dance. He played on his bamboo *pungi* and music swung here and splashed there, and suddenly he looked at her and her eyes and her breasts and the *nagaswara* went and became *mohaswara*, and she felt it and he felt she felt it; and when night came, he thought and thought so much of her and she thought and thought so much of him, that he slipped to the *serai* door and she came to the *serai* gate, flower in her hair and perfume on her limbs, but lo! Like the sword of God came a long, rippling light, circled round them, pinched at her nipples and flew back into the bewildering night. She cried out, and the whole town waked, and Moti Khan thrust the basket under his arm and walked northwards, for Allah called him thither.

'Now,' said Moti Khan, 'I have to find God. Else this creature will kill me. And the Devil knows the hell I'd have to bake in.' So he decided that, at the next saint's tomb he encountered, he would sit down and meditate. But he wandered and he wandered; from one village he went to another, from one fair he went to another, but he found no *dargah* to meditate by. For God always called him northwards and northwards, and he crossed the jungles and he went up the mountains, and he came upon narrow valleys where birds screeched here and deer frisked there but no man's voice was to be heard, and he said, 'Now let me turn back home'; but he looked back and was afraid. And he said, 'Now I have to go to the North, for Allah calls me there.' And he climbed mountains again, and ran through jungles, and then came broad plains, and he went to the fairs and made the snake dance, and people left their rice-shops and cotton-ware-shops and the bellowing cattle and the yoked threshers and the querns and the kilns, and came to hear him play the music and to see the snake dance. They gave him food and fruit and cloth, but when they said, 'Here's a coin,' he said, 'Nay.' And the snake was right glad of it, for it hated to kill Moti Khan till he had found God, and it itself hated to die. Now, when Moti Khan had crossed the Narbuda and the Pervan and the Bhagirath, he came to the Jumna, and through long Agra he passed making the snake dance, and yet he could not find God and he was sore in soul with it. And the serpent was bothersome.

But at Fatehpur Sikri, he said, 'Here is Sheikh Chisti's tomb and I would rather starve and die than go one thumb-length more.' He sat by Sheikh Chisti's tomb and he said, 'Sheikh Chisti, what is this Fate has sent me? This serpent is a very wicked thing. He just hisses and spits fire at every wink and waver. He says, "Find God." Now, tell me, Sheikh Chisti, how can I find Him? Till I find Him I will not leave this spot.'

But even as he prayed he saw snakes sprout through his head, fountains splashed and snakes fell gently to the sides like the waters by the Taj, and through them came women, soft women, dancing women, round hips, betel-chewed lips, round breasts—shy some were, while some were only minxes—and they came from the right and went to the left, and they pulled at his beard—and, suddenly, white serpents burst through the earth and enveloped them all, but Moti Khan would not move. He said: 'Sheikh Chisti, I am in a strange world. But there is a darker world I see behind, and beyond that dark, dark world, I see a brighter world, and there, there must be Allah.'

For twenty-nine days he knelt there, his hands pressed against his ears, his face turned towards Sheikh Chisti's tomb. And people came and said, 'Wake up, old man, wake up'; but he would not answer. And when they found the snake lying on the tomb of Sheikh Chisti they cried, 'This is a strange thing,' and they took to their heels; while others came and brought *mullahs* and *maulvis* but Moti Khan would not answer. For, to speak the truth, he was crossing through the dark waters, where one strains and splashes, and where the sky is all cold, and the stars all dead, and till man come to the other shore, there shall be neither peace nor God.

On the twenty-ninth night Sheikh Chisti woke from his tomb and came, his skull-cap and all, and said: 'My son, what may I give you?'

'Peace from this serpent—and God.'

'My son, God is not to be seen. He is everywhere.'

'Eyes to see God, for I cannot any more go northwards.'

'Eyes to discern God you shall have.'

'Then peace from this serpent.'

'Faithful shall he be, true companion of the God-seeker.'

'Peace to all men and women,' said Moti Khan.

'Peace to all mankind. Further, Moti Khan, I have something to tell you; as dawn breaks Maulvi Mohammed Khan will come

84

to offer you his daughter, fair as an oleander. She has been waiting for you and she will wed you. My blessings on you, my son!'

'Allah is found! Victory to Allah!' cried Moti Khan. The serpent flung round him, slipped between his feet an¹ curled round
his neck and danced on his head, for, when Moti Khan found
God, his sins would be worn out like the quern-stone with the
grindings of man, and there would be peace in all mankind.

Moti Khan married the devout daughter of Maulvi
Mohammed Khan and he loved her well, and he settled down in
Fatehpur Sikri and became the guardian of Sheikh Chisti's tomb.
The serpent lived with him, and now and again he was taken to
the fair to play for the children.

One day, however, Moti Khan's wife died and was buried in a
tomb of black marble. Eleven months later Moti Khan died and
he was given a white marble tomb, and a dome of the same
stone, for both. Three days after that the serpent died too, and
they buried him in the earth beside the *dargah*, and gave him a
nice clay tomb. A *peepal* sprang up on it, and a passing brahmin
planted a *neem* tree by the *peepal*, and some merchant in the village gave money to build a platform round them. The *peepal* rose
to the skies and covered the dome with dark, cool shade, and
brahmins planted snake-stones under it, and bells rang and cam-
phors were lit, and marriage couples went round the platform in
circumambulation. When the serpent was offered the camphor,
Moti Khan had the incense. And when illness comes to the town,
with music and flags and torches do we go, and we fall in front
of the *peepal* platform and we fall prostrate before the *dargah*, and
right through the night a wind rises and blows away the foul
humours of the village. And when children cry, you say, 'Moti
Khan will cure you, my treasure,' and they are cured. Emperors
and kings have come and gone but never have they destroyed
our village. For man and serpent are friends, and Moti Khan
found God.

Between Agra and Fatehpur Sikri you may still find the little
tomb and the *peepal*. Boys have written their names on the walls
and dust and leaves cover the gold and blue of the pall. But
someone has dug a well by the side, and if thirst takes you on
the road, you can take a drink and rest under the *peepal*, and
think deeply of God.

S. Mani 'Mowni'

A Loss of Identity

He awoke suddenly, wide awake in the night, clearly awake, as if something had startled him. Trailing across the edges of his consciousness like the tatters of a dream were the junctures and disjunctures, meetings and partings of his entire life. Outside in the breathless dark, the sibilant cry of some nightbird faded, answered by, or answering, the sharp scolding of the owls. The steps of a man, perhaps two, passing along the street in that unreasonable hour before dawn seemed to fade without disturbing the surface of the silence. Beggars huddled in sleep on the walk below. Far into the night, till sleep had come, they had gossiped, now and then shouting uproariously, coughing, coughing their way toward beggar death. Now they would sleep until daylight.

Why hadn't his life with *her* ended with the same sweetness it had had at the beginning? What had made events follow a course which confirmed the passing suspicion that had fallen between them? The world indeed blamed her, but was she really to be blamed for moving about in the world, showing her sweet beauty, delighting all who might see her wherever she went? He wasn't sure.

The blackness of the night in his room was overpowering. He opened the window, pushed aside the shutter, and looked out. The immense expanse of the universe seemed to extend before him. Town lights merged with stars, as if the stars had come down from the sky to parade in long lines in the streets.

He wanted to retrace in his mind just what had happened the evening before, to get a clear idea of how it all had gone. To do this, he would have to gather the long shadows cast by things to come and piece them together with memories of things long past and forgotten.

*

It had all started the evening before last when he had run into him at the corner of the side-street. That had been unexpected.

'Hello there ! What a surprise to find you here! I never dreamed ....' There must have been some meaning behind these excessive reactions. You could tell by his face, his manner, that he was living on top of the world. Could it be that *she* was living with him now? He had asked for his address, and noted it down, promising to call on him the following afternoon at half-past-four. Then he had hurried away. The dull yellow of the lowering sun had glowed for a moment in the street and quickly faded.

His upstairs room was larger than he needed for himself alone. From up there, through windows looking in all directions, he could see a long way into the sky as well as look down to see what was going on in the village. But he had to stumble and grope up a long steep staircase to get to his room. The anticipated difficulty of getting back up usually quenched his impulse to get out on the street and wander around the village. Holding the shutter, he gazed out into the distance. He could see the first grey of the dawn.

The evening before, from four o' clock on, in his excitement over the expected visit, he had begun to worry that the hour would come and the visitor not arrive. He had looked at the clock again and again. The effect of this had been to cause him to cease to focus on the exact time the visitor had promised to come, as if to console himself with the thought that it was not yet really late. And then, it often happens that, when one is waiting for someone, the identity of the person one is waiting for slips from one's mind.

Couples with their children had been pouring in a flood down the street towards the seashore. What a fuss they made, and how they decked themselves out to wash away the humdrum of their lives with a few minutes in the sea breeze! The sky too, as if preparing for a celebration in the heavens, held a special clarity, poised for sunset and the sharp plunge into darkness. The street-lights, not yet lit, ranged along the street in regular files to a distant vanishing point.

The time had come. The silence in the room had become a torture. It had been impossible to stay there quietly and wait. He had made his way down into the street. He had moved along staring intently at each passer-by so that his visitor would not pass without his seeing him. He had sidled up to a man wearing a wrist-watch and asked, 'Sir, the correct time, please?' The man had given him a side-long glance, looked at his watch, and mumbled something to the effect that he was always forgetting to wind his watch and it had stopped. Then the man had said, 'It must be about four thirty. In any case, it's not after five,' and had gone away.

He had considered going back to his room. Perhaps his visitor would already be there waiting for him, perhaps even sitting in his armchair, ready to chide him for having made him wait so long when he had arrived exactly on time. Walking along, pondering over how he would answer that, the idea of returning to his room had slipped from his mind. The thought came to him that, on coming out, he had only closed his door, not locked it. He had gone on walking down the road.

He had come to a house within a garden wall. Walking past, he had found himself watching a beautiful young woman on the verandah languidly turning the pages of a book. Her reading and the play of her imagination were reflected in her features. It had occurred to him to walk straight up to her and point out to her that he had come at exactly six o' clock as agreed, and that if she was bored, he was not to blame. But a doubt flashed in his mind whether he could become 'him' to her, and he had walked on. It seemed absurd that life should ensnare one in such hazards through unexpected occurrences. Cars whizzed past, along the street and across the crossings, sometimes even grazing him. The streetlights had not yet been lit.

Then the milk woman had come up to him in the street and he had stopped short. She had smiled at him and spoken 'Why sir, what on earth are you doing out so early in the evening! You even forgot I was coming to your room!' At first he had considered taking her back to the room with him. But what if his visitor should be there waiting for him? What if he should see them together? He had dropped the idea and considered whether to tell her to go there herself and leave some milk. Then he had said, 'I don't need anything today. You don't have to go to the room,' and had walked off, basking in the sun of her smile, 'Poor thing, how she loves me!'

*

Aimless wandering, earnestly pursued, finds its own goal somewhere beyond the limits of intention. The railway station was there before him, glittering with a thousand lights. He stood awhile looking at it. Then somehow he was caught in its pull and became an atom in its bustling crowd.

Railway stations usually give an impression of isolation and helplessness. Both in their empty moments and their crowded ones, they are essentially sheds for people coming or going on the railway. But a great railway terminus is the point of origin and the point of return for travellers. From here, trains move out in all directions and return here again. People set out from this place to everywhere; people come to this place from everywhere to take up new lives, new relationships. In such a place as this many people become detached from their essential natures, their souls, and here also those natures become lodged in other beings. A beginning-ending place, a place of crowds, noise, and straining, itself unshaken, a lofty, enigmatic shrine. At that moment there was a great surge in the crowd, an enormous confusion in which some arriving passengers became thoroughly mingled with a crowd waiting to leave. Noise seemed to come from everywhere. One seemed to be part of the noise. Forms seen and unseen, sound heard and unheard, all these rolled together into one great confusion, one great undifferentiated mass of noise, which rose and rose and broke as a wave breaks on the beach. Then each shape, each sound, each word or name seemed to have lost its harmony, slipped from its place, so that the senses could not grasp the message the mind seemed to be trying to convey.

One of the trains about to depart seemed to be waiting, delaying intentionally, purposely flaunting the temptation to travel. Its intended occupants swarmed and whirled about it, peering into it here and there, looking for a place. Some were already packed sardine-like inside the train, some were clinging to the steps and windows, others had even climbed onto the roof. Those who could not find a hold were giving vent to their frustration by shinnying up the posts, onto the platform shelter, even onto the roof of the station, like a frolic of blind monkeys. The engine stood belching smoke in a monstrous plume, snarling and gasping its exasperation at not being allowed to move, now that it was ready. The cars strung out behind it were a massive braid of human beings.

Departure was announced and the police moved in to impose

order. They dragged those they could reach off the train, beat them, and drove them away. Some of these circled back to get a new hold somewhere else. Jolting first back, then forward, the train lurched to a start, shaking off several passengers. Those who failed to gain a new hold, ran alongside until they dropped from exhaustion. In all this confusion, somehow or the other, he had got on the train. He was crouched in a luggage rack. He pulled his knees up, rested his head on them, and went to sleep. Whenever the train stopped or slowed down anywhere, passengers who had got on the train apparently for no particular reason, suddenly found some good reason to get off, and disappeared into the darkness. Now that he had more room in the luggage rack, he stretched out his legs and fell into a deep sleep. He opened his eyes and raised his body up. Shreds of dreams fluttered in his consciousness; he had the feeling that he himself was a dream-image.

A mischievous smile on a sleepy face was looking up at him from below as if waiting to speak to him. Smiling-face said, 'That conductor came through while we were sleeping. He thought we looked like people who would not be travelling without tickets, so he didn't disturb us. He won't come back... .'

He patted his shirt-pocket. No ticket there! He couldn't remember either buying or not buying one, or even starting out on this voyage. He suspected that if he had bought one, smiling-face had picked his pocket in his sleep. The conductor might come. He'd better get away from there. He dug his fingers into his scalp as if to drag himself off by his hair.

The train was crawling past a small flag-stop platform apparently uncertain whether it had been flagged or not. The carriage he was on came almost to a stop in an open field. He prepared himself, calculating its speed, and swung down neatly and expertly before it stopped. He had no luggage to hinder him.

As the train stopped and moved on, he looked sharply about and sensed, rather saw that there was no one else there but him.

But in that black void, the darkness itself seemed to glow and to illuminate objects and forms. Then this strange brightness would merge again with the dark. He heard a sound like the searing outcry of a soul parted from its body but still torn by its involvement, its bondage to earth and the flesh.

This dark, this death, this clarity, all gave the impression of being what they were not, as if slipping from their true natures. The severed head of a rooster, unable to find its own body, seemed to attach itself to whatever was near and unnaturally herald the dawn. A date-palm, a coconut tree, a goat, a cow, a man: in that eerie half-light might not any of them serve as cock's body, crow cock's crow? Even if one were aware of the cause of this slipping from role to role, how could one avoid it? Perhaps in perceiving the world itself as just such a slip, just such a mistake, one could.

*

A little before full daylight the milk woman knocked and shouted at his door, but he didn't get up. He lay as if immersed in the world of his dream, as if bemused with the thought that it might be an extension of someone else's dream. The milk woman called so loud he certainly should have heard, but he did not. It would be a mistake to wait for him any longer, the milk woman thought, and went on her way.

Translated from Tamil by Albert Franklin

Anita Desai

A Devoted Son

When the results appeared in the morning papers, Rakesh scanned them, barefoot and in his pyjamas, at the garden gate, then went up the steps to the verandah where his father sat sipping his morning tea and bowed down to touch his feet.

'A first division, son?' his father asked, beaming, reaching for the papers.

'At the top of the list, papa,' Rakesh murmured, as if awed. 'First in the country.'

Bedlam broke loose then. The family whooped and danced. The whole day long visitors streamed into the small yellow house at the end of the road, to congratulate the parents of this *Wunderkind*, to slap Rakesh on the back and fill the house and garden with the sounds and colours of a festival. There were garlands and *halwa*, party clothes and gifts (enough fountain pens to last years, even a watch or two), nerves and temper and joy, all in a multicoloured whirl of pride and great shining vistas newly opened: Rakesh was the first son in the family to receive an education, so much had been sacrificed in order to send him to school and then medical college, and at last the fruits of their sacrifice had arrived, golden and glorious.

To everyone who came to him to say, '*Mubarak*, Varmaji, your son has brought you glory,' the father said, 'Yes, and do you know what is the first thing he did when he saw the results this morning? He came and touched my feet. He bowed down and touched my feet.' This moved many of the women in the crowd so much that they were seen to raise the ends of their saris and dab at their tears while the men reached out for the betel-leaves and sweetmeats that were offered around on trays and shook their heads in wonder and approval of such exemplary filial behaviour. 'One does not often see such behaviour in sons any more,' they all agreed, a little enviously perhaps. Leaving the house, some of the women said, sniffing, 'At least on such an occasion they might have served pure *ghee* sweets,' and some of the men said, 'Don't you think old Varma was giving himself airs? He needn't think we don't remember that he comes from the vegetable market himself, his father used to sell vegetables, and he has never seen the inside of a school.' But there was more envy than rancour in their voices and it was, of course, inevitable —not every son in that shabby little colony at the edge of the city was destined to shine as Rakesh shone, and who knew that better than the parents themselves?

And that was only the beginning, the first step in a great, sweeping ascent to the radiant heights of fame and fortune. The thesis he wrote for his M.D. brought Rakesh still greater glory, if only in select medical circles. He won a scholarship. He went to the USA (that was what his father learnt to call it and taught the whole family to say—not America, which was what the ignorant neighbours called it, but, with a grand familiarity, "the USA") where he pursued his career in the most prestigious of all hospitals and won encomiums from his American colleagues which were relayed to his admiring and glowing family. What was more, he came *back*, he actually returned to that small yellow house in the once-new but increasingly shabby colony, right at the end of the road where the rubbish vans tripped out their stinking contents for pigs to nose in and rag-pickers to build their shacks on, all steaming and smoking just outside the neat wire fences and well-tended gardens. To this Rakesh returned and the first thing he did on entering the house was to slip out of the embraces of his sisters and brothers and bow down and touch his father's feet.

As for his mother, she gloated chiefly over the strange fact that he had not married in America, had not brought home a foreign wife as all her neighbours had warned her he would, for wasn't that what all Indian boys went abroad for? Instead he agreed, almost without argument, to marry a girl she had picked out for him in her own village, the daughter of a childhood friend, a plump and uneducated girl, it was true, but so old-fashioned, so placid, so complaisant that she slipped into the household and settled in like a charm, seemingly too lazy and too good-natured to even try and make Rakesh leave home and set up independently, as any other girl might have done. What was more, she was pretty—really pretty, in a plump, pudding way that only gave way to fat—soft, spreading fat, like warm wax—after the birth of their first baby, a son, and then what did it matter?

For some years Rakesh worked in the city hospital, quickly rising to the top of the administrative organization, and was made a director before he left to set up his own clinic. He took his parents in his car—a new, sky-blue Ambassador with a rear window full of stickers and charms revolving on strings—to see the clinic when it was built, and the large sign-board over the door on which his name was printed in letters of red, with a row of degrees and qualifications to follow it like so many little black slaves of the regent. Thereafter his fame seemed to grow just a little dimmer—or maybe it was only that everyone in town had grown accustomed to it at last—but it was also the beginning of his fortune for he now became known not only as the best but also the richest doctor in town.

However, all this was not accomplished in the wink of an eye. Naturally not. It was the achievement of a lifetime and it took up Rakesh's whole life. At the time he set up his clinic his father had grown into an old man and retired from his post at the kerosene dealer's depot at which he had worked for forty years, and his mother died soon after, giving up the ghost with a sigh that sounded positively happy, for it was her own son who ministered to her in her last illness and who sat pressing her feet at the last moment—such a son as few women had borne.

For it had to be admitted—and the most unsuccessful and most rancorous of neighbours eventually did so—that Rakesh was not only a devoted son and a miraculously good-natured man contrived somehow to obey his parents and humour his wife and show concern equally for his children and his patients, but there was actually a brain inside this beautifully polished and formed body of good manners and kind nature and, in between ministering to his family and playing host to many friends and coaxing them all into feeling happy and grateful and content, he had actually trained his hands as well and emerged an excellent doctor, a really fine surgeon. How one man—and a man born to illiterate parents, his father having worked for a kerosene dealer and his mother having spent her life in a kitchen—had achieved, combined and conducted such a medley of virtues, no one could fathom, but all acknowledged his talent and skill.

It was a strange fact, however, that talent and skill, if displayed for too long, cease to dazzle. It came to pass that the most admiring of all eyes eventually faded and no longer blinked at his glory. Having retired from work and having lost his wife, the old father very quickly went to pieces, as they say. He developed so many complaints and fell ill so frequently and with such mysterious diseases that even his son could no longer make out when it was something of significance and when it was merely a peevish whim. He sat huddled on his string bed most of the day and developed an exasperating habit of stretching out suddenly and lying absolutely still, allowing the whole family to fly around him in a flap, wailing and weeping, and then suddenly sitting up, stiff and gaunt, and spitting out a big gob of betel-juice as if to mock their behaviour.

He did this once too often: there had been a big party in the house, a birthday party for the youngest son, and the celebrations had to be suddenly hushed, covered up and hustled out of the way when the daughter-in-law discovered, or thought she discovered, that the old man, stretched out from end to end of his string bed, had lost his pulse; the party broke up, dissolved, even turned into a band of mourners, when the old man sat up and the distraught daughter-in-law received a gob of red spittle right on the hem of her new organza sari. After that no one much cared if he sat up cross-legged on his bed, hawking and spitting, or lay down flat and turned grey as a corpse. Except, of course, for that pearl amongst pearls, his son Rakesh.

It was Rakesh who brought him his morning tea, not in one of the china cups from which the rest of the family drank, but in the old man's favourite brass tumbler, and sat at the edge of his bed, comfortable and relaxed with the string of his pyjamas dangling out from under his fine lawn night-shirt, and discussed or, rather, read out the morning news to his father. It made no difference to him that his father made no response apart from spitting. It was Rakesh, too, who, on returning from the clinic in the evening, persuaded the old man to come out of his room, as bare and desolate as a cell, and take the evening air out in the garden, beautifully arranging the pillows and bolsters on the *divan* in the corner of the open verandah. On summer nights he saw to it that the servants carried out the old man's bed onto the lawn and himself helped his father down the steps and onto the bed, soothing him and settling him down for a night under the stars.

All this was very gratifying for the old man. What was not so gratifying was that he even undertook to supervise his father's diet. One day when the father was really sick, having ordered his daughter-in-law to make him a dish of *soojie halwa* and eaten it with a saucerful of cream, Rakesh marched into the room, not with his usual respectful step but with the confident and rather contemptuous stride of the famous doctor, and declared, 'No more *halwa* for you, papa. We must be sensible, at your age. If you must have something sweet, Veena will cook you a little *kheer*, that's light, just a little rice and milk. But nothing fried, nothing rich. We can't have this happening again.'

The old man who had been lying stretched out on his bed, weak and feeble after a day's illness, gave a start at the very sound, the tone of these words. He opened his eyes—rather, they fell open with shock—and he stared at his son with disbelief that darkened quickly to reproach. A son who actually refused his father the food he craved? No, it was unheard of, it was incredible. But Rakesh had turned his back to him and was cleaning up the litter of bottles and packets on the medicine shelf and did not notice while Veena slipped silently out of the room with a little smirk that only the old man saw, and hated.

Halwa was only the first item to be crossed off the old man's diet. One delicacy after the other went—everything fried to begin with, then everything sweet, and eventually everything, everything that the old man enjoyed. The meals that arrived for him on the shining stainless steel tray twice a day were frugal to say the least—dry bread, boiled lentils, boiled vegetables and, if there were a bit of chicken or fish, that was boiled too. If he called for another helping—in a cracked voice that quavered theatrically—Rakesh himself would come to the door, gaze at him sadly and shake his head, saying, 'Now, papa, we must be careful, we can't risk another illness, you know,' and although the daughter-in-law kept tactfully out of the way, the old man could just see her smirk sliding merrily through the air. He tried to bribe his grand-children into buying him sweets (and how he missed his wife now, that generous, indulgent and illiterate cook), whispering, 'Here's fifty paise,' as he stuffed the coins into a tight, hot fist. 'Run down to the shop at the crossroads and buy me thirty paise worth of *jalebis*, and you can spend the remaining

96

twenty paise on yourself. Eh? Understand? Will you do that?' He got away with it once or twice but then was found out, the conspirator was scolded by his father and smacked by his mother and Rakesh came storming into the room, almost tearing his hair as he shouted through compressed lips, 'Now papa, are you trying to turn my little son into a liar? Quite apart from spoiling your own stomach, you are spoiling him as well—you are encouraging him to lie to his own parents. You should have heard the lies he told his mother when she saw him bringing back those *jalebis* wrapped up in filthy newspaper. I don't allow anyone in my house to buy sweets in the bazaar, papa, surely you know that. There's cholera in the city, typhoid, gastro-enteritis—I see these cases daily in the hospital, how can I allow my own family to run such risks?' The old man sighed and lay down in the corpse position. But that worried no one any longer.

There was only one pleasure left in the old man now (his son's early morning visits and readings from the newspaper could no longer be called that) and those were visits from elderly neighbours. These were not frequent as his contemporaries were mostly as decrepit and helpless as he and few could walk the length of the road to visit him any more. Old Bhatia, next door, however, who was still spry enough to refuse, adamantly, to bathe in the tiled bathroom indoors and to insist on carrying out his brass mug and towel, in all seasons and usually at impossible hours, into the yard and bathe noisily under the garden tap, would look over the hedge to see if Varma were out on his verandah and would call to him and talk while he wrapped his *dhoti* about him and dried the sparse hair on his head, shivering with enjoyable exaggeration. Of course these conversations, bawled across the hedge by two rather deaf old men conscious of having their entire households overhearing them, were not very satisfactory but Bhatia occasionally came out of his yard, walked down the bit of road and came in at Varma's gate to collapse onto the stone plinth built under the temple tree. If Rakesh was at home he would help his father down the steps into the garden and arrange him on his night bed under the tree and leave the two old men to chew betel-leaves and discuss the ills of their individual bodies with combined passion.

'At least you have a doctor in the house to look after you,' sighed Bhatia, having vividly described his martyrdom to piles.

'Look after me?' cried Varma, his voice cracking like an ancient clay jar. 'He—he does not even give me enough to eat.'

'What?' said Bhatia, the white hairs in his ears twitching. 'Doesn't give you enough to eat? Your own son?'

'My own son. If I ask him for one more piece of bread, he says no, papa, I weighed out the *ata* myself and I can't allow you to have more than two hundred grams of cereal a day. He *weighs* the food he gives me, Bhatia—he has scales to weigh it on. That is what it has come to.'

'Never,' murmured Bhatia in disbelief. 'Is it possible, even in this evil age, for a son to refuse his father food?'

'Let me tell you,' Varma whispered eagerly. 'Today the family was having fried fish—I could smell it. I called to my daughter-in-law to bring me a piece. She came to the door and said no....'

'Said no?' It was Bhatia's voice that cracked. A *drongo* shot out of the tree and sped away. '*No*?'

'No, she said no, Rakesh has ordered her to give me nothing fried. No butter, he says, no oil....'

'No butter? No oil? How does he expect his father to *live*?'

Old Varma nodded with melancholy triumph. 'That is how he treats me—after I have brought him up, given him an education, made him a great doctor. Great doctor! This is the way great doctors treat their fathers, Bhatia,' for the son's sterling personality and character now underwent a curious sea change. Outwardly all might be the same but the interpretation had altered: his masterly efficiency was nothing but cold heartlessness, his authority was only tyranny in disguise.

There was cold comfort in complaining to neighbours and, on such a miserable diet, Varma found himself slipping, weakening and soon becoming a genuinely sick man. Powders and pills and mixtures were not only brought in when dealing with a crisis like an upset stomach but became a regular part of his diet—became his diet, complained Varma, supplanting the natural foods he craved. There were pills to regulate his bowel movements, pills to bring down his blood pressure, pills to deal with his arthritis and, eventually, pills to keep his heart beating. In between there were panicky rushes to the hospital, some humiliating experiences with the stomach pump and enema, which left him frightened and helpless. He cried easily, shrivelling up on his bed, but if he complained of a pain or even a vague, grey fear in the night, Rakesh would simply open another bottle of pills and force him to take one. 'I have my duty to you papa,' he said when his father begged to be let off.

'Let me be,' Varma begged, turning his face away from the pills on the outstretched hand. 'Let me die. It would be better. I do not want to live only to eat your medicines.'

'Papa, be reasonable.'

'I leave that to you,' the father cried with sudden spirit. 'Leave me alone, let me die now, I cannot live like this.'

'Lying all day on his pillows, fed every few hours by his daughter-in-law's own hands, visited by every member of his family daily—and then he says he does not want to live "like this",' Rakesh was heard to say, laughing, to someone outside the door.

'Deprived of food,' screamed the old man on the bed, 'his wishes ignored, taunted by his daughter-in-law, laughed at by his grand-children—*that* is how I live.' But he was very old and weak and all anyone heard was an incoherent croak, some expressive grunts and cries of genuine pain. Only once, when old Bhatia had come to see him and they sat together under the temple tree, they heard him cry, 'God is calling me—and they won't let me go.'

The quantities of vitamins and tonics he was made to take were not altogether useless. They kept him alive and even gave him a kind of strength that made him hang on long after he ceased to wish to hang on. It was as though he were straining at a rope, trying to break it, and it would not break, it was still strong. He only hurt himself, trying.

In the evening, that summer, the servants would come into his cell, grip his bed, one at each end, and carry it out to the verandah, there setting it down with a thump that jarred every tooth in his head. In answer to his agonized complaints they said the doctor sahib had told them he must take the evening air and the evening air they would make him take—thump. Then Veena, that smiling, hypocritical pudding in a rustling sari, would appear and pile up the pillows under his head till he was propped up stiffly into a sitting position that made his head swim and his back ache.

'Let me lie down,' he begged. 'I can't sit up any more.'

'Try, papa, Rakesh said you can if you try,' she said, and

drifted away to the other end of the verandah where her transistor radio vibrated to the lovesick tunes from the cinema that she listened to all day.

So there he sat, like some stiff corpse, terrified, gazing out on the lawn where his grand-sons played cricket, in danger of getting one of their hard-spun balls in his eye, and at the gate that opened onto the dusty and rubbish-heaped lane but still bore, proudly, a newly touched-up signboard that bore his son's name and qualifications, his own name having vanished from the gate long ago.

At last the sky-blue Ambassador arrived, the cricket game broke up in haste, the car drove in smartly and the doctor, the great doctor, all in white, stepped out. Someone ran up to take his bag from him, others to escort him up the steps. 'Will you have tea?' his wife called, turning down the transistor set, 'Or a Coca-Cola? Shall I fry you some *samosas*?' But he did not reply or even glance in her direction. Ever a devoted son, he went first to the corner where his father sat gazing, stricken, at some undefined spot in the dusty yellow air that swam before him. He did not turn his head to look at his son. But he stopped gobbling air with his uncontrolled lips and set his jaw as hard as a sick and very old man could set it.

'Papa,' his son said, tenderly, sitting down on the edge of the bed and reaching out to press his feet.

Old Varma tucked his feet under him, out of the way, and continued to gaze stubbornly into the yellow air of the summer evening.

'Papa, I'm home.'

Varma's hand jerked suddenly, in a sharp, derisive movement, but he did not speak.

'How are you feeling, papa?'

Then Varma turned and looked at his son. His face was so out of control and all in pieces, that the multitude of expressions that crossed it could not make up a whole and convey to the famous man exactly what his father thought of him, his skill, his art.

'I'm dying,' he croaked. 'Let me die, I tell you.'

'Papa, you're joking,' his son smiled at him, lovingly. 'I've brought you a new tonic to make you feel better. You must take it, it will make you feel stronger again. Here it is. Promise me you will take it regularly, papa.'

Varma's mouth worked as hard as though he still had a gob of betel in it (his supply of betel had been cut off years ago). Then he spat out some words, as sharp and bitter as poison, into his son's face. 'Keep your tonic—I want none—I want none—I won't take any more of—of your medicines. None. Never,' and he swept the bottle out of his son's hand with a wave of his own, suddenly grand, suddenly effective.

His son jumped, for the bottle was smashed and thick brown syrup had splashed up, staining his white trousers. His wife let out a cry and came running. All around the old man was hubbub once again, noise, attention.

He gave one push to the pillows at his back and dislodged them so he could sink down on his back, quite flat again. He closed his eyes and pointed his chin at the ceiling, like some dire prophet, groaning, 'God is calling me—now let me go.'

Chunilal Madia

The Snake Charmer

Jakhra, a snake-charmer, was playing his flute studded with white, flower-like shells. He was playing it so loudly, it was as if he was puffing at the bellows of a blacksmith. And he was blowing so hard that it seemed his cheeks would burst. The show was at its climax. The male and the female cobras, which he had caught hissing from the ant-hill in the reef of Ujadia, were now swaying in the midst of that tightly packed crowd. The snakes were raising themselves in mid-air, spreading their hoods wide like sieves.

The more the snakes swayed, the more Jakhra, who was kneeling when the show started, raised himself up and up. The muscles of his face became more and more tense every minute. It looked as if he was dragging air from the deepest hollows of his stomach and stuffing it in his flute.

And, there was justification too for all this, for he had dragged into his basket a divine pair of cobras that would never have come under the spell of any spirit. And, even if they had, they would never have remained prisoners in the basket. Jakhra had achieved that difficult feat through the magic power which he had inherited from his dead father and which, at least in these parts, had not been equalled. At the instance of the head of the village, he was giving his first public performance that afternoon.

The cobra pair was swaying and moving in the direction of the alluring music of the flute. Their movements were like the motion of ears of *bajra* (millet), full with fresh big grains, swaying with the wind passing over the fields. The audience was deeply absorbed in what they saw. All eyes were fixed on the pair. The two snakes, with their graceful curves near their heads, looked like two lean bodies, standing bent at the waist.

This was the supreme moment of Jakhra's life. It was the moment of fulfilment of that sacred power which his father had passed on to him, and for the attainment of which, the worshipper had to adopt arduous restraint.

Jakhra's quest had begun, many years ago. Old Ladhu, who could not maintain an all-round purity, initiated his only son into the sacred power so that it should not be forgotten. At the same time he warned his son about the difficulties and dangers of the path. He said the pursuit of the path demanded purity that would go beyond the austerities of the yogis of Jullundur. He emphasized that the threefold purity of mind, body and speech was absolutely essential if one wanted to follow this way. The slightest deviation—and one would roll down to the valley from the heights of attainment.

Jakhra was then very young; yet he was not inexperienced in the field. When his father went from village to village with the basket of "animals" on his shoulders, Jakhra would accompany him carrying the bag of tarpaulin in which would be stuffed the flute, the bowl and the snake-charmer's bag and many other odd things. When the show was on, his father would concentrate his eyes on the snakes. And Jakhra with his sharp eyes, would pick up small coins thrown by the onlookers in the dust. He made all the preparatory arrangements before the show began—such as playing the little trumpet to draw the crowd—first the children and then the grown-ups, clearing the place for the show, pulling out the mongoose from the bag and fixing his nail in the ground. In the meanwhile Ladhu would smoke *dhattura* to prepare himself for his arduous work. At the end of the game, when he gave threatening orders to the children to get some flour from home (and cursed their mothers if they did not bring any) and when the fear-ridden children did at last bring some leftover stuff, it was Jakhra who collected all the bits and pushed them into his bag.

It was the unwritten, universal practice that the father and the son should get out of the town by evening. They had to face the police if they failed to do so.

Actually, when they left the border of the town, they had to allow the guard to inspect all their paraphernalia—in case they were hiding in one of their baskets a high-caste child!

The father and the son would go far into the forest and take out the crumbs of bread. If there was not enough to eat, Ladhu would make Jakhra eat even if he himself had to go hungry. He would pour milk in a shallow bowl for the snakes. At times, when the rays of the moon, filtering through the thick, vast tamarind tree, played hide-and-seek on Jakhra's rosy, charming face, Ladhu thought of Jakhra's mother who was as rosy and as charming. But the asceticism in Ladhu would check his emotions and bring him back to his senses. He would say to himself: 'You were mad about her; as such you lost your hold over that magic power which is worth a lakh of rupees. Can the pursuer of this path ever afford to be mad about a woman? It needs strong will-power. If you make a slightest mistake, in no time it would take your own life. It is difficult to master the art. But it is more difficult to exercise it even after you have mastered it. You can cool the milk of a lioness only in a gold bowl— for it won't cool in an earthen pot. When the Ganges was brought down to the earth, was not the great Mahadev himself present on the scene in person?'

And at moments like these Ladhu's irrepressible ambition would begin to stir and whisper in his ears: 'Let your son fulfil the unfulfilled desire of your heart. You learnt the magic with great difficulty. Let it not be forgotten. Let your son do what you could not do and put to shame all the charmers of the entire area.'

Prompted by pride and ambition, he ordered Jakhra to remain a *brahmachari*. An ascetic's life is full of hard tasks and sacrifices. Right from his childhood Jakhra had been living the hard life of self-denial. He would not even look at a six-month-old female child. All women were looked at as a sister or a mother. He would not eat forbidden food. Again, he would not drink the water polluted by someone else. He would keep his body clean. He would not slip his feet into his shoes without tapping his shoes thrice to shake off the dust and reciting the ordained *mantra*. And if, even by mistake, he touched an "unholy" man, he would promptly have a bath.

Jakhra grew up to be very handsome—graceful like a peacock. He was a well-proportioned mixture of his father's manly strength and his mother's charming grace. Rigorous training of the mind and a vigilant control over the senses gave a lustre to his shapely, handsome face. Every line of his body spoke eloquently of his ascetic power and the dazzling expression on his face spoke of his attainment in his art at so young an age.

He put to test his knowledge of the magic by experimenting on a pair of cobras. It was rumoured that the pair was living in an ant-hill in a field at Ujadia. Great snake-charmers had been playing on their flutes till they could play no more, but those snakes had not so much as raised themselves out of their ant-hill. Jakhra went there and began to play his flute which was studded with shells, white and pure like two rows of teeth. Two days passed but nothing happened. But on the third day the cobras could no longer resist the sweet melody of the flute. They could not help swaying their bodies to the sweet tunes. Majestically, the pair slid out of the ant-hill. Jakhra suddenly brought them under the spell of his *mantra*. By the spell of his music the cobras lay stiff like pieces of wood and were at last closed in Jakhra's basket.

In his last moments, Ladhu had said: 'God will be pleased with us only if we think of even the animals as our own flesh and blood. A snake should be held captive for fifteen days and released on the fifteenth day. If held even a day more it will amount to harassing dumb creatures and God will punish us.' Guided by this counsel, Jakhra was aware that once the poisonous gland of the snake was removed even a child could safely play with it. Still as one who was proud of the maddening melody of his flute, he felt that he could control the deadliest of snakes without pulling out their fangs. So Jakhra had not bothered doing this with the pair of cobras in the basket.

The wind carried the news that Jakhra had caught a new pair and through his flute alone had kept them under his spell. The news reached the elders in the village and they sent for him.

Jakhra set the stage for the play. The swelling audience was rapt in attention. All eyes were concentrated on the cobras as they swayed in ecstasy. But there was a pair of eyes that was fixed not on the flute, nor on the swaying cobras, but on the handsome player of the flute. To those eyes, the one who could sway the cobras was more charming than the swaying snakes. They were the eyes of Teja Ba who was hiding behind the balcony door at the gate of her castle. She was the new Thakarani. Teja Ba was the very fountain of charm and grace. The entire village was under her spell. Teja Ba was so proud that she did not even care to glance at great princes. But it was Teja Ba's greatest despair that she had not yet come across anyone who matched her. When she saw Jakhra, she at once felt that he was the man she would most certainly like to have.

Jakhra, puffing up his cheeks as big as coconut shells, was swaying and with him was swaying the pair of cobras. In the centre of the hood of the male cobra was a lovely pale black mark. And that dark, beautiful hood on the bluish white neck of the cobra was very charming indeed. It reminded one of the *chhatra* over the *Shivalinga*. And the female cobra, swaying by the side of her male, expressed her mighty power through her majestic curve which was very much like the arch of Puradwar. Jakhra's eyes, ears and nose, his entire self were now concentrated only on the snout of the male cobra and on the brightly shining eyes of his female. Jakhra had become one with his flute.

Those eyes that were stooping in that evocative silence—why didn't they rise up just once, just for a moment ?

Finally, Teja Ba brushed her bangles on the door—so that those stooping eyes should be diverted to her.

And at the tinkling sound, for a moment, yes, only for a moment Jakhra's eyelashes rose.

And in that wink of a moment, just in that brief moment Jakhra had an experience of his lifetime.

The cobra pair had reached the pinnacle of joy when the notes of the flute had reached their climax. To bring them back from their ecstatic swaying, the tempo of the flute music was to be gradually slowed down. Instead, there was a sudden break—and that disturbed the absorbed cobras. The resultant agony was terrible. And the wrath and the consequent poison were still more terrible.

With a frightening hiss the hood of the cobra struck Jakhra's palm, and its sharp teeth made a wound there. The flute slipped from Jakhra's hand. There was confusion in the crowd. But Jakhra was still alert. He somehow managed to get the cobras back in the basket.

Very soon a glass-green round mark rose where the cobra had stung. The coins that the appreciative audience had thrown for him remained untouched, and Jakhra, resting his head on the basket in which he had just shut the cobras, fell into a swoon.

Promptly the news spread all over the town that Jakhra had been bitten by the cobra.

One of the people in the crowd remarked: 'You may bring up a snake on milk, but it is a snake after all ! It does not give up its nature so easily as all that!'

'And then,' came another remark, 'however small, a cobra is always a terrible thing. Poison will always kill a person. It may be a small quantity or it may be big—poison is poison.'

And again: 'Is it not said that a mason would die as he is building and a pearl-diver would die in the stormy sea? In the same way, the snake-charmer too would meet his death through his snakes!'

'Is it a joke, keeping such enormous snakes in such big baskets? It is a task as difficult as walking on a razor's edge. One must do penance like the most austere yogis—and one must deny oneself lots and lots of things. Only with the power of such purity can these "animals" be kept under control. It is, after all, not easy to shut the dwellers of the ant-hills in a basket!'

'Moreover, an elderly, experienced snake-charmer, may at least try to do something. This Jakhra is a mere boy. What could he do?'

'And believe me, this profession of snake-charmers is an art by itself—and it is a very difficult art at that. You must look after the snakes as if they are your own children. If you catch them, you can't keep them in your basket longer than a fortnight.'

'Even within that limit, is it a joke to have a pair of cobra snakes dance to the tune of the flute just for the sake of a few coins! You must have a heart of steel. And, it is not easy to have a heart of steel. Your mind must be pure. And your eyes should be clear like pouring oil. Even a little impurity can do a lot of harm. Snake-charmers are destined to beg and so they have got to hold out their hand at every door. But their eyes must be always stooping. Even if the bracelets of the lady of the house jingle, the eyes of the snake-charmer should never look up.'

'That is how you can go along the path of knowledge. And knowledge is like mercury. Only the deserving and the learned can digest it. Moreover, it is an art to tame the snakes and to make them dance. The meek and the weak can't hope to do it. It is easy to learn the trade of the snake-charmers; but it is difficult to acquire real mastery of the art. Only a genius can do it!'

The *bhuva* of Vacchda, who was the greatest expert in the whole area, came to relieve Jakhra of the pain of the poisonous sting of the cobra. He chanted *mantra* after *mantra*, and he tried his very best, but he was still unable to bring any relief.

People were disappointed. Jakhra was lying stiff, as if in deep sleep. He seemed to have no consciousness at all!

The audience expressed its disappointment in various ways. They were like a challenge to the *bhuva* who now started chanting his *mantras* desperately. But his efforts were still futile. He tried the final remedy against snake-bite. He took a long piece of cloth and recited some more *mantras*. And then, he gave one last warning to the snake. Now everybody expected that the poison from Jakhra's wound would come out. If not, the *bhuva* would start tearing that piece of cloth from end to end and the snake too would get torn like that !

People sitting beside Jakhra's body heard him mutter something in his semi-conscious state. He was supposed to have said: '*Bhuva*, why are you harassing those dumb creatures in the basket? Had it been only the poison of the snake, it would have gone long ago. But with that poison is mixed that other poison which is sweet and yet sour—and there your magic won't work.'

And, even before the *bhuva* could properly try his last trick, Jakhra lay lifeless.

But those two eyes, glistening bright behind the balcony door, remained fixed on Jakhra's dead body.

Translated from Gujarati by Sarla Jag Mohan

P.S. Rege

Savitri

Whomsoever I desire, him I make bold,
him the knower, him the seer, him of sharp intellect.

Rig-Veda (X; 10; 125)

I

Tirupet: Coorg
April 1939–July 1939

We were not even acquainted. I wrote to you and you responded in the same impulsive manner. How shall I introduce myself to you? I hardly know myself how I grew up—motherless and close to Appa, who was always engrossed in work. The first thing I ever learnt was to forget myself. The name you know already. Some call me Sau. But Appa once said: Child, you are joy itself (the word used by Appa was *Anand-bhavani*, which suggests joy-unfolding). Words like these come to him without effort—and since then I am like this (as you thought me in the beginning), joyous. You wrote and said—unreserved.

When I was a child Rajamma had told me a story: An old woman and her little grand-daughter, Lachhi, lived by a wood far away from the village. One day a peacock came near the old woman's hut. When Lachhi saw the peacock she began to dance. The peacock danced too. Lachhi insisted the peacock be tied in the courtyard. The old woman asked: How can it be? Where have we the corn to feed him? The two couldn't decide on anything. So the peacock himself said: I will stay here close by. I don't need the corn. There's the wood all around. But there is one condition. Whenever I come, Lachhi must dance. Lachhi agreed at once. The old woman was also satisfied. But dancing was no easy matter. If one must dance to order, the mind must be tuned. After that Lachhi was always joyous. One couldn't really tell when exactly the peacock would come. Later on she wasn't even aware whether the peacock had come and gone.

Rajamma never tells you the point of her stories. I often think she makes them up herself and in the telling gives them imperceptibly the shape of grandma's tales.

I said: if one wants a peacock, one must become a peacock oneself. Whatever it is one wants, one has to be that oneself.

It will be long before I leave this place. I will come to you some time, just like that, without letting you know.

II

In the train you expressed 'surprise' that I spoke in two different languages to the children with me. You fondly called it a marvel. But actually it was quite effortless. One of the boys belonged here, so his language was Tulu. The other was very small—two-and-a-half-years-old—his language was Konkani. I had been entrusted with seeing them to their homes. In a way I am multilingual. But it has always been my experience that language is not much of a problem in dealing with children.

I bought you some tea—what's wrong with that, any way? Where has it been decreed that you alone must buy it? You helped me to get the luggage out of the train. Was that a small matter?

III

For two years I was in Bangalore and yet how is it we never met? To tell you the truth, I got to know a lot of people during those years. The Ladies' Hostel is of course my own. The women who work there come to me whenever they need anything. I never participated much in college life though. It's not that I had my nose in books. Somehow I just didn't feel drawn to those routine activities.

Professor Gurupadaswaami had once referred in class to your Prize Essay. He praised you too. Every year the prize goes to someone; for me it merely meant that you had won it that particular year. If you had been in our class, this information might have roused more interest! But you were a post-graduate student and we had just joined college. Gurupadaswaami is a good teacher, don't you think? I managed to get full marks from him in the first year exam. But there, I have begun my own tale.

It is perfectly restful here. Appa works all day. He is writing a new book. At times like these he can't bear anyone, not even me, near him. I then occupy myself with the house—which means that I take great care to do everything without disturbing Appa.

The other day a young professor of Linguistics from Poona had been here to see him. He has a doctorate from the Sorbonne. He stayed with us for two days. He had come to discuss his new theory of aesthetics with Appa.

Appa listened carefully to everything he had to say. He discussed a little with him. But the question he raised at the end I thought very suggestive. The Durga of Navaratri, the Rama-Lakshmana-Sita images of Ramalila, the clay idols of the Ganesha festival—the craftsman who fashions all these knows that their existence is brief and still expends all his art on them. Why?

The professor's view was that in such cases the artist is not at all concerned with whether his work of art has a brief or a long existence. All his attention is centred on perfecting his creation.

Appa, it seemed, was hardly satisfied with this answer. 'Oneness'—'Samadhi'— he fights shy of such words. His usual comment on such an explanation is that it is mere paraphrase.

I was around and ventured to say. This is *my* Durga, this is *my* Rama, this is *my* Sita, this is *my* Ganesha—it is with this feeling that the craftsman works.

I felt that Appa approved of this explanation. He added : The maker perfects *himself*. Colour, bamboo, paper, clay, stone—it is not enough to call them mere instruments. If these are instruments, the maker too is an instrument. These are actually other aspects of the maker himself.

I am writing this specifically for you. Your thesis was on a similar subject.

IV

This happened on the day I lost my guitar. I had frolicked about a lot that day with wild flowers in my hair.

Some of us went on a picnic to a small, rather thickly wooded hill nearby. Actually it is not one hill, but a cluster of seven hillocks, merging into one another. Round these parts they call it the House of the Seven Virgins. There is quite an intricate legend about it. Seven young girls of seven *okkas* (a group of family households) couldn't find husbands and they were also harassed at home. So they left the village and each of them made a home for herself here. After some time such thick woods grew round the houses that they disappeared from sight. Later there wasn't a trace left of them. In their place rose these seven hills. Young girls have to offer prayers to them. Men are not supposed to go anywhere near them. If they do, they get lost in these woods. There are instances of a few who have even disappeared.

One of us had brought one of our brothers along. He and I lost our way. He was scared, but he didn't show it. I remained quite calm. It was impossible to turn back. One walked following the slope—but then again right in the middle rose the hump of a big hill. Heaven knows what happened eventually. We got down exactly at the point where we had begun the ascent. The rest of them had been waiting anxiously.

We didn't mention this to anyone at home.

V

After waiting for six days, I am writing this letter. You haven't misunderstood my innocent words, have you? I am worried, perhaps needlessly. Please forget what I wrote.

Quite often I fail to understand the implications of my actions. I do something naturally and unreservedly. But then somebody makes me realize later that it just doesn't mean what I had in mind. I am quite used to this now.

Henceforth I shall learn to behave like the rest.

VI

Yesterday's letter from you reassured me a lot. All my fears were unfounded then!

Now all of a sudden I find I am bored here. Couldn't you come down for a few days ? There is a lot to see near the place. Besides, the Bhadrakali festival is held about this time. In this district it is quite an important event.

Do come. I shall be your guide.

VII

Never mind if your thesis is a little delayed. Perhaps there are more chances of its getting an impetus here. You might even light upon some unexpected sources of art.

Appa's book is now taking further shape. For the last ten days he has been writing all the time. He begins with 'Experience'. We 'experience' a new thing or a situation—that is, we move forward from the past. An 'experience' undergone is a graph drawn with the assistance of memory by going backwards from the existing state. In both cases present existence is not taken into account at all—that is what he says. I am trying to grasp all this.

Let me know what things I can do to drag you here.

VIII

I am so happy you have decided to come. Rajamma is in a greater flurry than I am. (She thinks you are coming to 'inspect' me.) When I spoke to Appa he said : If he's a friend of yours, let him come. And then he asked me casually if you could type. Really, can you? But don't panic. He has no intention of making you sit and work, and I, none at all.

But in the temple festival, as is the custom here, you will have to take part in the music and dance.

IX

I must give you detailed instructions about how to get here.

This is a hill country. You get off the train at Rajnad. There you board the Tirupet bus and travel thirty miles into the interior. From there another two miles in a *buggy* to our house. I shall wait for you at Tirupet on Wednesday. We shall get here in our *buggy*. You will recognize me, won't you? These thirty-seven days we have got to know each other very well through our letters. Actually we have met only once, on that day.

I shall have my favourite pale purple sari on. There will be two choice flowers in my hands to greet you. When you see me, raise the stick in your hand.

We won't go straight home from Tirupet. I shall carry lunch with me. We will take your luggage and go to the Kannir lake which is close by. There is an old Hoysala temple near the lake. We will have our lunch there and then go home. Whenever I go to Tirupet, I always visit that place.

Now your programme! You say you will stay only a week. That's a bit of a problem. I had fixed a fortnight's programme for you. On Wednesday—nothing at all, just enough to overcome the fatigue of the journey. You will meet Appa at dinner time. He may not say a word. Or he may ask a string of questions. I should be prepared for any of these eventualities. Even if he doesn't speak at all, he observes everything closely. If our hospitality is found wanting, even in the slightest detail, he will scold me later.

On Thursday morning we shall visit our plantation. You can see all the oranges you ever wanted to see. We will lunch there by Venkappa's raised hut and enjoy his hospitality. We shall be back home by four in the afternoon. After dinner, there is my *veena* recital—by special public request.

Friday morning you will have to be on your own. On Friday I go and teach in a girls' school here. With you here, I shan't be able to teach. On that day Appa will chat with you on his own. You will get to know each other well. In the evening we will go out for a walk. The bazaar and the houses here will be quite new to you.

Saturday is the tenth day of the great festival. That evening everybody takes part in the dance. I have tidied up Appa's old costume for you.

Sunday, I have kept free for visitors. On Sunday night, if you feel like it, we could go and watch a folk-play. It will remind you somewhat of the Yakshagana.

On Monday evening you will lecture at the Local Association. I have suggested the subject—'The Art of Man'. You could, of course, change it to 'Shakespeare's Heroines' or 'Ocean Plants'.

Since you yourself have decreed that you will return on Wednesday, I have kept Tuesday free again—for you to do whatever you want to.

When you come, don't bring anything for me.

X

I have drawn up some rules for myself on the eve of your arrival.

1. To be up before everyone else; to be the last to go to bed.
2. To speak softly to the servants.
3. To guess what the guest would prefer without asking him.
4. Not to be needlessly flurried.
5. To use one's conversational skill in moderate proportion.
6. Not to burst into song needlessly.
7. To leave the guest to himself sometimes. (You must have noticed that I have kept this in mind while drawing up your programme.))
8. Not to take as literally true what the other says about oneself.

XI

The last four days I was anxious because I hadn't heard from you. And now the letter that arrived today has left me utterly disappointed. Why did you change your plans all of a sudden? You say that you are going to England. But that's still a long way off—there are nearly three months to go. You don't need that long to get things ready. The real reason could perhaps be something quite different. How shall I know it? And in any case, who am I to want to know it? 'Heart, be comforted!' I don't have the courage to say even this—and the right, none at all.

When we were children, my friend's brother was once to have come from a far-off place. I saw her weep because he didn't come. I even teased her. Then I too sat and wept with her. Today I didn't weep. Why? Because I am beginning to learn that one shouldn't look too far ahead nor try to reshape what has already taken place. What has happened must be left as it is—far away. By holding on to it, the shades tend to grow faint; that's all.

Now I have started remembering things, one by one. After coming back here for the holidays, I have hardly written to any one. I haven't really met people either. I had no idea how time passed.

XII

Just recently while re-reading one of your letters, I laughed at myself. I don't know what ideas you have formed about me! I am not as orderly as you think. You might perhaps have thought so because I am by nature a little cold and not so easily flustered. Even now, today, I am writing to you calmly, am I not?

You were kind enough to enquire about Appa's book. These five or six days his work seems to have slowed down, too. He has gone to spend a few days with Mr Edgeworth, an English planter who lives nearby. At one time Mr Edgeworth was at Appa's Oxford, which accounts for the warmth of their friendship. Every month or so he comes to Appa for a day or two or else Appa goes and stays with him. I have known him since I was a child. He still declares that I have often pulled his brown whiskers. He is more than fifty-five-years-old and still a bachelor. He works and reads to his heart's content and mixes freely with all the people around. Appa has already conferred upon him an honorary membership of our *okka*.

Edgeworth has his own peculiar notions. One of these is about rebirth. He believes that he was a Coorgi in his last birth. For has he not spent some thirty to thirty-two years of his life in Coorg, wholly engrossed in and at one with the life here? He declares that if this were not so he would never have come to this part of the world at all.

I once asked him in fun: Where is the Coorgi wife you married in your last birth? He was serious for a while and then he said : Sau, they didn't find me a wife in my last birth. I said to myself : Not in the last birth, so not in this. Does that mean there will be no marriage for him in any of the future births? An unaccountable sadness came over me. But he laughed almost immediately and said: In my next birth, I shall come here again. But as a Coorgi woman. Then I will be married off soon. Isn't that right? Appa laughed too; and they began chatting as usual.

How far have the preparations for your departure progressed? You say you will teach for a term. Which means that you might perhaps take our class.

XIII

Professor Joshi from Poona (I had once written to you about him) arrived here yesterday, via Nimbal. I have given him your address in Bangalore. Please introduce him to Professor Gurupadaswaami. He is keen to meet you as well, because you are one of Gurupadaswaami's pupils.

In the letter that came yesterday, you complained that I don't write much about myself. On the other hand, I often feel that I speak only about myself all the time—and then I become embarrassed at the thought of what you must think of me.

What shall I write about myself? Just now I am awaiting the results. (You have promised to wire on the 16th). Like you, I shall do Philosophy for my B.A.—because without doing so, one can't be serious. At the moment *veena* playing has more or less come to a stop. Some time ago I used to be pretty regular. I am going to practice regularly again from next Friday. Everyday I wait for your letter.

My next letter will be all about myself.

XIV

I was glad to hear that you are coming after all. This time no set plan has been chalked out for you—as a lesson for me.

Do you play tennis? If you don't, special instruction will be arranged.

Today is Monday, tomorrow is Tuesday, and Wednesday is the day after.

XV

I don't even know how these last five days flew. In a sense it was good that you came, because seeing me at close quarters must have shown you that most of your notions about me were not founded on fact. Let me know at once if I did make a mistake anywhere.

Edgeworth liked you a lot. He wants you to write to him once, before you proceed to England. He is going to suggest a few things to you.

I was also very happy to see that you got on well with Appa. Write and tell me when you can what you both sat and talked about for two whole days.

But you have completely 'fallen' in my esteem! They say a person oughtn't to be so calm...and yet this calm guise suited you all the more.

XVI

In a day or two the rains will come. I am waiting for the examination results. I don't hope to get a first, so one might as well say that the results are out. In any case, please send me the wire as planned.

At times I feel that I haven't understood your mind at all. I keep on re-reading what you have written and everytime I read a different meaning in it. The other day you said that every moment is unique. Does this mean that the same words denote a different meaning at different moments? Perhaps you might say that there is no 'meaning' as such. The structure of language, the associations of a particular time create a semblance of meaning, that's all. I want all this spelled out in everyday speech. I want to get to understand my own mind. When I get to understand it, I shall then understand yours as well.

I am still in the last week. How much better it would be if there were no remembrance of the past, no yearning of what's to come! This would also set at rest Appa's problem of 'experience'.

XVII

It is ten days since I heard from you. You did send the wire as planned, though. I didn't think I would get a first. I had a feeling that a letter of congratulations might follow the wire. Has the letter disappeared somewhere?

Sometimes the feeling comes over me that it's many days since you were here.

Edgeworth is with us again. He came just yesterday. Appa called him over specially. When his writing work is completed he needs someone like Edgeworth to listen to what has been written—someone not easily swayed by an opinion. Edgeworth listens to everything and then puts in a sly question in his typically English manner. When this happens Appa does get a little perturbed, but he soon demonstrates how he has drawn his entire conclusion taking into account the very point that has been raised. Occasionally he realizes that his line of argument is weak and right away notes down the point. Appa has called his book *Experience and Growth*. According to Edgeworth it's going to be a revolutionary book.

XVIII

Your two letters came together. It appears from the post mark on the envelope that the first one was posted later.

Please don't write such nice letters. Because then I don't feel like writing myself. My own letters seem to me just dry reports. No highlights, no poetry. Your mind is like a deep pool of water. Though one sees in it the changing colours of the sky, its own colours remain quite different. A colour gets to be unfamiliar even before one has learnt to get familiar with it. It smoothly sets off another.

What would you rather have me write? Love, affection, desire—words like these have no fascination for me. I feel we use them as banners to pitch ourselves somewhere. Their colours have long since faded. I am attracted to you—but what does that mean? I have made you mine; made myself yours. Is there anything beyond this? With this give and take are we to be something more or are we to build new walls round us?

If you get to understand the mould of my mind, you should not find it difficult to construe me wholly. Your simplicity, your slightly diffident nature, your conspicuous sense of justice in dealing with others—even talking about them, your gift for welding smoothly together what's happened and what's to come and leaving on it a stamp of your own—all this has now become mine. Is there nothing at all that I have given you?

College will soon reopen now, but I am not sure that I shall come to Bangalore and join. Appa has an invitation from Japan. If he goes, I shall have to go with him. Of course nothing is certain yet.

I shall soon answer one by one the queries you raised in your second letter.

XIX

This letter has been delayed a little. I hope you won't mind.

In English universities the session begins in October. Do you have to go there right now in the middle of July? There shouldn't be any difficulty getting admission to Oxford. Besides Edgeworth has already written to a tutor he knows. We shall know the position in about two weeks. I grant that going earlier in person might speed up your work. And yet you will certainly be rushed by your present plan of starting so early.

Do you still want the answers to all your queries?

So we are going after all. Appa has finally decided to accept the invitation to Japan. At Kyoto there is an old religious institution called the Anand Mission. Actually it wouldn't be quite right to describe it as a religious institution. It is a centre for seekers. People come there from all over the world to study and exchange ideas. It was founded by a Ceylonese monk some fifty years ago. Appa and the Mission's present head, Professor Namura, have been corresponding from time to time. Recently Appa had sent him some parts of his new book for his comments. Professor Namura felt that before publishing the book Appa ought to deliver the annual lectures organized by his Mission and speak on its main topic. These last twenty years Appa hasn't travelled much. So he wasn't too keen to embark on this new venture. But Edgeworth took the initiative and got him to agree.

Professor Joshi is here. He came down specially when he learnt about this. He says he will take leave from work and come with us for some days at least. He has made some study of the Chinese and Japanese languages. So the first few days he will be a great help. I would have asked you to come too. Will you? At times there is also some fun in not doing certain things at the appointed time.

I have not forgotten to answer your queries. I am waiting to see if in the meanwhile you yourself find the answers.

XXI

She is full of just two words in a letter. Very often she is quite lost. Where and how did the strands get woven? Who were the birds that strung the notes together?

The day is a marvel to her, the night a tracery of flowers. But her mind is such as will not bear the strict pattern of words.

She had said: I will come some time—just like that. And the days passed and she did not come.

Then who was it he met in the park on the way? Who had started out for whom?

As they walked together, the steps did not falter. The eyes

never lingered anywhere. The path became familiar and the trees around built arches of shadows. The dry leaves underneath had not even a trace of early memories left.

When she sat by the bank of the river, she did not startle anyone by casually tossing a stone into the water. A crane lighted smoothly on the grass along the bank; his reflection in the water hardly stirred.

When the first shower came down unexpectedly, she just stood there, drenched, dripping.

While walking with him in the precincts of the temple, she simply did a turn of the festival dance and, for a moment, musical instruments that weren't there resounded in rhythm.

While she sat at the raised entrance of the house, stringing flowers, she found a place in the garland for even those that were a little withered.

Where did all this happen?

These are five consistent answers to someone's sixty cherished questions.

XXII

Sayama Maru
22 July 1939

This is just a line of greeting from the boat. The weather is terribly monsoonish. Professor Joshi who affirmed that he has never felt seasick hasn't left his cabin these last four days. Appa is in very good spirits. He wants to try and see if he can still enjoy a game of bridge. I like the food here very much. I am going to write to Edgeworth: I have started feeling that I was really a Japanese in my previous life.

Where will this card reach you? At Bangalore, or at Simhachalam, or in London ?

Travel...and more travel: From where and to where! I am terribly happy.

XXIII

Kyoto: Japan
August 1939–October 1941

On my arrival here I found your three letters awaiting me. You are admitted to Oxford—so it means you have got what you wanted. I am glad you visited Edgeworth once again. His exterior is a bit rough, but he does care for everyone. He gave you his overcoat—that bodes well. He has a magic touch and his speech augurs blessing. He believes that ones affection for another is not quite perfect unless one gives the other something one has used oneself. He has given me the most ancient of his walking-sticks. I still use it when I go out for walks with Appa.

The Anand Mission is in fact an old Samurai palace. It's been fitted up for the purpose. There is a spacious lecture hall. Adjoining the hall are a library and study rooms. Namura and two of his colleagues live here in the palaces. They have arranged for us to live in a small house in the palace compound itself. The palace, with its surroundings, is extremely beautiful. It's outside the town. So one gets a feeling of space.

I was worried whether the climate would agree with Appa. But fortunately it looks as though it is going to do him a lot of good.

Joshi is quite at home here. He knows the language—that's an additional advantage. He lives in the university hostel because that's more convenient for study. He spends his Sundays with us or when we all go out on a trip he joins us.

In her capacity as the Mission's house-keeper, Mrs Namura is in-charge of all the arrangements. It looks as though one of her husband's colleagues, Mrs Imoto, will soon find a help-mate for her. Another of his colleagues is a Tibetan Lama. We call him 'Sudhamma'.

At present there are eight students studying here at the Mission—five Japanese, one Norwegian, one Englishman, and one Ceylonese. As yet I haven't been able to get to know them well. A lot of outsiders also come and attend the public functions and lectures.

Namura is a fine person. His eyes are clear like a child's. The slightest nuance of his mind finds itself reflected immediately in them. With his brown and grey beard and his perfect Japanese attire, he looks very impressive. His English is excellent. But when he speaks Japanese, he sounds more effective. It could perhaps be that when one is listening to an unfamiliar language, one is very sharply aware of its sound effects. He liked my name very much. But he pronounces it Sha-u. Appa has christened him Sandipani (he who kindles). When one sees how good he is at kindling with ease the light of knowledge, the name seems just right for him.

You will say I have written nothing about myself. But I am still looking at things around.

The papers tell us that the drums of war have begun to beat in Europe. One feels anxious on your account—and then one thinks that all of us need to be anxious about all the others.

I received a copy of your thesis. Wherefore the debt of gratitude to me in your preface?

XXIV

For a long time there was no letter from you; and the one that came today was all too brief. You must now be right in the middle of the din and smoke of war. Of course I am anxious, but less so after your letter. It is only right that you should have decided even in these circumstances not to return but to stay on there and complete your work. What is going to happen could happen anywhere.

Here too the atmosphere doesn't give one cause for much optimism. One never knows what might happen and when. But Appa seems to be happy here. His health too has improved a lot.

Professor Joshi says he is going back to India at the end of December. During his stay here he concentrated mainly on studying the Japanese language. At the moment he is busy visiting the important sites here. I like this characteristic of his very much. He does even the smallest of things with a lot of enthusiasm—conferring on it the same amount of care he might bestow on his study or meditation—or even a shade more. He never lets go a single opportunity. You are now already acquainted. With his study and interests, he could be of great help to you.

Appa has received a very pathetic letter from Edgeworth. Edgeworth fears that the war will last long, that there will be large-scale destruction. He fought in the last war and even won a DSO. Today there is nothing he can do himself. He can no longer grasp why the people of the world, instead of coming together as a result of material progress, should be increasingly pulled apart from one another. In India itself the situation today is explosive. The Viceroy and the Governors have everywhere taken over all the administrative powers into their own hands. The country's entire economy and its machinery will now be exploited for Britain's war effort. Edgeworth has, from the very start, never approved of the governmental policies and the social code of his compatriots. He came to India and became rooted in one corner of Coorg. Our people have never thought of him as an outsider. But now there is an upsurge of national feeling everywhere. What guarantee can one give that everyone will behave with understanding? Edgeworth is not anxious for himself. He wants to preserve the countless links that have been forged, the close ties that have grown out of them. Friendship is what he cherishes most. So it's not surprising in the circumstances that he should miss Appa all the more—only he hasn't written this in so many words. He has merely hinted to Appa that it would be a good thing if he were to come back soon. There are two months more to go before Appa's lectures commence. He too finds himself in something of a dilemma. But his nature is a little stubborn in matters like this. He does not undertake anything lightly, but having undertaken a thing he does not give it up either.

I have begun to feel that there is no point in being scared of all these sudden happenings that have come about. Big problems don't get solved by our applying to them the measuring rod of profit and loss. And besides I tend to be a little fatalistic. (This might have come down through tradition or it could also be the influence of what Edgeworth has been saying through the years.) It's not as though there is going to be some revolution in Japan as a result of our coming here. But what has taken place will mean that my identity will be lost all the more.

I am bringing to a close this more than usually prolonged letter. Day by day getting letters and receiving them intact is going to be more and more difficult. If one kept to one note: I want you; I am yours; it might work. But if in place of Sau's story, one were to interpose the story of *Kau* (the crow) and *Chiu* (the sparrow) our bright officials might draw the most impossible inferences. So, for the present, only this much.

It's the truth, I haven't forgotten you.

These last seven days I have been ill. The fever hasn't come down yet. The doctor says there is no cause for worry. I myself am in good spirits. Mrs Imoto, who has newly arrived here, does all the nursing. So Appa is not anxious either.

Normally I never fall ill. And if I ever do, I can't bear to watch other people do every small thing for me. When the fever rises, one almost vanishes. . . one feels one is a point or grain somewhere, that grows gradually, expands and envelops everything. This amuses me no end. There is a lot of commotion going on inside the body. There is almost a class war between the white and red blood corpuscles. The blood deliberately raises its temperature, assumes a dire aspect to kill off the disease germs. The various glands are at their strategic points—doing God knows what! But I have read this some time or the other and explained it to my examiners. After an illness the head and the body become lighter. I like that very much. . . .Even while writing this, I have started feeling much better.

You say there is a double advantage in having found work in the Bodleian. But really can a librarian ever find the time to read? In fact I even think that since he is always in contact with so many books he must feel that he doesn't want to read at all.

The date of Appa's lectures is now approaching. I have taken it on myself to produce a small play for the Mission's annual function which is held about the same time. I have written the play myself—but that is a secret. I have based it on one of Rajamma's stories (not the one about Lachhi's peacock) and made a few changes. Namura liked the story very much. I shall first write in English—in my English—and then he will translate it into Japanese. A rather roundabout business! Fortunately the play will be short; the words few. The rest I shall fill up with action, sound effects, all kinds of cries and suspense. The Noh drama here and our Yakshagana will have reason to fear this new creation.

Joshi ought to have reached India by now. There is no news from him yet.

Why did Professor Gurupadaswaami leave the college so suddenly? You have merely written about him in a general sort of way. It's not very enlightening.

After writing all this, I really feel much better. The fever has come down, so Mrs Imoto says.

XXVI

Lore, a Swedish girl, has recently come here. She diverted me greatly when I was ill. Her father is the Osaka representative of their shipping company. She wants to stay in Japan for some time and then go to India. She is my age, but awfully sweet, with the tiniest of lips and the most enormous of eyes. I have asked her to return with us. She is passionately keen on Indian art. To scare her a little in the initial stages, I have given her your thesis to read. I am sure you will like Lore.

I have just heard that Joshi reached home safely.

Find out in the enclosed picture which is Lore. Second on the right is Imoto. The one sitting on the floor, with his finger on his chin, is Olaf. If you haven't been able to recognize Lore, turn what's written below upside down and read:

Rehearsals for my play have now begun. Olaf will play the King. His beard is a BIG qualification. I have managed to get a few children of the neighbourhood to play the birds. There is a part for a tree in the play. Namura himself will do this role.

I learn that Professor Gurupadaswaami has gone to live in Simhachalam for good. Is this true?

I really feel well now. Sometimes I think: What am I doing here? But then again I feel that all this wouldn't otherwise have taken place. . . I wouldn't have met Lore.

Write in detail about yourself. You could leave out trifles.

XXVII

As I told you before, the story of the play is not very long. The play is in just three scenes.

The birds begin their chirping even before the curtain rises. When it goes up, we see before us a huge, ancient tree. Children wearing masks of different birds enter from all sides frolicking. They dance for a while and leave. The chirping continues.

All of a sudden, there is a loud noise—like that of an earthquake. For a minute it appears as though the tree is also shaken. *Enter the King, cheated of his quarry, indignant, surrounded by his ministers*. Because of the chirping of the birds his quarry has slipped away. He orders the ministers to kill off the birds. The four ministers put forward four different suggestions. One says, light a big fire. Another says, put poisonous manure at the root of the tree. A third says, climb the tree and destroy all the eggs and the young ones first. The fourth one says, axe the tree itself. Each one dances and expresses his intentions. The King's decision is not yet made. While all this is going on, the birds too enter occasionally. They dance and make their entreaties. The King and his ministers threaten them, each with his own plan of action.

Finally they decide to cut down the tree and even decide to build a house out of it. The ministers and the King begin to sharpen their axes; they swing them aloft like clubs, balance them on their shoulders and dance.

Suddenly the sounds from the birds cease. Where the tree stood there now stands an old man holding up his hands and entreating them: Don't kill me, don't pull me down. Some of the frightened birds come to him. He takes them to himself. But the birds are torn away from him. The blows of the axe begin to fall. The tree is felled.

Here the first scene ends.

Scene Two: Where the tree stood there now stands a wooden house. Some of the birds are now children. Some are birds still. All of them play and run about. The house has four doors and they run in and out of it, singing and dancing together.

Very soon there is another loud noise exactly like the previous one. The house shakes and the King enters with his ministers. The King's attire is medieval. The ministers are now different. There is a steward, a craftsman, a judge and a soldier. The children and the birds continue to play as before.

The King sees the birds; he is furious. He seeks to separate the children from them, but the children will not listen to him. The soldier utters threats. The steward makes his requests. The craftsman tries to board the doors with planks. The judge tries to weigh a bird and a child on the scales of a huge balance.

The craftsman cannot board the openings of the house. The King cannot decide one way or the other. No one can hold back the birds and the children. The craftsman says: We don't need the wood. The house is old. It must be pulled down. A new tall one can be built—where there will be no birds, where the children will not be able to play.

All of them fetch hoes and spades and begin their dance. Just then an elderly woman emerges from the house. The children and the birds snuggle up close to her. (Lore will do this role.) She says: I must have this very house. Children live in it. Birds too live in it. But her plea goes unheard. Everyone is dragged away and driven off. And while the house is being pulled down, blows rain on the elderly woman too.

When the curtain rises on the third scene, we see a very tall building. It has no eaves, no place where the birds can sit. Children and birds are not to be seen anywhere. *Thud, thud*, one monotonous sound is heard.

Very soon the King, his ministers and a few children—now grown up enter. Of his ministers one is a salesman, another a hotel-owner, the third a lawyer, and the fourth a government official.

Everyone is in high spirits. They dance. The dance is quite mechanical and automatic. The older children have by now forgotten how to play.

After a little while, there is a loud sound of circling planes. Gradually the sound grows louder. Everyone is frightened. The building begins to shake. They seek to steady it.

Birds enter, wearing the masks of aeroplanes. They carry out air exercises. All around there is panic. The building tumbles down.

The old man in the first scene and the elderly woman of the second scene emerge from the building with little children and birds. Some of them have branches in their hands. Others hold all kinds of peculiar musical instruments made of wood. They dance and gambol as they did before. They sing and play their music.

Slowly the building that has tumbled down disappears from view. In its place there are innumerable other tiny houses and trees. The curtain comes down.

The play is named: *The Singing Tree*.

XVIII

Appa's lecture series is over. Before the lectures were delivered they were translated into Japanese by Imoto and the translation was sent out to the invitees. The lectures themselves were of course in English. They will be published sometime in November in book form.

One result of these lectures is that our stay here is going to be prolonged. Appa has an offer from the Kyoto University to stay here for a year and lecture on Comparative Philosophy. Appa has agreed to stay on. We might leave this place and live in Kyoto or alternatively live nearby if we can find another house.

Edgeworth has written to me this time. The letter is quite different from his previous one. There is no mention in it at all of the war or of the present situation. I have specially copied out an important part of the letter for you.

> The trouble with us is that our minds don't work quick enough. They are not trained to consider every situation as unique. This is the real tragedy of the world. We can only hope to overcome it by developing a sense of immediacy. And I have begun to feel that this is possible only if we give up the categories we have built into our mind and its ways of thinking—categories of time, of space and all manner of social and personal habits which we call values.

How can I comment on this? I know only one thing, which can perhaps contain all these: to forget oneself. When this is achieved, the limitations of time and of space do not exist. In the old days they called it 'dedication'. Edgeworth is saying the same thing in different words. When do we really go wrong? When we merely cling to these ideas. We are not possessed through and through by the urge of immediacy that Edgeworth speaks of—the urge that encompassed Radha, the urge that was Urvashi's in the *Rig-Veda*. As a result, the questions that lie ahead assume a greater importance; nor does one escape the vigilant eye of the past.

I must congratulate you on your being able to recognize Lore. She sends you her regards. After reading your thesis, she gets me to read (and interpret) your letters, line by line. You won't raise problems of copyright, will you?

Professor Joshi has just got married. His bride is a well-known tennis star from Poona. She used to be his pupil. But he says there was no love or anything of the sort before. From this one might safely conclude that their life will be happy. Going by the photograph, she appears very smart and practical.

After your letter, I am now even more anxious to know about Professor Gurupadaswaami.

Next week I am going to stay at Lore's. Her stay here has also been prolonged. The whole family might probably go to Sweden from here.

At the moment, there is no more news about me. *The Singing Tree* was liked by many people. The play was very well produced. Some people saw a different meaning in it. I had tried to set forth a simple story. There was nothing else whatsoever in my mind.

XXIX

You have asked me how it was that I always met 'the good' and whether I had, in this world, never had occasion to deal with the wicked. In fact, when you asked me the question I became aware of this for the first time. I had thought that everyone was like oneself. (Don't we consider ourselves 'good'?) Perhaps the circumstances in which I was brought up, the people with whom I came into contact must have been on the whole just like me. Envious, quarrelsome people have never been my portion. There were no brothers or sisters in the house. I grew up happily alone. Those around me gave me their affection; I received it. All this just came about. But I still believe that I am what I am—thus, not because of this. What we term happiness in the usual sense does not always make men happy. (You might say: What's new in this? Haven't the saints been saying the same thing all along?) But as there is a joy beyond suffering, so too there is a joy beyond joy itself. The joy that lies beyond joy holds within itself both joy and suffering. Kunti asked of Krishna: Let adversity be with us always. For in adverse times Krishna was bound to be remembered. But I would say that this is not true. If Krishna is to be remembered, then he must be remembered naturally and intensely even in the most ecstatic moment of joy. Anyone can turn to him in adversity. That I am able to find the company of the good is partly through my good fortune, and partly through the makeup of my mind. I never reject anything and what I finally accept, I make my own. Good, wicked: we are so ourselves.

As a child, on one particular day I was terribly obstinate. Now I can't even recollect what it was all about. Even Appa, who never loses his temper, was extremely angry. Rajamma, Venkappa were all frightened. And all of a sudden it struck me this was all on account of me. I calmed down immediately—not because Appa would have hit me; had he hit me, I might have flared up even more. Since that day I have never been angry, never been obstinate. This could perhaps tell you something.

Of course I have not yet met a scoundrel, a thug, or an inherently wicked person. I am as eager as you are to see what happens when I do meet one. But does this mean my life has been meaningless? All our efforts are designed to make the world a place of the good. Isn't that what we believe in? It's like calling a play or a novel worthless because there is no villain in it. If conflicts rise only out of the struggle between good and evil and if this is to continue forever, then history will have nothing more to do than changing names. Novels and plays will have a still easier task. It should be enough just to make black and white puppets dance. Really one ought to try and see if a novel or a play can be written without a single of the villains you seem to have in mind.

Query: Was the King in *The Singing Tree* a wicked man?

Answer: I think even the birds were a little wicked. They too should have thought of the needs of the King. What harm was there in asking a pact with the King: We shall chirp only at fixed time; we will not come in the way of the hunt? Didn't the birds get more and more wicked and violent through every scene? Who destroyed whom in the end? Will the problem be solved if we say that the King learnt a good lesson?

Having written this, I have become quite 'wicked.'

Next month Lore and her father will leave here in a Swedish boat for America. Many of the Europeans here are leaving for America by this boat. At times I think: I too should go; if possible go to England and meet you. But how is that possible in all this commotion? Appa will say: Don't go deliberately into the war zone. But if war were to break out here tomorrow? Let me not

131

think far ahead. For the time being, Lore will be my messenger. If it's possible, she will meet you at Oxford.

XXX

Lore left yesterday. I don't feel like staying on any longer either.

We had to give up our plans of living in Kyoto, Namura wouldn't agree. He was literally on the verge of tears. Of late he always looks sad. When you look at him you feel something is amiss and is going to be somehow more amiss.

It seems you didn't get three or four of my letters sent some time ago. For I saw no reference to them anywhere in your letters. Of late your letters too have been arriving here at longer intervals. To whom and in what manner should one complain when the world itself has come to us with one big complaint? Even so for the sake of convenience, from now on let's number our letters—one, two, three. . . I have put the number 'one' on this letter. Henceforth I will number them consecutively two, three, etc. It will be easy for you to know whether a letter is missing. You could do this as well.

One feels better when one hears that you are well. Leaving Oxford and working in India House in London entails more risk. The problem of getting a decent meal will also become more acute. I feel sad that nothing has turned out as you wished. In an equal measure there is a feeling of admiration and surprise that you yourself should not feel this.

Write again immediately.

XXXI

It's almost a month since Lore left. During the time she was here, the two of us got on famously. I learnt a lot from her. Being with her I experienced truly what forgetting oneself means. As a child there were moments when I wanted very much to be like someone else. Then a thought struck me: How do we know that the other person is another, and not oneself? Then I started enjoying this game very much. I used to assume various forms. I began to look at myself through the eyes of another. This childhood experience had long since faded out. It was Lore who brought it back after childhood had come to an end. I used to have an old painting of the Mewar School. In it Radha became Krishna, and Krishna, Radha. This was the artless way in which she behaved. When I told her this, she felt she must have this painting. To get it out here from India was a difficult proposition. We went out and looked for it in the university library here. We searched for it in Tokyo too. But it wasn't to be found. And then quite unexpectedly, while I was arranging Appa's notes, I found it in one of my notebooks. It had appeared in the *Studio* and I had cut it out. Mrs Imoto made a lovely frame for it and we gave it to Lore. Tell me what place you reserve for pictures like this when you assess the inspiration behind art. Don't use mere adjectives like religious, spiritual, erotic, etc.

I want to tell you a lot about Lore, but later, some other time. Without reading your letter, or even before it arrived, she used to tell me what it was likely to contain. Sometimes she had a hand in the letters that went out to you. The questions and answers on *The Singing Tree* were hers. There were other things as well. She used to change a word or a sentence and make it more meaningful. If you meant to, you can detect these places.

A new item of news: I have begun a ballet on the theme of *Chaurapanchashika*. This story itself is familiar in Japanese folk-literature in a slightly altered form. That's why I chose it. In the *Panchashika*, a prisoner, who is led to the gallows for daring to love the King's daughter, starts describing his moments of intense love, re-lives the love again, and secures a reprieve. Such is the story, in brief. It is as though his life-force saved him. I am going to present it in a slightly different way. As the prisoner relates each experience and moves ahead, his beloved, who is following him, asks each one a question. No one is able to answer her. The King follows, looking for her. In the end she asks even the King a question. But he too cannot find an answer. Now only one answer remains and that is to free the lover before he climbs the gallows. The King issues the command, the messengers speed away—but by then he has already been hanged.

XXXII

Appa has not been keeping well of late. Every evening he runs a temperature. We have tried out every medical remedy. It looks as though he is now feeling the strain of the work he put in these last two years. As a result, Namura looks even more sorrowful. For no reason at all, he has a feeling of personal responsibility about Appa. It is not possible now to go back to India from here. There is no news from there. It's now eight months since Joshi wrote. I have no news from home either. I don't know whether the letters I wrote have reached them.

I didn't receive two of your recent letters—numbers four and five.

Lore's letter has just arrived—from San Francisco. They may have to spend some days in America. The letter covers everything: the flurry in the boat, the frightful atmosphere, the children's pranks. They even spotted a submarine once. But Lore's handwriting cannot be deciphered clearly at times and her manner of writing too is often quite cryptic.

.She hasn't given up the idea of going to India. She has enquired after you.

There are times when I think we won't meet at all....If that happens, think of Lore as me.

At the moment, my ballet is still an idea. After reading Lore's commentary on it, my enthusiasm has cooled down considerably. She feels its basis is unduly logical. Nothing is ever decided by questions and answers. The original poem sets forth just one situation. There is nothing before it and nothing after. She has suggested another story to me : that of *Narcissus and Echo*.

XXXIII

Tirupet: Coorg
March 1946–June 1947

After the war ended and before returning home from Japan I had sent you two letters—one to the London address and one to your home. It seems you received neither of these. There was a six-month-old letter waiting here. I am writing now to the address given in it, trying to see if it can reach you.

At the start, I must give you an account of all that has happened, because a good deal has happened in the last four years.

I had of course written to you about Appa. He didn't live

much longer after that. His name is now forever linked with the Anand Mission. Those last days every single person tried to give me strength and comfort. Even the government did not treat us as aliens.

Then a few days later a new wave swept across all the countries of the far east occupied by Japan. Netaji's INA (Indian National Army) came into being as a result of this.

In the beginning I used to live at the Anand Mission, but soon I began working as a nurse in the Osaka Military Hospital. Close to the hospital were my living quarters. All this experience was, in a sense, quite new to me. But Coorg is a land of martial people, and I am a daughter of Coorg. So very soon I was one with the work. I had in particular to look after the needs of Indian soldiers and officers.

Major Agnimitra Sen, the medical officer attached to one of the INA units, was now with this military hospital at Osaka. In the course of our work I often came in contact with him. He was a man of few words. Occasionally he would ask a question or two. Otherwise he was engrossed in his work. Later when he knew my whole background and history, he began to take more interest in me. But he never quite gave up his former distant attitude. I used to be curious about him. But those were days when one couldn't get too close to others.

After a few days, I learnt that he was married to one of the Japanese nurses in our hospital. Once when I had gone to see him in his room he himself introduced me to her. When she left he told me: You will have to take more care of her now. I knew why. She was going to be a mother soon.

After this Major Sen seemed less reserved while talking to me. I too began to call on Mrs Sen when I had some free time. She had become extremely weak. There was still a month-and-a-half to go for her delivery. I, and even Mrs Sen, could understand why he was anxious.

And one day all of a sudden during the bombing of the docks Major Sen was reported missing.

This shock caused Mrs Sen to deliver prematurely and she died in child birth. Her daughter survived—she is Bina, now two-and-a-half-years-old. She has been brought up by me and is here with me as my daughter.

You came into my life and I had to go and lose my cherished

self; I met Lore and found a dedicated and live companion—one who asked for nothing, offered nothing. Bina brought me unawares a sense of fulfilled motherhood. The joy about which I had written to you a long time ago thus came flying towards me through all the intense joy and suffering of the last six years.

I found yet another mystery in this. Edgeworth died here in 1943 on the 3rd of January. Exactly eight months later, on 3 September 1943, Bina was born. It is as though it was for him I went to Japan and brought back here a Coorgi girl, born of a Bengali father and a Japanese mother.

I pray that you might at least get this letter.

XXXIV

I got your letter. I am terribly, terribly happy. I am more in raptures now than I was when I got your first letter.

I knew you were somewhere, safe. But sometimes my strength would leave me and all manner of thoughts would trouble me. Today I made much of myself with your dear familiar handwriting.

Must you still stay there, now that the war is over? You say you need to spend a year-and-a-quarter there to complete your interrupted studies. There is some point in this. But then what must others do?

Professor Joshi came here with Malan and Subhash as soon as he got my letter. Bina and I spend the time happily in their company.

My main activity at the moment is putting together Appa's papers and arranging for the publication of his manuscripts and drafts. The publication of *Experience and Growth* was delayed at that time because of the war. Now Wilson and Todd of London are publishing it. Joshi has promised to come in the next vacation and help me a little.

Edgeworth's solicitors in London have written to me. In his will he has left me his entire estate here....Such love, so much trust!

So Lore did meet you! What did she say? How long did she stay? Write and tell me all in detail.

When I am a little free, I shall go to Simhachalam and meet Professor Gurupadaswaami. We will all go.

You have asked me what exactly it is I want. I could have asked you the same question. Quite often I believe that we read a lot, discursively, and forget our own problems. Observed superficially, my feelings about you at the beginning and my feelings now—six years later, appear to belong to two different planes. In the first, one might discern an intentional separateness and, in the second, a disinterested oneness. But in actual fact, there's nothing of the kind. Though the dimensions of my world have widened, they have also become sharp in the same measure. What has taken place is not a mere photographic enlargement. And also, it is not as though more areas have been included. The particulars of each part have become more significant. The disinterestedness one senses in it arises because those sensations have been experienced more intensely.

You shouldn't find it difficult to accept this. Change by itself is of no consequence—everything changes. The consciousness emerging from it is, I feel, of greater importance.

XXXV

I was really glad to learn that my last letter did not satisfy you. I can only interpret this to mean that your thinking processes are more alert.

You want love, and I don't want it? What is it that I have given you these six years? Only I did not get entangled in the nomenclature of what I wanted, of what I still want—that's all. You ought to have carried me off, dragged me away—yes, I am writing what's true, what's absolutely true. Nothing is ever gained by analyzing things. We only become strangers to our own selves.

I too can speak the language of psychology. I can work out a convenient scientific interpretation of my own behaviour. I grew up motherless—hence a very strong attachment to the father. This attachment, this father-fixation, indicating in a corresponding measure a lesser attraction towards another man. On this very basis, you would then interpret my feelings for Lore, and going a little further you could analyze my maternal sentiment in relation to Bina. But supposing one were to believe in all this, can our problem be solved by it?

At every moment we make an unalterable decision. When I

wrote to you in the beginning, I made one. I made another when I invited you to Tirupet. After you had been and gone, when I gave you that string of answers to your questions, then again I made a decision. I have not altered it. The psychological basis of my behaviour did not come in the way of this. Only I did not get the response I wanted. Had I got it, I would have come anywhere with you, done anything for you. Every girl, the instant she is born, comes prepared to leave her mother and her father.

You might perhaps say that you too expected a response and that you did not get it. How can I give an answer to this? To tell you the truth, one ought to be able to arrive at these decisions without resorting to the language of appeal and response.

Now, after writing all this, I feel embarrassed. If reading this causes you any sorrow then forget me for all time.

XXXVI

You wrote instantly and started at once to return. In this itself I found the answer to my question. But I am going to be a little patient. And I am going to tell you to be patient too.

Lore has come here suddenly, unannounced—not to see India, but to see me. We haven't yet finished talking. She and Bina are great friends. This solves many of my problems at home.

So you got a copy of Appa's book even before I got one. I am still waiting here for a copy. Joshi says that a lot of Appa's material is still lying here. It must be sorted out at leisure. He is coming back during the vacation to do this.

Very often I feel sad that Edgeworth is not here now amongst us. I don't feel that much even for Appa. Edgeworth was universally liked here because of his open nature and because he could get on effortlessly with others. I am going to turn his house into a House of Play. It will be a house of drama, of ballet, of crafts, of music and of story-telling. My last ballet remained unfinished, but Lore has now begun work on it with enthusiasm.

Bina says she is going to write to you—she has just begun to recognize a few letters. Mother writes—so she too must. Shall I ask Lore to write to you too? Then you will be really hedged in from all sides. (Or does she already correspond with you?)

Because I asked for nothing, I have received everything.

P.S.:- Bina's letter is enclosed. One must make out the words. Where the letters are missing, one must supply one's own. To make things clear, she has drawn on the right a muscle of the Sun. The two bird-like figures to the left are houses—one is hers, one is mine. You are outside standing in the sun.

XXXVII

As days go by, old memories assume new forms... I am playing once again my lost guitar...I am listening to Rajamma's story, freshly revised, my head on her lap. (She still thinks I am a child, even though Bina is around)...Edgeworth has got hold of some simple argument to tease me...Appa's body aches and he will not let me press his limbs....You have alighted from the train and are flustered on seeing two girls exactly like me...I am ill and Lore is somersaulting madly to make me laugh...Appa's first lecture is over and Namura embraces him warmly...After three days of continuous toil, with eyes strained, Major Sen is still working at the operation table, his deft fingers opening and closing swiftly...I have just returned from Japan and am gazing at the plumeria in full bloom outside our door . . . .

Bina is delighted, 'reading' the letter you remembered to send her. She forces everyone to listen to the story you have written for her. Draupadi tore off a gorgeous sari to bandage Krishna's injured finger. I know why you selected the story.

Lore hasn't made up her mind yet about the ballet. She has ruled out the *Chaurapanchashika*—at least till you arrive. *Narcissus and Echo* will probably not be understood here easily. (So she believes; actually it won't be so.) Just now I am on the look out for some tale about a roguish Prince Charming. Otherwise there is always our Ocean of Stories—Rajamma.

Did you get the spicy 'sweets' that were sent? The idea and the execution—both were Rajamma's.

Try and find out if they can give you a degree without your doing an exam.

XXXVIII

Lore has begun to build a tiny house for you on the hill behind.

139

There will be verandahs at the back and in front, two spacious rooms. And, if you are serious about cooking, then a small kitchen. The right amount of light. No undue fuss is made about windows. In the sitting-room a bed-cum-*divan*, a low, long table (which, however encumbered it might be, will still have some space left on it). And if it is considered absolutely necessary, a rack for books. Lots of mats, a few small stools and, so that you won't be too inconvenienced, a mirror and a cupboard for clothes. Lore declares: When furniture collects, people are pushed out. Edgeworth once said: I prefer two men to one man and one chair.

I am sending you two select reviews of Appa's book that have come from the publishers. How far do you agree with the verbal point raised by the reviewer in *The Hibbert Journal*? In his opinion, in tune with the main thesis of the book, its title ought to have been *Experience : Growth*. By calling it *Experience and Growth*, one gets the impression that the author considers experience and growth two separate entities. But he wants to say something quite different. Experience and growth are processes on two different levels. Their connection is not one of cause and effect, it is more of a relationship. This view of the author ought to have found clear expression in the title. I tend to agree a little with this. The review in *Nature* is favourable, but I found it rather brief and matter of fact.

Next month Professor Joshi will give up teaching and go to Delhi to take up a post in the External Affairs Ministry. It appears that our new Government has greater need there of his multilingual talent.

Next time don't forget to write to Bina.

XXXIX

At long last Lore has made up her mind and, as I had predicted, it was Rajamma who came to our rescue. We decided to inaugurate the Edgeworth House of Play (Edge House, for short) with a dance on the theme of Lachhi's peacock. Bina will be Lachhi, Lore old woman. The role of the peacock has come to you. The script and the music are mine, the direction is Lore's, the background music and words Rajamma's. As soon as you come here in July, the rehearsals will begin. You can't avoid this now. No excuse will work. Arrangements will be made for full instruction in dance. (The battle now is against all of us.) When you come to think of it, does the peacock himself know how to dance? He lifts up a foot...then loses his balance, and to regain it he sets it down...and then lifts the other. This goes on in the same fashion over and over again, *ad infinitum*. Those who look on call it a dance. (So I have read somewhere.)

Note down right now the date of the performance : 15 August 1947.

Translated from Marathi by Kumud Mehta

Thakazhi Sivasankara Pillai

A Blind Man's Contentment

Pappu Nayar accepted Bhargavi as his wife. He was blind from birth. Her reputation in the village was not good.

No one questioned the propriety of his visiting that house of evil repute. Was he not a blind man? Bhargavi's mother was fond of hearing stories from religious mythology. Pappu Nayar would narrate to her all the stories he knew. His mother had twice prohibited him from going there. Finally Bhargavi became pregnant. Pappu Nayar acknowledged responsibility for this.

Pappu Nayar's mother told him he would not be allowed to set foot in her house. He had an answer: 'My younger brother is not going to lead me around all the time. I need someone to look after me.'

His mother asked : 'How are you going to support her?'

'I don't have to give her anything. She'll make a living sweeping some compound or pounding rice.'

'What about you?'

'She will look after me.'

'She has had three abortions.'

'Nothing of the sort ! She has no peer on earth.'

And thus Pappu Nayar's expulsion from home became permanent.

Bhargavi was working as a sweeper and cleaner at a brahmin household. She was given two meals a day and a *para* (five measures) of rice every month. Besides this, she was permanently engaged by two families to pound rice by hand.

She looked after Pappu Nayar well. She would make *kanji* (rice gruel), and feed him the rice while she contented herself with the water. She was an obedient type. She hardly ever talked. Misery appeared to have wiped out all traces of cheerfulness from her face. At twenty, her sunken eyes and cheeks and falling hair made her look ten years older. There was always a shadow of sadness over her features. She never laughed out of a sense of inborn happiness. Occasionally a derisive smile would play over her dried-up lips, when she looked at her more fortunate companions.

Nearly always she managed with a thin loincloth tied around her waist. She had hardly any other clothes to change into. But she never hid her semi-nudity in shame.

Into that lifeless and drab atmosphere had come Pappu Nayar with his light-heartedness and his wagging tongue. She never talked to him much.

Pappu Nayar would say: 'Bhargavi has a boy in her womb. He will grow up and recite the *Ramayana*.'

She would reply: 'I want a girl.'

Bhargavi gave birth to a boy. Nayar's happiness was unbounded. He would not stir out of the room. He would tell all the women who called there, 'It is as I wished. Bhargavi wanted a girl.'

He wanted to fondle the baby all the time in his lap. He would ask it: 'Well, little fellow, will you read the *Ramayana* to your father when you grow up?'

The blind man's face would light up with delight. He would frequently say, 'Bhargavi, don't you kiss the baby?'

She would reply, 'Your tongue is not idle even for a minute.'

'Woman, our good days have come. What more do I want? He will take me to Kasi and Rameswaram. Won't you, son?' Pappu Nayar would stroke the child and kiss it.

'*Aswathi, Makham, Moolam*, seven to *Kethu*,' thus he would start calculating the horoscope.

'He is under the influence of Venus even during his youth. He is very fortunate. Bhargavi, we must name him Gopika Ramanan.'

He said Bhargavi should learn the old lullaby *Omana thingal kidavo* (Oh, child of the darling moon).

She named him Raman. He asked: 'Why, didn't you name him Gopika Ramanan?'

She said: 'Oh, for a boy born to beg. . . .'

'Don't say that, woman. His horoscope is that of a *kesari*, a leader.'

She did not learn the lullaby either.

The child would wriggle about on Pappu's lap and cry loudly. Pappu would get excited and shout for Bhargavi. She would gnash her teeth and shout, 'The brat was born to scream.'

Bhargavi would beat the child. Pappu Nayar would be

stunned. She went to work and would return only in the eve-ning. He would lose his peace of mind and would start muttering to himself that the child's throat was getting parched.

His affection was heart-rending.

'My son has great good fortune in store. Below his left breast there is a mole, like a lotus, a sign of divine grace.'

He would ask the women from the neighbouring houses: 'Does he look like me?'

The women's eyes would be wet with unshed tears. He saw a mole in the darkness that engulfed him! He thought the child was like him. One day one of the women asked him: 'Can you see?'

'I can see my son,' he replied.

And he went on seeing him. When he kissed the child he would sometimes say: 'You little rascal, your laugh!'

He even saw the silent laughter.

The women in the village would say: 'Well, she is a bad one all right. Does that child look like him?'

It was time for Raman to be given the first ceremonial feed of rice. Pappu Nayar desired that he should perform this auspicious act with his own hands. But Bhargavi would not allow it. She told her mother that he had too large an appetite. Her mother said, 'Then we must get it done by someone else. He should not grow up with a large appetite and an outsized tummy.' 'I did not know I ate so much rice,' Pappu Nayar said and laughed in genuine amusement at this joke.

The child grew up. Things started getting worse for the family. Bhargavi lost her job with the brahmin household on an accusation of theft.

'Don't keep the child hungry. Give him my share,' Pappu Nayar would tell Bhargavi.

It was *Karkatakam*, the traditional month of scarcity. It was three days since even rice gruel had been cooked in the house. They managed one day eating cooked bean leaves. The second day they managed with rice bran. On the third day, their neighbour Kesavan Nayar gave them two-and-a-half *chakkrams* (about ten paise). They bought a little rice which they made into gruel. Bhargavi, her mother and her son ate it up. Pappu Nayar was sitting on the verandah having the *Ramayana* read to him by a neighbour. He was not aware of what was going on in the kitchen.

That night he was light-heartedly singing couplets from *Kuchela Vritha*. His gnawing hunger would not let him sleep even after midnight. The neighbours could hear him reciting the verses and beating time. Bhargavi became angry: 'What madness is this?'

'Was I not singing *Bhagavan's* praises?' He stopped and prayed silently.

Bhargavi became pregnant again. Pappu Nayar told her that this time she would give birth to a girl.

The elder child began to talk a little. He would call his mother Amma and his grandmother *Ammoomma*. But even the basic sounds for Father never came from him.

'You little fellow, why don't you call out "Father"?'

And then Pappu Nayar would console himself that the word for 'Father' was difficult to pronounce.

Bhargavi fell ill many times during this pregnancy.

Pappu Nayar continued to say that their miseries would all be over. Raman would not leave his mother's side. He would go nowhere near Pappu Nayar. Pappu Nayar would tell him that his mother was expecting a younger sister for him and he would ask him to kiss her where it was.

Bhargavi gave birth to a girl. As before, Pappu Nayar cast the child's horoscope and said that she was destined for a happy marriage in her fourteenth year.

'My daughter looks like her mother, doesn't she, sister?' he asked Kuttiyamma from the next house. She laughed and a broad grin spread on her face.

'Yes, I think so,' she replied.

The neighbours discussed and decided who was the likely father of the girl.

Now there were two children. The poverty of the family increased. Bhargavi's health was shattered. She was too weak even to go to work.

Pappu Nayar consoled Bhargavi and told her that their poverty would soon end. She wanted to escape from all that misery by committing suicide. He argued that the children would be left orphaned and suicide was foolish. But not even a tear dropped from Bhargavi's eyes. She would just grind her teeth in helpless misery. Her lustreless sunken eyes sometimes lit up for a moment with inhuman brightness, but presently she relapsed into helpless acquiescence. One day she told him: 'Why don't you go out and beg?'

'Woman, you are right. You are talking sense. But I will have to leave the village. The problem is how I can be away from the little ones.'

Bhargavi was again carrying. This time she was too ill even to get up. For many days there was not even a fire in the kitchen. Pappu Nayar would send Raman every noon to the neighbouring brahmin house. The mother and the children would take the rice gruel they gave. Pappu Nayar would have some if there was anything left. He would say, 'When I hear the *Ramayana*, I want neither food nor drink.'

He would thus spend the day listening to the *Ramayana* read to him by someone. At night he would repeat such lines as he could remember.

The hungry children would cry. Bhargavi would not utter a word. Pappu Nayar would say, 'All this misery will end.'

The children were left to themselves uncared for. Raman was not to be seen during the day. He went from house to house begging. The girl fell ill. He would borrow rice from some neighbour and get some gruel prepared for her. Raman would return home at dusk. He would be asked to recite *namam*, words in praise of God, but would not pay any heed. Pappu Nayar would make him sit beside him and tell him stories from religious mythology. He would go away, while Nayar continued his narration. He would realize of Raman's absence only when he heard his voice from the kitchen.

The baby born to Bhargavi was a boy. He died on the fourth day.

In a way that was a blessing. How would they bring it up? Pappu Nayar consoled himself with this thought. He told Bhargavi, 'It is my responsibility also to bring up the children. We have two children now. How will they live? We do not want any more children.'

Raman was now six-years-old. Pappu Nayar decided that he should be taught reading and writing. He was put to school in the ensuing month of *Edavam*.

Bhargavi got back the job she had lost at the brahmin household. Pappu Nayar said it was the good fortune of the child which had died. Thus the family had the means for one meal a day. But it brought no comfort to Nayar. He continued to starve. Every noon and night, mother and children would eat the food brought from the brahmin *madom* (house). Nayar would be sitting on the verandah reciting prayers or listening to the *Ramayana*. Occasionally, he was given something to eat. He never asked for food. He took what was given.

Raman was not going to school. His mother had asked him to stay away. She said she could not afford the expenses. Pappu Nayar admitted she was right. All the same his children should learn to read and write. After all, the boy was only six. He said they would wait for the next year.

And the children? They had never called him Father till now. They would laugh when they saw him groping around in his blindness.

'Daughter, come here,' he would say and stretch out his hands. The girl would not go near him. She would stand at a distance and make faces at him. Once he told Raman: 'Son, bring me some betel-leaves and nuts to chew.'

Raman spread lime on the betel with a generous hand. The cunning lad put some pebbles in place of areca-nut. Pappu Nayar got his mouth burnt. Raman clapped his hands and laughed. Nayar also laughed at the prank.

One day Pappu Nayar stepped down from the verandah to the front yard with the help of his stick. Raman who had walked out in a huff from the kitchen after quarrelling with his mother knocked off the stick. Poor Nayar fell on his face. He would describe these events to passers-by and praise the boy's high spirits.

Two years passed thus. Raman had still not been put to school. Several times Pappu Nayar talked about this to Bhargavi. She would say: 'With your glib tongue you can say anything you like.'

'But, is there not something in what I say?'

She would say nothing in reply. She would indifferently go about her work. Raman was involved in some petty thieving. Nayar asked him: 'Is that right, you fellow?'

'I'll take care of that,' would be the reply.

After all he was a boy. He would be all right when he grew up, Pappu Nayar consoled himself.

Bhargavi again became pregnant. That surprised Pappu Nayar a little. He asked her: 'Bhargavi, how is this?'

She didn't answer. At this time Bhargavi sent Raman to some house to work as a domestic help. Nayar complained about this to the neighbour Kuttiyamma: 'Was it right to send him away thus? Should he not learn to read and write?'

'My dear, yes....' and then Kuttiyamma checked herself. Kuttiyamma had been an eye-witness to many of Bhargavi's goings-on. She had grieved over the way Pappu Nayar had been ill-treated by Bhargavi. She had seen her eating her fill of rice and curry while the blind man was starved. She had seen it and wept. Besides she had now come from Pappu Nayar's mother with a message for him. People around were talking of the sad state of affairs. But out of sympathy no one would talk to him directly of such things. And so the evil side of life lay hidden from him behind the perpetual darkness in which he existed. People were afraid that he would not be able to bear the burden of the hell in which he lived if it was revealed to him. His unbounded affection for Bhargavi wrested admiration from everyone. At the same time his unshakable optimism was a matter of surprise. The world bowed before his sincere and enviable spirit of sacrifice. He had not spoken one word in anger to Bhargavi. How could he be made to face the stark reality?

Kuttiyamma could not bring herself to spell it out. Pappu Nayar said: 'My son is a clever fellow. He is working for a big office. He will learn to read and write.'

'Pappu Nayar, he is not your son.'

'No, he is a child of God. Is not this world itself an illusion created by God?'

Kuttiyamma did not say anything to that. She did not have the strength to do so.

Bhargavi gave birth to a boy this time. Nayar was very happy at the new addition to the family.

He said the child would be a companion for him. Another day, Kuttiyamma came again. She said: 'You are lucky you cannot see. You do not have to see the misery and evil in this world.'

'There is no evil in this world. True, there is poverty but that will end. If there is sorrow, there is happiness also sister.'

'No dear, not that....'

'I am not unhappy; God has not sent down any sorrows for me. Of course I am a little uneasy about my children. Raman has not even written me a letter.'

'You would not feel like this if you had seen those children.'

'I see my children.'

'If so, are you their father?'

Kuttiyamma's heart missed a beat. She had blurted out the truth without thinking. Pappu Nayar hesitated, fumbling for an answer. The next moment he said: 'They are children.'

'What do you know, Pappu Nayar?'

'You may be right, sister. The present child—it—I am not a fool, sister. Blind people have an excess of intelligence. I know many things. One night I heard the jingle of coins from inside the house.'

'You sit in this verandah. She is a demon.'

Pappu Nayar did not answer immediately.

'What of it? At least the world will not say that the children have no father.'

'Do these children call you "Father"?'

'No. But I love them. Look, my Raman and my Devaki are standing before me. How lovely they are! The little darlings! They are my children. Should I not do something for them?'

'She has been deceiving you.'

'She is to be pitied. How much has she starved! Perhaps this is her only way of subsistence. She requires a husband to show to the world. At least I have been of help to her that way.'

Kuttiyamma had no answer for him. His heart was large, wide as the universe. He was not someone groping about in the dark. His mind was a luminous crystal with a perpetual inner light. Many, many worlds flitted about playfully in its prismatic brilliance.

Kuttiyamma left in silence. That night also the neighbours heard him reciting the *Kuchela Vritha*.

Translated from Malayalam by V. Abdulla

Mahadevi Verma

Ghisa

If it were not so hard to understand how, even in these latter days, some unconscious association may still evoke a certain forgotten episode out of my past with all its power to stir my heart, then perhaps I could also explain why it brings with it the poignant memory of a certain small, sad, timid village schoolboy, who with all his youthful freshness, watered my life's parched shores like a little wave and then vanished again into the infinite ocean.

I have always been so inexplicably attracted to the ruins of Jhansi and the surrounding villages that lie across the Ganges that, noticing my feelings, people have started remarking sarcastically that probably this attraction has something to do with past lives. After all, such an attraction is a strange thing! The leisure time which other people like to spend visiting old friends, taking part in festivals, and enjoying other pastimes, I not only spend on the banks of the Bhagirathi bewailing these ruins and their crumbling foundations—but I spend it there happily.

The crowd of women who come to fetch Ganges water, bearing their old discoloured jars or their new, red clay ones, or their glittering brass and copper vessels from their houses—some of which are old and dilapidated, and others newly plastered, all scattered about like children's sand-houses—I have become acquainted with all these, too. Some among them wear saris in which tears are widening, and others have new ones; some have clean clothes, and others have garments so soiled that it is impossible to distinguish the fabric from the dirt; some have red-printed ones, and others wear plain black ones. In the middle of the parted, oiled hair of one woman a vermilion streak, the width of a finger shines like the rays of a setting sun; and the dry, matted hair of another, unacquainted with even the cheapest mustard oil, hangs in little strings around her face, seeming to focus on her sadness. On the plump, dark wrists of some the artificial jewels—crude glass bangles bought in the city—shine like diamonds; and on the bony wrists of others, dirty hollow bangles of lac look like thick stripes of sandalwood paste on black rocks. Some are embarrassed that their bracelets are made only of nickel, and keep trying to hide them behind their pots as others carry on their conversation to the rhythm of their jingling bracelets of real silver. On the ears of some, lac ear-rings costing only a few pennies peek out from time to time from under their head coverings, while the long chain ear-rings of others seem to link cheeks to necks. Silver anklets on the tattooed, wheat-coloured feet of some seem to enhance their symmetry, while the broad toes and dirt-smeared white heels of others make the humble anklets of tin and pewter look like shackles of grey iron.

They wash their hands and faces first; then, wading into the water, fill their earthen pots. Next they set their pots on the bank and, settling their round pads carefully on their heads and glancing toward me—variously embarrassed, spontaneous, showing the suffering of hardship or revealing with a laugh a story of happiness, they all smile. They are aware of the distance between our social conditions, and it may be that they do not fail to link the opposite shores with a bridge of smiles.

The cowherds' children, noticing their grazing cows and buffaloes drifting my way, pick up their switches and begin to retrieve them; the shepherds' children, seeing a sheep or goat from their herds also straying toward me, snatch it by the ears and drag it back quickly; and even the boys who loaf about playing pick-up-sticks the whole idle day do not forget, peeping out here and there, to appraise my mood.

The cowherds coming or going from selling their milk in the city on the opposite shore, the labourers going to work in the fort or returning, the oarsmen casting off or mooring their boats and occasionally bursting into the song *I would colour my scarf red* might catch a glimpse of me, and becoming embarrassed, fall silent. Some, priding themselves on being a little better bred, even manage a shy *namaskar* for me.

I cannot tell when or how there occurred to me the idea of providing some instruction for the children of these people. But without even taking a vote to elect somebody to make preparations, without any choosing of the members of a selection committee, without forming any organization, without making an appeal for money, in short, without any of the familiar political ceremonies, my pupils assembled around me under the thick

151

shade of a *peepal* tree, and I was nevertheless able, even though with great difficulty, to assume the attitude of seriousness proper to a teacher.

And how can I ever tell you how eager they were to learn! Some wore ornaments in their ears and bangles on their wrists, and in their laundered shirts and dirty loincloths looked like an incongruous mixture of city and village. Some reminded one of scarecrows set up to guard fields, wearing oversized shirts borrowed from their older brothers. And some, with their protruding ribs, swollen bellies, and weak, bent legs, could be identified as human progeny only in the technical sense and by the loosest comparison. And in the pathos of the wan, scabby, grimy faces of some, in their intensity and their lucklustre sallow eyes, convened the neglect of a whole lifetime. But among them all Ghisa was nevertheless unique, and even today he alone comes into my memory.

I have still not forgotten that one evening, that very hour when the cows, returning homeward, stirred up a cloud of dust. It seemed as though night had strewn a handful of eyeshadow over the spreading mantle of the sunset, splendid in red and gold. My boatman was glancing a little uneasily at the waves. My loyal old servant, chuckling loudly, had gathered up my books, paper, pens, and other paraphernalia; but now she was muttering at the gathering darkness—or at me, her eccentric mistress—it was hard to tell which. The poor thing had spent ten long years putting up with me, and by her service had begun to acquire a sort of proprietary relationship to me; but what reward had she ever had for enduring the often unfortunate results of my whims? Suddenly my heart was filled with gratitude. But as my feet moved in the direction of the boat, I saw the form of a woman advancing towards me from out of the thickening dusk and, startled, I stopped. Gradually her dark, prominent lips became clearly visible. Her eyes were pinched, but still moist with sadness. Her neglected limbs were modestly covered by her soiled *dhoti* of coarse cloth with no decorative border; but there was nevertheless a hint of shapeliness to her body. Her hand was resting on the shoulder of a frail, half-naked boy, who was clinging to her legs. I could not see him very well in the deepening twilight.

From what the woman said, haltingly, with a few words and

gestures, I gathered only this: that she had no husband; that she went out to work at plastering and painting the houses of others; therefore, this only child of hers was left to roam about untended. If only I would allow him to sit with the other children, then he might learn something. On the next Sunday I saw him sitting alone behind the others, withdrawn to one side. He had a dark complexion, but was rather well-formed in body; his face was dull, and his pale, lacklustre eyes seemed to have been engraved into it. The strength of his thin, firmly shut lips and the rebelliousness of the shaggy little hairs bristling on his head contrasted with the shy, pure delicacy of his expression. His thin arms, held up by drooping shoulders and ending in hands with roughly cut nails and dusky palms, dangled from the protruding bones of his shoulders like the artificial extra arms of an actor playing Vishnu in a play. Only the feet that carried his wiry body seemed unusually tough because of his incessant running about. But enough—that was Ghisa. There was poetry in neither his name nor his form.

Yet in his searching eyes was—it is hard to describe—such an eagerness! His attentive gaze remained focussed on my face like the stare of an unrelenting clock, as if the aim of his life were to drink in all my knowledge and understanding.

The other boys always drew somewhat apart from Ghisa. It was not simply because he was of the lowly weaver class, but more specifically because some of their mothers, the grandmothers of others, or their aunts or other watchful female relatives, had impressed upon them, grasping them by their ears, the utter and urgent necessity of staying far away from Ghisa. Again and again these women had emphasized this—and also the secret of Ghisa's name as well, ugliest of all. There had been no father, even before his birth. Because there had been no one in the house to tend him, his mother had gone about with him clinging to her like a monkey baby. She would lay him down to one side while she went about her work; and crawling after her, dragging himself along on his belly, the child had acquired this apt name along with his earliest experiences of life. Ghisa...the dragger.

The other women, moreover, pausing in their comings and goings, began to acquaint me by degrees with the disgrace of Ghisa's birth and life, using all sorts of telling gestures and curiously allusive language. But somewhat contrary to their hopes, I gradually lost interest in anything about him but his name.

His father had admittedly been a mere weaver, but a proud and spirited man, eager to advance. He had abandoned the work of making baskets and the like, and had aspired to learn a little carpentry. And not only that: one day he quietly took a young wife from another village—thus, not only disappointed all the pretty girls of his own caste from his own village, but also by his marriage crushed the hopes of their mothers and fathers. This was really the full measure of the man's touted deviance. But the wrath of the Lord upon such transgressions is very well-known. Perhaps, too, he had become a little presumptuous, for after having made doors and door frames for village houses, or having finished whitewashing the homes of the gentry, he began to find some pretext or other to linger there. But suddenly the excuse of cholera called him away, and he went to that place where he needed no pretext to go, a place neither his intelligence nor his pride could conceive.

But his wife also appeared not a little proud. Many lonely and unmarried weavers, from a simple desire to be helpful, were willing to assume the responsibility of steering the boat of her life to the other shore. Yet she gave them no simple, bland refusal, but on the contrary a biting one, mixed with pepper and salt. She said, 'How could I become the mate of a jackal who has been the consort of a lion?' And when she shed tears of lamentation silently, letting down her hair, smashing her glass bangles, and wearing a plain borderless *dhoti*, she began to assume the bearing of a widow of a great house; then indeed the whole village society began to be consumed with uneasiness, afloat in an ocean of dismay. On top of this, Ghisa was born after the death of his father. His birth was, in fact, six months after it. But within this span of time what will ignorant people not say, people for whom a minute sometimes passes like a year, and a year sometimes vanishes like a minute? So if that term of six months got stretched out like rubber until it reached the span of a year, then how could the villagers be blamed?

This story was recounted, with many added embellishments, to influence my mind. By some guidance of providence, however, my heart did not incline toward the tellers of the tale, but rather went out to its protagonist; so Ghisa came even closer. Perhaps he himself had never come fully to understand the

154

infamy attached to his life; in any case, it had not had even a partial influence over him. Perhaps he was also shielded to some extent by the fact that he never so much as let his shadow touch anyone—as if he had some contagious disease.

No one was as clever as he in his deep and serious sense of responsibility for the pursuit of his own little work, his studying, his being the first to understand, his mindfulness of the hour for the preparations, the way he never let even one blot fall on his book and kept his slate polished. Because of all this I sometimes used to wish that I could beg him from his mother, and keeping him with me make some proper arrangement for his education—but I rejected this idea, for he was the only comfort of the neglected but dignified widow. She would not consent to desert her husband's place, this I knew very well. And how empty her life would become without her child was also not hidden from me. Moreover, seeing how devoted the nine-year-old Ghisa was to me, only his teacher, I had no doubt about his affection for his mother. And so Ghisa stayed on in that place, in those harsh circumstances where as a pure *jeu d' esprit*, a most cruel fate had placed him.

Every Saturday, with his own frail little hands, he used to plaster the shady area under the *peepal* tree with a mixture of cowdung and clay to make it smooth. Then on Sunday as soon as his mother had left for work, and after brushing and sweeping yet one more time the shady area under the *peepal* tree he would go and sit on the bank of the Ganges, hugging to his side some coarse unleavened bread tied up in a torn, dirty cloth along with some salt or a little parched grain and a bit of raw sugar, and shading his sallow but eager eyes with his thin, dark hands, he would gaze far into the distance. As soon as he could catch a glimpse of my blue and white boat he would fly like an arrow on his skinny legs, and calling to his companions without using any names, crying 'Guru sahab, Guru sahab,' he would arrive at the tree, never knowing how many times he would have to repeat this process of sweeping and cleaning the ground before I would actually arrive. The small, wooden writing-board would be taken out from a low-hanging branch, then cleaned and set on the ground. The inkpot of crude black glass with the ink dried up, along with the disjointed brownish-green penholder and broken nib which I never used, would be taken from a hollow in

155

the tree and set in its appropriate place; and then, the quaint principal and unique student of this quaint school would come forward, saluting me for my proper reception.

I had only four days in a month to spend there, and sometimes even less than that because of my workload at home; but even in such a short time, no more days than you could count on your fingers, I gained so much understanding of the heart of this boy that he seems as eternally fresh as an album of pictures.

Even now I have not forgotten that one day when, without taking into consideration the paucity of their clothes, I committed the blunder of explaining and stressing to those poor souls the importance of cleanliness. On the next Sunday they were all present, somehow or the other; but some had plunged their heads into the Ganges in such a way that the dirt had become partly dissolved and ran down in numerous, distinct streaks; others had scrubbed their hands and feet so, now that they were clean; they seemed to have been attached separately from the rest of their grimy bodies; and some, for the sake of exemplifying the proverb "You can't make a bamboo flute if there's no bamboo," had left their ragged and dirt-stained shirts at home, and had come to class in a form so skeletal that it seemed to say of their life breath, "It is a wonder that it abides; what surprise if it flees?" But Ghisa was missing. Upon my enquiring, all the boys became uneasy and either whispered the reason for his absence to one another or became restless to tell me the reason for it. Hesitantly, one word at a time, it came out that ever since the last class Ghisa had been asking his mother for laundry soap to wash clothes—but at that time his mother had not received the wages for her work, and the shopkeeper would not trade grain for soap. She had finally got paid the night before and at dawn, ignoring all her work, had gone out to buy soap at once. Now that she had come back, Ghisa was washing his clothes, because Guru sahab had said that one should bathe and wash and come wearing clean clothes. And what clothes that unfortunate child had! An old shirt donated by some charitable person, with one sleeve half gone and a kerchief like a torn rag. When Ghisa arrived after bathing and stood before me like a delinquent, wearing a half-drenched shirt and his folded kerchief, my eyes became moist, and my whole body glowed with pity. At that moment I understood how the master archer Drona had

156

been able to inspire his aboriginal Bhil pupil to sacrifice his thumb.

One day—I do not know why the impulse occurred to me—I came bringing ten or twelve pounds of *jalebi* sweets for my pupils. But somehow, partly through the honesty of the trades-man weighing it out, partly through the watchfulness of the customer having it weighed out, and partly through some pre-liminary snatching and grabbing when it arrived, there turned out to be not more than five pieces of *jalebi* left for each boy. One of them whined 'I got less than the others,'; another told me, 'Someone took mine away,'; a third wanted some for a little brother asleep back home; a fourth happened to remember some other excuse for demanding more. But amidst this noisy crowd, each one taking his share, where had Ghisa slipped off to? No one could tell. One urchin was whispering to his companion, 'That son of a gun has a puppy. He must have gone to feed him....'; but seeing my raised eyebrows, he stopped complaining. And just at that moment Ghisa came back. All his accounts tal-lied; he had folded up two of his sweets in the cloth he used for straining drinking water and stored them in the hut for his mother; one he had fed to his puppy and two he had eaten him-self. I asked him if he wanted more, but his shy eyes dropped, and his lips trembled a little. It seemed that he had had only a lit-tle for the puppy . . . perhaps Guru sahab might like to give one more, just for the puppy . . . .

And one incident before the Holi festival is imprinted on my mind with so deep a dye that it could not easily be washed out. In those days Hindu-Muslim tension was slowly growing, and it seemed that some day it was bound to reach a climax. Ghisa had been lying ill with a fever for two weeks; I had medicine sent but had not been able to make any good arrangements for nursing care. His mother herself had sat home three or four days; but she had to go to work and found a blind old woman to sit with him.

On Sunday evening I said good-bye to my pupils as usual and set out to see Ghisa; but I had not got fifty paces from the *peepal* tree when my heart became distressed to see him stumbling towards me, tripping and falling with unsteady steps. For as long as fifteen days he had not had enough strength even to get up, so I suspected that he was delirious now. A shock of excite-ment was running through his dehydrated body like bright

157

lightning; his eyes were even more brilliant; and his face looked like a piece of iron slowly turning red in the blaze of a forge. But even though he was gasping for breath he managed to get out the story of what was most burdening his mind. He had got up because of thirst but had found no water near at hand; and not knowing any polite way to get the attention of the blind woman, who was saying her prayer beads, he had resigned himself to suffering the discomfort. Meanwhile, Mullu's uncle who stood at the doorway had told the blind woman that a riot was going on in the city; then the thought of Guru sahab had suddenly occurred to Ghisa. He got up very quietly so that the blind woman heard nothing and as soon as Mullu's uncle had left he had escaped in this direction, bracing himself sometimes against trees and sometimes against walls. Now he would remain here clutching the feet of Guru sahab, who must not under any circumstances go across the river.

This presented a very complicated problem. It was necessary for me to return to the other shore; but now, besides that, I also had to give some explanation to the sick Ghisa which would not exacerbate his condition. But never before had there appeared such an outburst of insistent and resolute strength in the usually reserved, meek, and obedient Ghisa. The year before, upon a similar occasion, he had seen two badly wounded sailors. And now perhaps his brain, inflamed by his fever, was heightening the colours of those earlier mental pictures and thus making an already complicated matter more difficult. But in trying again and again to explain to him, I suddenly struck one chord in him whose sound was new even to me. As soon as he heard that there would be a number of students waiting for me who had come from far away by train, who got a chance to see their mothers only once in the whole year, and who would be left alone and confused if I did not go, then, all of Ghisa's obstinacy, all his opposition dissolved as if it had never existed. And, indeed who could have a capacity for understanding equal to Ghisa's? Those who are not able to be with their own mothers in the evening, Guru sahab must be with them. Ghisa would not make her stay behind, lest the Lord be angry with him; for seeing him wandering alone and idle, He had sent Guru sahab . . . and so he went on. As I remember his explanations, my heart overflows even today. But the measure of amazement in my soul was much greater on that day when I took Ghisa home and made him lie down on his broken little cot, he who had come to save me from troubles, dragging his powerless body burning with fever.

Subsequently Ghisa recovered. Then began his daily battle with the hot breeze of summer. Bundling up the dust and dry leaves and wandering about as though demented, it began to tease the perplexed boy. That schoolroom which he had swept again and again the wind would refill with dust and dirt. It would wrap itself in a veil of leaves, brown, yellow, sometimes green, then tangle this in the skeletal remains of the branches. These would cry out to the dry leaves, moaning with the scorched whistling of the wind. Thereafter I decided to remain there from afternoon until early twilight; but I came to know that Ghisa, rubbing his itchy eyes and brushing the dust off his book, would stay there the whole day as if he were some homeless, ascetic brahmin from ancient times, whose austerities the hot blasts of the *loo* came to defeat.

Thus, the days went by; and time, like a boy racing towards the target, swiftly placed its finger on the day when I had to leave those people, and my heart became heavy. Some of the children were sorry, and some were happy to have a vacation for play. Some of them wanted to know if they should keep track of the days during vacation by adding a dot of lime solution on the wall each day, or by marking them off with charcoal. Some wondered how they would keep their eight-page schoolbooks dry during the rains ahead, when the houses would surely leak. And some wanted a solution to the problem of mice nibbling their papers. Ghisa thought it made no difference whether he stayed or went amidst this noisy clamour, so on that day, as often before, I could not manage to find him. When, rather anxiously, I left there, my heart was becoming heavy and a sort of mist was slowly clouding my vision. In those days my doctors had begun to suspect that I had a stomach ulcer and would have to have an operation. I kept wondering whether I would ever be able to return to that village again. As I looked around me again and again, my gaze lingered on those familiar scenes which it encountered.

The mud-brick-houses were sinking up to their eaves in the dusk which seemed to rise from the earth like a sigh—only their roofs, of moldy straw or clay-coloured tile or dark thatch, still showed like old boats in the water or the debris in the rain-swollen Ganges.

The fields of muskmelons and ripe watermelons stretching away to the horizon over the sandy soil of the alluvial plain looked like some sort of primitive islands floating in the water, with their straw-huts for the watchmen, their hedges, and their wattle fences of grass and reeds. Here and there amidst them a few lamps glowed. Suddenly I was aware of a small, dark form approaching from the distance. Surely it must be Ghisa—I knew him even at a distance. No doubt his little heart, with all its capacity for feeling, knew that he had to say good-bye to his Guru sahab. I had no doubt of it. But I did not yet comprehend how much simple, honest affection this boy's heart held for me, nor how deep was his anguish at our separation.

As he drew near, his dark form stood out against the dusky shadows of the twilight like a black ink mark on almond-coloured paper. He was carrying a huge watermelon in both hands. A section had been cut from it, and the redness of the inside, just visible, contrasted with the dark rind like a bunch of full-blown, bright pink blossoms against deep green foliage.

Ghisa had neither a garden nor any money—then how...! He must have stolen it! For a moment I actually yielded to this suspicion; but I soon realized that the Lord, who had concealed the pure gold of life in that grimy body, was like the old man who hid his gold coin in an adobe wall and ceased to worry about it. For Ghisa believed that to tell a lie to Guru sahab was to tell a lie to the Lord. He had noticed the watermelon a few days before and had had to go alone to the field to ask for it, as he did not know how late his mother might come home. He found the field owner's son there, a boy who had been eyeing Ghisa's new shirt for several days. As Ghisa went on with his story, the other boy had said that it seemed insane to him that one whose hunger was supposed to be appeased by eating other's leftovers was being served happily by his betters. The boy had said, 'If you have no money, then give me your shirt.' And Ghisa explained that he had to take the watermelon that very day, for it would be useless to him the next. So he handed over his shirt. But Guru sahab needn't worry, he explained, for he didn't wear that shirt in the summer anyway, and the old one was good enough for everyday use. He had had to cut the watermelon open to be sure it was good, and to see whether it was sweet or not, he had had to scoop some out with his fingers.

If Guru sahab would not accept it, then Ghisa would cry all night—indeed, would cry the whole vacation through; and if she would accept it, then each day he would bathe and wash his clothes, and would review and memorize the lessons he had learned from Guru sahab under the tree, and would copy the whole book onto his slate and show it to his teacher after the vacation.

I laid my hand on the head of this boy, who had been made so bold by his devotion, and stood motionless in the grip of intense feelings. I cannot believe that any teacher ever received such a tribute from a student as was offered to me on that riverbank; and all the other gifts I have ever received seem trivial to me in comparison.

I made some special arrangements for Ghisa's welfare, then went away from home and stayed several months before returning. During that time I was unable to get any news about him. And by the time that I was finally able to find enough leisure to go that way again, his Lord had already given Ghisa a rest from studying forever. Even today I have not the strength to repeat the whole story. Perhaps when today will have turned into yesterday, yesterday into many days, days into months and months into years, I will at last be able to describe the neglected end of this little life with the stoic resignation of a philosopher. But at present, all I can do is go on searching for his likeness in other pathetic little faces.

Translated from Hindi by Sudha Chandola and Susan Tripp

O.V.Vijayan

The Wart

This was once my garden, the garden I had tended, but today its giant grasses dwarf me. I cower amidst them listening to the awesome rumble of the spiders' chariots, awaiting the wind that would lift me on its brown wave of dust and leaves, and speak to you my brother in the far generations. My time is draining away, and I have sinned the sin of the gentle and the pious, and so must make amends. I must communicate..... I go back to the wart, drawn to revisit my sin. My sense of time fails me, I cannot recall with any measure of certainty when it all began; it is just as well, because, through this story runs a perennial truth whose beginnings go back beyond the times we have known. I remember my wife Suma discovering the wart, tiny as a seed, below my lower lip. I remember too the surgeon who said he could scissor it away, and how I declined, because my people had never needed surgery, all their healing came from the riversides and the mountainslopes, whose tender shooted specifics were revealed to them by the sage Dhanvantari, the Lord of Health. Generations of my people had meditated on this seer with trust, and I could see no other path for me as well. This was my sin, and this now my moment of unburdening.....

*

I remember the morning when my razor blade had made a cut on the wart, which bled a little. Suma thought it was a mole, a sign of luck, and it seemed to excite her while we made love. It was many days later, in bed with me one night, that she asked, 'Do you think this is contagious?'

'I don't,' I said. 'It's just a wart.'

'I was wondering....'

'I'm positive it isn't.'

'Still it is better to remove it. We ought to be telling Aechchu Menon.'

We forgot this conversation. Aechchu Menon was the young

162

surgeon, whose clinic was six or seven miles away. He lived close by, a mere mile if you took the bridle path over the hill and the stretch of paddy, but quite some distance by road. I could have walked over to his house, but had felt reluctant. I was confident that my body, the child of gentle generations, would get back its wholeness through the benediction of leaf and root. In my house there was a crypt-like chamber where much wisdom had been stored away, inscribed on palm-leaves; there, one day, I searched for the cure which would rid me of my excrescence. The sage Dhanvantari had laid it down; I walked towards the stream beside which were the dense herbal beds. I plucked the leaves and roots I needed and brought them home.

When Suma saw the green pulp of the medicament over the wart, she said, 'I'd rather you got it scissored away.'

Unni, my eight-year-old, overheard her and seemed upset. I drew him close.

'Don't scissor it away,' he said.

'Why do you say that?' I asked.

'It will hurt.'

'As you wish,' I said, and smiled. 'We shall try these medicaments.'

These snatches of memory come alive without sequence.... Now the wart had grown large, with a glistening scab around its stem. One night, making love, I found Suma's play reluctant and her climax impersonal. Suma who lay with her eyes closed seemed far away. Something told me that she had made love not to me but to my other self, the one without the wart, an adulterous fantasy which sank me in despair. I sought to get back to her with a show of concern.

'Suma,' I said. 'Are you not well?'

'I'm all right,' she said, 'just tired.'

'Shall we tell Aechchu Menon?'

'There is no need.'

'Shall I give you one of my potions?'

'No,' she said, and turned away, a gesture the import of which I had no desire to understand. These bouts of distemper passed, and I revived.... Ours was a country mansion, a granary fortress a hundred years old. Our estate had dwindled, but there was enough to ensure a life of leisure and contemplation. I did not know the extent of the lands nor how much grain they yielded, but Chaaththan, the head serf kept count of things for me as had his father for mine. Suma disapproved of this, complaining often of my ineptitude, but I would tell her that Chaaththan knew better. Everyday I would rise early and bathe, and say my beads, and sit down to spin. Unni would soon be off to school and Suma to the kitchen; when I had spun for the day, I would wander over the extensive lands that lay around our house, taking in its compassionate noontide, its gentle browning of leaves, its bird noises and the ancestral camaraderie of its snakes. Towards the far south of the compound was the giant banyan and the barren patch where my fathers had been cremated. Here I would sit and marvel; soon it would be time to eat and then to lie down for a little sleep in the afternoon. In the evening I would take Unni for a long walk which ended in the temple of Shiva, where the priest would have kept for Unni his share of the consecrated offering, the palm sugar and fruit and coconut. Thus were my days spent in peace.

During one such visit to the temple, Unni stood for a long time before the idol, his eyes closed and palms joined. He opened his eyes when the old priest came up with the offering and tapped him on his shoulder.

'Should we watch the waterfowl?' I asked as we stepped out of the temple.

'Yes,' said Unni.

This too was another ritual of ours, a secret covenant; we would sit on the stone steps of the temple tank, their sunset granite warm, and the face of water mystic, the migrant waterfowl seared furrows of phosphorescence across it. As usual, we were alone.

We heard the last gongs from the temple; the sanctum was being closed. Unni had lain on the stone, his head on my lap and was soon asleep in the gentle tank breezes. I let him sleep on; the moon had risen when he got up, and the mist was falling. On our way back I asked him, 'Unni, you prayed long today. What did you ask the Lord?'

'To make me a good child,' he said.

'And what else?'

'Well,' he said, 'that's a secret.'

'It doesn't have to be a secret, Unni. What's it?'

'I shouldn't tell it to anyone, or it won't come true.'

'Not really,' I coaxed him. 'It doesn't always have to be so.'

'Well then,' he said. 'I asked the Lord to take your wart away.'

Involuntarily I felt below my lower lip. The wart had grown, its hem of ooze become wider. When we got home, Suma said reproachfully, 'You've kept the child out in the cold so long. The mist is condensing.'

The next evening Unni complained of a sore throat. Suma did not fail to remind me of my negligence.

'Suma,' I said, 'children do catch these colds. A little soup of pepper should make him all right.'

'I suppose you would like the cold to become a fever.'

'What do you want me to do?'

'Can't you show him to a doctor?'

I didn't have a car, and had I walked Unni all the way to Aechchu Menon's house in the evening, surely his cold would get worse; for it would be well past sundown by the time the doctor returned home, the dew would be falling thick over the hill. There were of course the herbs, but Suma was insistent.

'Let the child stay home,' I said. 'I could go and get the medicine from the doctor.'

'Forget it,' said Suma. ' I'll make the pepper water.'

'But Suma,' I pleaded, ' this is too trivial an illness to call the doctor over.'

'Who's arguing? If that's the way you feel, you don't have to call him.'

She spoke with sullen vehemence; silently I went out of her presence and set out for the doctor's house. I waded across the stream, and reaching the hilltop, stood awhile to breathe in the free breezes; the sun had set and the sky was lit with a scarlet afterglow. The village was quiet, its winds free; the hill stood like the incarnate Shiva, and the birds flitted against the red, wind-blown clouds that were his matted hair. But soon amidst these hills and sunsets I would be enslaved by fear and my sorrow imprisoned without communion. To you who watch the rise of the hill and the calm of the sunset, I say this: fear will return to hunt again amid the trees of this hillside, that is why these brief moments of communing are precious.... As I went downhill I felt the wart with a new sense of forboding.

Aechchu Menon was back from his clinic already.

'I finished early today,' he said.

I sat uneasily in a chair in front of him. The young doctor made me conscious of my crumbling manor and my ignorance; he was the son of a family of parvenus, the first man in our countryside to have mastered the medicine of the English.

'Doctor,' I said, 'Unni has a cold.'

'A cold? That's nothing to be upset about,' he said with a smile. 'I hope he isn't running a fever.'

'No.'

Aechchu Menon went into an ante-room, returning soon with a strip of packaged pills. I took the pills from him and slipped them into my pocket and said hesitantly. 'You must pardon me if I cause you inconvenience, but it's because of Suma's insistence. Could you come home?'

'Certainly. We'll drive down.'

I felt guilty about the drive in particular, because unlike the trek over the hill and across the paddies, the road was a long detour. Soon we were on our way....Suma met us on the doorstep. She apologized to the doctor, and he mumbled a pleasantry. Aechchu Menon followed Suma into the bedroom and I went in after. Unni lay under a blanket. He woke up and smiled at us.

'That's a naughty child,' said Aechchu Menon. 'Did you play about in the water?'

'No,' said Unni, 'I just sat watching the waterfowl.'

'It was the mist,' said Suma. I sensed the secret bitterness in her voice. Aechchu Menon laughed.

'My kinsman here,' he said, bantering, 'believes in remedies of rain and dew.'

Words rose within me only to ebb away; what could have I said about the gentle realm of leaf and root, of the secret covenant between father and son listening to the gongs of Shiva and watching the waterfowl streak through the dusking water?

Unni had fever that night. The fever lasted five days. In his fever, he threw his arms around me and said, 'Father, you won't let them cut up your face, will you?'

'Why do you keep thinking of it, son?'

'I'm afraid.'

'If it makes you afraid, we shall not let them operate.'

'We shall get medicine from the hillside.'

'We'll do that, little one. Now go to sleep.'

Today, I recall my words in sorrow, and know, my son, wherein I had failed you. You were pure and young, ignorant of the ways of the microbe; I ought to have armed you with that knowledge....

Suma had barred me from nursing Unni. 'Stay away,' she said. 'Do you want the child to catch the disease?'

My hand rose to my wart, it was sticky with the ooze. I withdrew to the bath and washed the ooze away, then looked in the mirror. The wart had grown the size of a gooseberry. Unni got well in a fortnight. Aechchu Menon had visited him everyday during his illness, and even after he recovered made it a practice to visit us and enquire after the child.

The wart was now growing faster. One night I woke in great pain. The ducts of the wart had given away; I had the sense of an enormous slush, like the yellow ooze of riven rocks. I felt the wart, and realized that it had grown alarmingly. When it was morning I made my way to the hillside and plucked the leaves I needed, pulled out the rarest of roots, and together ground them into medicament invoking the grace of Dhanvantari. But now the wart seemed to suck in the very medicament, to feed on it and grow. Soon it grew to the size of a lemon. If I dropped my gaze, I could see its shadowy contours; the pace of growth quickened. I realized too that though Aechchu Menon kept visiting us he talked of the wart no more.

Imperceptibly a change had come in my relations with people. It was a curious idler first, a man I encountered in the village library who stared hard at me; then another and another and another, until I found myself driven gently but relentlessly into a prison of their awareness of me. Still I could have carried the wart, now as big as a tomato, in the hammock of my lip, and trudged to the hospital in the town, but barring my way was all that I and my forebears had lived by. And now Suma began to stop my son coming near me. 'It's a disease,' she told Unni. 'A contagion.'

I chose not to hear my son's reply, the strength for that knowing had gone from me, and slowly I climbed up to the panelled attic, which would henceforth be my home.... One night in the attic, lying on the ancient cot of rosewood, I communed with the ancestral shades around me. *My fathers*, I said, *these riversides and mountainslopes bear witness to your freedom, and yet what has befallen*

*me, your offspring? You bequeathed to me the precious palm-leaf with
its arcana of healing, and yet why have these leaves and roots failed to
prevail over this invading spore?* In the aged panelling, and in the
walls of our sprawling home, they awoke and listened and
answered me with a great tide of sadness.

I lay long thus in the stream of my fathers, when I was aware
of someone moving stealthily through the attic's dark. It was
Suma. I rose and moved towards her. She had an earthen pot in
her hands.

I took the cold bowl from her and smelt the aromas of
Dhanvantari's medicaments.

'Merciful Lord,' I said.

'I got them from the *vaid*. This is his prescription. Take it.'

A multitude of beneficent things were within me, they lit me
with cool and gentle lights; so she had gone to the *vaid* despite
her awe of the apothecary, she had come up to the attic overcom-
ing her revulsion of the giant carbuncle that sat on my lip. I
threw my arms around her; she did not resist, but when I bent
over to kiss her, she said, 'We should not. It is not for me, but for
our son that I deny you so.'

'Suma,' I said, 'this is no contagion. This is a wart.'

'It's a wart,' she said.

'Come,' I said.

She stood reluctant in the dark, then barred me gently. When I
took her face in my palms, her cheeks were wet.

'Oh, god!' I said.

With a sob she came down on her knees, and unable to lift her
up, I sat down beside her.

'Unni does not eat,' she said. 'He's pining away.'

My memories fade here, it is merciful they do; I remember
that unspoken words moved on like a procession of termites
from me to her and from us to our child, until the termite tracks
were deserted and there were nothing but the attic's dark and
the earthen bowl which held Dhanvantari's gentle medicament. I
sat awhile to gaze into the vessel and be overcome again by
weariness and sleep. I woke again, the moon had risen in the
window. The ancestral shades on my walls were now vibrant. I
rose and paced my prison with the righteousness of my fathers.
It was then that the moon shone in on an ancient razor's edge.
My great-uncle Koppunni had shaven himself with this blade

and here amid derelict artifacts it had lain these long years. The knife blazed, and I remembered my great-uncle. We were gentle and pious people, but our genealogy was punctuated by proud and regal ancestors as well. Koppunni Nair was one such. He had stridden the hillsides in the rain, and grown to power in the green nutrients of the recurring seasons. I could see him sit down before the serf-barber for the ritual tonsure; this was the knife, on no other did the barber use it; it cleansed the scalp round his tuft and the base of his phallus, so that he was shorn anew into nakedness and would romp down the hillsides to seek out wedded matrons and in them sow the seeds of bastard sovereignty; and their children, in the unknowing of their ancestry, would chase and mate with one another. The wildness of it roused me, and I went to the shelf in the panelling and picked up the knife glistening in the moon. I did not know what followed; perhaps the knife and its power compelled me. The suicidal violence of my great-uncle welled up within me along with the futile resistance of the gentle and the pious, and in that great mingling I held the wart with my left hand and with the right drew the knife along its stem.

*

The swoon must have lasted months. When I came to, it was another season in the skylight. Instinctively, I raised my hand to feel the wart. There it was, defiant and invincible. It was the size of a coconut, and around it, like stalagmite or coral, was glistening scab and fester.

Chaaththan came up to the attic. 'We had given you up, master.'

'Chaaththan....'

'What is it, my master?'

I lay for a while in silence, to regain my words.

'How long,' I asked at last, 'did the swoon last?'

'Three months, master.'

In the corner of the attic I saw heaps of drying herbs and felt their gentle aromas.

'Have you been nursing me with these?' I asked.

'You've taught us to minister thus, my master.'

'Chaaththan....'

'Yes, my master.'

The words as they formed inside me sounded portentuous, I held them back awhile, then spoke them trembling.

'Chaaththan,' I said, 'where is Unni?'

Chaaththan did not reply. He rose from the cross-beam of the doorframe he was sitting on, and slowly walked to a cupboard in the panelling, and took out a sealed letter from a casket within.

'Here, master,' he said, 'this is the mistress's letter.'

'The mistress's letter?' I repeated, incredulously.

Chaaththan looked away and was silent; I tore open the cover and read; in disbelief I skated back and forth over the rounded script. *I am going*, she had written. *You and I can only console our-selves that such is our destiny. I am going away to a far country with Aechchu Menon. I shall put no more in words, lest it cause you more pain. I ask your forgiveness, so does he.... Unni will live in my ances-tral home, my brothers will look after him. Afflicted as you are, I shall not burden you with his care....*

Darkness descended on my eyes, and as they cleared, I felt the wart twitch.... On the walls the ancestral shades had fallen quiet. I looked for Koppunni Nair's knife, but it was nowhere to be found.

Slowly, like the fading and oncoming of seasons, I experi-enced a new quiet and a new acceptance. I came down from the attic, and every day at dawn I walked over the grass in the gar-den wet with the night's dew. Before the sun was up Chaaththan would come to me with the goings-on in the fields and the orchards, and do the reckoning. After that his young sister-in-law, Naani would bring in the milk, steam a banana for my breakfast, cook for the day, and depart. Sometimes at night, Chaaththan would come up to find out how I was keeping. That was the last thing for the day, after which I was left alone with the wart. The old house sprawled, enormous and cheerless, its rooms far flung, inaccessible like far provinces, where the ver-min multiplied and broke the sleep of my fathers with malefic noises.... The wart grew larger.

Chaaththan's concern was now slackening, and Naani began slipping up. I questioned her when she turned up after one of her truancies; after much insistence she answered, 'There was work at home.'

It was folly to question her further, it was folly for me to demand anything, I told myself. I remembered Suma's great reluctances, the freezing love-play, the nights which gave us the final knowledge of our alienation. I was thinking of Suma again. What at this moment might she be doing? The sun was climbing high, and soon it would be noon, when in the land of her refuge it would perhaps be midnight. Starting out of her sleep now, she was making love again; I sensed the wet of her lips, the felt and unseen breasts, the thighs, and the fair disc of the belly rising to meet the man's desire again and again. And then the interminable sleep, the interminable nakedness. I must have sat still for a long while, all this smouldering and dying within me. Naani had left.

All day long I chased Suma's memory with horrendous lust. As the night advanced I quietened, and in its place came a great tenderness for my son, and like a little boy, I cried myself to sleep.... Early next morning, I walked out of my compound gate and waded into the stream. There were no other bathers, nor any people in sight. I stood naked in the flowing water. Only my face had been claimed by the wart, my body was still mine, and limb by limb, it was sturdy and beautiful.

The wart was now a slab of meat. I felt the burden within as well; in vain I sought a place in my mind where I could rest it awhile. Thus I went one day to the boundary fence, beyond which lay the serfs' tenements. It was noon already, and I had not eaten since morning. I called out for Naani. She came to the fence.

'Has Chaaththan gone to the fields?' I asked her.

'Yes, my master.'

Naani was now looking hard at the wart.

'My master,' she said, 'it has grown big.'

We stood on either side of the fence, we stood close to each other.

Then I asked her, 'Naani, why have you stopped coming?'

'The chores at home,' she answered without conviction.

We fell silent again.

'Naani,' I said, 'did Chaaththan stop you from coming?'

'Yes,' she mumbled.

'Did he say it was contagious.'

Again, sadly, she nodded.

Naani was young, and beautiful in the manner of aboriginal women, her limbs strong and her skin the deep colour of honey, her lips black and glistening a healthy wet, windblown ringlets about the temples, the hair of an ancient race. Then as I stood looking at her, the wart's crust cracked and there was a great gush of ooze. Paralyzed, I stood by the fence.

On an impulse, Naani pulled off her upper cloth and held it towards me.

'Take this, my master,' she said, 'and wipe it.'

I took the proffered cloth, her bared breasts now basked in the sun. I wiped the ooze with the fingers and returned her the cloth unsoiled.

'Naani....'

'Yes, my master?'

'Will you come?'

She did not reply.

'Naani....'

'Yes, my master.'

Silence again.

'Naani....'

'Yes, my master?'

'Naani,' I asked her again, 'will you come to work?'

Quietly she said, 'I shall.'

I lumbered back into the house and sat behind a fretted casement and waited. I did not have to wait long; I saw her crossing the yard. She entered the room uncertainly and stood before me.

'Naani....'

'Yes, my master.'

'Are you repelled?'

I bent my head and averted my gaze, she did not reply.

'My master,' she said, 'when is the mistress coming back?'

'She is not coming back.'

Naani asked me nothing more; her eyes wandered about the room, and soon she was aware of nothing but the little things, the cobwebs, the drying peel of banana, the crumpled ball of paper in the corner. She picked a broom and began to sweep.

'I am back, my master,' she said. 'Be at ease.'

'Naani....'

She leaned the broom on the wall and came over to me. I had premeditated nothing that I might tell her, but I found myself

172

saying, 'I want to bathe. I want a warm bath.'

She moved into the inner rooms, noiselessly. Soon there rose the scents of medicinal oils warming over the hearth. She came back and called me, 'Your bath is ready, my master.'

I walked towards the bath, and she followed me with the oils and the pulp of gram. She entered the bath after me, and began to rub the oils on my hands and legs.

'My master!' said Naani.

I was crying. She pressed my face against her belly, and in my sorrow and dependence I began disrobing her. She pressed me harder against her body's transluscence of honey. I closed my eyes, and behind the shelter of those lids I was whole and handsome again....My eyes closed, I kissed her on her parted lips, my sorrow spilled over her and was spent. The wart twitched.

That night, for the first time in many nights, I slept deep. When I woke up the next morning I found the wart grown inordinately. I could hardly lift my face, and I began walking about the house with my head bent, with the sorrow of a lowly hog. Thus I went to the mirror, and in great pain raised my face to it. As I studied the image, I saw a red slit across the wart, and two black spots. For a moment I was relieved; I thought the wart was sappurating and bursting.

In this renewed hope that day, I plucked more leaves and roots and ground them into medicament. When I spread it round the wart, it smarted as it had never before, and I had the uncanny feeling that it was moving and wriggling. When the medicament dried and peeled away, the wart appeared even larger.

About ten days after Naani had given me the bath, it became difficult for me to hold myself up. When she brought me my milk one morning, I was lying crushed by the weight of my face.

'Are you in much pain, my master?' asked Naani.

I made a vain attempt to rise, then gave up and lay down.

'Let me hold you, my master.'

She held me and propped me against the cushions.

'I can't bear this burden anymore,' I said.

She pressed the palm of her hand between her large breasts, eyes closed; I saw her lips move in prayer. After that she disrobed me gently, and keeping her eyes away from my disfigurement, began caressing my healthy members. A great desire rose in me, swamping the pain and the burden of excrescence; I desired Naani to anoint me, desired that we should anoint each other on the cold tiles of the bath. Soon we were covered with Dhanvantara, the ancient unction of the sage, we went down on the floor like twining serpents. Thus does the unfree man seek freedom, in lust; like the condemned prisoner who spends his last moments not on God but mating with empresses in his fantasy. There occurs one moment when someone peeps into your prison cell and tells you he can cut away the tumid flesh; but you turn away to your roots and leaves, like the condemned one to his empresses; the moment has slipped by, never to occur again....I was preparing to make love to Naani when the wart twitched violently, and I fancied I heard a noise like a fish plummeting into water, and a scream of pain rose from Naani.

Piercing through the pus and scab, an enormous phallus had come out of the wart. I fell away, but felt a miraculous power pulling me up. It was the wart, drilling down beneath my scalp and holding me up in an unseen lasso. I found myself lying on Naani once again, my face on her underbelly. I felt the black phallus rise; the wart was taking Naani!

I am appalled by the enormity of my sin as I recollect how the wart had risen and fallen over Naani, carrying her to a tumultuous climax, and how I had shared the experience with the wart. I had till then considered the wart an alien impurity, but from now I was to know that this thing which I had fostered with nutrients of my body and folly of my piety, was the flesh of my flesh. The interminable orgasm caused a sleep to come over me, and when I awoke my limbs had grown cold on the tiles of the bath. I sat up with great effort. The cheerless dusk and the cold tiles filled me with a sense of derelict things. Then I realized that Naani might catch a chill if she slept long on the floor.

'Naani,' I said, shaking her, 'wake up! You'll freeze.'

The violence of the orgasm had apparently exhausted her, and, lips slack, thighs apart, the palms of her hands resting on her breasts, and blood and ooze drying below her navel, Naani slept. Then once again the wart's lust became mine. My senses spun, and I drifted into a swoon.

It must have lasted many days; it was a strong stench that awakened me. I sat up and looked at Naani; nothing had changed in the tableau of rape: the parted lips and thighs, the palms resting on the breasts. I touched her thighs, the flesh had begun to rot, and as I took my hand away, I heard an eerie laugh like the cackle of a woodpecker. I was alone with a corpse and its mortuary odour. The unseen woodpecker laughed again. Fear gave me the energy to rise and move; I went up to the mirror to take a look at the wart. It hung from my lower lip like a sea turtle. The red patch I had seen and which I had mistaken for an inflammation and possible decline, now opened up into a mouth, and the black dots into a pair of eyes, vampire lips drooling spit and pus, and little eyes winking at me from the mirror. The lips moved now, and once again I heard the spectral cackle of the woodpecker. As I listened intently the cackle defined itself into words of frenzied and obscene abuse.

Now the last spaces of my freedom vanished, the spaces I had conjured with my desperate lust. The prison closed round me once again, and I was left alone with the wart, my prison warden. And now the wart began to communicate to me its commands, helplessly I obeyed. Whenever I failed to decipher the woodpecker's cackle, the wart squirted pus on me. With patient industry I trained myself for this new listening, and soon I was lost to the speech of free men. Tugging with secret reins at my mind, the wart now put me to work. There was a lumber room on top, and one night the wart commanded me to climb up there. It was pitch dark inside, but pointers of a denser darkness led me on. Disturbed out of their ancient trances, tarantulas spiralled dizzily up my legs and down and away. The wart directed me to rummage in the junk. I thrust my fingers amid sodden and rusted things, amid hidden venoms, until at last I touched cold steel. It was Koppunni Nair's razor. I could not figure out how it had got to the lumber room. The wart directed me to pick it up. We climbed down the lumber room with the weapon.

There was a pall of mist outside, the moonlight full of disquiet. I remembered my fingers tightening round the handle, I remember the first paces of a murderous sleepwalk; then the long swoon took over. When I awoke the knife was still in my hand, and I was covered with black and red stains. The wart asked me to get up: we walked to the old well. It directed me to fling the knife into the well. As the knife shot through to the depths and pierced the deep lens of water, I sent up a prayer to my ancestors. The wart crouched and listened, and desecrated

175

my prayers. I sought consolation in the knowledge that the wart was still my excrescence, that it had once been a lowly knot of ducts on my lip. At that the woodpecker's cackle spoke, not in my ear but within my mind, *you transgress the law*.

Wherein do I transgress? I asked.

Memory, the wart said. *Memory is a crime against history*.

I spoke with sadness into my mind, *you were born of my flesh. Why did you take away my freedom, the freedom of the one who gave you your being?*

The wart writhed in great rage, and flung searing lances of pain into my bloodstream.

Spare me, spare me, I cried out.

When you speak to me hereafter, the wart said, *you must call me your brother*.

Brother, I said.

Not that way, the wart said.

Teach me how? I asked.

In this manner, the wart said. It gave me the knowledge of willing servitude. Brotherhood was a word of freedom, but from now on, words would change, and so would everything that came from the sacred grottos of the mind.

That night the wart ordered me to the gate of our manor: from some distance away came the noises of people. There were policemen with red berets on the rampage. I remembered the knife and the blood on my palms; a great distress came over me, and I asked the wart, *where is my loyal serf, and where is his wife?*

You need not know, the wart said severely.

I need not, I repeated. *Brother*, I called the wart, in a snivelling of the mind. I accepted my sovereign.

I knew the wart smiled. *Good*, it said. *It's time to feed. Move on to the bath*.

The stench in the bath had grown so dense that it was the colour of the moss of death, of a death unredeemed by rebirth. I dragged myself inside. The wart asked me to lie down on Naani's corpse once again for the funereal mating. The wart kissed the black parted lips, then I heard a noise like the snip-snipping of barber's scissors. Naani's lips vanished , I knew the acid taste of rot. A skeletal grin flashed where the lips had been, soon the eyes and cheeks and nose disappeared, and then there was a noise of the crushing of bones and of their softening in the alchemy of spit. Then followed the monotonous slurping of trea-cle. When it was over, I was given the command to rise.

I stood on the tiles of the bath. Naani lay headless at my feet, her thighs apart and her hands folded over the swollen nipples. Like a delicate pall over it all was the patina of mold. From all over her underbelly came fearsome secretions, while within it grew the foetus of death.

To the mirror now, the wart said. Now I saw the wart had sprouted supple tendrils, hands of the wart!

God, I said.

No sooner had I uttered that word, the javelins burned through my blood and my endurance gone, I cried out in suppli-cation, *brother, brother*! The javelins were called back.

Brother, my just and all-powerful brother! I chanted. The wart was pleased.

With its new grown hands the wart began to hunt; it gave chase to wild cats and the bandicoots, from the lumber rooms it caught the bats, preyed on them. The headless corpse had by now become a frothing, bubbling puddle. The wart mated with it again and again.

One night my thoughts dwelt on Suma and Unni with an intensity I had never before experienced. I sought them in the scalding darkness of my sorrow, I floundered and fell, and wept. The wart listened. Once in everyman's lifetime, once perhaps, his sorrow rises to enormity, and like the will of a king, sweeps away everything before it. This was my moment of my grief and power. The wart stood by and watched. When my lamenting subsided, I waited for the punishing javelins. They never came. Now the stench too had gone; after one last union the wart had licked up the puddle with great gluttony. The javelins never came, but I was to be punished yet; all nutrients were withheld from my bloodstream. Within me grew a hunger like an unseen fire that licks through mountain crevices. I began dwindling fast, even as the wart grew by leaps and bounds; I became a mere appendage. Then one day the wart battered down the doors of our chamber of palm-leaf manuscripts and sought the arcana of Dhanvantari. The wart was then lost in study for a while, after which it went out to the hillside for leaves and roots. I watched it make the medicament and lay it thick around the stem of my dimunitive body. There was searing pain, followed by numbness and sleep.

I woke up amid flaming dandelions, the sun was bright overhead and the wind blew with the aroma of living plants. I realized I was in my garden. I saw an enormous creature roll in from behind the house. It was the wart! The medicaments had worked, and I had shrivelled and fallen off the wart's great body. There was a weird change in the scale of things, the grass blades were like towers and dragonflies descended on them like airships. I had shrunk to the size of a worm.

The wart rolled about in the garden. The sun climbed to a blazing noon, then set and rose again. The spiders hunted amid the grass. The wart was growing and changing. Its black hide shone. It had four legs, great flapping ears, a trunk and a pair of tusks. The wart had become an elephant.

Down the hill came a band of brahmins, and saw the elephant frolicking in the waters of our stream.

'A truly majestic elephant,' they said.

'The temple could use him for the procession.'

'Whose elephant is it?'

'Koppunni's.'

'Koppunni was indeed a connoisseur.'

'Look this way, elephant....'

In my worm's voice thin like a pupal thread I cried out, *pious brahmins, this is no elephant, this is a microbe. I shall tell you its tale.* But the brahmins were gone. The wind rose and the dead leaves rustled.

The elephant took the offerings of the temple, the fruit and the palm sugar and the tender fronds of the coconut, and on its back glittered the idol of the temple god. The sorrows of the pious and the gentle were forgotten, and so too the death scent of the merciful woman. But I had my freedom, the freedom of the castaway. The wart had given me my freedom, the wart, my prison warden. Then like a deluge came the awareness of the living force which fulfilled itself as much in the toxic microbe as it did in the seeds of life. Skies unfolded in my tiny head, and in them shone a benevolent sun.

> *Om bhoor bhuva swawaha*
> *Tat savitur varenniyum,*
> *Bhargo devasya dheemahi*

Almighty Light, pervader of the earth and the sky, of the gross and the subtle, illumine my intellect....

Once again, the leaf and the root of the gentle exuberate in the bounty of the Sun.

It was in my folly, my Lord God, that I forgot your perennial becoming. You are the prisoner's door.

Translated from Malayalam by the author

Bhisham Sahni

We Have Arrived in Amritsar

There were not many passengers in the compartment. The Sardarji, sitting opposite me, had been telling me about his experiences in the war. He had fought on the Burmese front, and every time he spoke about the British soldiers, he had a hearty laugh at their expense. There were three Pathan traders too, and one of them, wearing a green *salwar kameez*, lay stretched on one of the upper berths. He was a talkative kind of a person and had kept up a stream of jokes with a frail-looking *babu* who was sitting next to me. The *babu*, it seemed, came from Peshawar because off and on they would begin to converse with each other in Pushto. In a corner, under the Pathan's berth, sat an old woman telling beads on her rosary, with her head and shoulders covered by a shawl. These were the only passengers that I can recollect being in the compartment. There might have been others too, but I can't remember them now.

The train moved slowly and the passengers chatted away. Outside the breeze made gentle ripples across the ripening wheat. I was happy because I was on my way to Delhi to see the Independence Day celebrations.

Thinking about those days it seems to me that we had lived in a kind of mist. It may be that as time goes by all the activities of the past begin to float in a mist, which seems to grow thicker and thicker as we move away further into the future.

The decision about the creation of Pakistan had just been announced and people were indulging in all kinds of surmises about the pattern of life that would emerge. But no one's imagination could go very far. The Sardarji sitting in front of me repeatedly asked me whether I thought Mr Jinnah would continue to live in Bombay after the creation of Pakistan or whether he would resettle in Pakistan. Each time my answer would be the same, 'Why should he leave Bombay? I think he'll continue to live in Bombay and keep visiting Pakistan.' Similar guesses were being made about the towns of Lahore and Gurdaspur too, and no one knew which town would fall to the share of India and which to Pakistan. People gossiped and laughed in much the same way as before. Some were abandoning their homes for good, while others made fun of them. No one knew which step would prove to be the right one. Some people deplored the creation of Pakistan, others rejoiced over the achievement of independence. Some places were being torn apart by riots, others were busy preparing to celebrate Independence. Somehow we all thought that the troubles would cease automatically with the achievement of freedom. In that hazy mist there came the sweet taste of freedom and yet the darkness of uncertainty seemed continuously to be with us. Only occasionally through this darkness did one catch glimpses of what the future meant for us.

We had left behind the city of Jhelum when the Pathan sitting on the upper berth untied a small bundle, took out chunks of boiled meat and some bread, and began distributing it among his companions. In his usual jovial manner he offered some of it to the *babu* next to me.

'Eat it, *babu*, eat it. It will give you strength. You will become like us. Your wife too will be happy with you. You are weak because you eat *dal* all the time. Eat it, *dalkhor*.'

There was laughter in the compartment. The *babu* said something in Pushto but kept smiling and shaking his head.

The other Pathan taunted him further.

'O *zalim*, if you don't want to take it from our hands, pick it up yourself with your own hand. I swear to God that it is only goat's meat and not of any other animal.'

The third Pathan joined in: 'O son of a swine, who is looking at you here? We won't tell your wife about it. You share our meat and we shall share your *dal* with you.'

There was a burst of laughter. But the emaciated clerk continued to smile and shake his head.

'Does it look nice that we should eat and you should merely look on?' The Pathans were in good humour.

The fat Sardarji joined in and said, 'He doesn't accept it because you haven't washed your hands,' and burst out laughing at his own joke. He was reclining on the seat with half his belly hanging over it. 'You just woke up and immediately started to eat. That's the reason *babuji* won't accept food from your hands. There isn't any other reason.' As he said this he gave me a wink and guffawed again.

'If you don't want to eat meat, you should go and sit in a ladies' compartment. What business have you to be here?'

Again the whole compartment had a good laugh. All the passengers had been together since the beginning of the journey, a kind of informality had developed amongst them.

'Come and sit with me. Come, rascal, we shall sit and chat about *kissakhani*.'

*

The train stopped at a wayside station and new passengers barged into the compartment. Many of them forced their way in.

'What is this place?' someone asked.

'Looks like Wazirabad to me,' I replied, peering out of the window.

The train only stopped for a short time, but during the stop a minor incident occurred. A man got down from a neighbouring compartment and went to the tap on the platform for water. He had hardly filled his glass with water when suddenly he turned round and started running back towards his compartment. As he ran the water spilt out of the glass. The whole manner of his dash was revealing to me. I had seen people running like this before and knew immediately what it meant. Two or three other passengers, who were queuing at the tap also began running towards their compartments. Within a matter of seconds the whole platform was deserted. Inside our compartment, however, people were still chatting and laughing as before.

Beside me the *babu* muttered: 'Something bad is happening.'

Something really had happened but none of us could figure it out. I had seen quite a number of communal riots and had learnt to detect the slightest change in the atmosphere; people running, doors shutting, men and women standing on housetops, an uncanny silence all round—these were signs of riots.

Suddenly the sound of a scuffle was heard from the back-entrance to the compartment. Some passenger was trying to get into the compartment.

'No, you can't come in here,' someone shouted. 'There is no place here. Can't you see? No, no. Go away.'

'Shut the door,' someone else remarked. 'People just walk in as though it was their uncle's residence.'

Several voices were heard, speaking simultaneously.

As long as a passenger is outside a compartment and is trying desperately to get in, he faces strong opposition from those inside. But once he succeeds in entering, the opposition subsides and he is soon accepted as a fellow traveller, so much so that at the next stop, he too begins to shout at the new passengers trying to get in.

The commotion increased. A man in soiled, dirty clothes and with drooping moustache forced his way into the compartment. From his dirty clothes he appeared to be a sweet-vendor. He paid no attention to the shouts of protest of the passengers. He squeezed himself inside and turned around to try and haul in his enormous black trunk.

'Come in, come in, you too climb,' he shouted, addressing someone behind him. A frail, thin woman entered the door followed by a young dark girl of sixteen or seventeen. People were still shouting at them. The Sardarji had got up on his haunches.

Everyone seemed to be shouting at the same time: 'Shut the door. Why don't you?' 'People just come barging in.' 'Don't let anyone in.' 'What are you doing?' 'Just push him out, somebody....'

The man continued hauling in his trunk, while his wife and daughter shrank back and stood against the door of the toilet, looking anxious and frightened.

'Can't you go to some other compartment? You have brought womenfolk with you too. Can't you see this is a men's compartment?'

The man was breathless and his clothes were drenched with perspiration. Having pulled in the trunk, he was now busy collecting the other sundry items of his baggage.

'I am a ticketholder. I am not travelling without tickets. There was no choice. A riot has broken out in the city. It was an awful job, reaching the railway station....'

All the passengers fell silent except the Pathan who was sitting on the upper berth. He leaned forward and shouted, 'Get out of here! Can't you see there is no room here?'

Suddenly he swung out his leg and kicked the man. Instead of hitting the man, his foot landed squarely on the wife's chest. She screamed with pain, and collapsed on the floor.

There was no time for argument. The sweet-vendor continued

to assemble his baggage into the compartment. Everybody was struck silent. After pulling in the heavy bundle he was struggling with the bars of a dismantled *charpoy*. The Pathan lost all patience.

'Turn him out, who is he anyway?' he shouted.

One of the other Pathans sitting on the lower berth got up and pushed the man's trunk out of the compartment.

In that silence only the old woman could be heard. Sitting in the corner, she muttered abstractedly, 'Good folk, let them come in. Come, child, come and sit with me. We shall manage to pass the time somehow. Listen to me. Don't be so cruel....'

The train began to move.

'Oh, the luggage! What shall I do about my luggage!' the man shouted, bewildered and nervous.

'*Pitaji*, half our luggage is still outside! What shall we do?' the girl cried out, trembling.

'Get down. Let's get down. There is no time,' the man shouted nervously, and throwing the big bundle out of the door, he caught hold of the door-handle, and hurried down. He was followed by his trembling daughter and his wife who still clutched at her chest and moaned with pain.

'You are bad people!' the old woman shouted. 'You have done a very bad thing. All human feeling has died in your hearts. He had his young daughter with him. There is no pity in your hearts....'

The train left the deserted platform and steamed ahead. There was an uneasy silence in the compartment. Even the old woman had stopped muttering. No one had the courage to defy the Pathans.

Just then the *babu* sitting next to me touched my arm and whispered agitatedly, 'Fire! Look! There is a fire out there!'

By now the platform had been left far behind and all we could see was clouds of smoke rising from the leaping flames.

'A riot has started! That's why the people were running about on the platform. Somewhere a riot has broken out!'

The whole city was aflame. When the passengers realized what was happening, they all rushed to the windows to get a better view of the inferno.

*

There was an oppressive silence in the compartment. I withdrew my head from the window and looked about. The feeble-looking *babu* had turned deathly pale, the sweat on his forehead was making it glisten in the light. The passengers were looking at each other nervously. A new tension could now be felt between them. Perhaps a similar tension had arisen in each compartment of the train. The Sardarji got up from his seat and came over and sat down next to me. The two Pathans sitting on the lower berth climbed up to the upper berth where their compatriot was sitting. Perhaps the same process was on in other compartments also. All dialogue ceased. The three Pathans, perched side by side on the upper berth, looked quietly down. The eyes of each passenger were wide with apprehension.

'Which railway station was that?' asked someone.

'That was Wazirabad.'

The answer was followed by another reaction. The Pathans looked perceptibly relieved. But the Hindu and Sikh passengers grew more tense. One of the Pathans took a small snuff-box out of his waistcoat and sniffed it. The other Pathans followed suit. The old woman went on with her beads but now and then a hoarse whisper could be heard coming from her direction.

A deserted railway platform faced us when the train stopped at the next station. Not even a bird anywhere. A watercarrier, his water-bag on his back, came over to the train. He crossed the platform and began serving the passengers with water.

'Many people killed. Massacre, massacre,' he said. It seemed as though in the midst of all that carnage he alone had come out to perform a good deed.

As the train moved out again people suddenly began pulling down the shutters over the windows of the carriage. Mingled with the rattle of wheels, the clatter of closing shutters must have been heard over a long distance.

The *babu* suddenly got up from his seat and lay down on the floor. His face was still deathly pale. One of the Pathans perched above the others said mockingly: 'What a thing to do! Are you a man or a woman? You are a disgrace to the very name of man!' The others laughed and said something in Pushto. The *babu* kept silent. All the other passengers too were silent. The air was heavy with fear.

'We won't let such an effeminate fellow sit in our compartment,' the Pathan said. 'Hey *babu*, why don't you get down at the next station and squeeze into a ladies' compartment?'

The *babu* stammered something in reply, and fell silent. But after a little while he quietly got up from the floor, and dusting his clothes went and sat down on his seat. His whole action was completely puzzling. Perhaps he was afraid that there might soon be stones pelting the train or firing. Perhaps that was the reason why the shutters had been pulled down in all the compartments.

Nothing could be said with any sense of certainty. It may be that some passengers, for some reason or the other had pulled down a shutter and that others had followed suit without thinking.

*

The journey continued in an atmosphere of uncertainty. Night fell. The passengers sat silent and nervous. Now and then the speed of the train would suddenly slacken, and the passengers would look at one another with wide-open eyes. Sometimes it would come to a halt, and the silence in the compartment would deepen. Only the Pathans sat as before, unruffled and relaxed. They too, however, had stopped chatting because there was no one to take part in their conversation.

Gradually the Pathans began to doze off while the other passengers sat staring into space. The old woman, her head and face covered in the folds of her shawl, her legs pulled up on the seat, dozed off too. On the upper berth, one of the Pathans awoke took a rosary out of his pocket and started counting the beads.

Outside, the light of the moon gave the countryside an eerie look of mystery. Sometimes one could see the glow of fire on the horizon. A city burning. Then the train would increase its speed and clatter through expanses of silent country, or slow down to an exhausted pace.

Suddenly the feeble-looking *babu* peeped out of the window and shouted, 'We have passed Harbanspura!' There was intense agitation in his voice. The passengers were all taken aback by this outburst and turned round to stare at him.

'Eh, *babu*, why are you shouting?' the Pathan with the rosary said, surprised. 'Do you want to get down here? Shall I pull the

186

chain?' He laughed jeeringly. It was obvious that he knew nothing about the significance of Harbanspura. The location and the name of the town conveyed nothing to the Pathan.

The *babu* made no attempt to explain anything. He just continued to shake his head as he looked out of the window.

Silence descended on the passengers of the compartment once again. The engine sounded its whistle and slowed its pace immediately. A little later, a loud clicking sound was heard; perhaps the train had changed tracks. The *babu* peeping out of the window looked towards the direction in which the train was advancing.

'We are nearing some town,' he shouted. 'It is Amritsar.' He yelled at the top of his voice and suddenly stood up and, addressing the Pathan sitting on the upper berth, shouted, 'You son of a bitch, come down!'

The *babu* started yelling and swearing at the Pathan, using the foulest language. The Pathan turned round and asked, 'What is it, *babu*? Did you say something to me?'

Seeing the *babu* in such an agitated state of mind, the other passengers too pricked up their ears.

'Come down, *haramzade*. You dared kick a Hindu woman, you son of a ....'

'Hey, control your tongue, *babu*! You swine, don't swear or I'll pull out your tongue!'

'You dare call me a swine!' the *babu* shouted and jumped on to his seat. He was trembling from head to foot.

'No, no, no quarrelling here, 'the Sardarji intervened, trying to pacify them. 'This is not the place to fight. There isn't much of the journey left. Let it pass quietly.'

'I'll break your head,' ' the *babu* shouted, shaking his fist at the Pathan. 'Does the train belong to your father?'

'I didn't say anything. Everyone was pushing them out. I also did the same. This fellow here is abusing me. I shall pull out his tongue.'

The old woman again spoke beseechingly, 'Sit quietly, good folk. Have some sense. Think of what you are doing.'

Her lips were fluttering like those of a spectre, and only indistinct, hoarse whispers could be heard from her mouth.

The *babu* was still shouting, 'You son of a bitch, did you think you would get away with it?'

*

The train steamed into Amritsar railway station. The platform was crowded with people. As soon as the train stopped they rushed towards the compartments.

'How are things there? Where did the riot take place?' they asked anxiously.

This was the only topic they talked about. Everyone wanted to know where the riot had taken place. There were two or three hawkers, selling *puries* on the platform. The passengers crowded round them. Everyone had suddenly realized that they were very hungry and thirsty. Meanwhile two Pathans appeared outside our compartment and called out for their companions. A conversation in Pushto followed. I turned round to look at the *babu*, but he was nowhere to be seen. Where had he gone? What was he up to? The Pathans rolled up their beddings and left the compartment. Presumably they were going to sit in some other compartment. The division among the passengers that had earlier taken place inside the compartments was now taking place at the level of the entire train.

The passengers who had crowded round the hawkers began to disperse to return to their respective compartments. Just then my eyes fell on the *babu*. He was threading his way through the crowd towards the compartment. His face was still very pale and on his forehead a tuft of hair was hanging loose. As he came near I noticed that he was carrying an iron rod in one of his hands. Where had he got that from? As he entered the compartment he furtively hid the rod behind his back, and as he sat down, he quickly pushed it under the seat. He then looked up towards the upper berth and not finding the Pathans there grew agitated and began looking around.

'They have run away, the bastards! Sons of bitches!'

He got up angrily and began shouting at the passengers: 'Why did you let them go? You are all cowards! Impotent people!' But the compartment was crowded with passengers and no one paid any attention to him.

The train lurched forward. The old passengers of the compartment had stuffed themselves with *puries* and had drunk enormous quantities of water; they looked contented because the train was now passing through an area where there was no danger to their life and property. The new entrants into the compartment were chatting noisily. Gradually the train settled down to an even pace and people began to doze. The *babu*, wide awake, kept staring into space. Once or twice he asked me about the direction in which the Pathans had gone. He was still beside himself with anger.

In the rhythmical jolting of the train I too was overpowered by sleep. There wasn't enough room in the compartment to lie down. In the reclining posture in which I sat my head would fall, now to one side, now to the other. Sometimes I would wake up with a start and hear the loud snoring of the Sardarji who had gone back to his old seat and had stretched himself full length on it. All the passengers were lying or reclining in such grotesque postures that one had the impression that the compartment was full of corpses. The *babu* however sat erect, and now and then I found him peeping out of the window.

Every time the train stopped at a wayside station, the noise from the wheels would suddenly cease and a sort of desolate silence descend over everything. Sometimes a sound would be heard as of something falling on the platform or of a passenger getting down from a compartment, and I would sit up with a start.

*

Once when my sleep was broken, I vaguely noticed that the train was moving at a very slow pace. I peeped out of the window. Far away, to the rear of the train, the red lights of a railway signal were visible. Apparently the train had left some railway station but had not yet picked up speed.

Some stray, indistinct sounds fell on my ears. At some distance I noticed a dark shape. My sleep-laden eyes rested on it for some time but I made no effort to make out what it was. Inside the compartment it was dark, the light had been put out some time during the night. Outside the day seemed to be breaking.

I heard another sound, as of someone scraping the door of the compartment. I turned round. The door was closed. The sound was repeated. This time it was more distinct. Someone was knocking at the door with a stick. I looked out of the window.

There was a man there; he had climbed up the two steps and was standing on the footboard and knocking away at the door with a stick. He wore drab, colourless clothes, and had a bundle hanging from his shoulder. I also noticed his thick, black beard and the turban on his head. At some distance, a woman was running alongside the train. She was barefooted and had two bundles hanging from her shoulders. Due to the heavy load she was carrying, she was not able to run fast. The man on the footboard was again and again turning towards her and saying in a breathless voice: 'Come on, come up, you too come up here!'

Once again there was the sound of knocking on the door.

'Open the door, please. For the sake of Allah, open the door.'

The man was breathless.

'There is a woman with me. Open the door or we shall miss the train....'

Suddenly I saw the *babu* get up from his seat and rush to the door.

'Who is it? What do you want? There is no room here. Go away.'

The man outside again spoke imploringly: 'For the sake of Allah, open the door, or we shall miss the train.'

And putting his hand through the open window, he began fumbling for the latch.

'There's no room here. Can't you hear? Get down, I am telling you,' the *babu* shouted, and the next instant flung open the door.

'Ya Allah!' the man exclaimed, heaving a deep sigh of relief.

At that very instant I saw the iron rod flash in the *babu's* hand. He gave a stunning blow to the man's head. I was aghast at seeing this; my legs trembled. It appeared to me as though the blow with the iron rod had no effect on the man, for both his hands were still clutching the door-handle. The bundle hanging from his shoulder had, however, slipped down to his elbow.

Then suddenly two or three tiny streams of blood burst forth and flowed down his face from under his turban. In the faint light of the dawn I noticed his open mouth and his glistening teeth. His eyes looked at the *babu*, half-open eyes which were slowly closing, as though they were trying to make out who his assailant was and for what offence had he taken such a revenge. Meanwhile the darkness had lifted further. The man's lips fluttered once again and between them his teeth glistened. He seemed to have smiled. But in reality his lips had only curled in terror.

The woman running along the railway track was grumbling and cursing. She did not know what had happened. She was still under the impression that the weight of the bundle was preventing her husband from getting into the compartment, from standing firmly on the footboard. Running alongside the train, despite her own two bundles, she tried to help her husband by stretching her hand to press his foot to the board.

Then, abruptly, the man's grip loosened on the door-handle and he fell headlong to the ground, like a slashed tree. No sooner had he fallen than the woman stopped running, as though their journey had come to an end.

The *babu* stood like a statue, near the open door of the compartment. He still held the iron rod in his hand. It looked as though he wanted to throw it away but did not have the strength to do so. He was not able to lift his hand, as it were. I was breathing hard; I was afraid and I continued staring at him from the dark corner near the window where I sat.

Then he stirred. Under some inexplicable impulse he took a short step forward and looked towards the rear of the train. The train had gathered speed. Far away, by the side of the railway track, a dark heap lay huddled on the ground.

The *babu's* body came into motion. With one jerk of the hand he flung out the rod, turned round and surveyed the compartment. All the passengers were sleeping. His eyes did not fall on me.

For a little while he stood in the doorway undecided. Then he shut the door. He looked intently at his clothes, examined his hands carefully to see if there was any blood on them, then smelled them. Walking on tiptoe he came and sat down on his seat next to me.

The day broke. Clear, bright light shone on all sides. No one had pulled the chain to stop the train. The man's body lay miles behind. Outside, the morning breeze made gentle ripples across the ripening wheat.

The Sardarji sat up scratching his belly. The *babu*, his hands behind his head, was gazing in front of him. Seeing the *babu* facing him, the Sardarji giggled and said, 'You are a man with guts, I must say. You don't look strong, but you have real courage.

The Pathans got scared and ran away from here. Had they continued sitting here you would certainly have smashed the head of one of them....'

The *babu* smiled—a horrifying smile—and stared at the Sardarji's face for a long time.

Translated from Hindi by the author

Sunil Gangopadhyay

Shah Jahan and His Private Army

Suddenly one day a huge commotion broke out in the market-place at Gajipur. The sweet potato-sellers were forever sparring with the pumpkin-vendors on the choicest spots to set up shop, and from time to time things would rise to a feverish pitch. This time there was really more smoke than fire. So people yelled their heads off, while others gave vent to long nourished curses; there was plenty of pushing and shoving, and a few even went so far as to brandish sticks in threat of yet greater violence. But it was just one lone head that caught the blow of any of the sticks. And whose would that have been, besides Hazu's? Hazu sold neither sweet potatoes nor pumpkins; it was simply his nature to be in the middle of whatever was happening, no matter what.

Startled by the blood pouring out of the open wound on Hazu's head, the two warring factions stopped their quarrel at once and practically stumbled over each other in their rush to reach him. And what cries of lamentation they raised! As for Hazu, knocked on the head by someone's stick and thrown on the ground, he did not utter a sound. Cradling his sore head in his arms, he shot quick glances from side to side like a terrified wild animal. He acted as if the mistake was all his. And so, indeed, it might have been, for no sooner had the waves of pity rolled over him, when all and sundry began their abuses 'What were you doing anyway, sticking your head under flying sticks?'

Such had always been Hazu's luck. It was as if disaster courted him. There had been the incident right there in the marketplace at Gajipur when someone had given the tail of a bull a good twist and let it go. Straightaway it had made for Hazu, butted him with all its might and knocked him over. Everyone else had escaped without so much as a scratch. And then, way back even before the bull, Hazu had once gone to the lake to gather some edible grasses when a water mocassin had sunk its fangs into him. Needless to say, it was the very first time anyone in Gajipur had ever been bitten by such a snake.

You must be wondering by now what Hazu was doing wandering around the marketplace at Gajipur in the first place, and well might you ask. After all, he had nothing to sell and nothing to buy. The truth was that he was roaming around there for no good reason whatsoever. He wore a dark cloth, wrapped around him in the fashion of a sarong and an undershirt and he was still straight, which no doubt accounted for the impression that his arms and legs were far too long for the rest of him. He shaved just about once a week or so. Even odder, he had the habit of fixating on a face in the crowd, stranger's, friend's and just staring at it. Mind you, that is not to imply that there was anything importunate about his glaring; on the contrary, he seemed to want nothing from the world around him.

The marketplace at Gajipur was hardly a saintly place. Plenty of money changed hands there, always giving the vultures something to keep their eyes on. Nor was there any shortage of people ready and willing to cause friction between the Hindus and Muslims or instigate more serious trouble between them. Though the petty shopkeepers were mostly Hindus, their suppliers were Muslim. The latest local official was a Muslim, Sheik Anwar Ali, but his defeated rival, the Hindu, Visnu Sikdar, still had enough power. With all of this, the peace in the marketplace hung on a slender thread which could snap at the slightest pull.

It needed a clever man to make his way in such a setting, and even the smartest of men still needed something behind them, if not the power of a mighty mouth, then the power of muscle, and if neither of these, then at least the power of money. Hazu had none of these. Nor did he seem to be endowed with much commonsense. He knew neither how to ask something of another person nor how to give. When he had been just a bit younger, he could be seen to spend his days in a deserted field, perched atop a palm tree he had climbed, staring intently into the sky. As the sun set and a part of the heavens would sink into a sea of red, Hazu seemed to discover some particular meaning in all that splendour. There were even those who went so far as to wonder whether the boy would grow up to be some kind of a sage or a holy man.

And then one day Hazu fell out of his palm tree. That was the last of his sky-gazing from his lofty perch; from then on he had to content himself with staring into the reflection of the red sky in the waters of the irrigation channel.

When Hazu got his head split open that fateful day in the marketplace of Gajipur, his uncle's friend Mozammel Ganda made a poultice of leaves to apply to the wound. Then, pressing a cigarette into Hazu's hand, he asked, 'Think hard now. Who was it that hit you? Did you get a good look at him?'

Hazu Sheik just shook his head from side to side, 'No, uncle Mozammel.'

Mozammel shot him a look of contempt as he went on, 'Who says you're good for nothing? You stopped the fighting with that broken head of yours, at least. Who knows otherwise how far things might have gone. Go, go home.'

Puffing on his cigarette, Hazu set off for home. Mozammel's comments had not made the slightest impression on him. His head still smarted, and a stream of blood continued to trickle down his neck onto his back where it stained his undershirt red.

Hazu walked across the irrigation channel, dried out in the cold season, and ambled slowly across the field. No one had ever seen him walk any faster; everything in his life was governed by the same sluggish rhythm. That was the way God had made him; who was he to protest? And so he walked on underneath the afternoon sky, which he watched as it spread its shadow around him.

Though the son of a *mullah*, Hazu was as useless as a sterile cow to a Hindu homestead. There was not a thing he could do: not work in the fields, not work around the lakes, not even the simplest of household chores. At one time his incompetence had been the occasion for more than one sound thrashing from his uncle and father, but finally they had given up on him. For Hazu was not shirking; he really could not do a thing. Even when he was sent out to the fields to weed, all he did was squat there with the scythe in his hand, staring in silence at the weeds. It might have seemed that he was steeped in profound meditation, when the fact that he was completely and utterly emptyheaded was closer to truth.

Still, Hazu's life had followed the normal course; he too had been married off when his time had come. He had fathered four sons. But Hazu was not quite the husband other men were, nor quite the father, either. None of his sons paid him any heed and they always used a surly tone whenever they spoke to him. His wife, Sayeda, was a born complainer; she bickered and grumbled from morning till night, and when her mouth was dry from all her yapping she would just give out. Hazu did not seem to take much note of any of this; he neither got wary nor smartened up. He just stayed where he had always been.

Just before he reached home Hazu stopped to wash his feet in the lake. Slowly, deliberately, he rubbed the sole of one foot against the other. He hadn't the slightest cause for hurry; all he would do anyway until nightfall was to sit on the verandah and wait until someone brought him something to eat. Eating was in fact, the one thing Hazu seemed to care about; Hazu took real pleasure in food.

Nowadays Hazu did not always get his three square meals a day. When he was still a part of the larger extended family he would manage, by hook or by crook, to get whatever he wanted. Mothers somehow do seem to have an extra tenderness for skinny children, and Hazu's mother had felt an added twinge of concern for his son who did not seem to make his own way. It was a year now that his mother was gone; his father had died sometime before her. Hazu's eldest brother had broken away from the extended family and set up his own household, leaving Hazu unsure of how he would support his wife and children.

Sayeda was the first to notice. 'Do I see blood on your head?'

'Uh-huh. It is blood.'

'Now what have you done to yourself? Hm? Don't tell me you've gone and fallen again?' With each word Sayeda came one step closer and her voice grew louder and louder. Sayeda was strong and solidly built; to look at her you would never know that she had given birth to four children. She worked herself to death all day long, doing the work of two hefty men all by herself. And there was power enough in her tongue, too.

Hazu's eldest son was thirteen, though he had already learned to talk like an adult. He worked as a cowherd for one of the families in the village. Now he joined forces with his mother and added his own insults which he hurled at his father. One by one the other members of the household gathered until they were quite a crowd.

Hazu was calm and cool. He knew that this was just like any other day. They would all yell at him for a while and then eventually they would stop. The darkness of night would descend; jackals and nocturnal birds would cry, and then at last all would be still. Just like any other day . But Hazu had no inkling of the momentous change that was to shake his life this time.

It soon came out that Hazu had not, in fact, fallen and split his head open; someone had struck him with a stick. There were those present who were indifferent at that news; others were outraged and some just felt genuinely sorry for Hazu. They were all certain that a simple, kind soul like Hazu would never have done anything to deserve such a beating. But, alas, how strange are the ways of the world. It was, after all, Hazu who had got his head cracked open.

Hazu's hair was matted with blood in places. He listened to everything that was being said, though he revealed no change of emotion on his face. He bore no one any ill-will; he harboured no resentments. All he had to say was: 'Who knows why someone hit me. I felt this whack on the head and down I went. It's really not so bad, just a little blood, that's all.'

Sayeda's elder brother, Eklas had shown up earlier in the day and now heard Hazu's latest misadventure. Eklas himself had been burnt plenty in his own life; he had seen his share and he knew exactly how treacherous the world was these days for the innocent and unwary. He and Sayeda came from a village just two villages beyond Hazu's. Eklas had been living in the city for some time but kept his ties with home. His ears sharpened by his sojourn in the city, he seemed able to hear the village groan and creak as it crumbled into the dirt.

Eklas had just dropped in on his way back to the city, but see-ing how matters stood, he suddenly proposed that he would take Hazu to the city with him. In the city, he would make a man out of Hazu; besides, Hazu could work there and earn some-thing for himself.

At first no one even took Eklas seriously. Hazu was such a fool he was sure to get run over by a car in his first few days in the city. And as for his earning a living—well, that was hardly likely. After all, what did Hazu know how to do? Even in the vil-lage he had never been able to do a thing, and everyone knew that in the city it was dog eat dog.

Eklas had an answer to all these objections. Even a simpleton, he explained, would know enough to try to save himself from a burning house. And in the city, you might say, the house was always on fire. That would do the trick; Hazu would have to learn to save himself. And what was more, what use was the village to him anyway? After all this time in the village Hazu hadn't a penny to his name. In the city, even if he did nothing more than roll cigarettes, he could earn a good five rupees a day. No, no one went hungry in the city.

Hazu stared at Eklas's eyes taking it all in. He had no idea even what the city was. He had never gone outside the circle of villages that surrounded him, with Munsidanga on one side, Suleimanpur on the other, a total of eight or ten villages. And yet when Eklas turned to him to ask, 'Well then, Hazu, are you coming with me?' Hazu at once nodded his head and said yes.

They put off going until morning. Hazu bound his possessions in two coarse bundles; his face was radiant with smiles. Eklas assured Sayeda, 'Don't worry. I'll look after him. You'll see, in a month or two he'll be sending moneyorders to you.'

They had to walk as far as Adanghata before they could get a bus. It was a good seven miles. There was a new road made when they had dug the channel. It was a perfect morning. The sun was not too hot, and there was a light, refreshing breeze. Hazu sauntered along, watching the reflection of the sky in the irrigation channel. Eklas loved to talk; he kept up a steady stream of conversation, only half of which Hazu even heard. For Hazu seemed to be discovering for the first time the glory of the sky reflected in the shimmering water.

It was near Suleimanpur when Eklas turned to Hazu. 'Hey! Look over there. Down the field, Hazu, to the right.'

There was a procession coming from that direction, flags raised high. There must have been a good hundred-and-fifty people. They were shouting something, though from that distance Hazu and Eklas could not make out what it was. Another group had gathered on their side of the channel. They had their own flags, and sticks, shovels, and axes as well.

Eklas remarked, 'There'll be a real battle here today, I can tell you that. Come on, Hazu. Let's get going. We don't want to get mixed up in this one.'

But Hazu was by nature incapable of walking fast; anyway, he just stood there transfixed, staring at the procession with wide-open eyes. By now the procession had left the field and was making its way up the embankment, winding and twisting like a gargantuan serpent. Nearby was a bamboo bridge; clearly they intended to use it to cross the channel and then make for the open field. That was where the fight would start.

Hazu had been to Suleimanpur before but he'd never seen the bridge then. Now it held him fast; who has made it and why? Just for this very battle, perhaps?

Eklas quickened his steps. When he looked back he could see Hazu not far behind, but not moving. Hazu was concentrating on the procession with the same intense absorption he had for everything.

The people in the procession and those waiting in the field had begun their shouting not far from where Hazu was moored. Eklas retraced his steps and pulled the reluctant Hazu with him, yelling as they went, 'You idiot ! What are you staring at like that? I suppose you can't resist the chance to get your head busted again? Let's go. Come on.'

Eklas had to drag Hazu along. He did not dare stop until they were well past Suleimanpur, right by Ratan Agrawal's cold storage plant. Both of them were panting by this time and they needed a few seconds to catch their breath.

Eklas remarked, 'From what I saw, I bet there are already some corpses littering that field, may be five, may be even seven.'

And suddenly it seemed to Hazu that he could see exactly seven men right before his own eyes, some faces down and some faces up, all sprawled out back there on the field. And where there should have been crops he saw patches of blood.

Eklas interrupted his reverie. 'Do you know why men kill each other?'

Sayeda had always said that when Hazu was steeped in thought he looked exactly like a cow; with its faraway stare. So it was just then. Startled by Eklas's question Hazu could only answer, 'Oh, brother, you're asking the wrong man. What do I know of all that?'

'Why shouldn't you know? All you have to do is think about it a bit.'

'But I do think, plenty. You see, when I was just a baby a big *mullah* had said that I've nothing but burnt cowdung in this head of mine. That must be why I don't understand anything, don't you think?'

'That's rubbish. Now listen. People kill each other to stay

alive. If someone tries to kill you, you've got to lunge at him and kill him first. Otherwise you're a dead man.'

'But I've never so much as touched another person. Why would anyone want to kill me?'

'It's because you're such a fool. Come, let's get to Calcutta. You'll see, I'll make a man of you there.'

They cooled themselves off with a long drink from the tube-well in front of the cold storage plant. And then they started out again.

Eklas had rented a room on Darga Road, not far from Maulali.

There were some twelve to fourteen men living there in the two-storeyed mud-house. It was your typical city boarding-house; all the men had families back in the village. Here they cooked for themselves and were gone from morning to evening at their jobs.

With so many mouths to feed already, it was no problem to feed Hazu too, but they decided nonetheless that he should help in some way. At first they turned the kitchen over to him. But Hazu was hardly a cook; he not only burned the rice but was on his way to losing his hands as well. And he would sit there, just staring into the fire on the stove, as if he found in it a secret to behold.

Next they gave him all the dishes and the clothes to wash. When they got back in the evening, there were the dishes, piled up in the courtyard along with heaps of wet clothes. Hazu was just sitting there doing nothing. He seemed entranced as he stared into space or watched the water drip from the tap in a steady trickle.

Saiphulla, the leader among the boarders, worked as a mes-senger in a small claims court. He tended to take himself very seriously. Now after a hard day's work, to see Hazu like that was more than he could stand. He dashed at him and gave him a sharp box on the ears. 'You stupid idiot! You damn fool!'

Eklas was right there. He made his voice as grave as he could. 'I brought him here to make a man out of him, after all. And if it takes a few beatings, well, that's what it takes.'

And Hazu did grow up, practically overnight. That evening he washed all the dishes, and all the clothes. The whole time Saiphulla and Eklas stood guard; if Hazu so much as stopped moving a hand, they jabbed him in the back.

None of this bothered Hazu in the least. In fact he rather liked his new surroundings. Within a few short days he had managed to fit right in. All fourteen tenants of the boarding-house took turns teaching him to be a man. And if he happened to make a mistake at what he was doing, they would give him a sound thrashing. There were even a few in the group who were his son's age, but that did not stop them; they would grab Hazu by the neck and give him a good shove. Still, Hazu was happy there.

The house was empty during the afternoon, while the street outside teemed with life. Peddlers passed by with their varied wares. Hazu loved to sit on the verandah and watch them all go by.

There was a mosque in the neighbourhood which broadcast the morning and evening calls to prayer over a microphone. Hazu had never heard a microphone in a mosque before. It sent a thrill down his spine, as if the Great Lord on High were calling to him directly from heaven.

Once Hazu sat down to say his prayers he never wanted to get up again. Motionless, he would stare at the ground in front of him, hour after hour if he could. Naim or Kader would have to yank him up.

Eklas had promised his sister that he would find Hazu some work. And it was clear that Hazu could not stay dependent on others forever. There was a cigarette-rolling operation in the shanty town nearby. It took some doing, but Eklas got Hazu a job there. It was easy work, no big rush, no pressure, no heavy physical labour, not even the nuisance of having to listen to a boss complain. All Hazu had to do was stretch out comfortably in a corner of the room with a basket of tobacco fixings on his lap and roll cigarettes. The pay was six rupees per thousand cigarettes. Some people managed to finish fifteen hundred or two thousand cigarettes a day. But it would be enough for Hazu to do a thousand at first, even five hundred.

On his first day Hazu rolled five cigarettes. The next day he did seven. All the other workers teased him. From every corner of the room came their jeers, 'Well now, fine sir, you haven't fallen asleep have you?'

Hazu was not at all asleep. He was staring at the tobacco fixings, without so much as blinking an eye. He was completely bewitched by the aroma and the appearance of the tobacco, so much so that he could not move a muscle. Even after repeated scoldings Hazu never did roll more than ten cigarettes a day. The owner of the operation finally had to call Eklas and tell him that he could not keep a worker like that. He could not pay anyone who rolled a meager ten cigarettes a day.

Hazu was incapable of doing even the simplest of tasks that anyone else could do without thinking. Perhaps God had singled him out for some special work, of which Hazu was yet unaware.

The cigarette-rolling was not Hazu's last job. There were others that the men arranged for him, all to no avail.

Occasionally late at night Imtiyaz stopped by the boarding-house. He was a handsome fellow, a bit on the heavy side with a thick lush beard. Imtiyaz was an assistant cook in a big hotel. He and Saiphulla were from the same village. He enjoyed a good time and dropped in to amuse himself with his friends. And they were always glad to see him, for he never came empty handed. Imtiyaz always brought an ample pot filled with delicacies. There might be spiced rice, or chicken curry, ground goat meat or peas and chillies. No one even bothered to ask where he got all these dishes, whether they were stolen or just leftovers at the hotel.

Hazu had never eaten such food before, and he did so now with great relish. Imtiyaz took a liking to Hazu. He stuck up for him when the others got after him 'Shame on you. How many people like Hazu do you see these days, kind, innocent, simple? A man like that who doesn't even know what's good for himself, sure'll never stick his paws into anyone else's fancy fare.'

Saiphulla grumbled, 'Even if a thief crept in here in broad daylight our Hazu wouldn't stop him. He'd just stare at the culprit. He'd probably even decide he liked him.'

Imtiyaz gave a good laugh. 'These days, brother, it's not so easy to say who's the thief. Whatever, I'm going to get Hazu a job at my hotel.'

All of them were dumbstruck. Imtiyaz did not work in any ordinary hotel; he was part of a grand establishment where foreign ladies and gents stopped over and the rich from Delhi and Bombay came to stay. The hotel had a posh verandah; the very sight of it from afar took your breath away. Once Kader had got into a bit of a mess and had gone to the hotel to see Imtiyaz. The doorman had barred his way. No one was allowed out of the kitchen during working hours, and no outsiders were permitted to go in.

Many of the boarders had long been trying to get jobs at the hotel, knowing that there were always tips in addition to the set wages. So far Imtiyaz had not been able to do anything for them, and now he was going to get Hazu a job, just like that?

They all began to talk at once, when Saiphulla, as befit his status as the leader, gravely raised his hand to quiet them. He turned to Imtiyaz, 'You don't realize what you're saying. You'll ruin yourself. If you get that fool a job in the hotel, he'll break some of the things he touches, lose some more and destroy the rest. He'll piss in the guests' drinking water, and then you'll see if you don't lose your own job. A man who can't even roll cigarettes is not going to be able to do anything at all. Let him be, let him just stay here, minding his business. We can take care of him. He's one of God's creatures, useless as he is. We won't just abandon him.'

Even so, Imtiyaz was not about to give in. 'You don't have to worry about me. There's nothing to break in the job I'm going to get him. It's an easy job—the simplest job in the world.'

Kader interrupted him. 'Then in that case, why not give the job to one of us? I hear there's going to be a lock-out at the factory.'

Imtiyaz answered, 'You wouldn't be able to do it. Not everyone is fit for every job. The job I'm talking about is perfect for Hazu, but not for anyone else. All he has to do is stand at a certain spot and bow respectfully to the guests.'

At once Kader and Naim spoke up, 'He'll forget. He'll forget to bow.'

'And so what if he does forget a few times? It won't matter. No one will even notice. It'll do if he just stands there.'

Eklas turned to Hazu. 'What do you say, Hazu? Will you work at the hotel?'

Hazu nodded yes, without a minute's hesitation. It was as if he could already smell the intoxicating fragrance of all those delicious dishes, ground lamb patties, curried fish and meats, all sorts of marvellous concoctions.

Imtiyaz took it on himself to rush out and buy Hazu two pairs of pants and two long shirts at the Intali Bazaar. And then he escorted Hazu to the hotel.

In no time at all Hazu fell in love with his new job. It was an ideal job. He did not have to run around; there was no hard physical labour, not even a grumbling boss. And it was far easier than rolling cigarettes.

Hazu stood at attention along one wall of the glittering, white men's room on the first floor of the Hotel International. Whenever a gentleman pushed open the door he bowed low. And it goes without saying that no one ever really stopped to see if Hazu was bowing or not. Hazu listened as the streams of urine hit the bowl. Different gentlemen peed to different tunes, it seemed. Even the smells were distinctive. If a guest wanted to wash his hands at the sink, Hazu stepped forward with a towel and soap for him. Many of the guests did not bother with the soap and towels he held out; there were even some who did not stay to wash at all, but just hurriedly did their business and left.

Hazu was astounded at the luxury that surrounded him and all for a pissoir, not even a bath house. He could not help wondering if wise Saiphulla, with all his knowledge, would ever have guessed that people could make such a gorgeous room and only to answer the nature's call. The walls were so smooth that Hazu's eyes virtually glided down them. And the mirrors were so imposing. When there was nothing else for him to look at Hazu took to staring at himself in the mirrors.

Hazu was on duty from one in the afternoon till eleven at night. Except for two half-hour breaks, Hazu just stood there. He did not find the job at all onerous; being on his feet all that time did not bother him in the least. Finally he had found a refuge where he was free from taunts all day long.

None of the guests ever spoke to him. Many probably never even noticed him there. The occasional gentleman tossed him a few coins on the way out.

Things were quiet during the day. The guests did not really start to arrive until the evening. The hotel had two bars on the first floor, and as the night drew on and things got hopping, the door to Hazu's white room swung open more and more frequently.

Of course, Hazu had seen a few drunks in his lifetime. They sold palm liquor in the marketplace at Gajipur. Although it was true that Hazu himself never visited the toddy-shops, he had been there when some acquaintances had kicked up a row after drinking their fill. But the drunks at the hotel were an altogether different breed. There was no commotion, no rowdiness, no fighting. It was true that a gentleman might be unsteady on his feet; he might even talk busily to the wall or have a hard time buttoning up his pants, standing there rocking back and forth in his own steps. There was even the odd guest who got sick and threw up or the guest who stood in front of the mirrors seemingly unable to identify his own face as it stared back at him.

Through all of this Hazu remained like a statue, pressed close against the wall watching intently. He never even moved to help the sick guests. Imtiyaz had told him again and again never to say a word unless directly asked and never to approach anyone unless first summoned.

In the afternoon there was a pervasive odour of napthalene. As the day advanced other smells took over.

One night at quarter to ten two young men came into the men's room. Their eyes were red, their hair all tousled; they were clearly drunk.

By this time Hazu knew many of the regulars. He had never seen these two before. With every new face Hazu would watch all the more intently, listen all the more carefully, even though he never understood more than a fraction of what the guests said.

These two young men were poets. As a rule, not many poets came to the hotel, except for the rare occasion when a wealthy patron might invite his protégé.

One of the poets glared at the wall, as he muttered dejectedly, 'I can't stand it another minute. The longer I see him, the angrier I get.'

The second poet also addressed the wall. 'Who? That midget with the woman? He's just about talked my ears off. The next time he opens his stupid trap, I'm going to belt him one.'

'No, no, not him. I mean this stupid lavatory attendant. What's the use of making some poor fool stand in a pissoir all day long?'

'It's a legacy from the British. Another example of our disgusting servile imitation of all things British.'

'Do they still do such things in England?'

'They reserved all these repulsive practices for the colonies.'

'But this country's a Marwari colony now.'

The two poets made their way to the sink to wash their hands. One started to splash water on his face while the other stared at himself in the mirror.

Stone-faced, Hazu stood there with soap and towels.

Suddenly without warning one of the poets bellowed at him, 'Where are you from? Village? District?'

Frightened, his eyes like the eyes of a cow tethered to a post, Hazu just stood there. Startled by the unexpectedness of the question, he was at a loss for an answer.

But drunks can be strangely persistent. It now seemed that the man had to know where Hazu came from; without that information his drinking fun was over. And so the poet grabbed Hazu harshly under the chin and hollered at him, 'Why don't you answer me, huh? Where are you from?'

Trembling, Hazu replied, 'Gajipur, sir.'

'In what district?'

'Medinipur.'

'What's your name?'

'Hazu.'

'Hazu? What kind of a name is Hazu? I'm asking you for your real name, the name your mother called you.'

Everyone had called him Hazu ever since he was born. He did, of course, have another name. It was just that no one had used it all this time.

'Shahjan, sir.'

The poet was totally put off. 'That's a strange name. A strange name for a strange fellow, I guess. Did you ever hear of anyone called Shahjan before? Are you a Hindu or a Muslim?'

Hazu started to shake again. In a timid whisper came the answer, 'We're Muslims.'

At this time the second poet burst into gales of laughter. 'Don't you get it? Shah Jahan, hey, I mean Emperor Shah Jahan, Your Highness, who, pray tell, has taken you prisoner and locked you up in this pissoir? What happened to the fort at Agra?'

The first poet slapped his friend on the back. 'Let's go. Let's get out of this place. It's disgusting that we still follow such vile practices. I can't even go and give the manager a swift kick in the butt for it.'

'With five pegs of whisky in you, you'd probably like to, but tomorrow you won't give a damn. And what good would it do you anyway to kick the manager's butt? That'd just get you a kick for yourself when you show up at the door next time.'

'That may be, but one day I will kick his butt, you'll see.'

As he got to the door the second poet was swaying slightly on his feet. His speech was slurred as he said to Hazu, 'Prisoner, Emperor, once you were the sovereign ruler of all of Hindustan. Now you are a prisoner in this pissoir. Then again, perhaps this is your Taj Mahal. I bid you good-night.'

Nothing that either of the gentlemen said made any impression on Hazu. In fact, he had not understood much of it. Just the prattle of some drunks. For Hazu it was enough that they had not beaten him senseless or cracked his skull in two.

Nonetheless, the event left its mark. Not long after, another Bengali gentleman came in. Positioning himself and fumbling at his pants, he said, 'Hey, you, is your name really Shah Jahan? That's a good one if I've ever heard one.'

It looked as if the two poets were having a field day with his name back in the bar. Eventually they got so rowdy that they were asked to leave, but so it was that many guests came to learn of the name of the nonentity who worked in the men's room. From time to time someone would use it, yelling, 'Hey, Shah Jahan, give me a towel.'

Naturally it made no difference to Hazu that his name had become so famous. Plenty of times when the guests called him by name he could not understand what they were saying. They talked differently from Hazu's acquaintances and with a few drinks in them, some of them did not speak very clearly anyway.

Best of all, Hazu loved his afternoons. Except for Saturday and Sunday, there were days when no one at all came in between three and six. Hazu could have gone out then if he wanted to, but he never did. He just stood there, motionless, staring at the gleaming wall. For him there could be no more splendid sight in the world.

One afternoon he noticed a line of ants crawling down a wall. It was a long row of ants, all of them red, all of them marching in a strict single file, not one out of line. Hazu did not care what the ants were doing there on the bathroom wall or where they were going. It was just that the red ants against the white wall were so very beautiful. Hazu was mesmerized by them. He went on and on staring at them.

Suddenly Hazu remembered the procession he had seen in Suleimanpur when he was on his way to Calcutta with Eklas. It had followed the bank of the channel and then crossed a bridge to the other side. Now, didn't that look just like this?

Hazu wet his fingers under the faucet and drew a line of water on the wall. There, there was the channel. And the bridge. The water ran off the slippery wall. And so the next time Hazu used bigger water marks.

The row of ants suddenly stopped at the line of water. A few ants moved out in either direction at the front of the line, one or two then scurrying back as if to consult the rest.

Hazu was wonderstruck. Wasn't the procession of ants going to cross the bridge to the other side of the channel? Thrilled by the game, he whispered, 'My good little children, why go over there where the water is? What's the use of starting so much trouble? See, there's much room over here.'

He painted another water mark. The procession of ants turned around, taking another direction. Hazu had never been so happy in his entire life. They were listening to him. They were obeying him. Drawing line after line on the wall, Hazu continued, 'This way, this way.'

Translated from Bengali by Phyllis Granoff

Nirmal Verma

Deliverance

The schoolteacher was the first person I met in the small, neglected and remote town in the mountains. It was raining as I got down from the bus. In the last three hours I had travelled through three different types of weather: sunshine in Bhuvali, clouds over Ramgarh, and now the rain here. The bus had pulled up by the roadside in the middle of the town. My wretched luggage which I'd borne all the way from Delhi was hurled from the roof-carrier—an old hold-all that had belonged to my father and an outmoded tin trunk with torn labels from previous journeys still stuck on it like dead cockroaches.

I stood there by the roadside, my battered luggage soaked in its own poverty, around me. Rain has a way of stripping man and town of dignity. I clutched my briefcase to my chest not only because in that desolate place it seemed the only reminder of civilization and a symbol of my middle-class respectability but also for another reason: it contained the entire purpose of my journey, for which I'd left my home and come to this unfamiliar mountain town.

By and large, most small Indian towns can be very dreary and oppressive. Besides, it was cold and dark and raining. As the bus began to pull out, I was possessed by a mad longing to jump aboard and request the conductor to take me to Bhuvali and Haldvani on the way back to Delhi...to my secure familiar life, its light and warmth and safety. But the bus did not stop, nor did it turn back. It rattled away farther up the road. I watched it recede, its tail-lights like red splashes of blood across the sheet of rain.

I looked about me. There were some shops and cheap eating places across the road and, in the cliff behind them, three or four hollows, their darkness unrelieved by glimmering lanterns. In the lowest niche close to the bus-shelter was a tea-stall. Under its burlap awning sat some men on benches. I held my briefcase over my head like an umbrella, but my trunk and hold-all were in bad shape. Soaking in the rain on the roadside, they presented a sight more piteous than I.

As I looked at the group in the tea-shop I hoped someone would take pity on me. Perhaps I remained unnoticed behind the wall of rain: it seemed to have screened me off from the rest of the world. The few passengers who had disembarked with me had long since disappeared into the darkness.

Suddenly I saw an umbrella hovering in front of me as though unable to make up its mind whether I was a man of flesh and blood or a ghost. A hillman's lean face peered out from under it.

'Is that your luggage?' he asked, pointing to my trunk and hold-all on the ground.

'Yes,' I said miserably.

'Where do you have to go?'

'Isn't there a hotel near by?' I almost whined in my helplessness.

'A hotel? In this place?' He looked at me incredulously, as if I longed to reach heaven without having to die.

'Any place where I could stay?'

'How long?' A faint curiosity was reflected in his eyes.

At a loss for a ready answer, I just stared back at him. When I left home I had not thought in terms of days or weeks. Before I could say anything, he held his umbrella partly over me.

Formerly, I alone was getting wet; now, sharing the single umbrella, he also got drenched.

'There is a rest-house some three kilometres from here, but you will have to climb all the way.'

'Can I get a coolie?'

'In this weather?' His eyes took in the row of shops before returning reflectively to me. He picked up my trunk by its handle.

'Come with me,' he said.

He strode away without waiting for me. It was too late to ask him to stop. I had no option but to grab my hold-all and follow him. It was surprising how a man as thin as he was could walk so fast with a trunk in one hand and an umbrella in the other.

The bus-stand and the shops fell behind as we continued to climb. It was hard to keep pace with him. It seemed as if I was being dragged along behind him. Now and then my shoes got stuck in squelching mud and submerged potholes. Once he turned round and said something which I could not catch. I could only listen to the pounding of my heart, which got worse with each step. Sweat mingled with rain as it washed down my face.

Now when I think of that arduous climb I'm surprised I could make it at all, so soon after a tiring journey and despite a gnawing feeling of uneasiness. So far, I had only climbed in years, never a mountain. Indeed, mountain climbing isn't easy for a man whose biological alarm clock begins to clamour midway up a flight of stairs. For the first time in my life, much against my will, I had set foot in a town where I was a complete stranger. Had it been left to me, I wouldn't have crossed my threshold to come all the way here. I had no choice in the matter. The choice had been made by the person whom I had come to find.

*

He opened the door. 'Here we are,' he said.

It was so dark inside I could see nothing. I lingered in the doorway, trying to keep out of the rain. Soon there was a scraping and the flash of a burning matchstick as he lighted a hurricane lamp. Only then did I realize that he had not brought me to a *dharmshala*, hospice, or even a lodge, but to his own place. I hesitated at the door. A blast of wind pushed me inside.

Is there such a thing as will? Perhaps it is one of man's fondest illusions. Even as our will strikes out ahead, we lag behind, dragged along somehow. Our will goes on, cleaving us into several parts. One part of me was left behind at home and the other, powerless to move, stood inside the open door, shivering in the rain-soaked draught——while yet another watched on helplessly. The schoolteacher led me to his room in much the same way as the wind had blown me in. I had no say in the matter.

'Please, sit down,' he said, indicating his low-slung bed which, besides a stool, was the only piece of furniture in the room. He pulled up the stool and started to unfasten the laces of his sodden, muddy shoes.

'I'd asked you to take me to a hotel,' I said irritably.

'Come on now! Take this for a hotel room, if it helps any. Tell me, where would you go in this weather?' he said with a laugh. His laughter, the mean walls swaying in the lantern flame, my body spattered with mud—did any of this make sense? Of course, it had to make sense or I wouldn't be here, I told myself. I closed the door behind me on wind, rain and darkness, and walked into the room.

At a first glance it looked like a hovel, dank and gloomy, suspended in air, open to vagrant clouds which could enter at will, although the fumes of smoke within seemed reluctant to leave. It gave on to what looked like a godown where a kerosene stove on a wooden slab and some utensils could be seen. Evidently, he cooked his food there. In another corner were a pail of water, a brass mug and a low slatted seat, which meant it also served as a bathing place. There was a barred window in a wall strung with his washing, hung out to dry under the eaves; of course, now it was dripping wet.

He was lighting the stove, his back towards me; but he kept an eye on me to make sure I wouldn't give him the slip. I am not a heavy man but I sank so deep in his low cot that my bottom was almost scraping the dust on the floor.

He brought tea in glasses and squatted down cross-legged on a mat opposite me.

'This is your first time out here, isn't it?' he asked.

'Yes.'

'I could tell it the moment I saw you.'

I looked into his sallow face behind the plume of steam spiralling up from the tea in his hand.

'It wasn't hard to tell,' he continued. 'When you got down from the bus you kept standing there by the roadside in the rain. Anyone from this town would have hurried away at once.' He laughed, displaying yellow, but not dirty, teeth. His teeth went well with his pale, weather-beaten face.

'We have very few tourists around this time of the year,' he observed after a pause. He regarded me with rippling curiosity, as if he expected, at the mention of tourists, I'd confide in him the reason for my visit in this bad weather. I kept silent. I had already made a mistake in coming here with him. I did not wish to make another.

'How long have you been living here?' I asked, parrying his implied question.

'Five...no, six years.' He placed his glass on the floor and counted on his fingertips. 'I came to this place in the year when Shastriji died in Tashkent. I remember hearing the sad news here in a hospital bed.'

'You were hospitalized at that time?' I said as if offering my sympathy.

'My uncle, who was a doctor at the hospital, brought me over for medical treatment, although there was no dearth of physicians at Almora where I lived. Anyway, when I was up and about again I learned that the local high school had a vacancy for an English teacher. I got the job.' He smiled. 'I'd come here for a cure, little knowing it would solve my problem of unemployment also.'

'So you don't belong here? This isn't your own house?'

'Would you call this shack a house?' His eyes flitted mournfully across the room to the bucket in the corner, the stove on a plank, the wan lantern flame, and back to me buried in the bed: all objects of pity.

'Are you cold? Shall I make a fire?'

'No, please don't bother,' I said. 'I'm fine.' I was fine if fine meant growing numb, so numb that even fatigue fell back in despair. I could only see things on the surface—a rainy night, a leaking roof; but deep down inside, I felt nothing. He was upset at my aloofness, my lack of response, and probably felt guilty for bringing me to this place.

'There is a forest rest-house here, you know,' he offered helpfully.

'You have to have official permission to stay there, don't you?'

'That's true,' he agreed. 'But the caretaker isn't so fussy if one wishes to stay for only a day or two.... How long will you need to stay anyway?'

There was no hint of inquisitiveness in his tone this time. All he wanted was to be of help. His gaze rested on me, steady and even.

I could have confided in him then and there. I suspected he had already figured out that I was neither a pilgrim nor a tourist. Who was I? What was I doing here? I was suddenly overcome with despair and weariness. In order to make sense of what I had to say I'd have to go into my family history. I doubted if even then he would understand the compulsion of my visit.

I'm not sure what he saw in my face in the pale half-light. Was it the desperation of middle-age or something else?

213

Whatever it was he did not persist. He went to collect his dripping clothes and wring them in a corner of the kitchen.

Left to myself, I heaved a sigh of relief. I rolled out my bedding on the floor. The lantern was kept on a tripod by my head. In its yellow light I took out a sheaf of papers from my briefcase. I wanted to look them over one last time. I was like a student preparing for his examination who suddenly discovers that his notes are in a mess, devoid of meaning, worthless. The paper of the property deed left by father was already fusty and brittle with age. The deed itself looked all the more forlorn in the dimly-lit room. Among its pages were three letters, one from my recluse brother and another from our younger sister, both easily distinguishable by the handwriting on them. The third was folded and rather crumpled. Mother had sneaked it to me before I left for the bus terminus, and I'd hurriedly thrown it among my papers. I did not know what words had been used by mother whose lips quiver as she writes. I still had not read her letter nor did I want to. In the feeble light the letters of the living appeared as dead as the dead property papers bequeathed by a dead father. If I held out the sheaf of papers over the stove, our house and all the family, the pulls and pressures of relationships among the living and between the living and the dead, would instantly be consumed by the flames.... Only I would survive— and he, who I had come this far to see.

The schoolmaster's shadow fell across the papers in my hand. He was standing at the door of the kitchen, his hands wet, the sleeves of his shirt folded up above the elbows.

'Are you preparing to contest a lawsuit?' He smiled at me.

I returned the papers to the briefcase. He was right, in a way. I had to face the hearing tomorrow—after ten full years; I was seized with an insane desire to seek him out at once to get it over with and catch the morning bus back to Delhi. The schoolteacher broke in on my reverie, 'You should wash up. I've heated the water.'

*

I spent the night at the schoolmaster's. I had with me my own bedding, so it was not a problem; but he became insistent about who should occupy the cot. He insisted on sleeping on the floor himself and letting me have the privilege. I didn't have the heart to tell him that to me his rickety cot would perhaps only ensure a night full of hallucinations of earthquakes. I might yet have to endure one: I was afraid he would create a scene over the question of meals. My wife had packed my tiffin-box to last me a lifetime. I suggested to him that instead of cooking for the night we should do justice to the tiffin together. Owing to the cold weather, the food had not spoiled despite the twelve-hour journey. The food had the flavour of intimacy, concern and care of a distant household. When he saw the containers full of fried *puries*, pickle, vegetables and seasoned rice *pulao*, a wistful look swept over his face—as if he regretted having taken pity on one who apparently did not deserve it. He said nothing and left to warm up the food on the stove.

His room was as untidy as the kitchen was clean. Books covered with layers of dust and old magazines lay in a pile on the floor. The ceiling was black with soot. A discoloured cupboard stood against a wall, its drawers half-closed with his garments peeping out over their edges. On the whole, it looked as untended and cheerless as a room in a *dharmshala*. It must be terribly lonely for him to have to live in it all alone the year round. Maybe he had brought me along because he was too lonely. I wasn't surprised that he knew nothing about me. What was surprising was that having taken me in he should choose not to ask me who I was and where I had come from. I had a nagging suspicion that perhaps he already knew everything. That would explain why he had gone to meet the bus in such rain. Who could have told him to expect me—except the one whom I had come to see?

'Dinner is ready,' he announced, setting out a tray. 'Hurry up! It will get cold in a minute.'

'Won't you eat also?'

'I eat early in the evening before going out for my walk. It ensures sound sleep....Please, go ahead.'

He seated himself on a mat opposite me. As I ate, a vague sadness overtook me. My thoughts went to my family. By this time my wife must have gone downstairs to see mother, leaving the children to do their studying in their rooms. From this distant stark place, they might as well have been creatures from another planet. It was hard to believe we had all been together twelve

215

hours ago.

'Look, it has stopped raining. We'll have a clear day tomorrow.' He sounded as excited as a child.

My hand stopped short of my mouth as I turned to look. Little rivulets were still sloshing down outside from the sloping tin roof. There was a thin mist beyond the eaves through which the stars shone as if scrubbed clean by rain.

'Is your school nearby?'

'I forgot to tell you. In fact, we are sitting in the outbuilding of the school yard.'

'Don't tell me!' I looked around in amazement.

'Well, this room is a part of the school premises. The management let me move in because it had no other accommodation to offer.... Anyway, the school is closed at present for winter holidays.'

'Don't you go someplace during the holidays?'

'I don't really like to. However, I do go down to Almora once in a while.'

'Don't you feel lonely here?'

He was silent for a long moment. Then he said thoughtfully: 'In a way, yes. Sometimes. Still, I think I'm better off here than at Almora. Besides, if I feel like it, I can always go over to the *baba's*.'

'*Baba*...who's he?'

He threw me a searching glance. A thin little smile formed on his lips. 'There is but one holy man here.'

I could no longer restrain myself. 'Did he tell you anything about me?'

'About you?' He was obviously baffled.

'About my coming here.'

'Why, have you come to see him?' He looked genuinely surprised.

'I hear people come from far-off places to receive his blessings.'

'In this kind of weather?' He stared at me sceptically.

'I'd some leave to spare. I thought this was as good a time as any to visit him.... Does he live far from here?'

He sat brooding for a while. 'Not very far,' he said rather indifferently. 'Maybe a little over a kilometre uphill.'

It seemed he was annoyed. Perhaps he did not believe me, for one had to be a little crazy to come all the way in this weather to a little-known town tucked away in the mountains to see a local guru.

Later he gathered the dirty plates and took them into the corner where the pail of water was kept. For long afterwards the only sounds that filled the room were the clanging and clatter of plates and the splashing of water.

We did not talk about the holy man the rest of the night. Nor about anything else. We prepared for bed in silence. He did offer me his cot again but I'd already made my bed on the floor. As he was settling in with a novel, he spoke briefly to ask if I'd mind his keeping the light on.

In my long life, it was the first night I'd spent at a stranger's. I lay down, my head pillowed on my briefcase, and tried to sleep, but it was difficult. In my sleeplessness, the sombre night seemed to have ripped me from my family and my job. Had my wife been told that I would have to put up at a schoolmaster's my first night away from home, she wouldn't have believed it. She had always looked upon me as an incorrigible stay-at-home. Her one regret was that I had never once taken her on a holiday. Travelling for me had always been brief trips on work. I had never taken leave to go to a place of pilgrimage or a hill station.

This place was neither a place of pilgrimage nor a hill station. Set in the mountains, it could only boast of a veterinary hospital and a Shiva temple where he lived... where he still lives. When a person walks out of our lives, we quickly take our vengeance and relegate him to the past. We refuse to accept that he exists in his own present, outside and independent of our time.

I could not get to sleep till late into the night. The wind lashed at the walls and shook the roof. Whenever a bus passed by on the road below, shadows of trees conjured by its headlights swept along the wall. The hiss of the bus tyres on the wet road lingered in the air. Once, as a bus passed below, the schoolteacher raised his head off the pillow, squinted at the clock, sighed deeply, and said, 'This bus is bound for Bhuvali,' and again when another bus approached, blowing its horn, 'This is going to Ramnagar.' Eyes closed, I pretended to sleep—until the pretense was overtaken by sleep and I was dragged into a dream. When I woke up again, it was after midnight. The lamp had been put out and the room was submerged in darkness. For a moment, I couldn't place where I was or who this man was, sleeping on the cot, turned over on his side.

*

When I came awake in the morning I found an oblong patch of sunlight waiting at the bedside. A cool, bright day filled the room. The cot was empty. The tea-things lay on the floor round the stove. A breeze knocked and thumped outside.

The clock, unbelievably, read ten; I could not recall ever having overslept this long before. I washed up hurriedly, put my thermos and tumbler away, and riffled through the sheaf of papers which included a postcard he—my estranged brother—had written to me a fortnight ago. I went out to look for the schoolteacher.

He wasn't there. Instead, what hit my eyes was a stately mountain.

The mountain rose solid and rugged into the air, rooted firmly in the rocky ground, unmoving, real— so unlike yesterday's mountains that had cartwheeled at a distance as the bus sped by. It soared above the town nestling in its shade. The rain and the darkness had concealed it from me at night. Now, this instant, I awoke fully to its splendour. I was right here. This was not just another wayside town but my final destination: a world complete in itself, isolated but not lost in a dense forest—contrary to what we had imagined back at home: a self-sustaining town, it had a shopping centre, a bus-station, a hospital, a temple, a high school....

The school stood on flat ground. Yellowish clumps of trees sprinkled the town spread out above and below the shopping area. In a tree some way down below, I caught a glimpse of the schoolteacher with an axe in his hands... and then the mystery of the thwacking-thumping sounds that had woken me cleared up: the axe in his hand rose and fell rhythmically on the branches, which plopped down with a swishing rustle.

I set out downhill on the road we had come up yesterday. Soon the sunlit grey roof-stones of the shops below came into view. Smoke from the cooking fires in the sheds and the market noises floated up towards me. I went over to sit on a bench which was in the open, in front of the eating-places buzzing with flies. It was cold despite the sun: the sun merely cast a web of illusion over the ineluctable reality of cold. I ordered tea.

'Only one tea, Sahibji?'

I turned to gaze into a pair of drugged bloodshed eyes which were fastened on me. He was a holy man, stark naked but for a loincloth, lazing on a bench on which he was sitting. 'You're staying with the schoolteacher?' He came over to sit next to me on my bench.

I could do no more than mumble 'Yes,' to his question-statements. I thought he had an uncanny gift of reading one's mind. Were he to tell me that I had fathered two children and had come from Delhi, I wouldn't have been surprised. But he did not speak another word. His attention was rivetted to the tea in his hands.

'Where are you coming from?' I ventured to ask him later.

He set his empty glass on the bench and wiped his flowing beard on the crook of his elbow.

'Ask me where I am going. I am here only for a few days.' His red-streaked eyes reflected a carefree unconcern.

'Where have you set up camp, *baba*?'

For a moment I thought his little finger was raised heaven-wards but, mercifully, it came to rest short of the heavens and pointed to a summit beginning to emerge from the shimmering morning mist.

'Isn't that where the Shiva temple is?' I could not repress the flutter of excitement and curiosity that the temple aroused in me.

'Don't you call it Shiva temple! Call it Mahakal temple.' He threw me a glance of derision and reproach. 'Haven't you been here before?'

'This is my first visit.'

'The first? Are you sure?' He laughed aloud. 'How can you be so sure you haven't seen all this before somewhere? No, no! There is no first time.'

'I'm also seeing you for the first time.'

'Really?' he said, his sly eyes on me. 'And that thing over there?' He pointed to a swaying pine tree that climbed straight up from a ditch across the road.

'Why, that's a tree.' I was intrigued. 'What's there in it?'

'And what's there in me?' He pulled a *beedi* out from under his skimpy cloth and lit it on a live coal from a burning log in the mud and stone oven. 'What do you see in me?'

Acrid smoke curled lazily upwards from the glowing end of his *beedi*.

I ran my eyes over his naked body. All his bones stood out, gleaming in the bleached winter sun: a skeleton bound in coarse brown skin which withstood the cold without a shiver or goose-flesh but provided warmth to what it held together.... No, I had never seen this man before, but seeing him, I was reminded of the bundle of bones and ashes of my father I'd carried for immersion from Delhi to Kankhal. Had the jostling, rumbling train coach somehow put the bones together, the reconstituted form could well have resembled the live skeleton before me...and then it struck me that even if one had not seen a certain man before, the latter could still bring back to life another who was once alive and was now dead. What I was seeing in him was not the man who sat so placidly beside me on the bench but a reflection of another long since dead.

'Are you on a sight-seeing trip?' His watery eyes held me.

I kept silent.

He moved closer to me. 'You must have come for a *darshan* of the *baba*. Am I right?'

'Well,' I stared at him.

'Do you know the way?' He spoke very softly. 'He lives on the way to the temple. Go up the rock steps until you come to a track. Turn and follow it; it will lead you straight to him.'

'Will it be possible to see him now?'

'You can try. It should be no problem unless he has retired to his cell. If he is inside, don't disturb him. He is not keeping well.'

'Is he ill?'

There must have been something in my voice which irked him. 'Illness is all a part of life. The body is vulnerable.'

What he said gave me no cause for worry. I was a little surprised that he had not written a word about the illness in his letter to me. Was he afraid I would have brought our mother along? I laughed to myself at his fear. How could mother, who could not even climb the stairs in our house, have withstood the rigours of a day-long bus journey to a height of 2100 metres?

I rose to my feet without a word. The *aghori baba* looked up. 'What, leaving already!'

'How long will it take to reach there?'

'It will take a lifetime,' he smiled. 'But if you don't lose the way, you might make it in half-an-hour.'

I filled my thermos with drinking water from the tea-shop. As I took out my wallet to pay for the two glassfuls of tea, the *baba* said, 'Make it for three. I'll take another.' I did not even turn round but paid up and took the road uphill.

The mountainside inclined steeply upwards like a raised palm. There were trees all around but none beside the track to give shade. Before long, sweat ran down my body like a mountain stream. In addition to my fear of high blood pressure, the loud pounding of my heart rattled my ribs.

The market noises and the honking of buses carried up here sleepily. Then even these sounds were lost...and I found myself all alone—not a single man around, or animal, not even air. It struck me that even if I were to keep going up and up, the track would never come to an end—nor would I: I'd be struggling upwards forever, bathed in sweat, seeing nothing, my mind blank, my feet refusing to give a damn if I was exhausted.

Up ahead, the road forked into three prongs, like three outstretched fingers of an upraised hand. A sign mounted on a tree at the junction, pointing along the near right-hand path, bore an arrow in white chalk piercing through a four word legend: *To The Forest Rest-house*. I remembered the finger of the *aghori baba* aimed skywards at the Mahakal temple. If the right-hand path went off to the rest-house, the middle one could only lead to the temple. I headed up the middle path.

Long ago there might have been some sort of rock steps here, but now, in this season, the stones fringed with blades of grass were slippery with moss. At each step my breath seemed laboured. As I hauled myself up, the burden of my years sat heavy on me. But far heavier than this was the other burden I was carrying—the legal documents and the messages from the family. I could not help asking myself why it was necessary for me to take these papers to him personally: I could have left them with the schoolteacher, and gone back by the late evening bus. But then, how would it have looked to have come this far and then go away without seeing him...go away emptyhanded, as it were. After all, he had been living in this part of the world for ten years, and here I was, already despairing on the first day of my visit. He also must have climbed up these selfsame stones for the first fateful time ten years ago—but he was a young man then. I recalled his face from his latest photograph—in it he looked what they call 'cheerful' in English—in the newspapers over father's message (he was alive then) : *Please Come Back*.... He not only didn't come back, he didn't even write to us. We went in search of him. The police took us on several rounds of the morgues where we went up and down the rows of the dead in search of the one who had walked out on us as a stranger overnight.

Trying to recover my breath, I wondered if I would be able to recognize him when I saw him.

*

Sweat dripped into my eyes, weaving a curtain behind which a green pine forest glistened tremulously. At long last in a clearing, the temple came into view—whitewashed, serene, cool. I sat down on a step, letting the breeze dry me. It was quiet all round, no devotees, no *sanyasis* who may have renounced the world ... only a monkey which squatted on its haunches on a swinging branch of an ancient tree beside the temple. It regarded me with momentary curiosity, beating its metre-long tail before jumping onto the roof. A thud, a rustling of leaves—and nothing else; the silence returned. In the midst of a deep quietude, it seemed the monkey and I were the only two who sought refuge at the shrine of Mahakal, the Timeless One who presides over death. Sometimes the gods come to our rescue in the form of animals. So had the monkey, which had wiped out all my doubts with a swish of its tail, when I got up to go forward. I was light on my feet.

The temple was not far away. The ground had levelled off. A well-trodden path stretched ahead, cleaving the choppy green sea of pine. As the pine needles fell, a heavy scent diffused into the air. The *aghori baba* had been right: I had barely walked another hundred metres when I emerged into another clearing—like a patio, empty except for grass and rocks. A few steps onwards, a rock to my left caught my eyes. I stopped in my tracks as I realized it was not a mere rock.

On a second glance, what looked like a rock resolved, like a puzzle picture, into a cell built of stones, wood and mud: a fluent coming together of the natural and the man-made. Its rear portion was flush with a cliff.

A rock which jutted out from the cliff before sloping down to the ground on either side, formed a roof above three whitewashed stones, surmounted by a door.

I walked up the three door-stones. The chain-clasp on the door hung loosely, unhooked from its hasp. It was very quiet inside. I peered through a narrow opening in the door and at first saw nothing but blackness. A pale shaft of daylight entered from an invisible window, or perhaps from the opening in the door itself and penetrated the darkness. A grubby little patch of sunlight lay on the floor.

Perhaps he was ill or asleep on his bed somewhere inside. It could be that he had not received my letter and was not expecting me. Or, he might have waited up for me yesterday evening and afterwards presumed that I had put off my visit.... I reached out to rattle the chain but it swung open before I could touch it. I stepped backward to the lower stone, as if for a short moment I wanted to flee, even as he appeared in the doorway. It was possible that rather than fear, it was a nervous eagerness to see him better which made me want to fall back, as one does for a better view of a painting on a wall. Be that as it may, he reached out to grip me by my hand and pulled me up, and in the scramble my briefcase fell. It clattered down the stones and the property documents, letters, loose sheets—everything flew about and scattered. Mortified, I dropped to the ground to retrieve them. He knelt down beside me, carefully picking up the papers. I felt his hand on my trembling knee. I turned and saw his hand—not his face—for the first time in ten years.

I do not remember how long we sat hunched there. At last, when I raised my head I knew him instantly—his face, his watchful eyes—unmindful of the fact that I had never seen him in a beard. With his grizzled locks, he resembled a stranger halfway between a forgotten brother and a *sanyasi*.

Yet, in his hand on my knee was a warmth evocative of a distant household and a shared past preserved in frozen memory. The ice began to melt at his touch.

He leaned forward to pick up my briefcase. 'Come, let's go in.'

I followed him into his cell.

'Please, sit down.' With his hand on my shoulder he steered me to one of the two mats on the floor. He squatted opposite me on a rug, his back resting against the wall.

Time dragged by. I was sitting with him in his cell, yet I couldn't bring myself to believe I'd reached the end of my journey.

'Did you get my letter?'

'Yes, I did. You were supposed to come yesterday.'

'I came yesterday but the bus was late by three hours.'

'Where are you staying?'

'At the schoolteacher's. He took me home.'

I longed to ask him if he had sent the schoolteacher to meet my bus, but I didn't. I was put off by his impassivity and aloofness. He seemed to have drawn a line around himself which I dared not overstep. The thaw that I imagined had set in when he touched me at the doorstep had merely licked the outer layers: it had not reached the core of our being.

'Was it difficult to find your way here?'

'No, not at all. I met an *aghori baba* at a tea-shop. He gave me the necessary directions.'

'Did he? What else did he tell you?' He was rather amused.

'Nothing.' I looked on at him for a moment. 'Are you ill?'

'He must have told you this. It is nothing very important. It is the old breathing trouble; it gets worse in this weather.' He seemed to find talking about his ailment more distressing than the distress of living with it.

'Could this high altitude have anything to do with it?'

He shook his head in dissent. 'No, I don't think so. You'll recall I suffered from this trouble even when I was at home.'

At its mention, "home" crept silently in and sat down on its heels between us. He closed his eyes. Even if a leaf were to fall outside the sound of its falling would have broken the silence of the cell.

'Is everything over there all right?' he asked drily, his voice keeping its distance from home, yet hovering around it.

'Yes, everything is all right.'

'The ground floor must be unoccupied.'

'Why should it be?' I didn't understand him immediately, 'Mother lives down there.'

'Alone, you mean?' He looked hard at me, surprised.

'Yes.'

'Doesn't she live with you upstairs?'

'Well, she prefers to live on the ground floor.'

He stared at me as if he had no inkling of what had gone on at the house, although I'd written to him about everything I could think of. He had not seen it happen with his own eyes, and I who had seen it all saw it again from the outside—through his eyes—and began to understand why he was surprised: an outsider had reason to be surprised to see a woman with three grown up sons and a house spend her last days alone in a corner.

Outside, a tree branch creaked and rustled. Suddenly, there was a loud thud on the roof followed by a quick skittering away and loosening of dust from the ceiling. He went out. I heard his voice carry in the silence. I heard it rise towards the mountain peak and return, until echoing waves caught up with it and bore it gently away.

When he came back I asked him: 'Who was there?'

'A monkey,' he smiled. 'The monkeys come down from the temple to bask in the sun.... Have you been to the temple yet?'

'Not yet. I hear it's a very old temple.'

'Not all that old, perhaps. But the Shiva idol is. It was found buried in the mountainside here. I'll take you to the temple one of these days....Would you like to have some tea?'

'Who will make it? You?'

'Who else is there?' he laughed. 'It will be ready in no time.'

He walked across the cell to a curtain and gathered it to one side. It gave on to an underground recess which sloped backwards. There was a low wooden seat in a corner, and beside it stood an earthen pot and two clean brass tumblers. In the wall above it was an air-vent, which could pass for a window: it framed a gnarled branch of a tree, grey rocks, and a slice of the sky suspended in humming silence. Nothing moved but the wind. I thought to myself: he lives here, alone, day in and day out, in the cold of winter, the wet of rains, the heat of summer. It was a mere shadow of a thought, without substance, intangible, unconnected to the grim reality. When we see a dead man, we may think either of death or the man or of both and still fail to register the flesh and blood reality of the man meeting his death. Why was I thinking of death? He in whose cell I was sitting was very much alive, although I found it difficult to convince myself that he was the selfsame person whom I had come to see.

He returned with tea in two tumblers and salted *shakarparas* on a bronze tray.

'Why don't you move out of the draught?' he asked, setting the tray down on a low slatted board between us.

I took my tumbler and shifted back against the wall. Huddled opposite each other in the narrow cell, we kept to ourselves, while the wind rattled the door now and then and shook the trees.

'The tea smells of burning wood, doesn't it?' he observed.

'Don't you have a kerosene stove?'

'Kerosene is not readily available here, but there is plenty of firewood. I can collect enough during my morning walk. It also helps in keeping the cold away....Come on, take some *shakarparas*. It used to be your favourite dish.'

I took some, grateful that he should still remember such a trivial thing, although I'd have expected him to know little about us, living as he did mostly on the ground floor with mother. He would rarely come upstairs. He only met my children when they went down to the courtyard to play.

We sipped our tea in silence. He asked no questions about home, which was surprising. But perhaps it was all for the good, for what could he have possibly asked me about, or, at what point could I have picked up the narrative of the ten long years which separated us. It was enough that we had a few hours to ourselves. Already the afternoon was wearing on. The shadows had begun to descend from the peaks facing the cell.

A shadow reached out between us, dividing the room into two portions; half where he was sitting in fading yellow darkness and the other half where I sat opposite him, near the door. A thin strip of wan afternoon light sprawled over the threshold in a still moment.

'How are the children?'

'Fine,' I said. 'Munni has started going to college.'

'And the little one?'

'She is grown up now.' I grinned as I thought of her. 'She also wanted to come along.'

'Well?'

'She has never been to the mountains. She said she wanted to see where *tayaji* lived.'

'She was very small when....' he trailed off.

*When I left home....*I was prompted to complete the sentence for him but I didn't. I let it hang unfinished around the seed of pain in the heart of a deadened grief. Perhaps that is the way grief lasts a lifetime, buried deep down.

There was no further mention of the children. He picked up the tray with the leftovers and went into the recessed portion behind the curtain.

I sat alone in the dusky light of the cell. Outside, the shadows were thickening on the ground but the sun still lingered on the humped mountain. A flight of crows winged downward beyond the cell, shattering the placid atmosphere with their shrill cawing.

He came back in, a hurricane lamp in his hand. As he set it down on the squat board in the middle, he glanced up at me. In that brief moment it struck me that he had something important, something crucial on his mind with which he was struggling, which he wanted to tell me about. Hesitation got the better of him and he took his seat quietly.

He sat with his head bowed, the lamplight playing upon his thoughtful profile, the greying hair, the swell of his shoulders, the curve of his neck.... It was as if I was seeing my father again, the way he looked in my childhood, concentrating on the arithmetic sums on a slate for me while my fascinated gaze would keep wandering to his neck.

'Does he come to see you?'

'Who?' I was startled: Was he talking about father? The next instant I realized he was talking about our elder brother who had moved out to another part of the city. 'Oh yes, he does. Sometimes. In fact, it's he who sent me here.'

'What for?'

'He wants us to sell our home. I've brought the sale deed for you to sign.' At once, I felt relieved. The task for which I had undertaken the long journey was done. How incredibly, wonderfully simple it had turned out in the end!

He raised his head. His eyes ran over the briefcase lying on the floor. Slowly, an understanding of what the papers he had helped retrieve from his doorstep were all about, dawned on him.

He looked at me rather wearily. 'If you sold the house,' he said slowly, 'where would mother live?'

'It's up to her. She can live with either of us.'

'And what about you?'

'I'll have to rent a house. In fact, I've already found one.'

'So all the decisions have been made. What can I say in the matter now?'

'You too have a share in the property.'

'Do I?' He laughed. 'I left it all a long time ago.'

I looked at him in silence.

'Is it really necessary to sell the house?'

'Perhaps not, but our brother wants to buy property in Dehradun. He needs cash.'

'So he'd sell our father's house?' There was just an edge of sarcasm in his voice.

'How else can he hope to raise the money?'

'Father put all his savings and gratuity into it.'

'I know. But he is no more.'

'True. Still, how can his things cease to be his?'

I gazed at him. Amazing, I thought, and felt like asking why, having renounced the world, he was still concerned whether the house was sold or retained.

He leaned forward, a reminiscent smile on his lips. 'You know you were in the final year M.A. when father bought the house. We didn't have the electricity connection then and you'd study in the light of a lantern in your roof-top room.'

'Yes, I remember.'

'You were married in the courtyard below.'

The courtyard, the roof-top room—what was he driving at? Obviously, he wasn't talking about the house itself. What he was saying was something very different, but I failed to grasp it in my anger.

Out of the corner of my eye I saw what looked like the blazing eyes of some wild animal flash past the air-vent in the side wall. It gave me quite a turn. 'What was that?'

'A flash of lightning.'

My fear was now replaced with worry. 'I must leave. It's going to be difficult to go down if it starts raining.'

'You needn't be in a hurry.'

'The schoolteacher would be worried.'

228

'He knows you're here.' Then, after a moment's hesitation, he added: 'Why don't you stay with me tonight?'

I'd come ready with an answer. 'It's my blood pressure,' I said, trying not to sound foolish. 'It may not be good for me to stay overnight at such a height.'

I knew I was making a fool of myself, for I was going to spend the night in the mountains anyway. But the thought of spending it with him in his cell was unbearable. We can spend our nights with someone who is either known to us or is a total stranger. He was neither; I felt distant and close to him all at once—which was probably why I had been sent to see him in the first place.

I picked up my briefcase and got up to leave.

'Wait a minute. I'll be right back.' He went into the rear portion of his cell and emerged with an umbrella in one hand and a flash light in the other. 'Keep this,' he said, giving me the umbrella. 'Let me walk you part of the way.'

He stepped down the three whitewashed door-stones, reaching out his hand behind him to steady me at the same time. His touch, so gentle, surged in my veins in search of the timorous memories crouched out of sight even as the love and affection of yesteryears returned to illuminate the darkness....Was he the very same person who had left us for good?

I saw him stop and turn around. 'Well,' he said with a laugh, 'I thought you were following me.'

I hurried my steps. Darkness lay under a thin glowing veil cast by twinkling stars in a clear, dense sky. To think that only a short while ago there had been a flash of lightning! Unbelievable!

He walked effortlessly ahead of me, the spot of his torch picking out the way, the wayside bushes, trees, rocks. A bird flapped its wings among the leaves and flew away overhead, screeching into the darkness. Suddenly, as my tiffin-box bumped against the thermos in my shoulder-bag, I realized I didn't have my briefcase with me.

'My briefcase.... I think I've left it behind in your cell.'

'Never mind, it will be safe there. You can take it back tomorrow.' He stopped and turned towards me. 'Are any of your writings in it?' he asked impulsively.

For the first time during the day he had made a reference to my writings. I'd assumed that he must have long since forgotten that I ever wrote. Writing, for me, had been rather like an illegiti-mate activity, almost a private disease not to be openly discussed.

'No, there are none. It contains only the property documents and some letters meant for you.'

We resumed walking.

'I've not seen any of your stories in a long time.'

'I haven't written much. There is so much to do at the news-paper office....Do you get magazines here?'

'Not regularly. The schoolteacher brings some from the library from time to time....I remember seeing one of your stories in an issue way back.'

I kept pace behind him, my heart pounding away in shame. Several years ago I'd written a story which got into print—indeed it was, written for publication. It was not so much about the one who had left home as about those left behind. Both mother and father—but mother more than father—were hopeful that he would return immediately if he ever came across the story. Why speak of returning, he hadn't even dropped a misera-ble postcard.... I was glad he could not see my shame in the dark. I blurted, 'You didn't even write to us!' My voice caught in my throat and I was doubly ashamed. I had resolved before leaving Delhi that I would not ask him any questions of this sort—but now it was out there between us, past us, like the bright round spot of torchlight on the mountain path.

'It would have been futile,' he said.

'You know how we looked for you in all the likely places?'

No, it was useless to go on. How could he, from his peaceful summit, comprehend the torment of the scurrying beetles on the distant plains? He could not have known how it felt to go on endless rounds of the hospitals, the railway platforms, the bus-stations, or checking the updated police lists of missing persons, or staring into the faces of the dead in morgues, or placing ads in the newspapers: *Please come back. Mother is ill....*

'I still think it would have been futile.'

'You could have at least informed us you were safe.'

'Suppose I'd done it, would that have made it easier for you to bear the pain?'

'I'm not talking about pain.'

'What are you talking about then?'

I groped in my heart for an answer but I found none. I could not lay my finger on anything, neither pain nor mother's old age, nor my own failures—everything would still have turned out the way it had. More or less.

'What was the point then in writing home after ten years?'

He was silent awhile. 'Maybe, I shouldn't have.' He took a deep breath. 'I took all of ten years to write to you. Long enough, I thought, when it would no longer make a difference to you whether I was alive or not.'

There was the detachment in his tone—otherwise manifest in the trees, the rocks, the streams—which is above the pain and hurt of embroiled relationships. It had taken him ten austere years of solitude to acquire his detachment.

I heard a rumbling on the slope below us, as if a rock had come loose and was hurtling down.

'What's that noise?'

'It's a waterfall. I bring water from there.'

'Isn't it too far away.'

'Not really. As a matter of fact, the stream flows by just a short way below the cell. I'll show you the place tomorrow.'

So he fetched water himself. Instantly, my fatigue, my shame and the lingering hurt dissolved. The sudden quiet resounded with the splashing water of the hilly stream. The evening prayer bells tinkled in the temple above.

'You should go back,' I said. 'I can find my way now.'

'All right,' he agreed, but he made no move to go. I could not tear myself away, either.

'I'll come again tomorrow,' I said reassuringly.

'Is it all right at the schoolteacher's? He has only one small room. You can shift into the rest-house, if you like.'

'No, it will not be necessary. I'm quite comfortable there. Besides, it is only a matter of another day or two.'

Another day or two—the words had tumbled out from my mouth unawares. They swung to and fro, rocked by the wind and the temple bells.

I left hurriedly. I headed down the slope towards the bend in the path. As I reached it, I turned round and saw him still standing at the spot where I'd left him... still, and unmoving.

The lights were strung out in a festoon along the motorable road below. A mist hung over the sleepy town. Had he also gone to sleep by now, or was he up alone in his cell? I'd met him after a full ten years and still....Couldn't I have spent even one night with him? You are a writer, I told myself; yet you readily give a wide berth to raw reality when you encounter it, as if living was a thing apart from the truth of existence or that truth was a thing apart from writing—as if living and truth and writing bore no relation to one another: as if each hung like a cold corpse from its own separate gallows. If I had to run away like this, why did I stay for even a single night here? I ought to have hurried to get his signature on the documents and caught the return bus back home. What was the point in staying on in town if we had to spend the night under different roofs? Why did all of us, my brothers and sisters, dry up like a wilted stalk at the moment of reckoning? How was it that at a certain point all our love dowsed itself in sand and ashes? How could we leave one another to his or her fate and stand aloof? Wasn't it the tyranny of this sinful indifference which had driven him away from home?

Even as I plunged downhill, I sank deeper into the mire of guilt and self-recrimination. With every step that took me nearer the schoolteacher's quarters, I burned more intensely with a desire to become invisible or else somehow vanish in his cot for the night and leave for Delhi the first thing in the morning.

The schoolteacher was busy in the kitchen, and I got in unnoticed. I could not summon enough courage to face him right then. All I wanted was to change into my night clothes and burrow into the cot. A brazier glowed in the room. As I approached it I suddenly felt very exhausted and cold and feverish. In the core of my being my feverish heart and my body, shivering with cold tortured and played with each other, while "I" stood to one side uninvolved. This was good in itself, providing as it did some measure of relief to a layman, who may not renounce the world like the *sadhus* and *sanyasis* but nevertheless can, albeit briefly, walk out of his body and heart with their tensions, and disembodied, stand apart. But I was not in luck. I had barely stretched out on the cot when I started at a sound from the direction of the kitchen. I turned to see the schoolteacher standing in the doorway, staring hard at me as if he had caught me red-handed.

'When did you come in?' he asked.

'Just a little while ago. I'm not feeling well,' I offered by way of an excuse.

It mollified him somewhat and he came over. 'I told you last night to sleep on the cot. In the rains, the floor is rather damp and chilly.'

He placed his palm on my forehead and felt my pulse. 'No fever,' he concluded, 'but you must be exhausted. I have some brandy. I'll advise you to have a sip. It will relax you.'

He took out a small bottle from the cupboard and brought two glasses. I sat up on the cot. Opposite the two of us sat the glowing brazier like some mysterious hill deity whom we had come to appease. As we drank, a bird out in the darkness scattered the silence with its strange entreating cries.

'It's the *ninira* bird. Its call puts the children to sleep.' He took a swallow from his glass. 'Would you like to have a splash of warm water in your drink?'

'No, don't bother. This is okay.... Do you have liquor shops in the town?'

'None. I get my occasional bottle from Almora or Bhuvali, thanks to an obliging bus-driver.'

Thanks to the brandy and the brazier, my limbs began to loosen and the knots melted away. Although the feelings of guilt and of overwhelming disquiet did not vanish altogether, they withdrew a pleasant distance away to hover within my soul. I grew light-headed, dimly aware that the schoolteacher was regarding me with a quizzical expression on his face.

'Have you been to see *babaji*?'

I stared at his yellow teeth. Perhaps he did not suspect that the one whom he called *baba* could in some way be related to me. People hardly ever pause to think that holy men come from ordinary homes and have ordinary pasts.

'Was he in his cell?'

'Where else could he have been?'

'Anywhere. Until some time ago, he used to roam all over the place. He would even come down for shopping.'

'Doesn't he go out any more?'

'I don't know. I haven't seen him around lately, though. There was a time I'd go to see him in his cell and help him with the chores, but I found his behaviour rather strange and discouraging and stopped going there.'

'What did you find so strange in his behaviour?'

He gazed into his palm, as if the answer was written there. Then he took a sip from his glass. 'Last summer I used to fetch water for him,' he said, looking up at me, 'but he did not like it. One morning I was returning from the waterfall when he met me on the way.' "Could you gather some firewood for me?" he asked. 'Why not?' I said. Thereupon, he asked with a smile if I could cook his meals also. 'No problem,' I said at once. 'After all, he used to eat only once a day.' "And I—what would I do?" he asked. 'Why *baba*,' I said, 'you must spend your time in meditation and prayers, for which you renounced the world. Do you know what he said then?'

The schoolteacher fell silent, staring into the sibilant flames in the brazier.

'What did he say?' I demanded.

'He said: "How can you meditate upon one you know nothing about."'

'Did he?'

'I said if it was so, why did he leave his family to come here. Can you imagine what he said? He said: "I have left nothing; I only came away." There was nothing I could do then but leave the pail at the spot and walk away. I wonder, a man who does not like being served, how can you serve him?'

The schoolteacher sighed and resumed after a while: 'I also live here alone but I have a job to do. Why is he here? He does not read his scriptures, nor say his prayers, nor meditate, nor hold discourses. He does not even have a word of counsel for the visitors who call on him to pay their obeisance.'

'Still people go to see him?'

'They do. Remember you too came from far-off just to see him!'

'I'd heard about his fame,' I said lamely.

'So did others. Some come for wish-fulfilment or for receiving his blessings, some are merely curious.'

I felt the schoolteacher's penetrating glance on me. I looked into myself and found nothing—neither any wish nor curiosity—

but a loose thread of relationship dangling among the cobwebs, which neither the schoolteacher could grasp nor I pull down.

'Shall I get out dinner? It's already late.'

He went into the kitchen. I remained sitting on the bed. Outside, crickets chirped monotonously. The brandy had kindled in me a gentle, cosy fire; slowly its warmth spread to combat the frost in my marrow and the cumulative exhaustion of a lifetime of routine-bound existence.

'Have you dozed off?'

I came to, with a start; the warmth had indeed lulled me to sleep. He set down two trays of food on the floor: *dal*, a vegetable, thick hot *chappaties*.... He had prepared the meal himself. I envied his simplicity in extending hospitality to me without demanding to know who I was. I was so touched I wanted to confess to him that this unorthodox *baba* was none other than my own brother, but I got over the impulse immediately; it would only have embarrassed him....Some truths are wholly unnecessary and are better left alone.

'You'll stay here for a few days, won't you?' His manner was easy, friendly and eager.

'No, I must push off tomorrow,' I said, somewhat self-consciously. 'I could get only two days' leave.'

'Where do you work?' This was the first direct question he had put to me, and he sounded so genuinely concerned that I felt grateful to him. I told him about my work with a newspaper, about my children, my household. He listened quietly. After I'd finished he still didn't speak, I began to have doubts whether he had heard me at all. I looked up into his face. In the pale moonlight from the window, I saw his wide-open eyes fastened on me. It unnerved me. Whatever was going on in his head?

'Look, why don't you stay on for another couple of days? You've come so far away from home, it would be a shame if you had to go back so soon.'

'What's the point? What shall I do here?'

'You can be with *baba* that much longer. He is all alone these days.'

'Why don't you call on him more often yourself?'

'Well, I wouldn't know what to talk to him about.'

'Anyway, he left home on his own. And to live alone is not

235

such a great misfortune, either. After all, you also live alone,' I reasoned with him.

'It's different with me. I go away to Almora for a few days every month. If I could find a better house here, I'd even bring my family over.' As another thought occurred to him, a look of puzzlement came into his eyes. 'I don't understand something,' he said ambiguously. 'Many years have passed since *baba* came to live here. But, so far, no one from his family seems to have ever visited him.'

I had a lingering suspicion that he had known all along everything about me but had taken care not to show it in his face.

'Probably his family doesn't know he is here.'

'You mean in all these years they couldn't even discover his whereabouts?'

'They must have tried their best. It's such a vast country. How can one comb every part of it?'

He stared into the darkness outside, lost in thought. At last, he spoke up: 'Perhaps he never had much of a family. There are some who leave their homes in search of god out of sheer loneliness.'

'You should have asked him.'

'He tells us as little about himself as about god. Sometimes I doubt if he is a true *sanyasi*. I doubt if he has truly renounced the world and taken to god.'

What was he if not a *sanyasi*, I asked myself? Ten years ago he had left everyone at home crying; now, how could he leave god as well? The night held out no answer.

I lay down on my bedding on the floor while the schoolteacher stretched out on his cot, as he had done the previous night.

But unlike last night, the room was not completely dark: the moon hung low in the kitchen window, shedding a pale luminous dust on the things in the room. I lay awake for a long time. When my thoughts turned to my family, they seemed to belong to another world; and when I thought of my brother living the life of a hermit, his seemed to be yet another world unknown to us. These different little worlds abutted on one another, yet they were virtually millions of miles apart. How did these worlds become imprisoned in their isolation? The question was painful and frightening. I tucked it under me for the night, turning over on my side.

*

Crows wheeled overhead, scores and scores of them. Cawing shrilly, they descended through the air to settle on the rocks, the pathways, the branches, the tree-tops, everywhere. Their sharp cries chipped the sky.

The schoolteacher and I had gone to the bus-stand. In the attached shed, there was a small crowd of passengers. Stray dogs and coolies dozed outside the eating-places across the road. The schoolteacher made his way to the booking window. It was closed. He rapped on it with his knuckles several times before a head peered out. Soon he returned with the information that there was no advance booking. 'You'll get your ticket on the bus itself,' he told me.

'Did you ask what time it leaves?'

'There is only one direct bus to Delhi in the evening at six. Another leaves at eight, but you'll have to catch a connecting bus in Bhuvali.'

A lot of time to go till six o'clock, I told myself. I had already packed my things. In fact, I left my luggage at a sweet-shop nearby to save me a detour to the schoolteacher's on the way back from the summit in the afternoon. I carried with me only my duffel-bag and the umbrella my brother had given me the previous night.

'Come let's have another tea. You've a long climb ahead of you.'

We'd had our tea before starting out for the bus-stand. It was so cold out here that I couldn't resist the temptation of hot tea by the warm oven at the tea-shop.

The schoolteacher had been unusually quiet since the morning when he asked me again not to be in a hurry to leave for Delhi. However, he did not insist when I told him that I had to get back to write my column for the newspaper the next day. We did not talk about the *baba* any more; we seemed to have reached a tacit agreement to black out his cell, the temple, the forest rest-house everything higher up. The sky was overcast but it did not look as if it would rain: it promised to be one of those days when there is neither rain nor sunshine. A grey mass of spent cloud racks had piled up, trapped between the valley below and the peaks above.

'These clouds pass over Bhuvali to reach here,' the school-teacher remarked. 'The main rain-clouds are borne to Ranikhet and Nainital, while the dregs are banished to this penal settlement of a backwoods... to serve their sentence, as it were.'

'Well?' I took another sip of tea. 'Don't these clouds go on ahead somewhere?'

'They go nowhere. Only the crows do. Look at the swarms of them!' he said laughingly.

Indeed the crows were all over—over the peaks, the house-tops, the trees....

'Aren't there a lot of them for a small town like this? They say this place carries a curse that all its dead will be reborn as crows.'

'Still, people live here?'

'Yes, they do, because they also believe that these crows in turn attain salvation on dying,' he explained soberly. 'This town is a sort of a transit camp for men and crows on their way to deliverance.'

The schoolteacher was no longer smiling. With a pensive look in his eyes, he gazed quietly at the black legions of crows and the little town lost in misty clouds. A penal settlement, he had called it: for the clouds from Bhuvali, the farthest end of the earth; a province for the spirits of the dead and the crows. He had spent half his life here.

He didn't let me pay for the tea.

'Try to get back early. I'll see you here.' He hesitated a moment before adding: 'And pay him my respects also.'

'Why don't you come along? He'll be glad to see you.' I didn't want to go to him alone this time.

He was caught unawares. 'No, no,' he said evasively. 'I can always see him later. But for you this may well be the last opportunity.'

With that, he turned away abruptly and disappeared into the bazaar.

*

The road uphill was muddy, and a light drizzle had begun. It was midday, yet a darkness was creeping up. I unfurled the umbrella over my head and continued to walk with long strides.

By the time I reached the rock steps which led to the temple, I was panting. I felt like sitting down to recover my breath: it would not do to rush in on him gasping and sweating. On the other hand, the sooner I was on my way again the longer I could be with him before I had to get back in time for the six o' clock bus. I was up and off in a couple of minutes.

Below the path was a beautiful little cottage which must have been nestling there since the time of the English... a relic from the old familiar world: lighted fireplaces, the carefree laughter of girls in the passages, music on the radio. It called for a deliberate effort to think that up here in the outlands there lived ordinary happy people who had nothing to do with the secluded cell of my brother, the naked ascetic, or the loneliness of the school-teacher. Within similar four snug walls I'd spent the forty years of my life. But from these misty heights the familiar and the known seemed suddenly to sink into unreality.... And then, without forewarning, a fear gripped me: what would happen to me if, in a convulsive moment, my world were to turn inside out? I'd probably beat the darkness in vain with my inadequate wings like an insect nipped from the drawing room between thumb and forefinger and thrown out of the window at night, unable ever after to find its way back in. But, mercifully, the moment passed and I could laugh at myself. I reached into my coat-pocket and touched my bank passbook; I touched the muf-fler round my neck given to me by my wife on our last anniversary; my patent leather wallet carried photographs of both my children; I was a part-owner of a house in Delhi; and there were books with my name on their covers—all solid, incon-trovertible proofs of my earthly existence. I was born forty years ago, quickened by the essence of life everlasting. It seemed impossible that it should now betray me and let me be turned into a mere moth. No, there was no cause for fear. Reassured, I hastened towards the cell of my brother, glad in a few hours a bus would take me back to the world where I belonged.

I sighed with relief when the cell came into view. I almost ran up the three door-stones. Dull lamplight shone through a fissure in the door. As I made to rattle the chain, I heard his voice, and it sounded as if he were praying or talking to himself or mumbling in sleep or in a stupor of high fever. I looked in through the fis-sure and caught sight of him standing below the air-vent.

Even today I haven't been able to get over the scene—though, perhaps, scene may not be the word for it. The person I saw through the fissure was neither a hermit—heretic or otherwise— nor the brother I'd known. Completely oblivious of his surroundings, he was talking to himself and laughing at the same time. Awestruck, I stood glued helplessly to the door, torn between fear and old ties of love, even as another part of me pushed headlong in to cling to him, screaming at him in bewilderment as to what he thought he was doing, whoever was he talking to, whatever was he laughing at.

They say when the soul is rendered dumb the body speaks: the blood rumbles in the dead silence and we hear our heart beat. Something like this happened to me also. I do not remember when my hand, of its own volition, rattled the chain or when he opened the door, but I do remember the touch of his hand upon my shoulder and the sound of his words in my ears: 'What held you up? I've been waiting for you since morning.'

His voice was so matter of fact, calm and collected that my head jerked upwards. I was astonished to see him smiling serenely.

Was he the same person who only a minute before was laughing to himself and raving like a madman?

'You....' I started to ask him but changed my mind at the last moment and left the question uncomposed. A door inside me swung closed. In the past, too, I'd closed so many doors behind me that one more made no difference.

'Your hand feels very warm,' I said instead. 'Are you all right?'

Gently, he removed his hand from my shoulder and said as though he had not heard me: 'Come in. It's very cold outside.'

I stood his umbrella in a corner and took off my shoes. It was as cold in here as outside. The solitary lamp cast but a yellow smudge of light in the bare room.

'Where have you been so long?' he asked.

'I went to the bus-stand to book a seat on the evening bus.'

He did not say anything. In the wan circle of light, his pale face, his greying beard, his thick black eyebrows—nothing registered any flicker of emotion. The gaze he directed on me was impassive—neither intimate nor aloof.

'On my morning walk, I passed by the rest-house. I happen to know the overseer in charge of it. He can spare a room for you.'

240

'What's the use?'

'You can take a few days off. You need not be in a hurry to go back.'

His voice carried just a hint of insistence and a faint trace of a distant affection. His apparent self-control made the mild concern all the more difficult and painful to bear.

'Would it make you happy if I stayed?'

He laughed a little loud. 'Would you be staying for my sake alone?'

'Who else is here? I only came to see you.'

'I thought, maybe, you'd like to spend some days here.'

'Do you want me to?'

'What I want is irrelevant.' He fell silent. Then he added slowly: 'Why don't you give yourself a holiday?'

'Back home, they'd think I too have gone your way. Isn't one *sanyasi* in the family already more than a handful?'

'Do they really think I'm a *sanyasi*?' He smiled, 'I live here the same way as I did over there. There's only been a change of places.'

'Is that all? You think nothing else has changed? That you haven't changed either?'

'Have I? What do you think?' I thought I detected a glint of amusement in his eyes.

'I'd never imagined I'd ever see you again in this life.'

'In this life? What do you mean?' He looked at me in amazement. 'Is there any life other than this one?'

I gave him a cautious, searching glance: Was he playing with me? But his gaze was unwavering and steady and there was sadness in his voice.

'If we live but once and if living here is no different than what it was back home, what was the point then in...in your change of places?'

'There is a point,' he said slowly. 'Over there, I did not matter to anyone.'

'And here?'

'Here there is no one to whom I should care if I mattered.'

'How is it possible to...to give up your own folk?'

He was lost in thought. The daylight filtered into the small room. He let his head drop to his chest until only the thatch of his grey hair showed. The face that I'd seen creased into laughter

241

only a short time ago was now a flat shadow in a dark pool.

'No,' he spoke at last. 'It is not possible. That is why I wrote to you. It is not enough just to give up certain people or things and hope to become a *sanyasi*....'

He had leaned farther away from the wall. His eyes were closed. The door moved as a wind rose and swept leaves and dust inside.

'Just have a look. See who they are,' he said to me.

I went over and opened the door wide. Some three or four men stood outside. They were accompanied by two women. When they saw me, one of the men stepped forward to inquire if the *baba* was in.

Even before I could answer him I heard my brother's voice behind me: 'Please be seated under the tree. I'll be with you in a minute.'

At his voice, they folded their hands in humility. I moved over to let my brother pass. As he went down to the bottom step, the visitors took turns to come forward to touch his feet. The last one was the younger of the two women. She was very young and was draped in a black shawl. She looked up to the *baba*, sank to her knees and bowed until her head touched his feet. She remained in this position for what seemed a long time.

Throughout all of this my brother stood still. He spoke not a word, nor did he once hold out his hand in blessing.

Finally, he turned to me. 'Wait inside,' he said. 'It shouldn't take very long.' He looked rather ill-at-ease. Wearily, I watched him. Was he ashamed of me before the visitors?

I went back in and turned down the lamp so that the grey daylight could advance further into the cell. The group of callers were sitting with him on a low whitewashed platform beneath an old plane tree which stood over to one side. Fragments of their voices as they talked to the "*baba*" carried in, but I heard him say nothing in reply. I recalled, with a feeling of shame, the question I'd put to him about leaving the family. He had left us but would these strangers leave him alone? What did he have to offer to them? Why did they keep coming to him? Most certainly they got something from him in return about which I knew nothing. Was I looking at a stranger in the guise of my brother, asking him questions that had no relevance in this place? My mind floated back across several years to the time I'd done the rounds of the morgues in search of him. It seemed to me as if I was one of the many queuing up in front of the platform to receive his blessings... to catch a glimpse of him from close by. But it was another time, another place: instead of the platform there were slabs of ice on which corpses lay like dead fish. As I lingered by the slabs looking for him, the attendant in the morgue pushed me from behind. Hurry up, he said rudely: there are others too, who have to identify their dead: quick: move on, will you? Their dead... the other people.... I was jostled and pushed and carried onwards, on and on, up through the next ten years. I made out I was lying on a cold slab of a floor and he was leaning over me, concerned.

'Chhote !' he was calling out to me.

I heard him faintly and saw the lantern he held over me. It had been ten years since he had called me by that pet name: Chhote—the little brother. I sat up, startled. Where was I? Was I back home? I stared wide-eyed at him.

'You'd fallen asleep,' he said gently. I saw him more clearly now, and saw his blanket around me, warm with the heat of my body.

'Have those people left?'

'They left long ago.'

'This blanket? I don't remember....'

'When I came in I saw you shivering, as if you were lying on ice,' he said, smiling.

On ice, was it? I emerged from a ten year old dream. A faded yellow light reached out across the floor. The sun had come out of the clouds, readying to go down below the horizon. The peaks glittered in the late afternoon sun.

He spoke again, very softly, leaning over me: 'Do keep lying, rest some more. I'll make you some tea.'

I saw him, a slight smile across his mouth—as if he too had just got up from another slab of ice, his own, and come out into the light where his present blended with my past. In the lingering moment, my gaze and his silence were, it struck me, a kind of preparation—for this moment had instantly spanned the vast speechless desert that stretched away into the past: a preparation for both of us. Perhaps it was for this reason alone that he had called me over. He had wanted to break with us, with all of us, one last time. Finally. A clean break.

I rose slowly, folded his blanket and put it away in a corner. I crossed over to the door, put on my shoes and picked up my bag. I looked round at him. He stood there, with the lantern still in his hand, although, here in the doorway, it was not necessary.

'I must push off,' I said. 'It's nearly time for the bus.'

He looked at me in silence. Then he said slowly: 'Wait a minute. I'll be right back.'

He went away into the rear part and returned with my briefcase in his hand in place of the lantern.

'Aren't you overlooking this again?' he said smilingly, giving the briefcase back to me. 'I've taken the letters and....' After a momentary pause, he added: 'You can see I've signed all the papers.'

I saw him turn slightly away. The sun straining through the branches of the plane tree beside his cell, fell across his feet. I bent down at his feet to pay my respects, and felt his hand on my head, his fingers stroking my hair, his burning touch sending waves of heat through my body.

I raised my head. The cell looked empty. A black branch of the old tree hanging heavily over the air-vent cast a long shadow inside. A spot of the sun had quietly crept up close to his feet.... I'd reached the end of my journey.

I picked up my briefcase and came out.

*

This is about all; there's really nothing left to say. Later, of course, I climbed down the path clinging to the wooded mountainside, awash with the glow of a setting sun—and it led all the way down to Delhi and my friends, the newspaper office, the blazing summer afternoons and my make-believe stories.

The schoolmaster and the *aghori baba* saw me off at the bus-stand. With the passage of time, the misty heights where I met my brother for the last time and the schoolmaster and the *aghori baba* have receded in my memory, although sometimes, in unexpected moments, everything returns poignantly in my troubled thoughts.... The schoolteacher, who stood close by the bus window, asked me frankly, if the wish that had made me undertake the journey had been fulfilled. Before I could think of what answer to make, the bus pulled out. He ran alongside for a short

distance and then fell behind. When I looked round at the *aghori*
baba, I saw he had not moved, he had found something more
engrossing in the sky overhead: he stood stuck to his spot, looking up at the swarms of crows fluttering away over the tree-tops,
wheeling in the air above the pine forest and the temple of the
Timeless One, gathering into the clamorous darkness in a dark-
ening sky.

Translated from Hindi by Kuldip Singh

Devanuru Mahadeva

Amasa

Amasa is Amasa's name. Maybe because he is dark, maybe because he was born on a new moon day (*amavasya*), the name Amasa has stuck to him. If his parents had been alive, we could have found out why he came to be called Amasa. But by the time he could walk around on his own, the mother who bore him and the father who begot him had been claimed by their separate fates. Since then the Mari temple has meant Amasa, and Amasa has meant the Mari temple. But just because he lives in the Mari temple doesn't mean that he is an orphan. The Mari temple has offered shelter to many like him. Especially in the summer, the little temple becomes a regular camping ground for people seeking shelter from the heat. Now, apart from Amasa, there is also an old man living there. He's really ancient: so old that every hair on him, on his head, body and limbs, has gone grey. Nobody so far has seen him get up from where he usually sits. In a corner of the temple is spread a tattered, black blanket, nobody knows how old. He's always sitting on it, feet stretched before him, or leaning on a pillar, or with his hands behind him. Apart from these three or four postures, he doesn't seem to know of any other. It has somehow become his habit to sit like this, his eyes half-closed. He never sits any other way. Sitting like this, he looks as though he were lost in thought. Maybe it is his face, all wrinkled, that makes him look so thoughtful. Or perhaps it is his white moustache, thick as an arm, which comes all the way down to his neck from his shrivelled face. In all, he looks very thoughtful. By his side there is always a man-sized bamboo stick. It doesn't have much use though, since Amasa is always around whenever he wants to move about. But it would come in handy to chase away the hens, the sheep and the young goats that wander nearby.

We've talked of all this, but we haven't told you his name. Everyone in the village, from the youngest to the oldest, calls him Kuriyayya, Kuriyayya (Sheep Man). Was he named so at birth? That concerns neither you nor us. But this much is certain;

from the day he could stand on his own feet to the day his feet could no longer walk, he had herded the sheep of the village headman. Even now when he sits with his eyes half-closed, he counts the sheep, one by one, on his fingers, to himself. This goes on, six or seven times each day. And he hasn't missed a single day. Amasa began to grow up right in front of his eyes. He is now around ten or eleven. Whenever Kuriyayya calls, Amasa answers. Every evening as the night descends on the village, Amasa and Kuriyayya wait eagerly for the monastery bell to ring. The moment it strikes, Amasa grabs the plate and glass kept by Kuriyayya's side and runs. As the night has already fallen by then, you can't see Amasa running in the dark. But if you skin your eyes and peer into the inky night, you can see the darkness stir at his flight. One doesn't know for how long he's gone. It's only when his call 'Ayya' shakes the night that you know he has returned. Kuriyayya sits up if he's lying down. As always they eat the gruel from the monastery together in the dark. Amasa then goes to sleep. Though the village too has by then gone to sleep, the silence of the night is broken now and then by the barking of dogs and the hooting of owls. The old man unable to sleep stares into the night, mutters things to himself, calls out to Amasa a few times and, getting no reply, finally falls asleep.

*

As the Mari festival comes to all the neighbouring villages once a year, it came to Amasa's village too. It was only then that Kuriyayya had to shift himself to another place, for the villagers scrubbed the temple, painted it with whitelime and red-earth, and made it stand out. When it was done, all sides freshly painted in stripes of whitelime and red-earth, and as the morning sun fell on it, the Mari temple shone with an added brilliance. Only Kuriyayya's corner, surrounded by all this brightness, looked even gloomier. In the hall, a dozen men milled around, busily running back and forth, getting the torch ready, cutting paper of different colours for decorating the yard and a hundred other things. And since almost everyone there wore new white clothes, the Mari temple sparkled in whiteness. One of those present, Basanna, was a short, dark man sporting a

247

French moustache. He too wore new white clothes and in them he shone darker still. His big yellow teeth protruded through his closed mouth and reflected the lustre of his clothes. In his hand he held a broom. Basanna stomped over to Kuriyayya's corner and shouted 'Ayya'. Since Kuriyayya would respond only after he'd been spoken to a few times, everyone spoke loudly to him. Kuriyayya slowly opened his eyes and looked. He watched the white figures that kept coming and going in front of his eyes. As he watched, his old memories stirred and began to form in front of his eyes. The Mari festival meant the Tiger Dance. That meant him. The Tiger danced in front of his eyes. The drumbeat in his ears. Those were the days of the elder village headman. Kuriyayya was then a boy about as high as Amasa. The vigour of Kuriyayya's dance had impressed the elder. Giving him a gift of clothes, he had said: 'Till the end of your days stay in my house. You'll have your food and clothes. Just look after the sheep, that's all.' His shrivelled face blossomed; the brightness of the Mari temple and the people around glinted in every wrinkle of his face. Basanna shouted 'Ayya' in his ears, this time even louder. He turned his head and looked up. Seeing Basanna, he grasped the reason for his presence. With the bamboo stick in his right hand, he stretched out the other. When Basanna held the outstretched hand, he pulled himself up and slowly walked over to the other corner leaning on the stick and sat down. Basanna shook the blanket a couple of times and spread it out in the corner where Kuriyayya was now sitting. The dust shaken out from the blanket swam in the morning sun. Where the blanket was before, there now lay a thick layer of reddish dust and dirt. But as the morning sun fell on it, it too seemed to turn white.

*

It was noon by the time Amasa returned from his playful ramblings. He couldn't believe what he saw. All kinds of things were going on there. The smell of whitelime, of raw earth, and freshly smeared cowdung around the Mari temple crowded into his nostrils. Kuriyayya had been moved from one corner to the other. In the hall, some men had crowded round in a circle and were jumping up on their toes to look at something. In the middle was a man doing something. Amasa hopped over and

248

peeped. He saw diadems, two-headed birds and other such things being crafted out of coloured silver paper. Everything that had been made there seemed wonderful to his eyes. As the man in the middle crafted these things, the crowd alternately offered instructions and uttered appreciations: 'It should be like that... It should be like this... *Besh*! Ha!' and so on. A long while later, after his eyes had soaked in all that they could, Amasa went over to Kuriyayya and sat by his side. In a row on the other side and leaning against the wall were several large red and white parasols and whisks for the deity; they had been put out in the sun to dry. In a nearby corner was a tall coconut tree, gently swaying against the sky. Amasa's eyes ran up to the top of the tree, where seven or eight large bunches of coconuts weighed it down. When he ran his eyes down the tree he noticed that someone had painted the stem of the tree in stripes of whitelime and red-earth. He slid closer to Kuriyayya and said, 'Ayya.' Kuriyayya looked at him meaning to ask 'What is it?' Amasa said excitedly, 'Look Ayya! Look! Someone's painted your tree with whitelime and colour.' Kuriyayya peered ahead. He saw only a short distance, and then everything was lost in a haze. But what he saw was this: someone had used a coconut for sorcery and had buried it in the cremation ground. It had sprouted, cleft the earth and sprung up. He had plucked it from there and planted it in the corner of the Mari temple, saying, 'Let it be here; at least as mine.' It had grown in front of his eyes; sprouting leaves and shedding them, bearing scars on its body where it had once borne leaves. It had grown and grown, taller and taller, and now stood fully grown.

*

As the festival days went by, relatives and friends from around started descending one by one on the village. As usual they would first visit the Mari temple and then go about their business. Some would forget everything and settle down there to gossip. All the old scandals from the various villages would be dug up and updated. While all this was going on, in the yard Basanna was warming up the drum over a straw fire and tuning it. A bunch of kids were jumping around him like an army of monkeys. Amasa was one among them. As Basanna raised the drum to his chest and beat it, its sound rang through, *chad chad nakuna nakuna nakuna*, like a gong to the four corners of the village. Unable to resist, the kids around him started to dance. Basanna was inspired too and started to dance, beating his drum *dangu dangu dangu chuki*. The kids danced, Basanna kept step, all of them falling over each other and those passing by. Heaven only knows who taught Amasa to dance. He was stepping out the best of all. Everyone watched him in amazement. By then the women too had gathered around to watch. Bangari just couldn't take her eyes off Amasa. As she watched him, she felt again a deep desire to have a child of her own in her arms. It had been six or seven years since she'd been married, but so far nothing had come to fruit. Raging at people's taunts, she had even slept around a bit. Yet nothing had borne fruit. She couldn't afford medicine-men and things like that; she and her husband were too poor for that. While women like her were already old by their thirties, she was one who could pass off for a new bride. Men who saw her couldn't help wanting her, even if for a moment; such was her bearing. And yet, nothing had come to fruit. Things couldn't go on like this forever. For a long time, as the night set in, stones would start falling on her house, one after the other. Her husband would raise welts on her back, and hide himself in the house. The stones had since stopped falling, and the people had begun to forget. Now, in her eyes, Amasa continued to dance.

*

While all this was going on, two landlords dragged in two fattened goats. The crowds instantly split into two. Children ran this way and that. The goats panicked at the beating drum and started to pull frantically. As the men holding them faltered, two more joined in and holding on tight, stood them in front of the Mari temple. The frenzied drumbeat continued. The goats stood frozen, only their eyes rolling round and round. The temple stood in front, the silver deity shining through the open door. From within, billows of incense smoke wafted out. A man, wearing only a small piece of cloth between his waist and knees, came out with holy water and a garland of flowers in his hands. He stood in front of the goats, closed his eyes and started to mumble. His dark body was covered with veins. They seemed to throb in time to his mumblings. He then cut the garland into two and tied them around the goats' necks. Then he placed the loose flowers on their foreheads, sprinkled the holy water on their bodies and, joining his hands in prayer, said, 'If we've done anything wrong please swallow it, Mother, and accept this.' His shrill voice resounded throughout the temple. But for the distant din, everyone around the temple stood with bated breath. For a while everything stood still, except for the eyes of the goats that were turning round and round. Then all of a sudden the goats quivered. The drumbeat rose again and drowned all other noise. The group moved on. A bunch of kids, including Amasa, ran behind it. The elders drove them away, but the kids returned the moment their backs were turned. The procession reached an open field. There, a well-built man stood casually by a tree stump, a knife in his hand. As everyone was otherwise occupied, nobody noticed the kids who had once again crowded around. As two men held the goats by their fore and hind legs and stretched out the necks on the stump, the man brought down the waiting knife and severed the heads from the bodies in one stroke. Someone poured holy water into the mouths of the severed heads. They gulped a couple of times and then closed shut. On the other side the bodies were writhing. By now the heads lay still, eyes turned upwards. Blood spurted from the writhing bodies as they spun around drenching the earth red with their blood. Some fellow shot into the middle and pulled from the goats' necks the garlands of flowers dripping with blood. Not satisfied with that, he draped them around Amasa's neck and said: 'Dance!' As the blood drenched his throat and started to drip down, Amasa panicked and ran. Some others followed. Even in his sleep Amasa saw only this sight. Several times that night Amasa sat up frightened. They kept the lamps burning all through the night. The outsiders slept all around the temple, curled up in their white shawls. That night the Mari temple was lit up.

*

That was also the night that railway gangman Siddappa had one too many. He had come with his belly full of spirit. It wasn't actu-

251

ally his fault. It was the spirit in him that played around with him that night. If he closed his eyes a storm raged within him. So he staggered around leaning on his stick, weaving aimlessly through the streets. When he came to a lamp post he flew into a rage. He lashed out at it, kicking and flogging it with his stick. The fury of it shook the entire neighbourhood. Not contented, he made it take on the role of the local politician, the contractor, his railway boss or the money-lender Madappa, and yelled at it: 'Bastard! You think you are a big shot just because you go around in white clothes. You hide your face when you see me. Forget us, we are loafers. We hang out on any street corner.' He let out a long wail and wept. And then he continued with renewed vigour. 'Don't vent your anger on me. Look at him laugh at my words.... Laugh, laugh away. It's your time to laugh. What else would you do but laugh? You are, after all, the one who uplifts the poor. Laugh... let the communists come. They'll put an end to your laughter. Till then you can laugh, so laugh, laugh....' His laughter and shouts rose and fell, stumbled down the village street and whined through the cold, dark night. Unable to sleep through all this, Amasa woke up with a start every now and then. It must have gone on for a long while. Nobody quite knows when or where Siddappa finally fell. His laughter, his shouts, died out.

*

It was dawn again. The village spent the morning yawning. Every verandah was filled with people. But still there were many who hadn't woken up. For instance, Siddappa. At noon, the Tiger dancers arrived at the Mari temple. The headman's bond-servant came and said, 'The headman's house needs coconuts,' and before Kuriyayya could say yes, he had climbed the tree, plucked the coconuts, and was gone. Back at the houses, the women had oiled and combed their hair, decked it with flowers and were running in and out. The young men teased the passing girls and were chided in turn. The drumbeat of the Tiger Dance drew everyone to the Mari temple. Everyone was eagerly awaiting the arrival of the Tiger dancers. All of a sudden the Tiger's cage flew open. All eyes fell on it. A huge Tiger leapt out, biting a lemon in his teeth. The startled crowd moved back and formed a circle around him. A few more Tigers, a Hyaena and a Clown emerged one after the other. Among them was a Tiger Cub too. After all of them had come out, they stood in a row, joined their hands in prayer to the deity and accepted the holy water. The dance began immediately after. The Hyaena was the best of all, and his costume fitted him perfectly. Remember the man who had sported the knife so casually at the sacrifice yesterday? It was the same man. The crowds would run away when he strode towards them, keeping step with the drumbeat. When the dance came down the street, women and children clambered up the parapet and watched it with their lives in their hands. The dancers had only to turn towards them, and they would dash into their houses and bolt the doors. The dancers continued, entered the landlord's street and danced in front of the village-hall. All the worthies, even the upper-caste ones, like the headman and the priest, had gathered there to watch the dance. They made gifts to the dancers according to their status and expressed their appreciation. Long after night had fallen and the dance was long over, everyone in the village continued to see the dance and hear the drumbeat. Those who fell asleep and closed their eyes, and the men even as they undressed their wives, saw only the Tiger Dance along with the drumbeat *dangu dangu dangu chuki*. The village headman, unable to sleep, came out for a stroll. The bond-servant, who was awake, saw him and stood up. The headman put a *beedi* between his lips and struck a match. For a moment, his face glowed red in the dark and flickered out. He gulped the smoke in silence for a while and then turned to the servant. 'The one who played the Tiger Cub. Whose boy is it?' 'That's Amasa,' came the reply. 'Who's Amasa?' enquired the headman. 'That's him. The orphan boy that lives there with Kuriyayya. That's him.' The headman was astonished. 'My, when did he grow up so?' Before his eyes, Amasa's Tiger Dance came dancing its many and wondrous dances.

Translated from Kannada by A. K. Ramanujan
and Manu Shetty

A Note on the Authors

Premendra Mitra (Bengali) Born in 1904 (d. 1988), he published several novels including *Kuyasha, Panchashar*, and *Sagar Theke Phera*, a collection of poems which received the Sahitya Akademi Award in 1957. He was also a popular children's writer.

Amrita Pritam (Punjabi) Born in 1919, she has published over seventy books, both novels and short stories. She received the Sahitya Akademi Award in 1956 and was honoured with the Padma Shree in 1969. She was also nominated to the Rajya Sabha in 1986. She lives in Delhi and edits a Punjabi monthly, *Nagmani*.

Bharati Mukherjee (English) Born in 1942, she has published two novels, *Wife* and *The Tiger's Daughter*, two works of non-fiction, *Days and Nights in Calcutta* and *The Sorrow and the Terror*, and a collection of short stories, *Darkness*. Her collection of short stories, *The Middleman And Other Stories* was the winner of the US National Book Critics Award, 1988.

Gangadhar Gadgil (Marathi) Born in 1923, he has published over fifty books which include novels, collections of short stories, travelogues, plays and children's literature. He is the president of the Mumbai Marathi Sahitya Sammelan and a member of the executive board of the Sahitya Akademi.

U.R. Anantha Murthy (Kannada) Born in 1932, he has published several novels, short stories and plays, some of which have been made into award-winning films. His novels, *Samskara* and *Ghatashraddha* received awards in 1970 and 1978 respectively. He has also received the Homi Bhabha Fellowship for Creative Writing in 1972 and the Karnataka Sahitya Akademi Award in 1983.

Gopinath Mohanty (Oriya) Born in 1914, he has published twenty- four novels and eight volumes of short stories. In 1955 he received the Sahitya Akademi Award for his novel, *Amrutura Santana*, the Jnanpith Award in 1974 for *Matimatal* and was also honoured with the Padma Bhushan in 1981.

Raja Rao (English) Born in 1909, he has published five novels and two collections of short stories, among them the critically acclaimed, *Kanthapura*. He received the Sahitya Akademi Award in 1961 for his novel, *The Serpent and the Rope* and was also awarded the prestigious Newstadt Prize recently.

S. Mani 'Mowni' (Tamil) Born in 1907 (d. 1985), he published a novella and thirty short stories. He is regarded as one of the important contemporary Tamil writers. His story *Transformation* was translated into the French and published in *Litteratures De L' Inde*.

Anita Desai (English) Born in 1937, her first novel, *Cry the Peacock* was published in 1963. She has published several books for children and also a screenplay of her novel, *In Custody*. She received the Sahitya Akademi Award in 1977 for her novel, *Fire on the Mountain*.

Chunilal Madia (Gujarati) Born in 1922 (d. 1969), he published several novels, collections of short stories and plays. He began writing at an early age and is regarded as one of the foremost writers of his generation in Gujarati. He has been a recipient of several awards from the Government of Bombay for his works of fiction and drama.

P.S. Rege (Marathi) Born in 1910 (d. 1981), he was best known as a poet and was one of the important figures in modern Marathi literature. He was the principal of Elphistone College, Bombay for several years and was also associated with the Institute of Advanced Study, Simla. His story in this collection was first published in 1962 and is one of the few works of fiction the author wrote.

Thakazhi Sivasankara Pillai (Malayalam) Born in 1914, he has published fifty novels and several collections of short stories. He received the Sahitya Akademi Award in 1957 for his novel, *Chemeen*, the Vayalar Award in 1978 for *Kayar* and the Sovietland Nehru Award in 1975.

Mahadevi Verma (Hindi) Born in 1907 (d. 1987), she published over twenty books including novels, poetry, collections of short stories and her memoirs. She was awarded a fellowship from the Sahitya Akademi and also the Mangala Prasad Paristoshak from the Hindi Sahitya

O.V. Vijayan (Malayalam) Born in 1930, he has published in Malayalam, three novels, three novellas, five collections of short stories and several books of political essays. His novel, *the Saga of Dharmapuri* and a collection of short stories, *After the Hanging and Other Stories* have been translated into English.

Bhisham Sahni (Hindi) Born in 1915, he has published five novels, eight collections of short stories, three full-length plays and a biography of his brother, the actor and writer Balraj Sahni. He received the Distinguished Writer Award of the Punjab Government in 1974, the Sahitya Akademi for his novel, *Tamas* in 1975, The Lotus Award of Afro Asian Writers' Association in 1981, the Sovietland Nehru Award in 1983 and two awards from the Uttar Pradesh Hindi Samsthan.

Sunil Gangopadhyay (Bengali) Born in 1934, he has published several novels, short stories, poems, plays and scripts. His novel, *Arjun* was translated into English and *Aranyer Din Ratri* was made into a critically acclaimed film by Satyajit Ray.

Nirmal Verma (Hindi) Born in 1929, he has published several collections of short stories, essays, travelogues and novels including *Ve Din* and *Parinde*. He is regarded as one of the most respected writers associated with the Nai Kahani movement of the 1950s.

Devanuru Mahadeva (Kannada) Born in 1949, he has published a collection of short stories, *Devanooru* and a long short story, *Odalaala* which was also made into a film. Several of his works have been translated into various languages.

891.47 PEN

The Penguin book of modern
Indian short stories

MORE ABOUT PENGUINS

For further information about books available from Penguins in India write to Penguin Books (India) Ltd, B4/246, Safdarjung Enclave, New Delhi 110 029.

In the UK: For a complete list of books available from Penguins in the United Kingdom write to Dept. EP, Penguin Books Ltd, Harmondsworth, Middlesex UB7 0DA.

In the U.S.A.: For a complete list of books available from Penguins in the United States write to Dept. DG, Penguin Books, 299 Murray Hill Parkway, East Rutherford, New Jersey 07073.

In Canada: For a complete list of books available from Penguins in Canada write to Penguin Books Canada Ltd, 2801 John Street, Markham, Ontario L3R 1B4.

In Australia: For a complete list of books available from Penguins in Australia write to the Marketing Department, Penguin Books Australia Ltd, P.O. Box 257, Ringwood, Victoria 3134.

In New Zealand: For a complete list of books available from Penguins in New Zealand write to the Marketing Department, Penguin Books (N.Z.) Ltd, Private Bag, Takapuna, Auckland 9.